"Zombie mayhem gets an interesting modern American makeover in Ben Tripp's notable debut" (*Publishers Weekly*)

RISE AGAIN

New York Times bestselling author Cory Doctorow hails *Rise Again* as "not just a zombie novel—it's an indictment of the us-versus-them mentality that chooses authoritarianism and control over cooperation and compassion. As such, **it does more than scare—it both moves and enrages**, and transcends mere spookiness for something much more satisfying. . . . Tripp raises the stakes so high that the book becomes nearly impossible to put down."

"*Rise Again* would make a terrific action movie due to a strong cast of characters struggling to survive by choosing to become heroic or malevolent. . . . **A fabulous futuristic apocalyptic thriller.**"

—*Alternative Worlds*

"Danny's journey through a land of death to find [her sister] Kelley makes for a remarkable character-driven story, and **the final sentence takes it to another level.**"

—*Library Journal*

"**It will delight fans of zombie fiction** and post-apocalyptic stories, including Charlie Huston's *Sleepless* and Justin Cronin's *The Passage*."

—*Booklist*

RISE
AGAIN

BELOW ZERO

Ben Tripp

GALLERY BOOKS

New York London Toronto Sydney New Delhi

Gallery Books
A Division of Simon & Schuster, Inc.
1230 Avenue of the Americas
New York, NY 10020

First Gallery Books trade paperback edition December 2013.

GALLERY BOOKS and colophon are registered trademarks of Simon & Schuster, Inc.

For information about special discounts for bulk purchases, please contact Simon & Schuster Special Sales at 1-866-506-1949 or business@simonandschuster.com.

The Simon & Schuster Speakers Bureau can bring authors to your live event. For more information or to book an event contact the Simon & Schuster Speakers Bureau at 1-866-248-3049 or visit our website at www.simonspeakers.com.

Manufactured in the United States of America

10 9 8 7 6 5 4 3 2 1

Library of Congress Cataloging-in-Publication Data is available.

ISBN 978-1-4516-6832-2
ISBN 978-1-4516-6834-6 (ebook)

For Tucker

He could hear its garments rustling in the leaves, and every breath
of wind came laden with that last low cry. If he stopped it did the same.
If he ran, it followed—not running too: that would have been a relief:
but like a corpse endowed with the mere machinery of life, and borne
on one slow melancholy wind that never rose or fell.

—Charles Dickens, *Oliver Twist*

Questi non hanno speranza di morte.
These have no hope of death.

—Dante Alighieri, *Divina Commedia*

PROLOGUE
THE SILENT KID TESTIFIES

Everbode nos yu dont get neer th zeros, caus neer th zeros is neer th deth. We feerdem, but we nodem wel lik oldentiim salors gon to see but duno how to swim, th danjar al rown an them in thaar wuden ships liik us in owr caravan. Feerdem or feedem, gos th sayin.

Im telin this story bowt dany wo is non rown th worl for her derin egsploids agins th zeros bc noobode riits anethin down animor an wat she don changit everthin tords man agin from when th zeros rulit th worl. This story is imporn for that rezin alon, but also bc peepel think dany is a legint wen she was jus a huumin liik yoonme. Onle she was a speshil huumin hoo was not afraad to dy. An ii was lucky enuf to no hir that is dany adelman or th zombikiler or th ledir of th triib, an she no me aswel an tretit me good wen she cud av kilt me that firsten daa, th daa thay founit me bludy an dyin.

It was neer 2 yeer sin th worl endit an th zeros, or as yu miit cal em th zombis or th unded or th maneetirs, riz agin and startit ther nu worl on th runes of th ol 1. As preecher say al th sins of th worl maketh th dum clay of th ded bestir an riz agin an turnip on th livin woo askit for destrucshin on acownt of thay doan lisin to th wird of th Lord. Th Lord is alwaas angry alwaas kilin peepel for 1 thin or anuthr dependin on preechirs mood. U wud hav thot if th Lord was so disapoynit with his creashin, that beein mankind ii meen, he wud of just startit ovar anu. But th Lord is an meen ol sunbich he wantit to kepe sum peepel alive so he kin make em sufir. Dany she fot agin th preechir an th Arkitkt and savit mee.

B4tiim ii liv in a superb of a big sity, Kansis Sity in the graat staat of Kansis. Awr hows lookit like ever uthir hows in the hool street and the hool superb and proly th hool sity for all ii noon. Ii dint think abowt other plasis vary ofen or nevar rily. We wen on vacashan wunst or 2 tiims an seen other plasis but thay dint seem al that difernt from Kansis Sity esept as miit be thay hav sum hils or mountens or mabe th oshin shoor.

On th daa th worl endit ii was plaan in the yard of my hows. ii was proly 2 ol to be plaan with toys but shaam as ii am to amit it th truuth mus be sed. Ii ges in th tiim befor it was oka for a boy 7 yers ol to play with toys enstet of ril guns an niifs and expeshily slinshots. My toys war prety gud thay war mosly wepin kind of toys but not danjaris bc thay war onle faak. Th guns had ornj plastic narzils on th ends and went bakabakabaka until th bateris diid or ii leftem owtsid ovarniit and thay got ranit on or th sprinklars watrit them. Ii had also a rubir niif not danjris wotsowivar and mani arme men in lyfliik posis lokt in combat with my toy diinoosoors.

In the midel of th daa my mam cum owt an tel me there was sum weerd nus on th tevy bc this was wen we still had tevy U unerstant and cud wach muvis and shos my favrets beeng th 1s wif sooljars fiiten, ane sho as long as th sooljars was fiiten rily. Ii likit viilent shos ii am not shamd to amit that. Now I don liik vilent shos not evin to think bowt em. Ii seen enuf of vilens to las me th rest of my liif.

Th weerd nus was abowt peepel runin and scremin everwaar in th worl but th nus kep chanjin th subjec like thaa dint want to tawk abowtet adal. Prolem was thar was so much news abowt it, onle thing hapenin rily esep for 4th of July paraads an warnin peepel to be caarful of fiirwurks so they don't blo off thaar hands or get blinet in ther iis.

We dint see aneethin rong at 1st only sum nebers cum owt of thar howsis and lookit around like U cud chek if th nus was troo jes by goin owtsiit and luuken down th street. Our neber mises kirshner saad to my mam ii am worit abowt what ii seen on th nus do U no a chanil waar they show wat is hapnin I cant fine 1, and my mam saad no ii cant finger owt why they don't jus sho us wat is hapnin ii think it miit be a teristatak and mises kirshner put her hand ovar hir mowth an saad oh biit yoor tung margrit plees god don let it be a teristatak do U think it miit rily be a teristatak, and riit then our neber kid on tother side my frend jerry he liiten a hole string of fiirkrakers and they wen pakabang and my mam an mises kirshner both of them jumpit bowt 3 fut in th aar an scremit.

Anewa my mam she makit me cum insiid th hows an ii 8 a snak last snak evar in my lif that was a nordinry snak sitn at th cawntar betwen th livin room and kichin an tevy goin liits on fijrater humin dishwasher washen dishs—las norml daa in th worl an ii dint no it at th tiim ii jus aten my snak an wundar wen ii can go outsiit an pla some moar cus ii wantit to liit firecrakers with jerry. It was a gud snak tho it was strin chees thar isnt ane strin chees ane mor also krakers graaps an milk. It was 10 minits after ii was dun an mam wantit me to sta insiid but ii wantit to go out an pla with jerry wen 1st craazz persn cum runin down th street.

It was liik a sirin on a firetruk in olden daas U no when U heer a sirin cumin tords yor hows an U don no if it is cumin to neer yor haws only it gets lowder an lowder an then U start to think maabe it cum to yor blok an then maabe it cum to yor hows. Th craazz man was runin an scremin hands in th aar an he run riit pas owr hows. Ii run owtsiid to see an my mam she was escaart she grabit me an pul me insiid th haws and th man run pas an fel down ded riit in frunt of jerrys hows. Ii was jelis at th tiim cus jerry got th ded man in frunt of his hows not me an he that is jerry wud get on th nus an be famist. But ther was another craazz man cumin down th street an ii thot mabe he dy in frunt of my hows. He dint dy he kep runin. Ii was wachen from th livin room windo an my mam was on th foon we had telefoon bak then an she was telin my dad cum hoom don't caar wer yar jus cum hom dont caar if yor helpen yer frend get his vintij car redy for th 4tha juli paraad cum hoom an he sed he wud cum hoom but he nevar cum hoom proly he diid runin an scremin iil nevar no.

Lots mor scremin peepel cum runin down ar street an even sum of ar nebers 2 runin with ther hans up in th aar. My mam lokit th dor turnit of th liits an tukit me upstaars an we hidin in hir bejrum an lookit out th windoo at th craazz peepel runin. Mane of th peepel diid in th street 1 of them diid riit agins owr fens an another crashit into th fens an wen riit ovar th top an landit in my toy sooljars an la stil. That 1 was a laade a nold laade she had a merikin flag shirt for th holida. Ii saw wen she diid she pupit a big shit in her pants an ii laf an my mam hiten me on th hed an saa don be a nanimel peepel are diin this is no tiim for lafen.

Jerry my neber cum to owr door an nok an nok and he was scremit his mam diid so my mam wen down to let him in ii staad upstaars to keep

wachen th spetakl of a worl gon craazz owt th windo. But then my maam
dint cum bak upstaars so ii thot she was given jerry a snak but she nevar
cum bak upstaars. It was getin dark wen ii fiinly cum downstaars an th
reesin ii dint cum down suner was cus ii was scaart so much ii dint hav th
curij to cum down. Ii ges ii nu thar was a prolem or my mam wud hav cum
bak up th staars with jerry but she dint. Ater a wiil th scremin stopit an onle
ded peepel wur everwar not ane livin peepel ii cud see from th windoo.

Ii cum don an it was dark insiid th hows an ii felt liik ther wur spiidars
crolin on my skin. My hart was hamrin. Ii dint fiin ane siin of my mam or
jerry ii thot maabe they wen to jerrys hows so ii got a flashliit even tho it
wasn rily dark owtsiid yet an I saw al th ded peepel everywar a milin ded
peepel. Sum1 sed latir on ther was 100an50thosin ded in th graatr meter-
politin aarya includen saan lewis.

Ii gon ovar th fens between th howsis bc ii was so escaart of th ded laade
on th lon with th shit in hir pants. Ii wen into jerrys hows th dor was opin ii
wen in an it was qiiit in thar qiiit as th tuum as dad wud of sed. Ii luken
arown but ii was 2 escaart to go upstaars an it got dark so ii turnit on th lites
an was escaart al niit. Ii peed in my pants also so it wasn fune.

Th nx mornin ii wen owtsid an th ded peepil was on thaar feet. Sum survivars was luken for other survivars so ii calit 2 them an tha cum 2 get me. Ii
cud tel tha wer aliiv bc tha cud tok an th ded peepil wu got up agen tha cud
not tok. Noor hardle even wok or mov arown. The survivars jus push th
zombis owt th wa. Tha war zombis as u alrede no this so ii wil calit them
zombis even tho we dint no tha war zombis yet. Tha pushit th zombis owt th
wa an cum get me an I criid I amit it I criid lik a smal baabe and a laade survivar she strokit my haar an presit my faas 2 hir busim. She gavit me a smal
dog hu bcaam mi bes fren. We al got in a van an droov tween the zombis
wakin arown lik a videeyo gaam.

Ii don reemembar wen th zombis startit biiten al th peepil. Ii was sleepin
in th van ii was tiirit from not sleepin al niit. We stopit at a hows an the men
went to see if thar was a survivar, ii was tool that latar. A zombi biten 1 of th
men an blud went everwar an th zombis wen craazz an biten everbode wu
was owtsiid th van. We drovit awa vere fast then an aftar that mor an mor
peepel got biten on arms legs nex eers fasis or fingars ever tiim we stopit it
seem liik sumbode get another biit. Thar was so mane zombis.

Tha seem to cum up owt th grown or under evere rok or behiin ever tre
an bush. An ever tiim sumbode got biten tha turn in2 a zombi themselv an

so it got wurser evere da until thar war no mor survivars xep me an 2 othir in owr gruup. We seen othir gruups 2 but we kepit to owrselv then ntil ii was aloon in th worl. Maabe it war a mistaak an we shud av gon for strenth in numbars but in liit of what ii seen aftar that maabe our gruup did th riit thin aftar al.

Bc th onle cretur worser an moor cruul an vilent an bludfirsy than the zombi is man.

PART ONE

1

"You have the right to remain silent. In fact I prefer it. Anything you say would be held against you in a court of law, except there isn't one. You would have the right to speak to an attorney, but we don't have those either. There ain't shit except me. Do you understand?"

Danny Adelman had the man facedown against the pavement on the side of the road, his hands bound across his spine with a plastic zip-tie. Her attention was divided, but she'd gotten good at multitasking since things went bad. The zeroes were coming through the tall yellow grass. Slow ones. Moaners. Dozens of them, drawn out into the open by the burning wreckage, preceded by their long, sobbing cries of hunger.

"You can't kill me," he said. "You're a cop."

"I didn't say I was going to kill you," Danny replied. She knew where he got the idea: Her short-nosed shotgun was jammed up under his left ear. "I'm only judge and jury here. But the executioner is getting real close."

She and the perpetrator had another minute, at most. Then Danny was going to have to get to the Mustang Special police interceptor and bug out. The black smoke rising up out of the wreckage of the man's truck was shaped like a giant fist, with one finger pointing down at the scene of the action. The perp wasn't going to be any more ready to talk than he was now. Time to get down to business.

"Tell me something," Danny said.

"Fuck you," he answered. He was burly-shouldered, stinking of sweat, his lank hair clinging to his skin in oily strokes. There was a deep, unhealed gash across his forehead.

With patience she did not feel, Danny said, "You tried to steal one of our children. Why?"

The man barked a laugh. "You don't know? I guess not, if you're coming from the west." He wrenched his face into a mirthless grimace, trying to smile despite the asphalt against his teeth.

Danny thought about breaking his nose. "And you figure not telling me is gonna be satisfaction enough for dying?"

"Doesn't matter—you're going to kill me either way," he said.

"Tell me what I want to know and you get your hands back," Danny said. "Even with that busted foot, you can probably make it out of here. *Don't* tell me, and I leave you just like you are. Maybe you can still get away, even with handcuffs on. You could last for days."

"Fuck you," the man repeated.

"And if you say that just one more time, we move on to option three: I break your other foot. You got fifteen seconds."

The perp wasted ten of them weighing the alternatives. Then he said: "I was trying to survive, okay? There's a bounty. One kid buys you passage to the safe place. Got to be under twelve. Lots of people are doing it. Parents are turning in their own."

"And what happens to the kids?"

"They go somewhere else. An even safer place. I hear they're happy there."

"Then why the hell didn't you just ask nicely?"

Danny saw there were tears running out of the man's red eyes and dripping on the tar.

"Because somebody stole *my* son," he said. "I was taking him there, and this biker gang showed up. Called the Vandal Reapers. And now he's gone."

The man sobbed. Danny heard the grief, the real agony in his chest, and she knew he was telling the truth. For a few seconds, she listened to the man's sorrow hacking out of his chest, but the muzzle of her shotgun never wavered, and she did not relieve the weight of her knee upon his back. The nearest of the zeroes was within fifty yards by now. It moaned with renewed urgency as it came closer. A big male.

There was only death in the world now. Living death that could walk and hunt and feast, and barbaric death from outlaws and madmen. Death from the ruins of a shattered civilization. Death from disease and festering wounds. Danny could leave this man to die, or do something to help him. This man whose grief had made him crazy and convinced him to rush one of the Tribe's caretakers. Whose panic had led him to drop the child he'd grabbed, and drive away at top speed.

Danny's mind was racing. She was long past compassion for anyone who acted on behalf of chaos, even with the most personal of motives. But another man dead was another feeding for the zeroes. Another pair of hands that could fight back against the dead would be lost forever—or might become one of the enemy.

"Get in the fucking car," she said.

2

The police special slewed between the undead that shuffled onto the roadway. They were ragged, dark, indistinct things, like the piers of an abandoned dock revealed by the tide. Skulls with wet rawhide stretched over them, yellow teeth in black, gaping mouths. Eyes that stared out of deep sockets. Pale, lightless eyes. Butcher-shop eyes. They moved like people in pain, stiff-limbed and lurching, twisting around to follow the vehicle. As soon as the last one went by, Danny hit the throttle. Those assholes back at the convoy weren't answering the radio, probably because Maria, who normally operated the communications system, was the one this escapee had punched when he went for the kid. But once again, the Tribesmen had failed to follow protocol and keep communications open. Danny decided the prisoner's fate rested on whether Maria was badly injured.

"Drink some water," Danny said.

"No," her companion in the front seat said. It was a woman's voice, or nearly so.

"You need to drink water or you'll shrivel up," Danny said and pressed the plastic bottle into the gloved hands beside her.

They were barreling along Interstate 70 through Kansas. Not too many shrubs grew through the pavement and there were relatively few wrecks on this route; she could use some of the speed the police special was designed for. The wind whistled through the barbed-wire zero catcher bolted to the front fender and ruffled Danny's choppy red hair beneath her Smokey hat.

"I made a mistake and I'm sorry. Can't you just let me go? Drop me off here, I don't mind," the prisoner said. "Please." He sounded afraid. More than he'd been before.

Danny glanced in the rearview mirror: The man in the backseat couldn't take his eyes off the apparition riding shotgun next to her. His fear was justified. They made a peculiar pair, she knew. Danny could pass for good-looking from a few feet away, but there were too many scars on her face for up-close work. Most people, however, found themselves staring at her left hand. It ended in a mess of cauliflower tissue where three fingers should have been. According to some crazy story that was going around, Danny had once chewed them off with her own teeth to get free of a wrecked car surrounded by zeroes. Mutilations were not an uncommon sight in this time, however. Almost everyone had a couple of badly healed injuries or an untreated illness. It was a world of decaying teeth, greasy hair, and crooked scars.

Even so, Danny's companion was the eye-catching one.

It was understood among their fellow travelers that nobody was to ask about her, although Danny knew they talked about her when she wasn't around. Underneath a stained, shapeless muumuu with big flowers on it, the woman was bound from head to foot in dirty bandages, like a cartoon mummy. She was known simply as "the Leper," and she was untouchable in every sense of the word. Her presence was part of the price of being a member of the Tribe.

"Water," Danny repeated, not much interested in the man's feelings.

"I don't want it," the Leper said.

"You need it. Your condition's getting worse."

"So is yours."

Danny glanced at the mirror again. The prisoner was looking at her now. If he hadn't figured out what the Leper's condition was, he soon would. But he seemed like a bright guy. And scared to death.

As if thinking the same thing, the Leper turned her head to face him.

The bones in her neck creaked audibly. Mike could see himself reflected in her sunglasses. She took a breath, speaking through the exhalation.

"We all make mistakes," she said. "It's only human."

3

The radio opened up, grainy with static. It was a call from the White Whale, the immense motor home that formed the center of the Tribe's convoy. The voice on the radio was not Maria, but Patrick, another of Danny's original fellow-survivors from the desperate hours after the undead first rose up in another life.

"The kid's all right," Patrick said. "Nobody's hurt. Maria's got a shiner, that's it. Where have you been?"

"Got the perp. Over."

"We were calling you for the last half hour. Just so you don't feel like you need to lecture us about communication when you get back," Patrick said.

"It did cross my mind," Danny said. "Remember to say 'over' when you're done speaking. Over."

"Can't we pretend this is just a phone call? I really miss phone calls."

So the child was okay. The failed kidnapper had that in his favor. Danny hated to admit it—she hated to admit anything—but she didn't have a clear answer as to what should be done with this guy. She would have to put it to a Tribe vote or something. For now, she was silent with her thoughts.

They drove on through a broken country.

It was a year and a half since the onslaught of the undead plague: Lawns had become fields, pavement was buckling and sprouting with grass and sapling trees, and everywhere there were vast swaths of scorched earth and burned-out towns where fires had raged unopposed. Cities were unapproachable, swarming with animated corpses.

In contrast to the ruined places, the Tribe would sometimes pass through deserted neighborhoods that appeared not to have suffered at all—overlook the untrimmed yards, and the houses were just as firm as the day they were built. The windows cast back reflections of the clouds, the roofs shed the weather, and the walls stood straight and clean. But here and there a front door hung open in a litter of leaves, or there was a rotten shape in the grass with one skeletal arm outflung.

The Tribe had been traversing the western states, mostly, looking for supplies and safety. Neither one lasted very long. But they had seen a great deal of the changed America along the way. Of all the ruined things they saw, it was the cars that bothered Danny the most. She'd spent a long time fighting wars overseas, and had seen ruins and fire and death. But in those foreign places, everybody took the bus or drove shabby little cars and dust-colored pickup trucks. Here, though? This was *America*. The cars were supposed to be bright and clean and shiny, neatly parked along streets and in driveways. To Danny, who had once owned and loved a flawless vintage cherry red Mustang, cars were a projection of who Americans were.

Now these once-prized machines were scattered all over the countryside like discarded toys, many of them smashed and broken, doors sagging open. The vehicles had become colorful tombstones marking the death of an entire civilization. And many of them sheltered the undead. It might have been some dim reptile memory of their past lives that drew the zeroes to wait there in the vehicles, dormant, their eyes and noses hung with webs of mucus. Many of them had ceased to function and were now mummified in the driver's seats, truly dead. But others were simply biding their time, waiting like trap-door spiders for prey to come along. The dead sat in the cars and waited, and rotted, their sleepless graves made of steel.

4

No one but the scouts would have seen the child. The scouts had spent the last year looking for anything with two legs, anywhere they found it. Their eyes had become specialized, like big game hunters, like fighter pilots. They saw things differently. They saw man-shapes, no matter how well concealed.

The boy was around two hundred meters from the road, probably with a concealed bolt-hole nearby so he didn't feel he had to run to escape. Topper saw him first, and shouted to his wingmen, Ernie and Conn, over the crackle of their big Harleys: "Stander, three o'clock!"

They had a system. The spotter would stop to destroy the thing if it was a zero, or make contact if it was human; the others would continue on. Commonsense precautions: no leaving the paved surface in pursuit, radio circuits to be left open. If there was a problem, the other two scouts would double back and assist. Otherwise they were backing up the primary mission—seeking safety and supplies.

Ernie and Conn kept on going. Topper swung his bike around and let the engine idle, his boots on the asphalt. It was a big, windswept nowhere, this place. There was a railway line off in the distance with a train sitting on the tracks. Just the cars, no engine, like a giant decapitated snake. Topper watched the child, and the child watched back.

Topper had personally hand-dropped hundreds of zeroes since the crisis began. He had shot them, speared them, set them on fire, hacked them to pieces with axes, machetes, shovels, and meat cleavers. He'd run them over, blown them up, and bludgeoned them into ground hamburger with anything he could lift over his head. And yet dropping the kids still bothered him. Like braining Casper the fucking man-eating Ghost, as he'd explained it to Ernie. The things had been children once, and the tragedy of it lingered. They'd never grow any taller, get zits, or fall in love. They would just drift around the countryside like toy scarecrows until they found fresh meat or rotted off their feet. Children forever, and yet never again. Topper hated them.

Usually the living shouted something right away when a scout stopped to check them out; they called for help or news or offered what they had to trade, if they had anything. This kid didn't say a word. He had the dirty pallor of a zero, too, like sheet metal left out in the weather, and his clothes were falling off in blackened strips. Topper drew the rifle out of his saddlebag, scraped a couple of dead bugs off the barrel, and worked the action to get a round into the chamber.

The kid just stood there. Had to be a zero.

Topper sighted down the hunting scope on the rifle. It was a very nice piece of optics on a fine weapon—if you were a survivor, you could have the best of anything. The entire nation had become one vast half-ruined superstore with no employees to watch the stock. He trailed the scope along the grass and found the kid. The face jumped into view, big and clear. That always startled him. He checked the eyes, but they looked empty, like those of all zeroes. Then he saw the dog.

Holy shit, the damn kid had a dog. Some kind of little Buster Brown mutant dog with its face smashed in and no tail. Black and white with big spots. Frozen eels wriggled down Topper's spine. Jesus, was this a zombie dog? Had the disease crossed the species line? There was talk of that, some places they'd been. If it spread to animals, that would be the end of the remnants of mankind, game over, people knew that much. He let the scope fall on the dog, his finger leaning on the trigger.

But it was clearly an ordinary dog. The ugliest one he'd seen in quite some time, but still. It was shivering and turning circles around the kid's feet. Topper sighted on the kid again: The child bent down and put his hand on the dog's fist-sized head. There wasn't a zero in the world would do that. Topper let out a short breath of relief. It was a living kid after all. The only problem was, that meant Topper was probably idling his bike at the edge of a trap set by the boy's people—men with guns hidden in the ditch, explosive booby traps, cutthroat wires stretched across the road, a tiger pit concealed in the ground somewhere in front of the child. He'd seen it all. A working vehicle, a little gas, or a bottle of aspirin—your life was worth whatever desperate survivors could take off your corpse. The zeroes were killers, but men were still murderers.

Topper waited, feeling eyes crawling over him from behind every stalk of wheat. You could hide an army in that yellow grass. But he didn't get the sense anybody else was actually there. No sign of trampling, no broken stems or footpaths cut through the fields. Still, he wasn't going to leave the road. Rule numero uno: Never leave the road alone. There could be fifty people hidden on that broken-down train, for example, and then bye-bye Topper.

He rested his rifle on the gas tank and switched off the engine. The sound of the other scooters was long-gone, so his voice sounded like the bang of hammers when he called out to the boy: "Hey. Hey! Come on over here."

Predictably, the boy didn't move. He'd have to be a goddamn fool to do it. Topper wasn't a confidence-inspiring figure, even without the rifle in his hands. He was a big man clad in scuffed black leather, with a coarse, windscorched face surmounted by a forked black beard. In a land without laws, he still looked like an outlaw. Don't fuck with the Topper.

He thought about the situation. They didn't come across stray kids anymore. In the early days, there had been many, but then the zeroes got most of them, and the rest generally starved or met with accidents—or human marauders. It didn't seem possible that this one could have survived alone all this time.

"Kid, you hungry?!" Topper shouted.

The boy didn't say anything, but Topper could see the dog capering around out there, and he had an idea. "Dinner," he tried. "Uh, num-nums. Supper. Lunch. Breakfast. Food." The dog didn't react, but the boy's head tilted on its side in a doglike manner. So he could hear, at least.

"Come and get it," Topper tried, and that did the trick. Every dog had a dinner call. It took off like an arrow from a bow, charging straight for Topper through the grass and looking like a skinny soccer ball with those spots. Then the animal burst out of the grass, leaped the ditch, and was springing up and down on its hind legs beside Topper like a pogo stick, whining and chirping.

"Okay, okay, calm down, boy," Topper said, and fished a scrap of venison jerky out of his handlebar bag. He tossed it to the dog. "Jesus Christ, you look like a goblin's asshole," he observed.

The dog ran off a few feet and started tearing the meat to bits. Topper kept one eye on the boy during this operation, and was gratified to see the dog's changing sides had gotten the boy to react; he was trotting toward the road, obviously afraid for the dog's safety. Topper threw another piece of jerky on the pavement and gnawed one himself as the boy slowed down, caution setting in. Now the kid was at the edge of the tall grass. There was shorter stuff along the road, no concealment there. The boy's eyes cut between Topper and the dog, who was valiantly wolfing down enormous chunks of the jerky, gagging on half of them.

"Listen kid, I ain't gonna hurt you or your dog," Topper said. "You saw them other guys? We got a convoy of vehicles, couple hundred folks down back the road about ten miles. We're known as 'the Tribe.' I'm a scout. This is what we do. We find living people and zeroes ahead of the convoy. Look for traps and trouble. So I ain't got any designs on you, boy, but if this here *is* a trap meant for me, understand I'm gonna shoot you first and your confederates after. Are we clear?"

Topper said the last part loudly, casting his voice around to the sighing grass. If some slingshot-wielding relative was lying in wait, he might think twice now. Or maybe the kid was nothing more than bait, his survival of little interest. That was the gamble.

"So, you hungry? You look skinnier than a Jap's pecker."

The boy thought about that, watching the dog eat, and at length he nodded gravely. Topper produced a good-sized chunk of jerky and threw it knife-style in the general direction of the boy. The wind caught it, and the boy had to scamper along after it, climbing down into the ditch. Topper was patient. Results were happening. He observed as the boy ripped the jerky apart and hardly chewed it, swallowing big splintery pieces of meat dry. The pup was now licking the road with an immense pink tongue. Topper threw another chunk of jerky to the dog. Then he ate another one himself. It was good quality, no seasoning except salt, but the meat had a fresh game flavor. He'd bartered half a case of bug spray for the stuff at a fortified settlement ten days ago.

"My buddies should be coming back in a little while, unless they get killed. So you can think on it until then, and if you want to go tell your people about us, I'll parlay with 'em, maybe we can do some business. Maybe they can tag along with us. That's the deal. I ain't got more than that to tell you."

The boy was staring at the bag with the jerky in it. Topper thought the kid might come all the way over to him now, with the taste of food still in his mouth. But he wasn't going to grab the boy and throw him across the back of the bike. This was not a hostage situation. He'd have to wait for Danny to decide what to do, tedious as that could get.

Then something occurred to Topper.

"You do got people, right?"

The boy shook his head.

"You ain't got people? You can't be alone. I don't mean relations or whatnot. I mean . . . the others. Who's with you?"

The boy shook his head again. Not the talkative type.

"*Nobody* at all? You survived all this time without nobody?"

The boy extended his arm and pointed up the road with a dirt-black finger, the direction the other scouts had gone. Topper squinted at him.

"This ain't fuckin' charades, kid. Just tell me."

The kid dangled two of his fingers and wiggled them. Legs, he meant. Walking. Now he did it with all of his fingers: several people walking. Then he made two fingers and flung them over his shoulder. He did this several times, and then finished the performance with one pair of fingers walking through the air.

Then he pointed at himself and the dog.

Topper scratched his chin through his beard. "Okay, you saying there was a bunch of you and now there's only you and that dog there?"

The boy nodded again, almost a bow.

"What's that way?" Topper indicated the direction the boy had pointed.

The boy bared his teeth and went into a crouch, limbs jutting, fingers hooked into claws—and for a second Topper was looking at a hunter, one of the quick zeroes that could chase down prey in packs, like wolves. It scared him a little, as if the boy had thrown off a human mask to reveal the mummified cannibal beneath. But the boy had made his point, and just as quickly, he stood upright again and the monster was gone.

"Son of a bitch," Topper muttered, and got on the radio.

5

The Tribe's convoy, some fifty vehicles and two hundred souls, was parked along the roadside between a burned-out city to the west and an area that Danny had heard from fellow travelers was crawling with zeroes. That's where the scouts had gone. There were two ways to survive in the world: find yourself a fortress somewhere and defend it against man and zero, foraging ever farther afield for supplies, or stay perpetually on the move. The Tribe followed the latter approach. But it meant a lot more scouting. And waiting around.

Danny was the Tribe's leader, the closest thing to an authority figure among them. The informal hierarchy was pretty simple: Danny at the top, then the scouts, then all the specialists—Dr. Amy, the cooks, Maria the radio operator, the auto mechanics, gunsmiths, and so on—and after them the "chooks," or civilians, people without any particular skill who did grunt work, built fires, carried water, and stood sentry.

These days, a lot of the Tribe's people were just sick of traveling. It came up almost daily: They envied the folk who stayed put in fortified places and only had to risk their necks on foraging expeditions. But Danny sure as hell wasn't going to hole up somewhere and get surrounded. A number of dictators had learned that the hard way even before the crisis. The zeroes had a kind of homing instinct. They would gather from miles around, once they found a stationary group of the living. Drawn to the feast by some unknown telepathy. She was certain they communicated over long distances somehow. Black magic or pheromones, it didn't matter.

The people who agreed with Danny's assessment didn't like to stop moving for more than a day or two, no matter how secure the location. If they did have to stop, they liked to be somewhere with a clear escape route and high walls. Currently, they were halted in a shitty, indefensible nowhere, the only virtue of which was the surrounding grasslands. They could see for two miles in every direction. But the water was running low, the shallow trench latrine was starting to stink, and it was time to go.

There was an argument to this effect in progress when Danny pulled the interceptor up alongside the White Whale. Raised voices dropped low when she opened her door, and fell silent as she approached. She had that effect on people.

"What's the trouble now?" Danny asked, not wanting to know.

"Shirleen's got a feeling again," said Crawford, an older man with a big, grizzled mustache. The Tribe had found him holed up in a sporting goods store back in Colorado. He could do anything outdoorsy.

"Remember that Shirleen is mentally ill," Danny observed. "I got the kidnapper in my hold, but I don't want anything to happen to him, you understand? He's my prisoner."

"We should hang him," Crawford said. "Hang him with a sign to warn the next one comes along."

There was a great deal of anger floating around over the situation with the kids. Danny herself had to compartmentalize it; they were constantly losing children one way or another, and kidnappers weren't strategically worse than zeroes or disease. To think so was a distraction.

"He's just a symptom," Danny said. "It's a bigger problem than that. Hang on, we need to debrief."

Danny opened the rear door and dragged the man out. Now that he was back where he'd made his attempt at kidnapping, confronting his victims, there was no defiance left in him. He was meek and afraid, his shoulders sagging. She steered him to the rear of the motor home, where there was a ladder to the roof. She took the steel handcuffs off her belt and manacled his right arm to the ladder, then cut the zip-tie binding his hands with her hunting knife.

"Be right back," she said, and strode away to confer with the parents of the child who had escaped kidnapping. They needed to know the situation was officially handled.

A number of onlookers gathered around the prisoner while she had her back turned, and there was some ugly noise rising among them. Danny came back in time to overhear a couple of men making plans that would be fatal to the "fucking kidnapping bastard." She needed to make her ward seem a little more human, fast, or she would have to post a guard to keep him from getting lynched.

"What's your name?" she asked, loudly enough to be heard by the others.

"M-Mike. Mike Patterson," the man said.

"I'm Sheriff Adelman, Mike. And these here are my people. We're one big team. We look out for each other. If I say 'don't kill you,' they won't. But if I decide you fucked up too bad to live, I don't have to say shit. They'll take care of business without me needing to ask. Are we clear?"

"You can't just kill me. That would be murder." Mike was pale now, the gash on his brow as vivid as a torch singer's lips.

"Tell it to the judge," Danny said, and then turned to her companions. "Nobody touches him, understood? He thought he was doing himself and the kid a favor. He heard the rumor about the safe place, and somebody else stole *his* kid. I think the safe place is bullshit, but Mike believed it enough to risk ending up just like this here."

Crawford advanced through the crowd. "He won't be the last, Sheriff. We don't have the bandwidth to deal with this. We need to send a message."

Danny looked at him in mild disbelief, then called his bluff, offering him her knife handle-first. "Then kill him. Go ahead. I gotta take care of the Leper."

Crawford just stood there. Nobody could quite make eye contact with Danny.

"Where's Amy?" she said, when she judged enough silence had gone by. "Mike Patterson here's got a broken foot. Somebody make sure she looks at it."

Danny walked away. Nobody would kill Mike now, she thought. He was human again. At the thought, her eyes slipped over to the interceptor, inside which the Leper was sitting very still.

Topper returned to the site before Ernie and Conn. He'd had difficulty getting radio reception, so his arrival with the kid on his bike was unexpected. As always, anxious eyes searched along the direction he'd come from, looking for the other scouts. People had a way of disappearing all the time these days. See you later, then never see you again. Topper handed the kid to Maria; she was mother hen to the small ones. Another child to fuss over might make up for the black eye.

"I found this kid about ten miles along. Nobody else around. I think everybody except him got chewed and he's all that's left. Check this out," Topper added, and opened the fiberglass pannier on the side of his bike.

The weird little dog looked out, eyes bugging at the unaccustomed crowd of people around him. Danny had been out in the fields with the Leper, cleaning her up; they did everything at a distance for privacy's sake. Now she was coming back, although the Leper remained where she stood in the swaying grass. People were willing to put up with her presence, but only barely. She had to stay well apart, and even then, there were always eyes on her.

"Who's this?" Danny asked, when she saw the kid.

"He don't talk," Topper said.

"Silent kid, huh?" Danny pronounced. "I like 'em that way. What the hell kind of dog is that?"

"It's his," Topper said. "I never seen one like it."

"It's a Boston Terrier," Amy Cutter said, coming around from behind the White Whale. "Smallest of the bulldogs. A miniature breed, unlike the French or English Bulldogs, which are dwarf breeds. Mike's foot isn't broken, by the way; it's sprained. Did you make the cut on his head?"

"Do I carry a machete?"

"In your car, you have one," Amy said, kneeling.

The dog seemed to know she was an ally, because he immediately hopped out of the pannier and bounced up and down in front of her.

"Well I *didn't* cut him," Danny grumped. She often found herself bickering with Amy the same way they did as young girls. It was ridiculous, irritating, and comforting at the same time.

"Thanks for not smashing Mike too bad, Danny," Amy said. "He's scared out of his brain."

Amy gave the dog a quick examination out of old habit, checking ears, eyes, and abdomen; although she was the Tribe's doctor, Amy had been a veterinarian in the time before. Her straightforward brand of medicine was ideal for the life they led: She could set bones, stitch wounds, and sling antiseptic; she could do surgery in the back of a pickup truck. If somebody had cancer or a chronic illness, those were problems for God.

The dog inspected, Amy then examined the boy in much the same way: She soon determined he was suffering from ringworm and malnutrition. Amy was good with kids. They seemed to understand her better than a lot of adults did.

"You sure don't talk much," Amy said.

The silent kid said nothing.

Twenty minutes later, the remaining scouts came back: Ernie and Conn had gone on another thirty miles down the highway, with a detour down a southward fork that ended in a burning town they couldn't possibly get through, unless they waited for it to burn out. It looked like Mike's biker gang, the Vandal Reapers, had gone through that way. There were a lot of fresh corpses, some of them reanimated, the bodies hacked and shot. The Tribe could go straight on or straight back, and the rumors were true: The zeroes got real thick after mile twenty in the easterly direction.

"There's a big old truck stop about halfway," Ernie explained, mopping the grease off his spectacles with a blackened handkerchief. "There's a crossroads there, route goes north-south, but the fire closed the south end. We saw some travelers on foot, regular folk it looked like, coming the other way, but they bugged out when they saw us."

"So we got this kid," Danny said. "And a kidnapper. There's zeroes to the east and fire to the south. Marauders to the north. This party never ends. Okay," she barked, turning to face the main group, "we roll out at sundown, people. Let's get to the truck stop, and then we'll see if we can locate a route around the swarm and keep going east. If not, we backtrack three days. I'm going to do a little recon before dark. Now, can somebody figure out why the fuck our radios don't work?"

"I'm on it," came a response from the crowd.

Danny turned to the silent kid, who hovered not far away, his dog at his ankle. He reminded Danny of her sister Kelley when she was that age, big-eyed and quiet, worried.

"I'm gonna keep you safe, you understand? That's a promise," she said.

By way of reply, the boy raised his arm and pointed an accusatory finger at the crooked outline of the Leper. Danny bounced her damaged hand against her thigh, framing a response.

"That . . . that's my kid sister," Danny said. "Guess you figured out what's wrong with her. She doesn't bite, okay? I promised I'd keep you safe. She will not hurt you."

The kid lowered his arm. But like so many of the others in the Tribe, he didn't take his eyes off the Leper, either.

6

"Recon" wasn't in fact what Danny had in mind. She simply didn't want to discuss the real nature of the mission: It was time to take the Leper on a feeding trip.

For twenty minutes Danny drove through open country, then the fringes of a settlement, slowing down when they entered a light industrial area not far from the husk of a medium-sized town. A dead end by road, but with railway lines running through it.

"What are you in the mood for? Rats?" Danny said, as they rolled past shuttered repair shops, auto parts distributors, and warehouses.

"It's not funny," the Leper said, drawing breath for the purpose.

"You never did have a sense of humor, Kelley."

"Or maybe you were never funny. Do you know what rats taste like?"

They pulled up in front of a ransacked food distribution center beside the railway tracks. The place had been thoroughly trashed by survivors looking for sustenance. As much had been trampled underfoot as carried away. There was a lot of rotten garbage strewn around in front of the yawning warehouse doors.

And there were plenty of rats.

The vermin population had exploded since the outbreak. Most species except man were making a comeback, especially those that thrived on human detritus. There were millions of tons of hermetically sealed food out there, even after the better part of two years. Cheetos would be available for decades, entombed in airtight plastic. Most of all, two hundred million human corpses made a ready supply of protein. Rats and cockroaches and flies had inherited the Earth.

"I hate it," Kelley said.

"I ate a two-year-old candy bar the other day," Danny said. "It had turned white."

"No, I mean not just the rats. All of it. I'm coming apart, Danny. I'm peeling and rotting. Imagine you can't heal. Every little scrape." She filled her lungs again. "The skin on my fingers is worn almost completely off, and there's stuff showing through underneath. My gums are just rags. I can feel parts of the bone in back—I can feel where my teeth go into the bone."

"Wish it wasn't like this," Danny said, knowing it was a feeble response.

"I'm the picture of Dorian Gray."

"I don't know what that is," Danny admitted.

She waited while Kelley stepped carefully out of the interceptor. She had to move cautiously—her flesh was vulnerable.

"Go somewhere else," Kelley said. "The rats are afraid of the car."

"Good hunting."

She was already crossing the littered street.

"I'll see you in an hour and a half or so," Danny replied. "Be here, okay? Sundown is coming."

Danny watched as the bandaged woman lay down in the midst of the garbage in front of the food warehouse. The rats would smell death. They would come swarming. And Kelley would feast on them once they got too close. Danny had learned a great deal about the undead through her sister; she was one of them, a thinker, the intelligent variety.

Kelley had died in Danny's arms and come back different from the rest of the undead. She remained the person she had been, mostly. Danny had almost blown her sister's brains all over the farmhouse they had taken shelter in. If she had, she might have blown her own brains out, too. But Kelley had spoken. *I'm still me,* she'd said. And a pick of ice had been thrust down the center of Danny's brain that was as cold and sharp today as in that moment. She would never forget the horror of that. It had been seasoned by hope, somehow. Some crazy idea that the dead might not always be lost.

But Kelley *was* lost. She had returned with her memories, the record of her life, intact inside her mind. Just as her body was decaying, those things that had been hers were fading by degrees. Sometimes Danny thought she should have pulled the trigger. But she hadn't, and Kelley was now her constant responsibility. It was the price she paid for being a crappy sister, and for putting the Tribe at risk to go find her. Someday Kelley might attack Danny, or kill someone else in the Tribe. It was possible. They talked about it. But Danny didn't think so. Kelley had made some grim calculation and decided not to eat the flesh of men. She had never wavered, at least so far.

The Tribe didn't like it at all. Most of the small children didn't know the truth; the name "Leper" had stuck because it was the only way to explain the concealing bandages. It took new people a few days to realize what Kelley was, and most of the folks who hitched a ride for a couple of days never knew how close they came to a specimen of their worst nightmares. The thinkers they'd encountered were deadly. They could use weapons, lay traps, and make complex plans. They sometimes worked with hunters, the undead who had animal-like intelligence, using them almost like dog packs; the moaners, the stupid ones, were useless to them. But the moaners also seemed to fear the thinkers, and that's why Kelley was allowed to exist alongside the Tribe.

Moaners wouldn't come anywhere near her. They had superb senses of smell: Even the most rotten walking corpse would have fresh-looking tissue in its sinuses. Not pink, but marbled and purple. But it was vital flesh, sometimes so enlarged it bulged out of the nostrils or the hole where the nose used to be. The ones that came shambling toward the Tribe's halting places, though, would smell Kelley and immediately back off. Their incessant moaning would stop. They would slouch away and disappear into the landscape. The hunters were a little more persistent, and might circle a campsite all night, but they'd never come close. It was almost worth the price of having a thinker around. Almost.

This aversion to the scent of thinkers was why Danny escorted Kelley through a few tours of the perimeter wherever the Tribe had halted—the residual smell usually kept the stupider types away, as long as it wasn't windy. It was the same reason she guided her sister *away* from safety when it was time to change her diapers and clean up the spongy, half-rotten skin around her genitals. Danny always buried the baby wipes and diapers in the place she thought most likely to facilitate an attack. They worked better than land mines on the zeroes.

But Danny knew that her people were only waiting for the other shoe to drop. As if Kelley had some diabolical plan to kill them all and eat their guts. Every day, Danny spent a lot of her leadership capital ensuring her sister was safe from destruction by the living. That was one reason she took big risks: it was a show of fearlessness to remind them all who had their back. It kept the balance sheet firmly in her favor. If Danny wanted Kelley around, there must be a good reason: that was the message she wanted them to get. On an average day, she guessed they about half-believed it. Kelley wasn't dangerous—she craved human flesh all the time, but had never actually tasted it.

Danny had lost her sister once. She didn't intend to lose her again. Ever.

She drove aimlessly through the twilight. As long as Danny stayed in the vehicle, she didn't have much to fear from the undead; it reeked of her sister. But another thinker wouldn't hesitate to attack. They didn't fear each other. The Tribe had even found evidence of thinker teams destroying each other. She turned on the headlights and saw a kind of View-Master slide presentation of the apocalypse in exaggerated 3-D. Wrecked cars, burned-out structures, white femurs and rib cages winking out from beneath cars or strewn across the pavement. Sometimes a gallows figure crawling away, clothed in rags and filth. She drove until she came to a low hill, bare of trees or bushes; the entire hilltop had been flattened and paved a long time back, for what purpose Danny couldn't imagine.

She parked at the margin of the paved area in a position that gave her a good view of the landscape below: a town, completely dark and silent, the last of the daylight spread as thin as watercolor on the rooftops. Kelley was hunting on the opposite side of the hill where the uglier businesses had been built, away from the quaint charm of downtown. Danny thought to look at the map and find out what this place used to be called, but it didn't make any difference. Call it Deadville.

She had her elbow out of the open window, relishing the ice-cold air; if anything wanted to attack, she'd hear its feet on the broken pavement. So it was that she felt the sound before she heard it. The door panel was vibrating under her arm. She pressed her one finger against it and felt the rumbling in the sheet metal. Then the sound reached her ears: engines. A lot of engines, very far away. Was it the Tribe? Could they have come after her, for some reason? But no; they'd be on the other side of the hill. This sound was coming from outside the town. She permitted herself another minute of listening, until she was certain: motorcycles. A lot of them. It sounded like early morning on Bike Day back in Forest Peak, when the Harleys started coming in big groups up the mountain roads, audible ten minutes before they came into view.

Is it the Vandal Reapers? Danny wondered. *Maybe not worth finding out.*

Then there were gunshots—some single, some rapid-fire, punctuating the rise of the engine sounds. She dropped the interceptor into neutral and rolled backward away from the rim of the hill, lights out. Then she turned around and drove down the road she'd come up, maintaining darkness until she was among buildings at the bottom of the hill. She had to be sure she wouldn't light up the sky. Artificial illumination caught the eye in these times.

It took her half an hour to backtrack to the place she'd left Kelley to feed. She wasn't there.

Danny honked the horn a couple of times, then zipped up her jacket and retrieved the snub-barreled shotgun from the passenger foot well. Best not to remain in the vehicle in case it attracted unwanted attention. She checked the immediate area outside the warehouse for signs of other zeroes, then ran across the truck lot to a security booth. There wasn't any glass in the windows, but it would protect her from a rush, at least. She waited. After a couple of minutes that felt like days, Danny saw something move on the far side of the rubbish piled up outside the warehouse. It might have been Kelley. She waited, holding her breath. The light was poor. But she saw it again: a distinct human figure, hunched over, moving between the buildings. Then it was out of view.

She didn't think it was Kelley she'd seen; maybe a hunter. But any hunter would have fled at Kelley's scent. So if it was one of the wolf-smart zeroes, that meant Kelley was nowhere nearby.

Then Danny saw the pale ripple of the muumuu coming out of the warehouse itself. Kelley had been in there. Who—or what—had been nearby?

She tabled that aspect of the problem; her sister had reached the interceptor and was looking around. Or, to be precise, scenting the air. It disturbed Danny to think the thing that had been her sibling now operated more by smell than sight.

"Kelley!" Danny whispered, as loudly as she dared. The thin neck swiveled around. Danny saw Kelley's bandages were smeared with blood. She would have to change them before they returned to the Tribe. Kelley walked toward the interceptor and looked inside, then again scented the air with her nose tipped up. Danny emerged from the security booth, but kept most of her mass behind it, opposite where she'd seen the unknown figure move out of sight.

"Over here," she said. Kelley came swaying toward her, and Danny felt the same thrill of horror she experienced every time: All her instincts cried out that the enemy was coming. That she needed to destroy this thing.

"Whenever I come near, you hold your breath," Kelley said, when she was close to Danny.

"Because you stink," Danny lied. "There was another zero. I saw it."

"Yes," Kelley said. She never bothered to lie anymore. That was a thing the living did. If she didn't want to admit something, she simply remained silent.

"A thinker?"

"Yes."

"Did you talk to it?"

Kelley chose silence.

"Goddamn it, Kelley, I need to know."

No response.

Danny found her hand on the butt of her sidearm. Kelley's silences had become deeper, lately. It was hard to explain. Somehow she seemed to be retreating inside herself. Without her personality to hang on to, Kelley was just another sentient corpse; the thing Danny feared the most was an ambush by her own sister, if that glimmer of her old self ever went away completely. The factor that kept Kelley in touch with her past humanity might be Danny's determination to keep her that way. If Danny broke that compact, there would be consequences.

Danny let her hand fall into her pocket and retrieved the keys to the interceptor.

"The subject is not closed. But we need to get out of here. There's a shitload of motorcycles coming."

Danny drove back by a more direct route than the one they'd taken out. Kelley had removed the bandages that bound up her head—once there was blood on them, she was in danger of getting moldy underneath. Danny would rewrap her before they came into view of the Tribe's encampment.

She glanced over at her sister after a period of prolonged silence—the kind of silence that made Danny feel alone. The features of Kelley's face were recognizable, but discolored, sagging. The skin had tightened across the high bones—brow and cheeks—and lost its shape around mouth and neck. Kelley looked almost as if she had aged fifty years. Or, if Danny was honest, as if she'd died and begun to rot.

"So who was it?"

"One of my kind," Kelley replied. "But they're boring. They don't have any feelings."

"You understand that I consider that consorting with the enemy, right? Did you talk about the Tribe? Our defenses? Our route?"

"He wanted me to join his group. They've been hunting along the roads to the north."

"Did you talk about the Tribe?"

"No, Danny. We didn't. He already knew."

Kelley took a long breath that would have signified emphasis for a living person. But she was merely out of air for speaking. Danny found herself gnawing at the knotted skin over her fingerless knuckles. The instant she realized she was doing it, she took her hand away from her face—no good setting an example that way. *He already knew?* What the hell did that mean? *How* did he know? She wanted to ask but knew Kelley wouldn't respond to such questions. She didn't when she was alive.

"Okay," Danny began, speaking carefully, "he already knew about the Tribe. Probably rumors and stuff. So he just wanted you to join his group and kill the living for food."

"He also wanted to know how many kids we had," Kelley said. "Like, if we had too many."

"How many is 'too many' children?"

"I don't know. I said no."

"Okay," Danny said, as if she understood. "What else?"

"What else did we talk about?"

"Yeah."

"None of your business."

When Danny returned to the Tribe, Kelley's bandages refreshed, she moved into action without delay. She reported on the motorcycle gang and ordered everyone to saddle up immediately.

The Reapers, if that's who they were, hadn't followed her, as far as Danny could tell; at least, she hadn't heard any engine sounds when she stopped on the road to wrap up Kelley.

There were no surprises as far as the truck stop the scouts had found, but twenty kilometers after that, the landscape was writhing with the undead. Beyond the infested area, it was supposed to be completely zero-free for a day's drive or more. That was good enough for the Tribe. They weren't going to a specific destination. It didn't work that way. But the project of going eastward, the logistics of it, kept everybody occupied and gave them a common purpose. So rather than give up, they all focused on the problem of finding a route around the swarm—as if it was part of a long-term plan, and not merely another meaningless obstacle.

And for many, it did fit in with a plan of sorts. The rumors of a safe place came from that direction like the smell of a summer day comes off the horizon before the sun has even risen. It was something to hope for, a direction to go. Eastward, somewhere. They'd heard about this possible Shan-gri-la from hitchhikers and fellow-roamers. How far east, though, nobody could say.

Danny was out front in the interceptor with Kelley at her side as always; then came the scouts on their motorcycles, half a dozen of them. They rode herd, sometimes falling back, sometimes stringing out ahead, keeping an eye on the shadows. The main file of vehicles traveled in no particular order, except that the motor home was always in the middle, and the ambulance always at the back; the convoy was mostly heavy-duty pickups, SUVs, and panel vans. What people wanted was a heavy vehicle with a durable suspension and enough room to lie down inside. There was also a roach coach, which served meals for the entire Tribe, if there was food enough, and a lineman's repair truck with elevating basket that made an excellent sentry platform. One of the vans contained enough tools to perform almost any vehicle repair. Spare parts could be found wherever there was an abandoned car.

They had a dedicated vehicle for tagalong strangers to the Tribe, as well: the Courtesy Bus, a parking shuttle painted with black-and-yellow zebra stripes to make it easy to find at the airport. The driver sat inside an improvised angle iron and chicken wire booth, and the big windows made it easy to see what the passengers were up to from outside. Mike Patterson was handcuffed to one of the grab bars in the back of the shuttle, which very much interested the other outsiders aboard that night. The Tribe's policy was to pick up hitchhikers regardless of their appearance, as long as there were fewer than six in any one group. But they had to ride in the shuttle. The driver, Sue Baxter of Tulsa, Oklahoma, was prepared to drive the shuttle into a telephone pole if her charges tried to commandeer the vehicle. They'd never had any trouble like that, but after all that had happened so far, there was a tendency to prepare for the worst-case scenario.

They drove through the night, reaching the truck stop as the moon was emerging cold and hard above the distant hills.

It was one of those vast plazas of asphalt and concrete designed to get hundreds of vehicles and their passengers refueled and back on the road all at once, day and night. There must have been fifty gas pumps under a gigantic gullwing roof mounted on posts. At the center of the plaza was a sprawling collection of ransacked fast food restaurants and souvenir shops. They were surrounded by abandoned vehicles, mostly big rigs. There wasn't much left to forage for. But the Tribe wasn't looking for materiel, except fuel. Someday soon, all the gasoline would go bad—phase separation, contamination, and especially water getting into the ethanol-laced stuff. Gas had been around five bucks a gallon when the end came. Now it was priceless—and free of charge, if you had a siphon pump and a lookout watching for zeroes.

Besides gasoline, if there was any, what they needed most was a good place to wait a couple of days while the scouts went the long way around to find a route to the east. These big truck stop plazas were excellent for holing up as they were generally fenced on three sides and the acres of pavement around them meant zeroes couldn't attack from places of concealment. *Nice field of fire, head-to-toe beaten zone, and three-way enfilade potential,* as Danny had once described them. In better times it would have been lit up like the sun at night; now it was dark and full of black shadows that glittered with broken glass.

As the first vehicles in the convoy arrived, a flare went up from the foremost; men and women spilled out of the others with flashlights, dogs, and guns, reconnoitering every corner of the place beneath the wobbling red light of the flare. They looked inside the looted truck trailers, checked all the cars, team-cleared the restaurants and shops, and kicked all two hundred of the restroom stall doors open. They searched the overgrown landscaping and made a circuit of the fence. All clear. No living, and no undead. Danny had taught them the system, and it kept them alive, so they stuck to it.

A heap of mangled hunter corpses piled up among some abandoned big rigs suggested the place had been defended in the recent past—so maybe the local superpredators had been wiped out. The Tribe's dogs, mostly Shepherds, barked furiously at the remains. They had to be pulled off. It was Tribe custom to burn the corpses of the dead and undead alike, but most other groups weren't that organized—or didn't care. They would burn these ones in the morning. As an extra precaution, there were double watches posted on all sides of the perimeter.

Danny sent a team of lookouts five kilometers back down the interstate; they took the truck with the bucket lift. They'd spend the night in shifts at the top of the crane arm, watching in case the Vandal Reaper gang approached. The bucket was retrofitted with a .50 caliber machine gun, but they weren't expected to fight. In practice, the heavy weapon made the crane oscillate so violently it was useless, anyway.

Then she walked through the tall grass beyond the fence with Kelley, making a long, slow circuit of the plaza. Set the smell of a thinker out there like a moat. They'd do it again in the wee hours to make sure no expeditious corpses got too close.

In half an hour, the plaza was occupied, secured, and the Tribe was moved in. It was their equivalent of 1700 hours: quitting time, but not yet bedtime. In fact, it was 1:20 in the morning.

"Can we have a quick talk?" Danny muttered to Patrick on her way back from the circuit. He was headed toward the White Whale with food for some of the kids; there was a DVD presentation of several early *Ren & Stimpy* episodes on the TV in there, to keep the little ones out from underfoot a while.

"Ten minutes," he said.

Danny was at loose ends. Sometimes there wasn't anything to do, despite all that needed to be done. This was one of those moments. She watched the Tribe assemble its fires and begin meal preparations. There was young Michele, and beside her as always her brother Jimmy James, who was shooting up tall all of a sudden; they attached themselves in a general way to Maria, the radio operator, who had lost her husband in Forest Peak.

Danny remembered Michele as a blue-haired girl in deep shock when they'd first met. Now she came off as a grown woman, although she probably wasn't sixteen yet. Danny didn't remember her true age. A similar evolution had happened with Kelley, although Danny hadn't been around for that part of her life. She turned and squinted out into the darkness beyond the pavement where Kelly stood beside the interceptor, motionless except for the rippling of the muumuu in the light breeze. Kelley's head was tilted back; she was smelling the air.

Then Patrick was back, cleaning between his fingers with a dish towel.

"What's up?"

"You and that guy Beowulf . . ." she began, but realized she didn't know what the question was.

"So you want to talk about my old boyfriends."

"I got something on my mind," Danny said. "I can't—"

"Are you feeling inarticulate?"

"Yes."

"What's it about? I mean name names, and we can put it together."

"Kelley."

"Inevitably," Patrick said, as if he'd seen this one coming a long time.

"It's not like you think," Danny hurried to add, although she didn't know what he thought. "It's just—well. I took her out for a feed tonight. She . . . I need you to keep this a secret."

"I have never betrayed a confidence," Patrick said, stiffening his back. "Otherwise I wouldn't have scored as much as I did in my twenties."

"I'm not talking about sex. I'm talking life and death maybe. See, I saw her with somebody. You know we go off on feeding trips. I'm not there the whole time. I leave her alone. Tonight I ran across that biker gang and came back early to pick her up . . . And I saw somebody. Something."

"A person?"

"A thinker. *Another* thinker. They . . . they talked."

Danny felt as if she'd jumped off a cliff. Patrick had every right to run up and down through the plaza shouting this news, if he wanted to. But he wouldn't. Only Patrick. Even Amy might blab. This man had the instinct for discretion.

"Holy fucking shit," Patrick said. "I mean, holy fucking leaping shit." His hands went to his mouth, covered it like an injury.

"That's what I said. You can't tell *anybody*. Not yet. Maybe never. I have to find out what it means first."

"What it means is they're hanging out," Patrick said. "It means—I don't know what it means. Were they like passing a joint back and forth or anything? Dancing? I mean what do thinkers do when they meet?"

"I just saw it for a second. She doesn't deny it. She doesn't even seem to think it's a big deal."

"Maybe it isn't."

"Maybe. There's stuff she didn't tell me."

"As long as nothing happens, it's all good. But Danny? Why did you tell me about this?"

She looked around them, as if the whole Tribe was listening in. In fact, they could not have been more perfectly ignored. There was food and heat and bedding to think about. Nobody cared what the sheriff and her old buddy were whispering about in the shadows.

"First off, because you talk plenty, but you don't tell. And I needed to tell somebody."

"Yeah, but you mentioned Beowulf. Why?"

"That's the thing," Danny said. She was struggling so much with words. Her mind wasn't geared for this kind of abstract thinking. "I . . . I thought after you lost that guy Weaver in the early days, you'd never find anybody else. You were real busted up over it. But then you found Beowulf. And you guys were like really tight. I mean I guess in love, right?"

"Yes."

"And then a few months ago, you kind of stopped talking to each other."

"Yes."

"Were you *really* in love? Like, I want to spend the rest of my life with you?"

"Believe it or not, Danny, even homosexuals can experience the full gamut of human emotions," Patrick said, a little stung. "God, you're so un-reformed in so many ways."

"I didn't mean it like that. You guys were supertight and then you broke up. And he left the Tribe."

"Yep," Patrick said, tight-lipped. Danny realized his eyes were getting wet. It still hurt to think about. That erased any doubts she had about the extent of his feelings. "What does my failed relationship have to do with Kelley?"

Suddenly, Danny found the words.

"I'm wondering if me and Kelley are meant to be together anymore. I did right by her. I did my best. I *found* her. Now the two of us sit together all day like one of those old married couples and there ain't shit between us."

"Ah."

"And I'll tell you what. You know how it felt when I saw that other one there? That other thinker? It felt like I caught her cheating."

"Danny," Patrick said, and took her two-fingered hand in both of his. "Listen to me. Even after the end of the world, with humankind in ruins and zombies everywhere, people can still find love. I think that's awesome. But if we didn't fall *out* of love, too, we wouldn't really be people anymore.

I don't know what Kelley's up to, but you're just doing the hard work of being a fucked-up human being."

Mike Patterson sat on the Courtesy Bus and waited to find out what was going to happen to him. He'd been shackled to a pole since his capture, largely ignored except when people paused outside the shuttle to give him dirty looks. The three other survivors who had ridden with the convoy for several days had decided to take their chances on foot again, staying behind after a quick pit stop to replace a tire on one of the trucks. They had been unnerved by the hatred coming in through the shuttle windows, even if it wasn't aimed exactly at them.

So now Mike was alone.

He'd been able to listen to the driver singing tolerably well in her chicken wire booth, but now that the convoy had stopped, she was somewhere else, probably eating. He felt like a goldfish in a tank: The interior fluorescent fixtures remained on, so he was flooded with baleful green light while the rest of the world was in darkness. He had to pee something wicked. He was hungry. And he stank. Everybody stank, of course, but the sheer terror of having that wild redheaded woman come after him, driving like a demon, charging him, and then him believing she was going to kill him on the spot—he'd gone into perspiration overdrive. His armpits smelled like an electrical fire in an onion factory.

Most of all, Mike wished he could explain himself, or better yet, excuse himself and get the hell out of there. His first impressions of the Tribe were not positive. A lot of hard, unforgiving faces. These people took their cues from the top, and consequently they all displayed a little of the sheriff's badass swagger. After his capture he'd listened to them demanding he be executed to make an example for others who came along that road, and he'd tried to think of what to say that might cause them to spare his life. He'd tried to explain how there was a safe place only a few days to the east, a safe place where they could live themselves, and send the children somewhere even safer. They'd called him ugly names. Then the sheriff had reasserted command of the situation, marked him as hers to decide on, as surely as a panther marks its prey. Since then there had only been the mean stares.

The folding doors bumped open. Mike flinched. He'd been lost in thought; it was like waking up suddenly. For a long moment nobody came up the steps of the bus, and he wondered if someone was playing a trick on him. Then a small head peeked around the kick panel between the seats at the bus entry. It was that kid the bikers had brought back earlier in the day. Despite his nerves, Mike could relish the irony. If he'd kept on driving a while instead of making a run on the convoy, he might have seen this kid himself. And he could have taken him away, penalty-free. Nobody would ever doubt he was doing something good-hearted, in fact, even if it did happen to get Mike himself to safety as well. Instead he'd tried to grab one of the Tribe's kids and now he was on two hundred shit lists.

The dark humor of the thing evaporated when Mike realized what must be happening. The kid aboard the shuttle was a decoy. They were going to set him up and kill him, using the boy as an excuse. Mike turned his eyes firmly away—there wasn't anything else he could do, chained up as he was. He kept his eyes fixed on his own reflection in the back window, a steely outline filled in by darkness.

The boy didn't say anything. Mike had heard him referred to by some of the others as the Silent Kid, so this wasn't a surprise. But he could see the child advancing down the aisle behind him in the reflection. And *through* the reflection he could see the light of the shuttle falling on faces outside, watching at a distance. Angry, flat eyes and thin-set mouths. They were watching to see what happened. Maybe they considered this kid to be expendable. What did they think, that he was one of those child-cannibals or something?

The kid stopped two rows of seats away and stared at Mike. His small dog came along behind him but stayed well away from the stranger, preferring to shiver and flex his ears up and down in an anxious manner. Mike stared at the reflection, which the kid didn't seem to notice. They stayed like that for a long time, until Mike felt a serpent of icy sweat running down his neck.

Then a singsong voice cried out, "There you are!"

A moment later the Tribe's Dr. Amy came bustling aboard, followed by the blond man, Patrick, whose face looked like it had been pretty badly smashed at some point. The thick features didn't match his willowy build. He was missing some teeth. The Silent Kid turned to look at them, but Mike kept his eyes averted. This could all be part of their sting operation.

"Hey, kidnapper guy. Did anybody feed you yet?" Amy continued. Mike had met her when she'd splinted his foot shortly after his capture; it hurt abominably but she'd done a good job of immobilizing it, so the pain was more of a dull roar than a series of sharp crescendos.

"My name is Mike," he replied, still keeping his face to the window.

"That was it," Amy said. "Also, if you have to do a number one or two now is kind of a good time."

"God, he's not an infant," Patrick said. Mike knew his name because he'd assisted Dr. Amy with his foot. "Do you need anything?" he added, addressing Mike. "The sheriff told me to hook you up."

"He's not talking," Amy said. "He's caught the not-talking disease from this nasty little kid!" She gave the Silent Kid an unexpected tickle on his ribs. The boy jumped in the air and made a strange croaking sound, but didn't laugh. "Aha, you almost talked!" Amy crowed. The Boston Terrier leaped up and down.

Patrick cut in. "Seriously, Mike. Now or never. Grab something to eat while it's hot and so forth. I'll get you something. Are you allergic to wheat? Vegetarian? Anything like that?"

Mike realized the man wasn't kidding. He decided their attention must not be a trick. He said, "I'll eat anything. That would be good. And maybe I could stretch my legs a couple minutes and take a whizz."

Mike relieved himself at the edge of the darkness, facing outward into the night. There was a huge old man like a derelict yeti standing a few yards away. He had a fine hunting rifle in his hands. The Tribe called him "Wolfman." Mike felt pretty conspicuous—he was not far from the shuttle bus and its sickly light fell on his back, and people were still giving him the evil eye at any opportunity, even while he had his penis out.

He heard the Wolfman muttering to himself. He could also hear relaxed, everyday voices and the boom and crackle of campfires off in the distance. He smelled food cooking. Someone was playing a ukulele and singing. He heard the redheaded sheriff's hoarse voice at the far end of the rest stop, barking out orders to somebody—apparently there was a line-of-sight gap among the perimeter sentries in the form of a drainage ditch, and she was hollering someone into position to keep an eye on it.

"Okay," Mike said. "I'm done."

The Wolfman escorted him back onto the shuttle, but omitted the handcuffs; a minute later Patrick returned with a tin pie plate loaded with food. It was canned beans, Spam, and fruit salad in a little school lunch portion, barely a year past its serve-by date. The fruit salad knocked unexpected tears out of Mike's eyes. He'd put just such things in his son Kevin's lunch. Whatever these people thought, Mike was still grieving. Despite his hunger, he put the food down and pinched his eyes with forefinger and thumb to stop the tears.

"Are you okay?" Patrick asked. He was sitting up at the front of the bus. The Silent Kid was next to him, holding the little dog.

"I lost my boy, Kevin. Brave little guy. He went to the safe place, I guess. I hope. But he was all I had in the world."

"I lost my boy, too," Patrick said. "He was only forty-four."

Mike looked sharply at him, but Patrick's broken face was bent with genuine sorrow. Must have been a lover or something, Mike figured. Still, he couldn't eat. The hunger had been drowned by memories of his son. He rested his arms on the back of the seat and lowered his head between them.

He didn't want to talk. He didn't want to explain. He wanted to die peacefully by willing his heart to stop.

Patrick tried to open a conversation again, but there was nothing to rouse Mike from his thoughts, so he left the bus. The Wolfman stood sentry outside, scratching his ass. The Silent Kid and his dog remained there to observe Mike's bent shoulders. Eventually, after the food was cold, Mike looked up at the Kid. His eyes were bloodshot and tears had made clean patches over his cheeks.

"You can hear, even if you can't talk," Mike said. "My boy couldn't hear so good. He was maybe a year smaller than you. Deaf in both ears."

He left it at that for a while, his chin quivering while he tried to keep the sorrow back. There wasn't time for emotions now. He was still in danger, even if there were a few kind people among the Tribe. Then, when the Kid remained where he was, he and the squat-faced dog staring at Mike like he was the Mona Lisa, he decided to lay some home wisdom on the boy. Something he should have said to his own boy before it was too late.

"Listen . . . if somebody grabs you, you do everything in your power to get away, you understand? And get back where you were when they did it. People will come back, looking. God knows I sure did. I know that one patch of ground where they grabbed my boy better than the house I grew up in. But my boy didn't come back."

The Kid was silent. The dog broke wind.

"I don't know this here Tribe very well. You neither. They got a wrong side and I'm on it. So I don't think you should trust them too much. Mercy is something to look for in people. Hearts without mercy got a cruel streak instead."

Mike saw the sheriff amble up to the Wolfman outside the Courtesy Bus. They had a conversation in low voices, Danny pointing here and there, probably discussing vulnerabilities in their position. Mike's time to tell the kid anything useful was probably running out—he didn't want the child around, in case people got the wrong idea.

"Listen, okay? I'm not some kind of child-stealer or anything. I'm a regular guy, too, swear to God. But there are a lot of real kidnappers around. Stick with the sheriff. I think she might be the only shit-together individual on the road."

A few seconds later, a posse of men with loud voices marched up to the sheriff and Wolfman outside the shuttle. They were talking about Mike and it didn't sound like they wanted to invite him to a warm fireside chat. His heart accelerated: If they saw the kid in here they'd probably rush the bus and kill him on the spot.

"Don't let yourself get seen," Mike said, and to his relief, the Kid seemed to get it. He ducked down between the seats, dropped the dog, and snaked his way forward. The dog followed. They slipped down the steps, and moments later Mike saw the kid evaporating down the outer side of the caravan a few vehicles away, the dog's pale spots a semaphore in the shadows at his feet. The argument broke up outside after the sheriff raised her voice. Then she came aboard the Courtesy Bus and snapped the handcuffs around Mike's wrist and the pole again.

"It's for your own safety," she said, and threw him a blanket. Then she went back out into the night.

"The sheriff says there's a big-ass scooter club behind us somewhere," Ernie said. "But that ain't my concern. My concern is we're being shadowed."

The scouting teams were composed of outlaw bikers, and they mostly hung together in their off-hours; now they were sitting on the ground with their backs propped up on bedrolls, encircling a fire they'd built on top of a manhole cover so the asphalt wouldn't heat up and stink. A dozen of them, looking not much different than they would have before the crisis, except all of them were lean. You couldn't develop a beer belly in this world anymore. They wore scuffed leathers and old denim vests emblazoned with the names of their various clubs.

The biker subculture had completely changed: There were some huge gangs that rode around pillaging human settlements; that was likely what Danny had spotted, and surely the Vandal Reapers fell into that category.

But most bikers found themselves unaffiliated and came together in small bands, like the scouts of the Tribe. They had lost the rest of their local chapters, and with them, their allegiance to the bigger clubs, when the dead rose up. Women were treated as well as the men, too. That was another change in the zeitgeist. Like Charity, who had destroyed her resurrected husband with a broken kickstand. She bedded with Conn these days and would drop him, too, if he came back.

"We're being shadowed by what?" Topper grunted, and spat through the gap in his teeth into the fire.

"A Chevelle. Fuckin' early seventies SS unless I'm very much fuckin' mistaken."

"I mean what's driving it? Man or zero? A gorilla?"

"If I known that," Ernie replied with great dignity, "I woulda said 'we're being shadowed by a fuckin' gorilla' or whatnot, man. I don't know what's following us, except it's driving a sweet-lookin' Chevelle."

There were Vagos, Highwaymen, Hell's Angels, and Mongols present in the scout's circle, along with a number of previously unaffiliated riders. There remained only one old-school source of friction among the bikers: A couple of them rode Japanese machines. All but two of the scouts were men. The gender line didn't much matter anymore among the Tribe, but women didn't seem to take to the scouting lifestyle.

Although she didn't ride, they considered Sheriff Danny to be one of their own: a scout and the right kind of hard core.

Conn spoke, a sound like a castle gate grinding shut. "I didn't see nothing."

"You wasn't fuckin' looking is why you didn't see nothin'," Ernie said, his voice rising into a whine. "I seen it first time a couple days back. It was parked by the road. We scooted clean past it, and I noticed it 'cause my old man had the same model. If it's what I think it is, it's got the LS6 454 power plant. Highest factory horsage of any car as of that time. The Beast. Anyway it fuckin' turned *my* head."

Ernie and Topper were buddies from the time before; Ernie looked like a hairy, bespectacled skeleton held together with veins and horsehide. Topper was more of the big ugly type, and the lead man in the scouting outfit. He wasn't the meanest—that was Conn; Charity was probably second-meanest— but the smartest. Smart was back in style in those days, and in typically short supply.

"So you saw it another time? And it was the same one?" Topper prompted, when Ernie seemed to have sunk into a nostalgic daydream.

"Yeah. Yesterday we was going out on our scouting run and there was a road para-leel to ours and I saw it again, caught the color. Astro Blue. It was behind trees and bushes and shit. I only got a glimpse."

"Did you see it after that?" Conn said. He looked more irritated than usual, like a pissed-off sledgehammer, probably because Ernie's story didn't reflect well on his abilities as a scout.

"No. I *heard* it. Remember when we was coming back tonight and we stopped for a fuckin' piss? I heard it right as we shut down the scoots. Off in the distance real far. Then it stopped, too. But I know the sound 'cause I used to listen for it when my old man come home from the VFW. Had to be the same model. You-nique sound."

"We should tell the sheriff about that," Topper said.

"It don't mean shit," Conn rumbled.

"That's for her to decide, man," Topper said. "Ernie, go tell the sheriff. We don't need any more fuckin' baby snatchers sneakin' up on us."

"She'll just bitch slap me for not checking it out at the time," Ernie pleaded, his voice coming out of his red-tipped nose. "How come you kiss her ass so much, Topper?"

"You gotta learn the difference between rimming and being polite," Topper replied, and heaved himself to his feet. "I'll tell her. You owe me a beer."

You owe me a beer was the expression people said to mean *you can never repay me for this*, because there was no beer left in the world, except the occasional tub of sour home brew.

7

Topper walked through the Tribe's stronghold from campfire to campfire—they were kept going all night, in all weather—to the outer perimeter, nodded to the nearest sentry, and stepped off the pavement onto the dirt and into the darkness.

Topper located the interceptor, parked at a distance from the rest of the convoy in the gravel area reserved for overflow parking, now knee-deep in weeds, not far from the low perimeter fence. They usually arranged the Tribe's vehicles in a long crescent, so both ends of the line were visible from the center; certain vehicles were set a little apart, like the Courtesy Bus, fuel storage trucks, and the like. Danny always parked farthest from the rest, outside the range of firelight and voices. Most folks assumed it was because of the monster she rode with. Topper thought it was more likely she just didn't want to be around people.

The police Mustang squatted like a lion out at the edge of the property. He could see Danny doing something with the Leper—Kelley, he knew her name to be, but "Leper" was far more fitting. Sister or not. Ernie was half right about the ass-kissing: The sheriff could hold a grudge like nobody else. Better not to piss her off. She wasn't a physical threat to Topper, but she could turn disapproval into a painful weapon.

"Is there a problem?" Danny asked, when she saw who approached.

"Ernie thinks we're being paced by somebody in a Chevelle SS."

"And it didn't occur to him to hunt them down?" she said.

Now that Topper was close, he could see Danny was winding fresh bandages around the Leper's head. He caught a glimpse of matted hair and nothing else; her face was lost in shadows. He almost wanted to see her clearly without the wrappings. See what a tame thinker looked like up close. Almost.

"That's what I told him," Topper said. "You know how he is, he can't improvise unless I tell him how to do it. But the thing I'm wondering is why some asshole would be following us in the first place. Anybody can tag along. That's well known by anybody that's heard of us."

"Ernie's sure about this?"

"Yeah."

"Could be linked to those motorcycles I heard. Got to investigate that shit."

Danny said something to Kelley that Topper couldn't hear, and the gaunt undead girl walked away through a gap in the fence into the deep dark. She went straight out into the wild grass like there was nothing to fear. For her, of course, there wasn't. Then Danny went around to the trunk of the interceptor and Topper heard the clink of bottles.

"Drink?" Danny asked.

"Why the fuck not?" Topper said, although he could think of a dozen good reasons why not. Like Danny's temper got worse when she was drunk. But a couple of slugs wouldn't hurt.

She threw him a full bottle of Jim Beam and took one for herself, then went back around and sat on the hood of the car. "It's cold out," she said.

"Winter's almost here, I guess," Topper said, and took a couple of burning swallows of liquor. He let out his breath in a *hoo* as if he'd just eaten something spicy.

"Water?" Danny offered him her canteen. Topper wasn't sure if the Leper drank from it or not, so he declined it, and took another blazing pull of bourbon.

"Hood's still warm," Danny added, after they'd been silent a while. "Sit over here and keep your ass from freezing."

They sat on the hood of the Mustang with their feet propped up on the zero-catcher wire across the fender. Danny leaned back on the windshield and looked at the night sky; Topper rested his elbows on his knees and watched the distant campfires scattered around the truck stop plaza. He could see the outline of Wulf Gunnar atop the White Whale, a hunched shape with the barrel of a rifle sticking out of it. The old man spent most of his time up there. Somebody else must be guarding the prisoner.

Topper found himself wondering if he and Danny were friends. They were more like buddies in a military unit than friends, precisely. They'd each been in the Marines, if years apart, so maybe there wasn't much difference. Topper's tour happened before women had combat roles. He and Danny had gone through some heavy bonding experiences after everything went to hell. Their first meeting, she had damn near shot him for murder; since then she was usually mad at him for something or other, but she relied on him a lot, too. Topper kept the scouts organized and stepped in when there was trouble among the chooks. Now it seemed almost like she was reaching out to him, trying to be nice or something. Or maybe it was nothing more than she didn't want to drink alone.

They were silent except for the occasional hard swallow to get the raw spirits down. Danny could drink like nobody else Topper knew, excepting Wolfman Gunnar. But she was just passing the time on this occasion. She wasn't drinking for effect, as far as he could tell.

"So," Topper began, and said nothing more.

"I got too much on my mind," Danny said, once it became clear Topper was done speaking. "You guys deal with the Chevelle however you want. Keep him away from the convoy. I'm more worried about how we're going to get around those zeroes up ahead."

"It's bad," Topper said. "Where we turned around they were horizon to horizon out ahead, thousands of them. Like fuckin' two-leg cockroaches."

"They didn't follow you, right?"

"We'd be knee-deep in 'em right now if that was the case."

Danny spat in the grass. "There's something on the other side of that swarm. That guy I captured, Mike? I don't think he's bullshitting about doing the kid a favor when he tried to grab him. He says it's the real deal. Safe place for children, out east of here. The Dakotas, somewhere. We keep hearing about that from different sources on the road. I'd like to find it. See if it's true. That's why we have to punch through here."

"This would be a shitload easier if we had a phone. I miss having a fuckin' phone," Topper muttered, and drank deeply.

"I miss McDonald's," Danny said.

"I don't," Topper said, taking the canteen because his esophagus was on fire. "All it did was make me fart. And my sweat smelled like mayonnaise." It also made him fat and impotent, but he didn't particularly want to get into those details.

"What the hell does mayonnaise smell like?"

He considered it. "I honestly can't remember."

"We'll never have mayonnaise again. Think about that."

"There's about a hundred million unopened jars of it out there. Go nuts."

Danny coughed out her rough laugh. "Are you kidding? Eat mayonnaise after the sell-by date? That's *dangerous*."

They were silent for a minute. Topper couldn't relax around the sheriff. He felt like moving on. She was still lying back on the windshield when he stood up, like a cheerleader waiting for the quarterback, except not. She was looking at the firelight through her bottle. It cast a rippling amber glow on her face.

"I miss beer," she said, sadly.

"Oh, fuck yeah." Topper missed beer so much he even dreamed about it. He looked around at the gigantic darkness beyond the truck stop. "You sure you should be out this far from the convoy? Zeroes could come through that tall grass pretty sudden. It's dark as hell. Even with your sister around, seems like a risk to me."

He knew right away it was a mistake to mention it.

"Don't you worry about us," Danny said, after a silence. "She's keeping all our asses safe. Don't forget that."

Topper knew it was time to get out before the anger built up, so he held the remainder of his bottle out to Danny.

"Keep it," she said, and he did, and walked back toward the scouts' fire to pass it around.

Kelley came back, her bound feet swishing in the grass. She must have been waiting for Topper to move on.

"Catch anything?" Danny asked.

Her sister's slack lungs hissed in a long breath. "No," Kelley said. "I saw a jackrabbit, but they're too fast."

She stood beside Danny, looking at the fires and the silhouettes of the Tribespeople. Danny assumed the conversation was over. But after a couple of minutes, Kelley spoke again, using the same breath.

"I smell hunters."

"There's a shitload of dead ones over there."

"The ones I smell are not dead. They are like me."

"Which direction?" Danny slid to her feet and popped the latch on her holster, placing the bottle on the hood of the interceptor.

"It's faint, but everywhere. In the same way this convoy smells like living blood."

"Is there a threat? I mean, are we in immediate danger?" She opened the driver's side door and reached inside. If she lit up the roof lights, the entire Tribe would go to battle stations.

"You're always in danger," Kelley said. "You remember before, I talked to one of my kind? There's another one around somewhere. I can smell it. Almost like when you feel a car coming before you hear it. Just the smallest hint."

"A thinker? The fuck didn't you tell me this before?" Danny had her fingers on the switch box. She might throw some siren in for good measure. Her heart was starting to race.

"I could not say before, until I crawled on the ground and smelled the grass," Kelley said. "That's what I was just doing when I saw the rabbit. I tasted the dirt. The smells are hidden."

The living Kelley would never have tasted dirt.

"Fuck," Danny said. "Fuck. Okay, you told me, that's the main thing. Party time."

Better to raise the alarm and be wrong than take a chance. She rocked the switches and the lights came on, blue, red, and white throbbing over the dark perimeter. Voices went up around the encampment. About two seconds later, headlights glared on in the middle distance beyond the interstate, an engine revved, and the mysterious Chevelle came roaring down the road past the truck stop.

Gunfire erupted from the passenger window. Bullets whined off the pavement and hissed through the air. There were shouts of fear—shots and police lights so close together instantly plunged the camp into confusion. A scrap of light revealed a male profile behind the wheel.

Seconds later, Danny's interceptor was howling after the Chevelle in a spray of dust and flying gravel, siren screaming. Topper saw the sheriff's silhouette at the wheel, outlined by firelight for a moment, her face constricted in a snarl, the thin scarecrow of her sister in the seat beside her. The bottle was still rolling around on the hood of the car. As she reached the roadway it was flung clear, and shattered on the yellow line. Then they were gone in a red streak of taillights.

Topper ran for his bike. In under a minute, the scouts were on the chase. It was time to find out who was at the wheel of that Chevelle.

8

For several miles Danny fought to close the gap. The Chevelle was one of the muscle classics from before computers ran the engines. It must have been bored out and supercharged, because the interceptor couldn't gain on it, although it had a technical power advantage. And the driver was nerveless, precise, making superb use of the road. He turned his headlights off for long stretches to make himself invisible, but couldn't lose his pursuers because his brake lights still worked. That was all Danny knew about the driver, except he might have a confederate to do the shooting. But he might not. He hadn't been aiming for effective fire.

Danny, however, planned to make her next shot count. There were sabot rounds in her tactical shotgun that would punch right through the Chevelle from end to end, if she could get a clean bead on it: Sabots were sharp steel projectiles with fall-away boots around them to increase velocity and accuracy—like a two-stage rocket out of a gun. A gift from a SWAT locker in Nebraska. Right now she was mostly struggling to keep the interceptor on the road. The pavement was in rough shape, and at 95 MPH the steering wheel needed two complete hands, not the seven digits she was working with. She realized the unknown driver must have been waiting all along, concealed near the truck stop, knowing they would come that way. This was all part of a plan, and it might be a diversion.

"Smokey to scouts, go back and seal up the defenses," Danny barked into her radio handset. "I think this is a decoy, over."

There was a broken reply; she couldn't understand it. The damn radios were still clouded with choppy static. The scouts continued to follow after her on their motorcycles, so they hadn't gotten the message. Maybe they *all* ought to turn around, but Danny wanted to know the driver's motive. Then she wanted to crucify him on the roof of his own machine. It would be a public service message to others who came along, in case they thought her clemency toward Mike was some kind of standard behavior: *Hi, I'm Danny Adelman. Do not fuck with the Tribe.*

"If they're trying to lure you away," Kelley said, "it's working."

"No shit," Danny said, gripping the wheel like it was a venomous snake. "You worried about it?" Danny took her eyes off the road to look at the bandaged face, as if there was anything there to be learned.

"I'm already dead. Nothing to worry about."

The Chevelle's taillights were out of view between a couple of small, knobby hills. Danny thought she could make the curve between them faster than the Chevelle had, maybe get within firing range. Then she saw dust spiraling up in her headlights, and her foot went to the brake pedal. She battled to keep herself from flying off the road. The Chevelle must have left the pavement.

She lost some traction as the interceptor decelerated, slewing over the tar, and then she turned the wheel over so the nose of the vehicle was pointed up a dirt track that cut in a straight line far out into the rolling grass, well beyond the range of the lamps. A tail of dust boiled through the light, the Chevelle racing away down the track. Danny didn't punch the gas again. She waited.

The bike scouts rumbled up and put a leg down beside the interceptor.

"You have any idea what they're up to?" Topper called out, once Danny had her window down.

"Feels like a decoying action. You guys go back. I'll check this out."

"Alone?"

"I'm not alone," Danny replied. Topper threw a glance at Kelley, but didn't say anything. *Yeah, right,* the look meant. Danny was slow-burning now, but Topper waited.

"If you're volunteering, get in," she said. "The rest of you get the fuck going. Fast."

Topper pulled his bike off the road and laid it down out of view, then climbed into the cramped rear seat of the interceptor. Danny switched off the light bar on the roof, doused the headlights, and eased down the farm road into the darkness. The rest of the scouts passed a look around between them, but the sheriff had spoken. They turned their cycles in a half-circle and hightailed it back toward the truck stop.

The moon was thin and low, but starlight meant they could see shapes in the darkness. Danny pulled the interceptor off the track and she and Topper got out.

Kelley followed them. Danny raised a hand.

"Stay here. He'll back me up."

Kelley filled her empty lungs in order to speak. "I smell blood," she said.

Topper shifted on his feet. He was nervous, maybe thinking Kelley meant *his* blood.

"This is a fight for the living," Danny said. "If you catch a bullet or something, you won't heal. We'll be back in an hour or so. Just wait. Listen to the radio and honk the horn if anything changes back at the camp."

Kelley didn't respond. She'd told them what she knew. She was done.

Danny retrieved a cold-weather jacket from the trunk—it was midnight blue, and would hide her better in the dark than the tan windbreaker she was wearing. Besides, Topper was right: Winter had arrived.

They moved a little way off the shoulder so they weren't in a clear field of fire down the road, then hiked along parallel to it. There was a lot of tripping and cursing in the blackness, and twice they came up against wire fences that were invisible until they hit them.

They both carried shotguns and combat knives; Danny also had her sidearm and a hand grenade tucked away in her utility belt. The scouts had found caches of combat-grade hardware at abandoned military bases and at police stations, and there was a general rule that grenades, rocket launchers, and the like were not possessed by anyone except a few security personnel in the Tribe. It kept accidents and arguments from getting out of hand. In the trunk of the interceptor, Danny kept a black nylon backpack containing enough ordnance to sink a destroyer.

She and Topper stole through the night, getting quieter and more careful as they began to see more man-signs: trash caught in the fences, junked vehicles, wheel ruts going off to various unseen destinations.

Now they were crouching, breathing carefully, hands on their weapons.

Anybody who dared to keep a homestead these days put out security perimeters, the more the better. Mostly it was wires with bells attached to them, moats of broken glass and accordion wire, and walls made of assorted junk, but they might even find generator-powered electric fences, motion detectors, and infrared cameras. This one was different. They could see lights up ahead before they came to the first perimeter defense, and it wasn't much of an obstacle.

It was an old sheep fence with barbed wire coiled along the top on the inside. The idiots had made it easy to get in—the wire should have been on the outside of the fence. Danny tapped Topper's arm: stop. The handful of closely placed lights burning at the bottom of the next hill meant a building with windows. They were still a kilometer distant, but in that heavy darkness the lights stood out like beacons.

"You go around that way, toward the back. I'll come down the road. If I draw any fire, you rush in behind and get the fuckers while they're facing the other way."

Topper made a noise of disapproval.

"What?" Danny said.

"I still think it's a setup. That driver was trying to lure you down this goddamn road, and you know it. Now they got all the lights on and the windows ain't even boarded up, and you think you're just going to draw some blind fire? Hell no. This here is a big old fucking piece of mouse cheese."

"If they see me coming, they won't look for you, that's the whole point."

"I'm just trying to say be careful, Sheriff. Don't go and get yourself killed."

"I hadn't really planned on it."

9

Two minutes later, Danny had reached the dirt road again. Her boots crunched on the loose grit like it was breakfast cereal. She drew a steadying breath and began her march toward the house.

She was within rifle shot now, if it had been daylight. But they wouldn't be able to get a bead on her for a while yet in the dark—even a good night scope would have trouble picking her out at this distance. She kept on walking, her steps amplified in the cool, clear air. She passed through a broken-down gate, a continuation of the sheep fence they'd come up against. It wasn't even locked; there was a gap she could step through.

And as she did so, the floodlights came on.

Danny tossed herself back through the gate and crouched low against one of the crooked posts. Her eyes throbbed with the sudden brightness. There were lights mounted on the roof of the main building, about a fifty-second sprint from her location. They revealed a ranch yard: barns, sheds, a main house, vacant animal pens. Fences running every which way inside a taller fence that marked the borders of the ranch compound itself. No gunshots rang through the night, no shrilling alarms or shouting. Just the lights, staring across the dry grass like sunlight on the moon, colorless and severe with long inky shadows.

They must be automatic, Danny thought. If the occupants were truly looking, they couldn't have failed to see her. But they weren't doing anything about it. *Maybe waiting for a better shot.* Still, Danny's role here was to draw fire.

She hitched up her gun belt, took a few deep drags of air, and then sprinted through the gap in the gate, running zigzag for the nearest cover—a pickup truck on blocks near a cattle pen.

She got behind the truck without incident.

Now she stole along the margin of the pen, then broke cover and ran for a long, low shed. She got her back up against that and dipped around the corner.

No sign of life from the main house.

She drew her Beretta out of its holster and thumbed the safety up. She would use the pistol for cover fire to make her enemies duck, save the shotgun for when she got to the building and needed to clear a room.

She swiftly reached the house. Still nothing.

Okay, now things are getting weird.

It appeared nobody was home. Where was the Chevelle? She could still smell dust in the air; it *had* come this way. But it was not in the yard as far as she could see, and none of the outbuildings would provide sufficient cover. She decided to join Topper around the back, in case it was there.

She kept below the windows and skirted the house; at the rear corner, she risked a hissed signal and waved to Topper, who was hiding behind a stack of rusting natural gas cylinders. Always a good place to seek cover—

people were afraid to shoot at fuel tanks, as a rule, and they were made of heavy steel. No sign of the Chevelle, but there was an open gate at the back of the property and the long straight road continued into the darkness behind it.

They met in the middle of the back wall of the house and took up positions on either side of the back door, which led into a mudroom with the kitchen beyond.

"You see anybody inside?" Danny whispered.

"No, nobody," said Topper.

"Huh."

"Yeah, I know. Weird."

The lights in the house were blazing, the only sound was the hum of a generator running in one of the barns. They both raised their weapons. Danny pumped her fist three times, because she didn't have enough fingers on that hand to count to three, and then they stormed through the screen door, Danny first.

The only thing that came at them was the stench of rotten meat.

The original occupants of the ranch were long gone. Human beings hadn't taken their place.

It could only be zeroes that had squatted there recently—thinkers. Hunters wouldn't know to fire up the generator.

The air was dripping with a miasma of decay, heavy clouds of flies motoring through it. The mudroom was undisturbed. There were rubber boots, jackets, rakes in there. The kitchen was mostly untouched as well, mundane clutter under the bright fluorescent lights, dirty dishes, a coffee cup with a black crust in the bottom. Zeroes don't cook. Bloody footprints all over the floor, however, told of worse to come.

Sure enough, the next room—the dining room, it must once have been—was a scene from hell.

The fly-studded chandelier cast yellow light on a four-walled cesspool. There was a gelatinous coat of rotten blood halfway up the walls, the ceiling spattered with it, the floor toe-deep in the stuff. It was so rancid it bubbled in places, seething with maggots. They could hear it fizzing. No furniture in there, but in the middle of the room, a four-foot-high pile of animal remains. Human and sheep, maybe. Impossible to tell. Topper suddenly puked at the threshold of the dining room, his vomit diluting the stew of gore. Retching, he followed Danny around the perimeter of the room, boots sucking through the effluent, both of them covering their noses and mouths with their sleeves. Neither of them spoke. In the center hall, Topper went left and Danny went right.

She made it all the way to the front parlor before her own belly gave up, because that's where they'd hung the children.

Topper was somewhere in the back and Danny was alone in the parlor when she saw them. The cadavers were roped up on hooks in the ceiling. They had been eaten where they hung, nothing left of them but blackening red pulp in the shape of marionettes. Even then, Danny might have been able to keep her gorge down. But as she passed the swaying remains, one of them lifted its head.

It couldn't speak without lips, but Danny didn't need to discuss the options. The child tried to say something, its eyes staring from crimson, lidless sockets. How life remained in that skinless husk, Danny could not imagine.

"Mercy shot!" she shouted, breaking the silence.

She put a bullet through its brain, ran back out to the front of the house, and heaved her guts out.

If she hadn't gone outside, she wouldn't have seen the flare.

10

By the flickering light of the flare, Danny and Topper ran down the dirt road—the direct route back to the interceptor. But the interceptor was on its way to them. It never occurred to Danny that Kelley could still drive. But there she was, piloting the police car down that rutted strip with skill and considerable speed.

"Get over!" Danny barked as the vehicle braked to a halt beside her. A thick cloud of dust washed past them. Kelley slid across the bench seat and Danny took the wheel. Topper threw himself into the back, his heels up on the hard plastic seat. A chassis-banging power turn took them across the rough grass and then they were racing at high speed for the main road and the way back to the truck stop. Danny switched on the siren and the roof lights. They were going in hot.

"That fucking Chevelle is long gone," Danny barked. "What the hell happened?" There was a lot of confused gabble half-buried in static on the radio. Nobody was answering her calls. They were still several kilometers from the truck stop.

"I heard gunshots on the radio, and then screaming," Kelley said. "It sounded like the kind of thing you'd want a flare for. So I launched a flare."

"So nobody told you what it is? Do we know what's happening?"

"From the noises I heard, the convoy is under attack. But the signal is really bad." At the end of this speech, Kelley ran out of breath, and the final words were forced out of empty lungs in a rush. She didn't take another breath to replace it.

Topper was separated from the front of the vehicle by a thick acrylic partition; he'd never been so close to the Leper, partition or no—he kept her at a safe distance, about the extent of a machete swing. Danny glanced in the rearview mirror and caught his expression.

"She doesn't bite," she remarked, and immediately wished she hadn't.

"I'm still shitting myself about all that blood in the house," Topper said, changing the subject.

"You didn't see the worst of it," Danny said. She didn't expand on the subject. He'd heard the mercy shot. There had been a dying survivor; no point getting into the details. She had the outlines of a plan and preferred to focus on that.

"You saw that road out back of the ranch there. You figure the Chevelle went out that way?"

"Must of," Topper said. "I smelled exhaust when I got there, diesel and transmission smoke. Not just the Chevelle. I think there's a truck, too. They knew that shit in the house would slow us right the fuck down."

"We'll have to deal with them later. When we get back to the Tribe, we're entering a dynamic situation. We may have surprise on our side. If the road is clear, I'm going to drive by once so we can see what's going on, then we'll come in wherever it's hottest, okay? I'll pop the doors from up here. Come out shooting if that's how it is. There's the lights."

It was standard procedure to flood the Tribe's encampment with light if a zero attack occurred; there were spotlights on roof mounts for the purpose. Otherwise it was campfires only, to avoid attracting attention. Fires were a common sight at night—electric light, exceedingly rare.

The entire plaza was lit up now.

Danny raced the interceptor over the crest of a low hill and the scene was revealed before them like a Civil War diorama in a museum. Dozens of figures were running around, chasing long shadows across the tarmac. There was gunfire and smoke. Within moments, they could differentiate men and zeroes: It looked like the place had been assaulted by a big pack of the hunters. Their scuttling, apelike shapes were charging around after anything that moved. Danny saw someone go down under two of the things, and three of the living rushed to pull them off.

Then the interceptor was screaming past the scene. It took all the discipline Danny had not to crane her neck to watch what was happening—but there were people running across the road. She needed eyes front. There was a hunter capering after one of the fleeing figures—she swerved twice and slammed into it. The creature whacked into the hood, cut nearly in half by the wire across the nose of the car, and then was sucked under the wheels. Danny punched the brake and swung the car around, using its velocity to complete a 180-degree switch. Topper banged heavily against the acrylic partition behind her.

The scene was in front of them now. Chaos, hand-to-hand combat. She powered the interceptor forward into the melee, crushing another of the zombies in a spray of black fluid.

"No! You stay in here," she said to Kelley, who had begun to climb out. "Friendly fire." She popped the rear locks, Topper threw himself out of the backseat, and they were running into the fight.

The battle was impossible to make sense of. Everybody was everywhere, no sides. Several zeroes were going after the White Whale, but Wulf Gunnar was up on the roof of the RV, methodically dropping the creatures with his vintage bolt-action Winchester. It looked like he had several young children up there with him. Somebody was pushing them up through the skylight from inside. There were clusters of struggling figures all over the place.

Danny figured the only thing to do was to start killing.

She took down three of the things with ten shots. Guns weren't that useful against the hunters. They were too fast and a head shot was difficult because they ran with their heads tucked down almost to the ground. You had to hit them once in their center mass to stop them, and then shoot the brain. Danny kicked away another of the things that was tearing a meaty flap of skin off a woman who had joined the Tribe only a few days earlier. The woman would be dead by morning. Danny clubbed the rebounding hunter in the face with the butt of the shotgun, then struck it in the temple with a golfer's swing. Its head caved in. The wounded woman was trying to squash the wobbling slab of flesh back on her shoulder, as if it would glue into place. Blood streamed out from beneath it.

There was a lot of gunfire. A stray bullet zinged past her, close.

"Get your backs up against the Whale!" she shouted. Several people heard, and ran in that direction. The simple fact that their leader was on the scene galvanized some folks out of their panic. Wulf shot several more zeroes once people started to move in a consistent direction and he had clear fire. Word was passing around.

Danny ran for the RV herself. A man reeled across her path with a hunter clinging to his back. It hadn't bitten him yet, but he wasn't in any position to defend himself. He was one of the older guys in the Tribe. Danny got hold of one of the hunter's limbs, pulling the hard, dry bones to haul the thing off. It hooked its other arm around the man's neck and drew itself back in.

Its teeth found the man's throat. He shrilled a scream of fear and agony. Then a withered claw came into Danny's field of view from behind the hunter. Kelley. She thrust bony fingers into the monster's eye sockets and pulled its head back until the spine broke. But the thing's jaws didn't release even as it was destroyed; a jet of smoking blood sprayed out of the wounded man's throat and spattered Kelley's face. She lurched backward.

At the same instant, a bullet took the top of the victim's head off. He and the hunter fell in a pile and the blood poured out of him as from an overturned milk bottle. Danny shoved Kelley to the ground and covered her.

"That was meant for you!" she shouted.

Kelley didn't answer. Instead, the same claw, now black with hunter blood, caught Danny by the throat.

"The fuck!" Danny croaked, and slapped the hand away. The power in her sister's limbs was shocking, but she hadn't been hanging on at full strength. Those long yellow teeth were bared, inches from her face.

"The fuck," Danny said again, shoving Kelley away. The two of them sprawled on the bloody pavement. Kelley got her legs under herself first. For a few seconds, she crouched in front of Danny, no different than the hunters, head low, limbs bent. Then something snapped back into place inside her mind—that's how it looked to Danny—because in the next moment Kelley was running into the smoke and shadows. Danny expected to see her shot down, but all the gunfire seemed to be directed toward the outer edges of the action. She wanted to go after Kelley, and took a few steps in that direction. She couldn't see how the fight was going anymore. It was all noise and motion.

Kelley wasn't the main concern right now, or more people would die. Danny looked around, seeking some pattern. The hunters were working in pack formations again, trying to cut people off from the defensive line. She saw Topper and Charity join up with Ernie and some of the other mean sons of bitches she relied on most. They were felling the zeroes with machetes and sledgehammers, out of ammo.

Danny saw a string of the hunters hunching along behind the long row of gas pumps that formed the centerpiece of the plaza. They were going to get behind the Whale and attack from the far side. She shouted for someone to cut them off, but no lone voice was decipherable in the chaos. She broke into a run. It might have been too late already. Several of them seemed to have broken through the line.

Danny took aim with the shotgun, squeezing the trigger on one of the gas pumps. The weapon barked, a tongue of white fire leaping out of the barrel, and then the pump exploded in a mushroom of greasy orange fire. That ignited the next one, and the next. And then one of the underground tanks must have caught fire, because a jet of blindingly bright flame belched into the air and rained down on the hunters.

Danny had forgotten about the sabot rounds loaded in the shotgun. She might as well have launched an antiaircraft rocket. The creatures flailed in the flames.

She flashed back for an instant to the first time she'd fought the zeroes, a lifetime ago, when she'd blown up the gas tank of a car and nearly killed herself. The explosion *had* killed Patrick's boyfriend. A dozen of the hunters were blazing like fatwood now, scarecrows of red fire wheeling around setting others alight. Somebody in the convoy was shooting at them, dropping the burning ones.

A spidery shape came out of the darkness—Danny was still mostly blinded by the explosion—and knocked her down. For an instant she thought it was Kelley, and her guard was slow to come up. She felt dry, broken teeth latch on to her arm, tearing through her jacket sleeve. She had the shotgun across her chest, and used it to shove the monster away. It came at her again. There was something wrong with its skin—not just the usual decay and mummification, but weird, wormlike growths coming out of its face like a beard made out of long, thin warts. Its mouth was a dark crater in the middle of this stuff. The horror of that made Danny recoil. She got the shotgun into its mouth. Its head vanished in a fountain of black puke as she squeezed the trigger. Then she was running for the White Whale.

11

The fires were still burning bright when the last of the hunters was brought down. Danny demanded to know if anyone had seen how the attack started. She didn't mention her personal concern: Had Kelley lied to her? Had there been hunters waiting in a ditch, and she hadn't mentioned them? Nobody had an explanation—the zeroes were suddenly in their midst, as far as anybody knew—until Wulf came down off the White Whale.

"You son of a bitch," Danny said when he shambled up to her.

"Fuck off, Sheriff. Your sister gone bad and you know it. You think just because she dropped outta the same cunt as you she ain't a man-eating monster?"

"She's never eaten human flesh, asshole. You tried to kill her and you killed one of the *living*."

Wulf wouldn't look into Danny's eyes. He watched the tip of his rifle barrel hovering just above the pavement.

"He was already dead. Get out of my face."

Danny got closer, shoving herself up into his line of sight. She had enough adrenaline in her system to freak out a blue whale, and she needed a target, and he'd asked for it. She heard some familiar voices calling to each other in the background. She heard her name. It only made her angrier. She felt something pop inside her head, like a valve breaking, and white-hot rage flooded her limbs and made the darkness around her shimmer with supernatural light. She had to look at her hands to see what weapon she had. How she was going to kill him. Shotgun.

"Danny! Danny, what the hell?!"

It was Patrick. Covered in blood, grabbing her arms to control the weapon. He pushed it down, trying to keep it aimed at the ground. Danny jabbed him in the gut with the stock and he stumbled back, colliding with Wulf.

"Get out of this, Patrick!" she barked.

"I won't," he said. "Wulf's not the enemy."

"He tried to put Kelley down."

Danny considered shooting Patrick, too. She could hit them both with one shot. It would be cathartic to turn this thing into a dictatorship. It would only take a single trigger-pull, and she'd be the dictator.

"Kelley is a danger to everyone, Danny," Patrick implored. "She is. She is. Wulf's a dick. He's an awful person. But he's one of the living and we can't kill each other. He's Tribe. We got to stick together."

"Kelley's tribe, too, fucker," she said. The color was draining out of Patrick's face. He could see the murder in her eyes.

"Jesus Christ, Sheriff, calm down. You on the rag or some shit?" He clapped a paw on Patrick's shoulder. "Listen to this faggot. He's talking sense for once."

"Gee, thanks a lot, asshole," Patrick remarked.

The anger was exhilarating. All the things Danny worried about were gone. Consequences, responsibility, the *plan,* they were gone. There was only righteous fury.

"No. You listen here, you hairy old pile of *shit*. So much as *look* at Kelley again and I will put a bullet through your fucking brain, you hear me? You aren't worth jack to me. She is. You know what? Fuck it, why make threats. Say something else and I'll fucking kill you right here, right now. Say it. Give me a reason."

Wulf stuck his barrel chest out and spat on the ground.

"Fire away, then," he said. "I ain't got time for your little titty-baby feelings about some half-rotten zombie whore. You dumb fuckin' pussy."

A blade of pain slid down the cleft in her brain, pierced her corpus callosum, and twisted. It hurt so much she thought she might pass out. Then it was gone—only a moment had elapsed—and it was gone, along with the anger.

She saw what the old man was doing. He was baiting her. He'd overplayed his hand with the "whore" and revealed it was a ploy. He probably *wanted* to die. *Death by cop*. Danny was not going to give him that satisfaction.

She stepped back another stride and tossed the shotgun to Patrick.

"Thanks for sharing," she said. "Let's talk about what you saw from up on top of the Whale."

Even pushing seventy years old, Wulf was a superb lookout, a deadeye shot, and from his perch up on the roof of the giant vehicle, nobody had to smell him. Danny was right: From that vantage point, he'd seen how the attack unfolded. She put the issue of Kelley out of her immediate thoughts. Her sister might have been destroyed. She might still be out there in the darkness. Danny would find out soon enough either way.

She and Wulf—now sheepish and docile because Danny had controlled the anger he wanted to stir up—patrolled the scorched zone around the gas pumps. He indicated what happened as he'd seen it.

"That trailer over there where the dead zeroes were stacked up? Must be parked over a cellar or something. Heard a door bang. The zombies come out from under it. They were under the fuckin' ground. Come out in a swarm, like ants."

"So they waited all that time before they attacked? Just sat under there and waited?"

Wulf snorted dismissively. "Ain't in their nature. Seems to me they were locked in, and somebody released 'em. That's what I think. Some prick waited until your posse rode off, and then opened the door."

Danny was discreetly flexing her bitten arm. The hunter's teeth had deeply scored the skin but hadn't torn any flesh loose. Nonetheless, it was the kind of wound that could kill, if a secondary infection set in. Nothing filthier than the teeth of a dead thing. She pushed it out of her mind.

"So you heard a noise, and you saw them come up out of the hole. But did you see who let them out? I'd have thought you'd notice somebody moving around like that." She knew it sounded like she was blaming Wulf for negligence. Fuck it. Maybe she was.

"I wasn't looking for regular people, Adelman," the old man blustered. "I don't know every face in the Tribe, and I don't want to. If I saw him, he was just another civilian chook. If he went behind the trailer, he was just taking a piss. The fuck do I know? Who the hell expected this?"

"So he must have *looked* human, then." They were walking toward the trailer now. Danny could see a steel access door set in the ground. Sure enough, it had been flung open. The air was greasy with decay.

Wulf punched his fist into his palm with a noise like a baseball hitting a glove. "He must have *been* human. You think a fuckin' zero can just walk among us? Other than your pet sister, anyhow. You're right: I had her in my sights tonight, Adelman. Had a *bead* on her."

"You leave Kelley the fuck out of this. It won't work—I'm not taking the bait."

"Are you tellin' me you really believe she didn't have nothing to do with this?"

"She was with *me* when this shit started. She wasn't even *here*."

Wulf shrugged. He didn't give a damn what Danny thought.

They had reached the trailer, beside which was the heap of inanimate zeroes they'd found on arrival. The postaction mop-up crews had already checked it out; there weren't any more zeroes down there, but it stank like a flooded tomb. The trailer had been deliberately parked on top of some kind of below-grade sump pump room with a diamond-plate iron lid over it. There was a double door set into the lid, and the creatures had come up through that. Danny knelt beside it and studied the scene, her shadow swaying in the light of the burning gasoline.

"So they stacked up their own dead right here on top of the hidey-hole. That's why our dogs didn't smell these ones underneath. But this is the tell. See that piece of rusty pipe? See the fresh scratches on it? I bet somebody threaded it through these door handles to keep 'em closed, and pulled it out when the time came. But there's no rope or anything, so he must have been standing right here. If it was a man, he'd have been the first one they killed. So I think our perpetrator *is* a zero. A thinker. And I'll tell you what else: so is the Chevelle driver who's been following us around. I'm sure of it."

It all came together in Danny's mind. The thinkers were using the hunters like dog packs.

Draw the most competent defenders away with a diversion and spring the trap. This had been a coordinated attack. And it had almost worked. The enormity of the idea was terrifying.

"Bullshit, pardon my fuckin' French," Wulf said. He spat on the ground. Most of it ended up in his yellow-white beard. Danny looked sharply at him, surprised at the objection.

Wulf squinted past his crooked purple nose at Danny, as if he was only now seeing her properly. "Sheriff, you and me go back a ways. Probably you don't remember when this whole thing started and we saw our first zero, but I do. I said it was a *zombie*. You said bullshit yourself. Turned out I was right. Well, now I'm gonna say your latest theorem is bullshit, and *if* it turns out you're right, I'm real sorry."

Danny did remember that first zero, the mindless, stupid thing with a fly walking across its unblinking eyeball. Wulf had been absolutely correct, and nobody, least of all Danny, had wanted to believe it at the time.

"You don't buy that the Chevelle driver is undead, or you don't believe they could put together an ambush like this?"

"There's ones that are plenty fuckin' smart, Adelman. Ain't denying that. You'd know better than most. Thing is, they're not *that* damn smart. They're caveman smart, not you and me smart. Hell, that one of yours, she don't hardly talk."

"She's smarter than you, old man," Danny said. "Why can't you believe it? Just tonight, she drove my car and fired a flare gun. Tell me how that's not smart enough for this."

"That thing's getting to be a liability, Sheriff. You gotta do something about her. What if she was in on this job? Just 'cause she didn't open the doors herself don't mean she wasn't passing information to some other nasty-ass rotten fuckers. No offense."

Danny thought again of the distinctly undead figure she'd seen slipping out of view in Kelley's feeding ground. Had they been conspiring? But it couldn't be true: This trap was set up long before Kelley had gone anywhere.

"You let me worry about that," she muttered. "She's on our side. You saw it through your goddamn rifle scope. She was killing hunters same as the rest of us. Alls I'm saying is you underestimate the thinkers and you got a problem."

"That's why I can't believe it. If they're good enough to set us up like this, we're fucked."

"We fought human enemies, you and me. Thinkers are the same as that."

Wulf shook his head slowly, as if at a funeral. "Except human enemies have a weakness—they got a desire to stay alive. These fuckers don't. 'Cause they're not."

He fished a pint bottle of whiskey out of the front of his pants, drained half of it with six loud swallows, and belched fragrant, invisible fire. He shivered.

"Losing my touch," he said. "Can't drink like I used to." He offered the flask to Danny. She took the bottle between finger and thumb like a dead rat, wondering if the liquor was strong enough to defeat Wulf's bacteria.

"Don't get lit, Sheriff," a rough voice interjected. It was Topper, a machete still in his fist. He was soaked in the oily black blood of the undead, like Danny was. They both stank unmercifully. Danny tossed him the flask.

"We got a problem," Topper said, taking a grateful swallow.

"No shit," Danny said, her eyes on the team of men that was dragging the corpses of the zeroes into the fire.

"I mean, we got another one. I just found Maria back there—she's okay but she rounded up most of the kids, and four of 'em are gone."

"They're probably hiding out there in the tall grass."

"No, I mean they're *gone*. Maria saw some fuckers grab them. Two thinkers, she says."

"They didn't eat them on the spot?" Wulf said.

"They got away with them," Topper said. "Like that Mike guy tried to do, except these fuckers are undead. Maria swears it. She saw their eyes."

A sliver of fear stabbed Danny's belly. "That new boy, the Silent Kid, is he still here?"

"Somebody said his dog run off a minute before the attack, and the Kid followed. Ain't seen him since." Topper couldn't meet Danny's eyes.

Danny turned to face the scene of the carnage, took it all in. The ragged line of vehicles, a couple of them burning. The dead and wounded scattered around with Amy, Patrick, and anybody with a little medical experience doing their best to keep the fallen alive a while longer. There wasn't much hope for most of them in the long run. Blood spattered all over the asphalt. Even as Danny watched, someone cried "Mercy shot!" there was a pistol report, and one of the dying was hastened on his way out of the world.

The inferno must have been visible for thirty miles, a pillar of orange flame licking at the guts of the black smoke rising into the night sky. Every ambulatory corpse in the area would be on its way soon. The survivors were sweating in the heat, although it was a chilly night beyond the fire. The nearest building, the service center, was ablaze. Everywhere Danny looked, there were weeping, stumbling, hurt people. No direction, no defenses. They needed her. They might not be able to put themselves back together after this unless she was there to snap them out of the shock.

But she was also needed on the road. Those stolen children were still alive, getting farther away by the moment. Freshly yanked out of the arms of their protectors. Danny picked out the parents, the guardians. They were the ones searching everywhere, running back and forth as if the fight was still on. Imploring people to help. They would spot Danny soon and come to her and demand she *do* something, they way people always did. What could she say to them? That she'd seen other children hanging from hooks, devoured alive by the very creatures who had kidnapped their own?

"Sheriff?" Topper was watching her. Waiting for an answer. Danny shrugged. She didn't know what to say. Her bitten arm was swelling up, tightening around the tooth marks. They started back toward the survivors.

Amy was soaked in human blood, her own arms as gory as the skinned corpses back at the ranch. She left her work to Patrick when she saw Danny. Patrick wouldn't turn in Danny's direction.

"Ouchies?" Amy said.

"Nothing to speak of. Did you hear about the kids?"

"We lost some," Amy replied, and it sounded as if she thought that was an end to the matter. That was uncharacteristic.

"Topper says they were taken alive," Danny said.

"Zeroes don't do that," Amy said. "I bet you're just changing the subject. You're hurt, aren't you. I see a bite hole through your sleeve." *Amy doesn't want to think about the kids,* Danny realized. *It's too much.*

Wulf, who was following Danny around now like a bear looking for sandwiches, shook his shaggy head. "These ones do. Shit's getting worse."

Danny hawked and spat, mostly to buy herself a few seconds before she had to speak. They were all looking at her, and for once she simply didn't know what to do.

"It's a whole new fuckin' ball game if they're kidnapping the little ones," Topper observed. Despite everything, a plan was formulating in Danny's horror-stricken mind. There was action she could take.

Amy saw the look in her eyes and shook her head. "Danny, those kids are probably already dead. We need to grieve for them and move on."

"You didn't see the ranch we found tonight," Danny said. "There was barbed wire all around it but it was on the wrong side of the fence . . . I thought they just set it up wrong, but now I see—it wasn't to keep people out. It was to keep them *in*. We found . . . kids. That *fuck* is stealing human kids, and he has accomplices. That place was a slaughterhouse."

"But we need you here now. Nobody else has the nuts to keep this bunch together."

"Nobody else can find those kids. I found Kelley, didn't I?"

Danny was breathing hard through her clenched teeth. She wouldn't have bothered to explain that much to anyone but Amy. She would have decked them for daring to question her, at this point. And then she would have gone and done what needed doing. But part of her wanted Amy to come up with a good counterargument. Talk her out of it. Because the last time Danny had gone on a lone-wolf mission, it was to find her sister. Which was when disaster hit the people she left behind—Amy included. They needed her now, more than ever. If she was off on a wild goose chase and they stumbled into another trap . . .

Amy stared down at her red hands, turning them so the firelight glittered on the coagulating blood.

"If you're going after them, you better haul butt," she said. "They could be a hundred miles away by morning."

That was it, then. Danny had permission. Like she needed it. Fresh anger flashed into her mind, and she crammed it down. This was what she'd wanted, right?

"Amy, get the Tribe out of here as fast as you can. Just a few miles, but get away. Every zero in the territory must be on its way. Me and the scouts will find you up the road."

"What about Kelley?"

"I don't know. If she comes back, I . . . don't think I can keep her safe."

"Come back alive yourself," Amy said, and walked away.

Danny was on her way back to the interceptor when she heard someone coming up behind her. She assumed it was Amy, reversing her decision to let her leave without argument. But when she turned around, there was Patrick, again wiping his fingers with a cloth. But this time it wasn't food—it was a clotted glaze of human blood from the triage he'd been engaged in.

"So was it Kelley?" he asked. No point being subtle. He wasn't forgiving Danny yet.

"I don't think so," she said. She debated whether to leave it at that, but there was more to be said. And Patrick was one of very few people she felt she could talk to. She had to try.

"Listen: Kelley was with me when it started, and she kicked some ass in the middle of it. Wulf tried to kill her and he shot one of the wounded instead. That's what you walked into. I'm not going to ask you to put yourself in my position because that's bullshit."

"Are you *apologizing*?" Patrick said. He was frankly astonished.

"You're a good guy, Patrick. And Kelley is still my sister. She's *in* there, man. Somewhere. But I promise you, if she was involved in this thing tonight, I will destroy her myself."

Patrick nodded. Good enough for him. He glanced at his hands and used the cleanest one to grip her briefly by the shoulder. Then he went back into the firelight.

The motorcycles pulled out first. They could cover ground faster than the interceptor. Topper and Conn this time. Ernie had stayed behind to ride herd on the caravan. There were enough tough hands to fend off another attack, if it came to that. Fighters Danny trusted to defend the soft center. But no leaders. Not really. Troy Davis the ex-fireman came close, but he was more courageous than commanding. In fact he avoided Danny. She'd noticed.

She could only hope the retreat went smoothly and nobody was left behind. The Silent Kid would either come back or go his own way. He'd made it this long alone, although when hard winter set in there was no way he'd survive. He and his dog would freeze while hiding in a culvert or something. But it was up to him now. The wounded would be kept in the shuttle bus until they got better or died, usually a matter of hours. If the survivors didn't have time to burn them, the bodies of the dead Tribespeople were always wrapped up in the back of a pickup. They would be making a cremation stop tomorrow. For everybody else, it was business as usual.

Except Kelley, the unwelcome voice in her head remarked. *Maybe she's not part of the usual business anymore.*

Danny rolled slowly past the devastation at the truck stop, as always wondering what she could have done better, what detail she'd missed. They should have shifted the pile of hunter remains. That was obvious. But it was a world of corpses. They became part of the scenery, easy to ignore as long as they weren't moving—especially in cold weather, when they didn't stink so much and the flies were dormant. Danny would never make that mistake again.

The interceptor left the jumping ring of light cast by the fires and Danny turned her attention to the road ahead. Her foot sank the gas pedal halfway down and she felt the acceleration pushing her into the seat back. Then there was something coming into the headlights, a ragged bundle of limbs. She slapped the brakes.

Kelley.

Danny drew her sidearm and stepped out of the interceptor, keeping the door between them.

Kelley stood between the lights, her muumuu smeared with blood like an abstract painting. She had torn the bandages away from her head, revealing a face like an old black-and-white photograph.

"I think we're done," Danny said. "I think it's time for you to go."

"The blood," Kelley said, and sucked in a long-forgotten breath.

"Yeah, the blood. If you go back there I think they'll kill you. I won't be able to stop them. And I think—" she couldn't say what she thought.

"Are you going to kill me?"

Kelley had guessed it. Danny thought about her answer. She could chase

Kelley off, or kill her, or let her keep on existing at her side. Those were the options. Chase her off and she'd most likely feed on the living. Maybe start with the Silent Kid, if he was left behind, and then work on ambushing travelers on the road. Or join up with that other thinker, the one Danny had glimpsed.

If Danny killed Kelley, that was that. Danny didn't know what was left after such a thing. It would be the end of her, too, somehow. Maybe she'd kill herself. Maybe she'd go insane. There was only one option, until Danny knew the truth.

"I won't kill you unless you go for me again," Danny said. She fed her gun back into the holster.

Kelley made fists of her hands and stared at them with bulging gray eyes, as if they were a jury of bones and this was her confession.

"I tasted the *blood*. It was an accident. But I tasted it. You don't know. The blood, it tastes like God. It tastes like everything you ever wanted, Danny. I'm so hungry, my insides are on fire."

"I can drop you off somewhere far away. Eat rats or coyotes. Just don't eat people."

Kelley pressed her fists to her forehead like the heroine in a silent film.

"I can't face this hunger on my own. I'll do terrible things. But it makes me want to stay alive. Not alive, whatever I am. I want to exist."

Kelley hesitated, then reached for the passenger door.

"You can sit in back," Danny said.

"The hunger made me crazy. You have to understand."

"You can sit in back or you can walk. That's how it is," Danny repeated.

Kelley climbed in behind the partition and curled up in a ball on the backseat floor.

12

The headlights were white spikes in the darkness, revealing only that there was more road to travel. They drove until dawn.

Danny dwelled on the roots of the disaster they'd just endured. She'd drilled the Tribe so many times on what to do in an attack: pair up and fight back to back. Get up against something. Form larger groups. Predictably, tonight the chooks hadn't done any of it, and they got their asses kicked. Nobody was blaming Danny, but she still felt it. The blame thing ate her up like acid.

It was guilt, she knew. A long time ago, she had left them hanging so she could go off and look for her sister, and it had ended in disaster for everyone. Kelley died in her arms, and was resurrected as a zero. And that was the end of things. Danny ceased to have any other ties to the world than the Tribe. Since then, she'd focused entirely on its safety. The only reason she hadn't been there when this night's attack went down was that she was out doing the stuff most folks were terrified to do—on their behalf.

Still, the guilt sizzled inside her. Maybe the way the hunger worked inside Kelley. She glanced in the rearview mirror and saw only the hunch of Kelley's back. She was still curled up, rocking a little like a junkie on bad dope.

Danny turned her mind back to the Tribe. She decided they were going to have to get serious about combat training as soon as this current situation was handled. She needed these people to stop being chooks and become survival machines instead. If, as she believed, the thinkers were starting to make complex, coordinated attacks, the world had just gotten harder. They needed to get harder, too. She had the same thought several times before she realized she was only truly interested in Kelley. She raised her voice to be heard through the partition.

"Are you still with me?"

"I'm so hungry. Oh, God, it hurts."

"One more time, then I'm done asking. You weren't involved in the attack, right?"

"I told you. No. It was thinkers who set it up, but not me. It *hurts*." Kelley was out of air. She sucked in another breath, and it sounded very like a sob to Danny.

"Because nobody else could have gotten the hunters into that hole in the ground. And the dead ones were piled on top to hide the smell of them. Right?"

"I knew I smelled something else. Just didn't figure out what."

Danny looked at Kelley's slack, bruised face. Peeling and discolored, like Halloween makeup that was starting to rub off. Danny wondered if jealousy was hiding in there. If the eternal hunger for flesh gave her sister some admiration for the thinkers that went to such lengths to feed.

"What do we do about it? Maybe if we get you some rats or a cat or something?"

"Pull over!"

Danny stopped the interceptor on the shoulder and went around to the rear door, which had to be opened from the outside. She turned her hip so that Kelley wouldn't see her holster flap was open. Kelley tumbled out onto the ground and squatted on hands and knees, retching. Thick bile dribbled from between her yellow teeth.

"So hungry," she gasped. "It burns."

Danny felt like she had to do something. If Kelley had been alive, if there were no zeroes, they'd be on the way to the emergency room.

"What will help?"

"Nothing. Oh, God." More retching. Now thin black fluid spattered the pavement.

"What if I bled into a paper cup or something? I could give you something to live on for a while. Or maybe find an animal."

"Shut up," Kelley wheezed. After a while she got back on her feet, leaning on the interceptor. Danny closed the rear door, signaling that Kelley could get in front. She looked too weak to do anything much.

They drove on. Kelley cradled her belly. She drank some water without being coached. Then she spoke.

"I've never felt anything like . . . I don't know if that's true. Since I died, I haven't dealt with this. I kind of remember feeling alive. It's different now. I'm still alive, but my body isn't. Or it wasn't. But now it is."

She breathed, then: "I remember how I used to talk, and stand, and what I did. I know I used to love bacon and tomatoes. My favorite TV show was *The Prisoner,* which is like really old. I liked showers but not baths. I liked reading. I can't read now. That part of my brain doesn't work. I can see the letters but they don't join together."

"I hardly ever read." Danny didn't know what else to say, and didn't care. Kelley never talked like this. Not in life or afterward. She wanted it to keep coming.

"I thought I didn't care about eating anymore. I used to love hot dogs with brown mustard. Now I don't. Until the blood got in my mouth, I didn't care about anything. I was just sore all the time.

"But now I'm hungry. I'm hungry like I climbed a mountain with no breakfast, and at the top there wasn't any lunch, so I climbed back down and it was too late for supper—forever. And no matter what I do, there's no food. Forever.

"My stomach is so empty it feels like a black hole or something. Like it could swallow light. My fingers hurt. I feel like I'm eating my own bones. Like every nerve inside my rotten body has come alive. Like if I just eat human meat I can be alive again and maybe then I'll remember what hot dogs taste like and I'll care about anything except spurting hot blood and wet chunks of fucking flesh in my mouth, killing the hunger. Oh, fuck, to make it stop. Anything to make it stop."

Kelley had taken several breaths. The last words came out in a squeak, her lungs drained. She didn't breathe again for a while. Danny kept on driving, waiting. She saw there was gray, thick saliva bubbling through the bandages. A thought was fluttering around inside her head like a bat. She didn't want to acknowledge it. But part of her was thinking of the mercy shot.

Kelley spoke again, urgently.

"I don't think I can handle this much longer. I'm going to tell you what I know about my kind, okay? Because you need to know this shit. Thinkers, okay? I wasn't like the others and I didn't get it. Now I do. Remember early on in the disaster, the thinkers attacked everybody like maniacs? They were smart, but they did stupid stuff, just running at people and trying to kill them. I understand why, now. They were hungry like this. They were so fucking *hungry*.

"But the ones that got meat in their bellies, they started to think. They calmed down. They started making plans. Nothing's any good after tasting human blood, okay? Nothing even comes close. So only feeding mattered. Only feeding matters now. Nothing else will ever matter.

"Thinkers are teaming up. They're setting traps and making plans that would scare the fuck out of you. Taking over. That's what they want. The ones I've talked to? They all have a scheme. And now I get why."

The renewed hunger had brought some clarity to Kelley's mind. The other thinkers were insane from hunger when they turned, focused only on gaining flesh to eat. They couldn't think strategically. But once they had fed, they could think of the future. She had experienced this herself, although never the perfect release that came from devouring human meat. Any warm blood would do, but man-flesh was the finest thing, the reason to endure.

There were things she *hadn't* experienced. She was isolated from her own kind, her new species. She hadn't killed. So she hadn't passed through the postfeasting stage during which, with newfound clarity of mind, the thinkers developed rudimentary relationships with one another, and devised strategies and plans. These creatures, it seemed to her, never forged the strong pack behaviors of the hunters; rather, they were utterly selfish, only working together to achieve their individual ends, which happened to be always identical—they wanted to feed.

Kelley knew from the time before she changed that they had learned to capture people alive rather than butcher them outright where they fell. They had learned to hide the traces of their attacks, and how to conceal themselves before the living were lured in. She understood how it worked, now. Everything they had experienced in life was still there, memories as clear as day. But it was all jumbled. It had to be sorted through. She was doing the same thing right now. But she wasn't only obsessing about the kill back there (although now it dominated her thoughts). Now the things she'd been dwelling upon didn't seem to matter anymore. Who was she? What had she become? It didn't matter. Only the hunger mattered.

Kelley's thoughts turned into a long break in the conversation. Danny intruded, following the train of her own thoughts.

"Was it the one I saw you talking to?" she asked. "Was it him that did this to the Tribe?" She wasn't sure she wanted an answer. It would mean Kelley was complicit, if only through her silence.

"No. But that doesn't mean he didn't talk to the one who did it."

"I want you to stop contacting your kind, Kelley. Don't talk to them."

Kelley didn't respond. Which was an answer, after a fashion.

Morning found them on a long, empty highway. The farm road behind the ranch was on the map. It went nowhere for a while and then turned back to the highway several miles ahead. After that, the Chevelle could have gone in any number of directions, but Danny didn't think the kidnappers intended to stray far from the big road, which was clearly their hunting ground—and the fastest route of escape. In that case, they were somewhere ahead. And if Topper was right, they had a truck with them. It wouldn't be as fast as the Chevelle. With a little luck, she and the bikers could overtake them before midday.

"I can smell infection on you," Kelley said.

"Well yeah, I got bit," Danny replied, rotating her arm to show the rip in her jacket. She didn't want to talk.

"You will become like me someday. Then you'll understand how hungry I am."

"No, I won't, Kelley. It doesn't work that way. You know it." This was a subject Danny hated to discuss. Her sister had been bitten, and the infection killed her. She had died and come back. Danny, however, had been bitten badly enough to draw blood at least six times since the outbreak began, and she'd never gotten anything worse than a nasty bacterial infection.

"You say you're immune, but nobody just dies," Kelley said. She was watching Danny from behind her inky sunglasses, the bandages around her face fluttering in the breeze from the cracked windows.

Somewhere deep inside there was a tickle of fear that Danny wouldn't acknowledge. She was *afraid* of her kid sister. The way she'd gone wild during the attack. Maybe because the thing seated next to her wasn't truly her sister anymore. She couldn't tell.

"Yeah, I'm immune. We've been over this before. It's bullshit."

"I almost lost it when the hunters attacked. There was so much blood. I just wanted to eat a little piece off one of the wounded. But I didn't."

"Wulf would have shot you down," Danny muttered. "You so much as taste human flesh, that's it. That's our deal. That's what makes you different from the rest of your kind. One bite and I treat you just like the rest of your kind."

"You're afraid," Kelley observed. Danny glanced over at the sunglasses and saw only her reflection in them.

"Bullshit."

"You are afraid of me," Kelley persisted. "I can tell. Maybe it's because I'm hungry like you're thirsty. You should be able to understand that. Know how bad you want a drink? I want human meat a hundred times more. Maybe you can guess what it's like."

I need to stop drinking, Danny thought. She never had a good enough reason, but by God, maybe this was it.

"When you came back, you were the same person, only undead," Danny said, once the silence had gone on longer than she could bear. "But you've been changing. Don't think I haven't noticed. You're different now. I think you're waiting for something."

"Like an opportunity?"

"Well?"

"I *am* waiting. It's true. But I don't know what for." She drew breath, her lungs deflated.

"I been thinking," Danny continued, when Kelley didn't respond. "What if we split up? What if you went somewhere on your own?"

"You said that would never happen again."

"But one of these days, shit is going to go very wrong. Unless maybe we switch things up."

"Or very right."

"You mean like you'll finally get to kill me?"

"That's not . . ."

Kelley sounded uncertain for a moment. Her words trailed off, not for lack of air, but because she couldn't frame her next thought. There was a clicking in her throat. Then, rolling out in a series of sharp breaths:

". . . Has it ever occurred to you that the food chain just got longer, and I might be one link ahead of you? Has it ever occurred to you that maybe *my* kind is humanity, now? Huh? All this time I been rotting away at your side, not tasting what every goddamned fiber of my being craves as a fucking *favor* to you, and you have been acting like *you* are the boss. Like *you* are the last word. What if it's not you? What if it's me? What if this whole time I have been sitting here tolerating your anger and drunkenness and judgment because *I* am now the superior being, the one who sees the furthest and thinks the deepest and understands the way things are?"

Danny realized she hadn't drawn breath herself in almost a minute.

"You want to eat people's fucking skin and you think you're the superior one? Jesus, Kelley. You were a haughty-ass child, but this is beyond that. At the very fucking best, you have a serious terminal disease than makes you a danger to yourself and others. At the very fucking best. At worst, you're my tame fucking pet zombie and you exist at *my fucking pleasure!*"

She hadn't wanted to shout, but in the end Danny was raging, her spittle flecking the cracked windshield. Kelley was silent. Danny couldn't tell if it was the silence of the undead, or the silence of Kelley, the girl who sulked a lot. She almost expected to be attacked. But nothing happened, and all her cruel words disappeared into the silence.

She might not have gotten so angry if she hadn't half-believed what Kelley was proposing.

"Okay," she said, when the rage had metabolized into ordinary heartburn. "Let's say you're Humanity Mark II or 2.0 or whatever. Why don't you just try to kill me and we find out who's superior?"

"There's something I need to know," Kelley said, speaking in a slow, deliberate voice, taking short breaths. "It's the reason I remember who I am before I died, when most of my kind don't. Is it just because the disease hits people in different ways, and that's how I turned out? Is it because you were there, or because you said what you said?"

They drove past a three-car wreck from the early days of the crisis, the vehicles tangled together, rusting. Danny watched it recede into the distance in the wing mirror.

"What difference does that make?" Danny asked.

Kelley turned her head carefully, looked at Danny from behind the sunglasses.

"I woke up and there was only the hunger. I didn't know who I was or what I had been. I just smelled this hot, spicy fresh meat. But you said something then. You didn't know I had come back . . . and you were crying. You said 'I love you.' And it reminded me that I was something else before." Kelley was out of air. She breathed again.

Danny felt a couple of hot tears spill down her dirty face. Her chin was quivering. To hear it from this thing that had once been her sister—the pain of that moment tore open again, bright and fresh.

Kelley was choosing her words one at a time. "I need to know if I am still that person. If I am your sister. Or if I'm something new, and what I was before doesn't matter."

Danny's throat was constricted with grief, but she tried to sound matter-of-fact when she said, "What happens when you figure it out?"

"I kill you."

13

As she sat beside her sister in the front of the police car, Kelley dwelled on the hunger.

Her putrid guts were squirming with it. She could smell the blood on her sister's skin, smell the bacteria devouring the edges of her wounds. Inside that body there was hot, fresh meat, especially that beating heart, tough and rich. Her teeth would nearly break on it, but the muscle would yield at last, the blood would gush out of it in a stream that would fill her belly and spurt from her nostrils.

She wouldn't care if her sister was screaming or fighting or begging for mercy when she did it. The triumph of a full belly, her zombie metabolism racing so that her *own* heart might beat more than once or twice a minute, sensation returned to her limbs, body healing, the pain of starvation driven away—

She felt the bandages around her mouth grow gelatinous with thick saliva. She turned her thoughts away from the prey. *I love you,* Danny had said. And she continued to change Kelley's bandages and clean her body when it obviously repulsed her to do so. Kelley herself would do nothing she didn't wish to. Why would anyone do so? Living or dead, there were only needs and fulfillment of needs. Nothing else existed.

Or so it seemed to her. But the question itched at her hard-edged mind: Was there something more? If there were not, Danny would have destroyed her.

It was the riddle of the living. There was a kind of sacrifice in it, something beyond the self. The living version of Kelley would have said there was something greater in life just as there was something greater in a word than individual letters. But Kelley could no longer decipher written language, either. She felt an endless confusion that drove her thoughts in circles: She could not die, but she was lesser than the living. When she fed, it was the life in the rats and opossums and raccoons that sustained her, a spurt of electricity; but none of this mysterious element was manufactured inside her own body. It faded away as her digestion worked upon it. She felt empty, stagnant. The fire inside the living was what she most wanted, and the thing she couldn't have. To consume it was to extinguish it. There was only the tantalizing taste for a few seconds. Now that she had accidentally tasted human blood, that desire filled her mind and body completely.

Kelley could not precisely remember the sensation of life, but there were things that survived the transition from life to undeath. These things remained with her as memories of someone else. None of her old tastes had survived. She didn't care for grilled hot dogs with brown mustard anymore. It would have infuriated the living version of herself. As she now was, she didn't care. It was inconvenient but not important. She felt like a shark that remembered another life as a human being. The taste of blood had made her want nothing more than to be just a shark, feeding, always feeding.

This was the torment of the thinkers, when they were not hungry. They were perfectly alone, no matter how many gathered together to hunt men. And lost, driven only by appetite. They scarcely knew who they were. Only what they needed. Not long before, money had affected people like that, consuming the lives of the living. Never enough, every taste of the stuff making them want more. Making them forget who they were.

Then again—back in those days, nobody got paid for chewing the flesh off a human head.

Kelley clung to her relationship with Danny, such as it was, because it connected her to what she had been before. Now she was afraid that the hunger would replace everything she'd been clinging to. She had experienced a unique moment as she emerged from the brief sleep of natural death. It had shown her a lightning flash of her true self. Then it was gone. She sought to reclaim that light, to see the thing once more and take it back into herself. The hunger made it impossible even to conjure up in her mind.

Her thoughts moved at the same pace as before, but their purpose was different. Once, the future had occupied her attention; now there was only hunger or not-hunger, the two outcomes.

She had no use for abstractions anymore. Her thoughts were becoming more practical, more single-minded with every passing hour. Nothing should have intruded on her lust for bloody flesh.

But this one creature, her sister, was a riddle that she must answer. She was the key to what Kelley had become, the unbroken mirror in which she had glimpsed herself.

Kelley hoped she would understand soon, because the stench of her sister's body renewed her hunger with every passing moment. And once again, her thoughts were upon the flavor of Danny's blood, always circling.

14

The zeroes were getting thick. Swarming. There had been a city not far from the interstate, once a stop on the intercontinental railway and now a stop on the road. The area, as the earlier travelers had said, was worse than anywhere Danny had seen—and they were still only at the fringes of the swarm. All moaners, at least so far. No hunters or thinkers, or the stupid zeroes would have avoided them.

Danny rolled the windows down an inch. Not enough to let any clutching hands in, but enough so that Kelley's fishy, decayed smell was released outside the vehicle. It made the moaners recoil. They stumbled over each other to get out of the way.

Kelley's words still rung in her ears. One of these days, probably soon, the hunger was going to get the better of her, and Kelley would try to kill Danny. She didn't doubt it for a moment. The only real question was how long they had left together.

Topper called Danny on the radio, breaking the musty silence. "There's too fuckin' many, Sheriff. We're gonna get knocked off our bikes. Over."

"Copy," Danny said. "Fall back and I'll see how far we can go in the interceptor. If I fuck it up, you may need to shoot your way in to us, can you handle that, over?"

"Aye-aye," Topper replied. "Over'n out."

It was clear they wouldn't be able to travel much farther. If the Chevelle and its truck had indeed come this way, they must also have avoided giving away their thinker scent; otherwise the roadway would be clear. But Danny didn't see how they could have progressed through the swarm in this area by any other means. The moaners lurched around like gigantic, bipedal termites in a nest, moving in dense crowds, aimlessly, sometimes scattering until they were spread out, the way strangers spread out on train platforms, but eventually massing together again. Often they would crowd together until they were jammed cheek to rotten cheek.

She saw one with big yellowish knobs all over its exposed skin, like veiny mushrooms. There was another that looked like it had been shot in the face with raisins—they could almost have been huge blackheads, erupting through the gray flesh. Then they passed one with fleshy filaments growing out of its face, like that which had bitten Danny the previous night. It resembled a mask made of week-old hamburger. Most of the zeroes were clad in slack, dead skin of the usual kind, but these few stood out for their hideous originality. Maybe there were zero diseases going around. A whole new biology.

Equally disturbing was that a great number of the undead here appeared to be the remains of children. Thin, gray little things with yawning mouths.

"The wind has shifted," Danny said aloud, not expecting an answer. "It's coming out of the west now. That's why the radios are working, I think. It's the only variable. I wonder what that means."

The radio was the least of her worries, however. The city wasn't near enough to explain the swarm. Danny was able to drive as far as an overpass into town, but the narrow area beneath the bridge so concentrated the zeroes that there was no way to physically push the car through the throng, not even if they smelled the thinker inside. They couldn't get out of the way. The vehicle would be overcome, like driving into a mountain of cow carcasses. Greasy handprints slathered the windows and doors. The cacophony of their muddled voices filled the stinking air.

"They didn't come this way," Kelley said, ignoring the moaners outside the glass like a celebrity snubbing the paparazzi. "If they did, these ones would still be retreating."

"And you don't smell them?" Danny asked.

Kelley didn't respond for a while, and Danny thought maybe she was giving one of her nonanswers, the closest thing she had to a lie.

But then she said, "No. I can only smell the blood inside your skin."

Danny hooked the steering wheel over and made a slow, bumpy U-turn through the swarm. A couple of them went under the wheels. A skeletal child scraped the stumps of its arms over the hood. Then they were pointed back the way they came, and the undead thinned out.

The blood inside your skin.

Danny considered the options as she slalomed between the moaners, steering like a cartoon drunk through the widest gaps in the swarm, heading back the way they'd come. The ones that had smelled Kelley before were struggling up the embankments and through the fields to get away.

"Kelley? Where do you think the other driver has gone?"

Kelley was silent a while, then inhaled carefully and said, "That way." She pointed north.

"Away from the city?"

"Yes."

Danny wasn't sure how many questions Kelley would take before she said she didn't understand and shut down. But it was worth asking.

"Why did he go north?"

"He couldn't go that way," she said, and indicated the direction from which they had come—the heart of the swarm. After that, she didn't respond to further questions. Danny was baffled.

Was she lying by omission, or just lying? Danny wanted to wring the thin, mushy neck. Demand answers. It felt sometimes like Kelley already knew the entire big picture but only hinted at it to keep her guessing.

Then again, it could also be that Kelley didn't have anything else to say. She'd been silent in life, too.

Danny decided to take Kelley's word for it, as far as it went. The zeroes were thinned out to the north, swarming thickest to the east and south. It made sense to carry a cargo of children in a less-infested direction, after all. Danny had seen swarms overturn buses and trucks. They'd go mad at the sweet stink of unwashed kids. So the Chevelle might very well have veered north, rather than punch straight through the thickest part of the swarm, even if that was the most direct route to the zero-free zone beyond. On their own, thinkers could pass through the swarm like a razor through the belly of a rotten dog. That might change with a cargo of human flesh behind them.

A few minutes beyond the fringes of the swarm, Danny saw one highway exit that looked like the best way north; she asked Kelley if that was the way the others had gone, but there was no reply. It had to be the one. Long, straight road, plowed through the abandoned cornfields, which were fallow because all the mutant genetically engineered corn was sterile. Weeds taking over, Roundup be damned. The road was two lanes, ran due north, and although she saw a couple of scratchy silhouettes of undead moving across the fields, there wasn't any particular energy to them. They were individual walking corpses, not part of the swarm. She would herself have gone that way, if she were the kidnappers. At least, it was a place to start.

She radioed the bikers, and the signal got through, for once. They rendezvoused at the off-ramp and headed up the road, bikes first, Danny a little way behind. She watched the motorcycles, admiring these tough, nononsense men. They were scared shitless half the time, the same as her, the same as everybody. But they strapped the fear down tight and kept on doing what needed to be done. She was grateful. They made a lot of crap decisions, of course, but that was human nature. Danny did, too. She was beginning to think that was the foremost quality of leadership: the willingness to make decisions, good or bad, and insist others work with them.

After a few kilometers, they reached the train tracks that ran parallel to the interstate. In places the tracks came much closer, as each mode of transport found different ways around features in the terrain. At the tracks, running alongside them, was another two-lane road—probably the original route the interstate replaced. Danny could see an abandoned motel and a no-name gas station not far away. The places that had been knocked off the main route when the interstates went through had never recovered, three-quarters of a century later.

Danny and the scouts stopped at the intersection of the two roads. Kelley raised herself out of the vehicle and stood a little distance away, facing down the road they'd come along. Danny stretched her always-stiff back.

"Nothing could have got through that swarm," she said.

"I never seen anything like that," Conn said, his voice grating like stones.

"But," said Topper, turning a slow circle, "which way did they go from here?"

"No point going west," Danny said. "That's where these fuckers came from. Tribe's there. The swarm is south. So that narrows it down to one-half of the fuckin' compass—east or north."

"Your sister have an opinion?" Conn asked.

"North, she says," Danny muttered. They rarely mentioned Kelley by name. It was always unnerving.

Danny spat on the ground and walked in a wide arc around the intersection. Brown grass sprouted from the cracked pavement. Winter was coming fast, so the plants had gone to sleep, but in the spring this road would be half-overgrown. It amazed Danny how fast things were breaking down.

"Sheriff . . ." Topper said, "if the kidnappers *ain't* zeroes, and the price is one kid per adult to get into the safe place like that prisoner says, then it makes sense. Could be a human gang, and once they got enough kids collected for all of 'em they drive to the safe place and get in, right?"

"But the kidnappers *are* zeroes," Danny said. "You saw that ranch. They were holed up there at least a couple of weeks, waiting for somebody like us to come by. Eating their prisoners. We scared them off. But they still got our kids with them, and probably more, if they got a truck. That means they're gonna eat them, too."

"So they could of gone anywhere. Or maybe they're hidden behind that wall over there, waiting for us to go away," Topper said. "They got nothing to fear from moaners, if they're thinkers. So we ain't got a thing to go on. The trail is stone cold."

Nobody had anything to add. There wasn't much left to do but acknowledge failure. Conn leaned against his immense Harley with his legs stuck out like a kickstand. Topper stood in the center of the intersection and continued his slow rotation around the compass. Danny walked in her circle.

Then she stopped by the railway tracks, frozen in position. Both men knew what that meant. She'd seen something, or had an idea. Danny stepped over a broken candy-stripe signal arm, then knelt beside the nearest rail.

"Do you hear that?" She placed the flat of her hand against the rusty steel.

"No," Topper said.

"It's over here. The rail is kind of singing. It's real faint. But I can feel it."

This got the bikers' attention. Topper and Conn hustled over to the tracks and bent down to feel the rail.

"Train coming?" Topper said.

"Who the fuck would run a train out here?" Danny shook her head.

But what else could it be? The rail beneath her hand was vibrating, although in such a subtle way it felt more like a mild electrical current than anything else. And they could all hear it now. A faint, high keening sound, possibly the vibration of the sand and pebbles against the track, or steel against steel.

"If that's a train," Conn said, "it's a long goddamn ways off. But it could be those kidnapping assholes took off by rail. Or maybe they're on this here road and the rails are picking it up."

This was the longest speech Danny had ever heard Conn make. Even Topper looked surprised.

"Fuckin' detective," Topper observed. "One-man FBI."

"Fuck you," Conn said.

"It's a good idea," Danny remarked, ignoring the witless banter. "Makes sense. They're on the rails, traveling west or east."

"You know what," Topper said. "I'm an asshole. I just remembered there was a train west of here where I picked up the Silent Kid. It was on this same line, I'm pretty sure of it. No engine, just some cars."

"So if there's a working train," Danny said, "it's going east."

"Or headed for a high-speed crash."

"I'm gonna make the call," Danny said, squeezing the air with her one good fist. "We follow the tracks east. We're already falling behind by the minute."

"You think somebody got the trains running?" Conn said, doubtful. He was squinting down the tracks, his stony forehead crumpled with concentration. "That would be a hell of a thing. Zeroes couldn't stop a train. Might be a kick-ass way to travel."

They drove onward. Danny's mind was racing. So many possibilities. There was no question that *something* was moving on those rails, or close beside them. She couldn't remember how far that kind of vibration traveled, although she had some dim memory of learning it in high school. A unit on waves of energy in water, air, metal, and stone, and as she recalled it was water that sound would travel through the farthest. The rest was a blur. She was more interested in sex back then. And beer.

But it seemed to her that noise could run a long, long way down a railway line.

How far would they have to go to find out? The lives of those children probably depended on the answer. She remembered that hideous, bloody thing hanging in the ranch, unrecognizable but still alive. No more. Not on her watch. She'd told the Silent Kid she would personally keep him out of danger.

Was he among the stolen children? He must be, unless he just ran into the darkness. In which case, he'd probably been eaten anyway. Nobody could keep him safe. Danny was just another bullshitter.

The zeroes got thicker as they drove east; they were a couple of kilometers north of where they'd reached the swarm on the freeway. If this was part of the same mass, the swarm was colossal, the biggest they'd ever encountered. It got so infested the bikes had to fall back behind the interceptor, which was equipped to ram the undead.

They moved through a couple of small two-story towns that once served as suburbs for the city up ahead, although they were run-down little places, mostly having dealt in lottery tickets, auto parts, and cheap food, as far as Danny could tell. Now they dealt in nothing, of course. There was a skeletal woman hanging from an upstairs window, half-in, half-out, as if someone had hung her out to dry. There was hardly any flesh left to hold her remains together, a matted flag of yellow hair dangling from her partially exposed skull. The roadway was mostly free of abandoned vehicles, presumably because everybody took the interstate to get out of there. But the undead were out in force, lurching through doorways, out of alleys, and crawling from beneath parked cars at the sound of the approaching humans.

The motorcycles were a liability again. Danny pulled over into a fenced tractor dealership parking lot; Kelley climbed out of the vehicle and the moaners stopped in their tracks, sucking the air to taste it. The bikers pulled up alongside.

"You guys get on back to the convoy," Danny said. "I'll keep pushing through. Zeroes gonna get one of you at the rate we're going."

"We can keep on," Topper said. He was invested in the mission.

"Tell you what," she said. "Take that route north we saw back there at the railroad crossing. Odds are just as good they went that way. But one of us has to report back to the Tribe. The radio is fucked again. The wind changed around before, did you notice that? And then the radios worked. It was blowing east for a little while. Anyway, it's blowing this way again so we're gonna have to hand-deliver word back to the Tribe. Conn, you comfortable splitting up?"

"Do I look like a fuckin' delivery boy?"

"You look like alligator balls. I'm asking you, go back and tell the chooks to saddle up and get closer. We might find a way to punch through the swarm, and they don't want to be too far away if we do. This is a highly dynamic situation."

Danny was aware she was giving both men a lot more choice in the matter than she would have in the past. They seemed a little put off by it, like they didn't know what to do. But she couldn't make every decision. She needed these two to start doing more of it, so she could focus on her own tasks. And she was sure those children were somewhere directly down the railway line. Her instincts told her this was the trail.

"I'll go north," Topper said, much to Danny's gratification. "Conn, you get back to the Tribe. Sheriff, good fuckin' luck."

Kelley took her time getting into the car; Danny had to choke back a complaint. There was no criticizing the undead. They simply did not give a shit.

Danny hit the gas, tore the legs off a zero in the entrance to the parking lot with the cable overrider on the bumper, and drove hell-for-leather alongside the railroad tracks, racing due east.

15

The swarm simply vanished a few kilometers farther down the track. The zeroes got so dense it was almost as bad as the interstate—and then there were a lot of fallen ones, rotten, sprawling everywhere, and none standing, and for whatever reason after that there were just empty shells of buildings, and fields and prairie glinting with naked bones. Danny stopped the interceptor. Whenever something major changed, it was time to take stock, as much as she wanted to rush ahead. Ten minutes, then back on the road. She turned to Kelley, who was hunched silently against her door, arms folded tightly across her belly.

"I'm going to climb up that grain silo over there and see what there is," Danny said.

No response, which Danny interpreted to be affirmative.

Danny backed up until she crossed a farm road that went over the railroad tracks, and a couple of minutes later the interceptor was parked in the shadow of a corrugated steel warehouse used to transfer grain into train cars that would never come. Rats everywhere.

"You hungry?" Danny said.

"Fuck you," Kelley said.

"Looks like an all-you-can-eat buffet. See you in ten."

Danny headed for the silo. She glanced back once and saw Kelley scowling out the window of the interceptor, eyes fixed on the rats scurrying everywhere through the debris.

Atop the silo's gerbil cage ladder, Danny scanned the horizon with her binoculars, her crippled hand aching from the climb. The sun was getting low. Lately the days seemed not so much to pass, but to leak out of the world. The wind, she noticed, was at her back again—west to east. So the radio might work. But she didn't have anything to report just yet.

Wait. There was a stationary train on the tracks a couple of kilometers away. She focused on that. The sun was beginning to reflect off the roofs of the cars in such a way that she could see the train wasn't as straight as it should have been. It looked like a derailment, in fact.

Was that the vibration she'd felt on the rails? But it couldn't be—the rails here didn't shine. If the train had been running recently, there wouldn't be rust on the tracks; they'd be bright as chrome. That film of rust meant the derailed train in her binoculars was the end of the line for anyone coming this way. The pieces fell into place in her head: two dead trains on the same track, twenty or thirty kilometers apart. So no through traffic. But trains could use the track to the east—for how far, she didn't know. Could be ten kilometers, could be two thousand. Whatever was making the rails vibrate, it was on the other side of this wreck.

Still, where would a pack of kidnapping zeroes be going, anyway? They could stop anywhere and eat the cargo at their leisure. There must be some greater goal. It was impossible to guess. Danny stared through her binoculars as if the answer was written on the train cars.

The train, now that she thought about it, looked familiar. It reminded Danny of the one she'd seen a year back in a small California town, abandoned by paramilitary contractors. Engine and cars painted in some kind of blocky digital camouflage. Not all of them, just the ones in front. The middle of the train was cylinder cars of some kind, gasoline or liquid nitrogen or (most likely, in this region) corn syrup. Several of these had come clean off the rails and were scattered around beside the tracks, burned black. There was a big delta of gray, dead vegetation—not simply brown, but scorched—spreading to the south away from the train. Some of the tanker cars must have burned. Danny saw a couple of fire trucks on the road by the tracks; they had given up in a hurry for some reason. Probably zeroes. There were skeletal human remains scattered everywhere.

Then she saw the symbol.

It was a big decal on one of the charred tanker cars. Its colors were mostly roasted away, so she didn't recognize it at first, but there was no mistaking it once she understood: *radiation*. Three wedge-shaped segments converging on a circular center. Vestiges of black and yellow. The car itself had split across its belly, and dull cylinders like egg cases had fallen through the twisted metal. The ground around them was ebonized.

Danny climbed back down as fast as she could, her mutilated hand slipping on the rungs of the ladder, and returned to the interceptor.

"We need to get out of here," she barked at Kelley, who had succumbed to her hunger. She was crouching over the mangled remains of several rats, shoveling bloody scraps into her mouth.

Thirty seconds later Danny was driving them away from the wreck as fast as she dared go—the moaners were thick on the road. But there had been none anywhere near the wreck. That had to mean something. Plenty of corpses, but no zeroes.

"Drink some water," she said to Kelley, and shoved a bottle into the gloved hands. Her sister didn't so much drink as pour it down the inside of her neck—she never swallowed—but the water seemed to metabolize and keep her from developing that intense dried-fish smell that reminded Danny that she was an animated corpse. They'd tried perfume, once. It was worse. This time, though, it was the smell of rat guts in Kelley's teeth that Danny sought to dilute.

"What did you see?" Kelley said, and belched like a raven croaking. It stank cruelly.

"There's a train wreck back there. So whoever we heard riding the rails, they must have gone around north and then hooked down well east of here. This is a hot zone."

"I don't feel hot or cold."

"Radioactive hot zone. You remember what radiation is, right? Invisible death? Looks to me like the train was thrown together to move some nuclear fuel or something . . . but they had an accident. Busted open the container and there was a big spill. We need to get away from here in case the wind shifts again. I don't know what it will do to you, but I know what it'll do to me."

"I know where we are," Kelley said, after a while.

"Southwest Nebraska?"

"I mean this train wreck. I heard about it."

"From your thinker buddies?"

"I'm still hungry."

Danny still couldn't get out of her head that ghostly figure she'd spotted in Kelley's feeding ground. She wanted to ask a hundred questions, demand answers. But further exploration would probably be a waste of time. Kelley only said what she wanted to, and always had. In life she had been a fluent liar. It was a cosmic irony that the unforthcoming girl had only been rehearsing for her role as an even less forthcoming zero.

"You're putting everybody in danger," Danny said. "You need to tell me what you know."

"I told you, I heard of this place. Radiation kills my kind instantly if it's close by. There you go. That's all I know."

"And that doesn't scare you? If the wind had changed, you'd be—"

"I'd be what? Killed?"

Danny couldn't think of anything else to say. Kelley kneaded her belly and belched and stank.

Danny stayed on the old side road for a while on her way to rejoin the Tribe. She needed to think. And part of her, as always, was hoping to find some scrap of normality hidden away somewhere. She'd have given a year of her life to drive past a working 7-11 with the sign lit up, lottery tickets on the counter, those nasty hot dogs rolling in their cooker, racks of chips and snacks, Slim Jims, cold soft drinks, crappy Top 40 music coming from the ceiling. Surely there must be such a place. Just one, somewhere in the almost four million square miles of America. But it didn't have to be as slickly packaged as that. A big working farm would do. One where the hands didn't have to plant fast in small areas, the zeroes coming toward them, and then leave for a few months, coming back only to see if anything took hold. A school would be nice, too. With clean kids and teachers who didn't have automatic weapons on their backs.

She was halfway back to the interstate when the radio crackled on.

"Come in, Sheriff," Topper said through a web of static.

"Read you," Danny replied into the handset.

"I got some news, where are you?"

"Okay for radio?"

"Let's meet."

They joined up at a burned-out filling station that had been destroyed in the early days of the crisis. Danny could tell this because the sign in front displayed gas prices in the five-dollar range. By the time things had been in chaos for a week, prices per gallon were fifty dollars and up. After two weeks, gas was free if you could pump it.

Kelley stayed in the interceptor, holding her head down low like she was trying not to vomit. Danny retrieved a pint bottle from the trunk and offered Topper a pull. It was Southern Comfort, sweet and awful. Just something to ward off the chill in the air. There didn't seem to be any moaners around. Danny signaled for Kelley to lower her window, just in case there were hunters or thinkers nearby.

"I found a radioactive train wreck," Danny began, as soon as Topper's engine stopped rumbling. "That's why the swarm is built up, I think. They can't get past the hot area. Radiation drops 'em. What have you got?"

"I found the Chevelle."

Danny was rocked back by this. Without thinking, she hooked Topper's lapel with her damaged hand and pulled him closer.

"You found the vehicle, but no kids? No kidnappers?"

"Easy there, Sheriff," Topper said, and disengaged her finger and thumb. "I found the truck, too. Medium-duty two-ton diesel job. The back smelled like people, you know? Like dirty skin and pee. Padlock on the outside of the cargo door. But nobody around."

He unfolded a map from inside his vest and stabbed a thick finger at the route. "Check it out: I went north and found a road east, like we figured. Hardly any zeroes. Couple few miles I take that road. Then I seen the Chevelle, parked next to a fuckin' saloon like the driver gone in for a fuckin' beer. And up an alley there's the truck. I did some ninja scouting and didn't see nobody around. Then down the road a piece I seen this wreck. Three cars, all the way across from one guardrail to the other."

"Go back to the Chevelle. Tell me—"

"Hear me out, Sheriff. These cars was put there on purpose to block the road, because ain't any debris on the ground and they ain't tangled together. Just kind of piled up."

"So can we clear the way and get through? That's perfect. No swarm."

"Ain't as simple as that. This here's why I didn't want to talk on the radio. I didn't want 'em to overhear us. See, the road don't go that far east. After a piece it hooks down to a train station on that same railway line. It ain't a passenger station, more like a freight depot. Ain't on the map so it must be private property. But here's the fuckin' kicker: It got lights, power, radio aerials, bobwire, the whole bit. And there's armed motherfuckers on the roof. Whole place is staffed up and secured. Trains, man. Somebody's running *trains*."

Hot damn, Danny thought. Something new.

"Did they see you? Hear you?"

"Hell no. When I saw the wrecked cars, I thought right away they didn't look natural, so I hid my bike and did the rest of the recon on foot. Thought it might have been an ambush."

"And you didn't call me."

"Didn't want to risk it."

Danny nodded. She was impressed by Topper's handling of the situation—so impressed she almost mentioned it. But she didn't.

"How many men?"

"Maybe eight or nine, maybe more. There's a few buildings. No zeroes around."

So her working hypothesis should be right: The kidnappers escaped by train. But if there were men at the depot, how had the zeroes gotten *aboard* the train? Maybe they weren't zeroes at all. Maybe the horror at the ranch was just a coincidence, and they'd been chasing ordinary men who happened to stop somewhere where evil had occurred. God knew there were plenty of those places.

But something else was on Danny's mind. She mulled it over. Topper stared off into the sky, occupied with his own thoughts.

"The station must be east of the radioactive zone," Danny said, after a while. "Other side of the train wreck. And the perimeter of the zone is swarming with zeroes like we've never seen before. Like tens of thousands of the damn things. Right?"

"Yeah," Topper said, unsure where she was going with the idea.

"So the safe place might *really* be safe. This might not be some urban legend bullshit. If there was a settlement that way, they wouldn't have to worry about attack from this direction, because the zeroes aren't going anywhere near the radiation. I watched them—the moaners are so damn stupid they'll walk through boiling water, but they aren't going anyplace near that stuff. Or they're dropping as soon as they get near, which amounts to the same thing."

"Okay," Topper said. He was intrigued, but he couldn't swallow the idea. "But you wouldn't want to take a train ride through there, either."

"Were the men you saw at the train station wearing protective gear?"

"No, just clothes. Nothing special. Civilian stuff."

"No respirators, even?"

"No."

"So," Danny concluded, "probably the hot zone ends before then. Prevailing winds are north-south, so it makes sense. Take the train straight through the hot zone with the windows up, check the Geiger counter now and then, and after a few miles you're in the clear."

"It still don't work," Topper said, shaking his head like a boxer. "You're the one figgered out them kidnappers is zeroes. The hell would zeroes want to get to the safe place for? Hell, they're fuckin' *thinkers*. *Everywhere* is their safe place, except human settlements. If there's a safe place, people would kill 'em on sight."

"Maybe they figured out how to pass for living. Maybe they didn't take the train at all. They could be walking overland. There would be no danger from other zeroes."

"In other words," Topper said, "our kids got stole by some fuckers who might of took a train, or they might of walked. And like that dude you captured said, the price to get into the safe place is one kid per person. So assuming they ain't zeroes, they're going to use them kids as tickets. Assuming they are, they're just packing lunch."

"That's how I see it."

"Then I say we go the fuck after them right now," Topper said, slapping his hands together. "Maybe hold those pricks at the station at gunpoint and get some answers. We could even make 'em stop the train. Then we light out and wreak vengeance on the kidnappers, old-school."

Danny laughed. "You sound like me, Topper."

"Your kind of bullshit rubs off on people after a while."

Danny made a sudden feint and play-punched Topper in his belly—a play-punch that would have knocked him down if she'd connected it. He was so surprised he laughed, too. For a moment, they both felt like normal people. He put his big hand on her shoulder and they both laughed, him like a bullfrog, her like a crow.

Kelley emerged from the interceptor and watched them. The mood drained out of the moment with that hungry presence hovering nearby.

"We do this by the book," Danny said. "If they're on a train, they can outrun us but we know where they're going to, and if they're on foot, we can catch up to them. So let's go back and get the Tribe settled somewhere it can stay till we get back: check real good for traps, maybe leave Kelley out on the perimeter to keep the moaners and hunters at bay. Then we book it across that empty zone and get the kids back."

Topper threw his leg over his bike and fired the engine, then switched it off again. There was more to be said; he was trying to piece it together in his mind.

"There's something we ain't thinking about. If this here train goes to the safe place, the whole fuckin' Tribe is gonna want to get aboard. Probably hand over *all* the kids. That's gonna be the end of this thing we been doing. This whole kind of journey we been on."

"Good," Danny said, with feeling. "I've had enough of it."

"What happens if we get there and they already got our stolen kids?"

"We tell them whose kids they are. Sort that shit right out."

"I hope it's that fuckin' simple," Topper said, and restarted the bike.

Danny didn't reply. *Hope won't do it,* she thought, but it didn't bear saying out loud. Her hopes had resulted in the undead thing that stood nearby, snuffling at the air, yearning for fresh meat.

16

The smoke rose lazily from a late-model station wagon that had been hit by what looked very much like a rocket-propelled grenade. It had blown the rear axle off; one of the tires was still burning. It reminded Danny of her beloved vintage Mustang, which had been similarly destroyed, although by a more powerful weapon. There was a fresh corpse on the road surface next to the car, a woman. It was clear that she had suffered before she died; her jeans were wrapped around one ankle and her shirt had been torn open, exposing pale white breasts. Her skull had been split from ear to ear by an axe or a machete. Danny felt the sting of bile in the back of her throat as she made a circuit of the scene, shotgun at the ready. Topper stayed on his bike, rifle across the handlebars. He kept his eyes on the scenery, looking for ambush.

Even before they'd reached the place, Kelley had been inhaling deeply, smelling the fresh blood. That had made Danny queasy enough. Seeing what made her sister's animated remains hungry was more than she could take. She spat a few times, and put her hands on her knees with her head down, and was able to master the sickness. But she never stopped listening for the sound of engines.

"Looks like we missed the party by ten minutes," Topper said. "The body is still steaming."

Danny retched.

"Thanks, Topper," she managed to say. "Let's not talk about it."

Danny wondered what this woman had been doing, traveling alone out here in the heart of nowhere. Nobody went alone, except the Silent Kid. Then she worked her way around to the far side of the station wagon, and the question was answered. There was a zero. A fresh kill, reanimated only a short while. A moaner now, but recently a man about the same age as the dead woman; there was red blood all over his clothes, and black blood flowing from his jaws. He hissed and snapped at Danny, but didn't attack. He couldn't—he had been shot with an arrow, and it had gone through his back and stuck into the car door.

Danny watched as the thing laboriously pulled itself along the length of the exposed arrow shaft, its grief and terror forgotten, only hungry. *This is how Kelley feels, every second of every day,* Danny thought. *But she doesn't attack. She's stronger than me.*

If Danny came back, even as a thinker, she knew damn well she'd eat the hell out of the first living person that came along. She didn't flatter herself. She'd probably rip Amy Cutter's head off and eat it, marshmallows and all. But Kelley was sitting there in the vehicle right this moment, with a feast of fresh meat in front of her, and hadn't so much as turned her head when Danny opened the door. Her sister had always been strong-willed, but this was something more than that. If she was like this in death, Danny had sorely misjudged her in life.

"What is it?" Topper called. He couldn't see the zero.

Danny was about to squeeze the trigger when she recalled that the attackers might not be far away. Just because they hadn't come running at the sound of a Harley didn't mean they wouldn't hear a gunshot. She picked up a broken stave of wood from a knocked-down signpost, jabbed it into the pinned zero's eye, and then leaned forward until the head thumped against the car door and there was the double *pop* of bone and brain yielding.

Then she went around to the female corpse and dragged it off the road.

"Let's get the fuck out of here," she said, and didn't bother to tell Topper about the arrow. They started their engines and hightailed it toward the interstate.

17

The Tribe was waiting on the interstate about halfway to the infested zone. Several zeroes had approached the convoy while it waited; they appeared to be headed for the swarm, driven by whatever inner sense guided them. The smoke of burning corpses drifted around them from the hasty funeral pyre that had been built in a field off the road to destroy the dead of the previous night. A couple of the undead stopped near the blaze, and seemed to stare at the fire, remembering. It was probably only the bright light that attracted them.

Wulf shot them down from atop the White Whale. The children, who were now kept together inside the RV while the Tribe was stationary, would put their fingers in their ears after each shot, but they didn't think much about it. Gunfire was customary to them.

When Danny and Topper returned, the rest of the scouts were already there; she whistled up an assembly, and within a couple of minutes the entire Tribe had gathered around, some on the pavement and others standing on top of their vehicles. It was a battered-looking group, Danny observed. A lot of bandages and dirty faces, blood-crusted hair.

Danny wanted to get this over with and start the hunt, so she skipped the preamble.

"Listen up. Two things. First, there is a motorcycle gang operating in the area. They're not friendlies. So we need to remain on high alert. Second thing: We have an idea of where the kids have been taken. They may be on the way to that safe place on the far side of the swarm. Whether that place is actually safe or not remains to be seen. I think it's probably bullshit. So myself and the scouts are going to head over that way. If we can catch up, we'll bring the kids back. If they get there first, we'll scope out the situation and report what we find."

"How far is it?" It was Crawford, the voice of doubt.

"I don't know," Danny said, trying to keep a lid on her irritation. "We'll find out."

"How do we get there?" a scraggly-haired woman said, unconsciously raising her hand. Danny didn't know her name.

"Don't know. The kidnappers might have taken a train. That's what it seems like. We found an operational station about forty minutes northeast of here."

Even as she spoke, Danny knew she'd made a mistake. There was a sudden alertness to the crowd; the word "train" seemed to have galvanized everyone. She hadn't anticipated this. A buzz of voices threatened to drown the central discussion.

"A train?" Crawford repeated.

Topper broke in with his bullfrog voice: "They might be on the train or on foot. We don't know yet."

The scraggly woman stepped forward, her hand still raised. Now she was looking at the others around her. "If there's a train, must be civilization, too. Need all kinds of stuff for a train."

"You don't," Danny said. "This isn't some magical good news, people. The sooner we can all get set up for a few days' stay, the sooner me and the scouts can get moving."

"Hell if you're going alone this time," Crawford said. "We're all coming."

The man to his right chimed in: "Ever time you leave, we get fucked over anyhows, so we all go."

"There's a damn *train,*" the scraggly woman interjected.

"Stand down," Danny barked. The woman lowered her hands and a lot of the side conversations ceased. "Let us do our jobs. You all get yourselves set up safe, form a perimeter and set watches. We'll report back in a couple of days."

"Bullshit!" another man yelled from the back.

"How about I fuck you up, bitch," Topper suggested.

"I don't like where this is headed," Crawford said, all of a sudden the reasonable one. "Isn't this a democracy? Let's *choose* who goes."

Danny felt her face turning red. The situation was out of control. She was furious, but needed to hold it down. They'd use her anger against her.

She raised her voice just below a shout: "Hold on! We don't know who is running that train, or why they're running it. We are still alive today because we have an advance team. If everybody goes, we're as likely to get the kids killed as anything else. Let us do our fucking jobs." It sounded feeble to her, like whining. Apparently the dissenters thought so, too.

"They're not your kids, they're our kids!" a short woman with a bandaged head hollered.

Danny turned to Amy, who stood a little way behind her. Amy looked cornered. She even shrugged. "Thanks a lot," Danny said.

"Danny, it's too late," Amy replied. She was correct: The crowd was breaking up. Already, several drivers had gone back to their vehicles, ready to roll out. More and more chooks were getting the message. They were pulling out, Danny's orders be damned. The safe place was within reach.

Crawford approached her, stopping slightly beyond arm's length. "Sheriff, you need to understand," he said. "We might be at the dawn of a new era here. Don't make us wait."

"It's your funeral," Danny said, and raised the lone finger of her mutilated hand in what she meant to be an obscene gesture.

"Are we gonna let this chook prick dictate Tribe policy?!" Topper said, and addressing Crawford directly, added, "Shut your fuckin' trap." Conn, who had been watching silently, stepped up beside Topper. He wasn't above beating somebody up if it would improve his mood.

"It's too late," Danny said, waving them off. It was always too late.

As she turned on her heels, glaring around in frustration, a grim thought occurred to her. She turned back to Topper. "What did you say just now?"

The biker thought she was looking for a target to vent upon. "I didn't say shit. Don't take it out on me."

"He told that fucker to shut his trap," Conn interjected. "Good fuckin' advice."

"The only trap gonna shut," Danny said, "is the one these assholes are driving into."

Half of the convoy was already on the move, the vehicles forming up into their crooked line, heading for the exit off the interstate that led north. The air was pale with exhaust fumes. People were still piling into cars and trucks and herding their children into the White Whale. Danny's heart was speeding up. That part of her mind that formed theories and plans of action had plenty to work with—she cursed herself for not seeing it sooner.

Most of the scouts had collected around her, looking for orders. This mutiny situation was new.

"Guys," Danny said. "Guys! Vandal Reapers—they've been working this area. Why? Think about it. Chooks come through here looking for the safe place. We've seen them all over. Dragging their poor fucking kids along. There's the train line and everything. It's the promised land. And these sons of bitches nail them before they get close. Mouse cheese. I think it's a goddamned *trap*."

"We gotta stop these shitheads," Topper said.

"They don't know where the place is," Conn pointed out.

Ernie chimed in: "Where is this place?"

"Not twenty miles from here," Topper said. "It's just about the only way to go. They'd find it by mistake. Sheriff, what do we do?"

Danny had been asking herself the same question. Kelley stood beside the interceptor a few meters away; as usual, people gave her a wide berth but otherwise ignored her. She wasn't a part of this situation any more than a vicious dog would be. But now she raised her skeletal arm and extended a finger northward, and the scouts all turned to look at her.

"Stop them," she said.

In ten minutes, the entire Tribe was on the secondary road leading toward the train depot. Thirty-five kilometers of wreckage and bad pavement. The first time in a while that the complete convoy had attempted to take a narrow route anywhere. It was a lesson often learned: never get into a tight place with a wide load. But these people had been driving to nowhere for almost two years. They had seen no specific progress except the ritualistic racking-up of mileage and a slow, aimless review of what was left of the great open spaces of the American West. If they had forgotten why keeping to the open spaces was a tactical decision, not everyone would blame them.

Danny did, however.

She, Kelley, and the scouts didn't race for the front this time. After flagging down individual vehicles proved futile, they stood back and watched the Tribe go by. Danny was seriously wondering if the time had come to give up on the entire project. She made only one further attempt to intervene: As it rolled past, she tried to flag down the White Whale, biggest of the vehicles, to keep it from joining the general rush. Patrick was at the wheel. He called to her out of the driver's window:

"We can't stay behind anymore, Danny. Divided we fall. I'm really sorry."

"It's a trap, you dumb bastard," Danny said.

"It's a cookbook!" Patrick shouted, and Danny had no idea what he was talking about. Then, as he was rolling past, he added over his shoulder, "We have to stick together. I'm not leaving the kids sitting out here without the whole Tribe around us. And to be honest, I'm tired of you always leaving us."

Maybe he is right, Danny thought. After all, the Vandals would attack half the Tribe standing still just as fast as they'd attack the other half moving. It was her instincts against everything else.

"Fuck it. We'll take up the rear for once," Danny said, and the scouts climbed aboard their bikes. "Stay off the radios!" she added, yelling above the thunder of engines. "Let's not clue anybody in if they're listening." By the time she and Kelley were in the interceptor, most of the traffic had already passed by.

"No matter what goes down, stay in the car," Danny said.

"We're past the point of you trusting me."

"We're past the point of me covering your ass, Kelley. Stay in the car."

They rumbled along in the stop-start fashion the convoy always did on smaller roads; somebody would hit the brakes and the entire enfilade would shudder to a crawl, then a bit of distance would open up and others would rush into the gap—only to repeat the process. The exhaust fumes at the back of the convoy were choking. This was the first time Danny had ever been in the rear guard, and she didn't like it.

There was a halt when someone ran over a plank with nails in it. The tire change took ten years, in Danny's estimation. She considered walking up the line and trying to talk individual drivers out of pursuing their quest, but by this time she was so angry about the situation she was almost reconciled to finding out what happened when she wasn't in charge. Maybe nothing. Maybe everything would be fine. Maybe she was only paranoid. But she had a feeling they'd fuck it all up.

They passed through an area she remembered—up ahead was a big modernistic church opposite a slaughterhouse, with two liquor stores in a row right next door to the church. Huge parking lots followed by endless fields of weeds. The convoy slowed to a crawl and Topper pulled up next to Danny's window.

"You sure you don't want us up ahead? I don't like this," he said.

"What difference will it make?"

"None, I guess. But we should of stopped these fuckheads. We're fifteen minutes from the place where that dead chick on the road is. Maybe that will slow 'em down."

Topper rode on anyway, weaving in and out of the traffic for a while, then falling back behind the interceptor. Danny hoped the murder scene would make some of these idiots think—if not of their own safety, then of what the scouts saw every day. She glanced over at Kelley, who sat motionless, her head turned to look out the passenger window. Or, more likely, to exclude Danny from her field of view.

"You think this really is a trap?" Danny asked, not expecting much of a response.

"Yes," Kelley said.

Kelley drew in a lungful of the exhaust-poisoned air, which meant nothing to her except as a medium to allow her to speak.

"What," Danny said, when Kelley failed to say anything for the better part of a minute.

"There is one thing I didn't tell you," Kelley said, speaking with care, as if the words were made of thin glass. "It's a secret. You keep grilling me about talking to one of my kind? He told me a secret on pain of destruction," she continued.

"Tell me now."

"And you won't tell anybody?"

"Who the *fuck* am I going to tell?"

Kelley took a hesitant breath and sounded, for that moment, almost alive.

"One for you, twenty for me," she said.

"What?" Danny didn't understand, but the goose bumps suddenly breaking out all over her arms gave away her deep unease. "Is that a riddle?"

"One for you, twenty for me."

"You need to tell me what the fuck that means," Danny said, her head throbbing. "I don't understand."

"You're in trouble," Kelley said, and pointed ahead.

"Incoming!" a voice shouted on the radio.

The Vandal Reapers were upon them.

Immediately there was gunfire and smoke. The bikes came booming out from behind the church and the slaughterhouse, which were dead center of the convoy; this placed the White Whale and the children at the heart of the attack. The vast apron of tar around the buildings made for a broad maneuvering zone joined seamlessly with the road. It was a perfect setup.

Danny couldn't see the action at first. She heard the bikes roar as they started up, bleating and crackling; then there were voices on the radio and confusion and gunshots. She wanted desperately to move up the file, but at the back of the convoy the road was still narrow, with guardrails on one side and cow pens on the other. So she shoved her entire upper body out of the window and waved the scouts forward.

"Do what you can!" she shouted, and then turned the wheel over and scraped along the guardrail, squeezing past the vehicles ahead, ignoring the shocked faces pressed to their windows.

"Hand me the shotgun," she said to Kelley.

Now she could see the fight. Most of the gang's bikes had riders in tandem, the passenger firing into the line while the one at the handlebars maneuvered in close. In the initial panic, Tribe drivers were slamming on the brakes or trying to speed up, depending on what confronted them. Plastic and metal crunched; broken trim began to fly. Vehicles piled up and gaps in the line split open. The riders moved in, cutting the convoy into sections. They'd done this before.

The Vandal Reapers, Danny saw, had covered themselves in animal remains—bones, hides, gristle. These weren't some *Road Warrior* disco renegades; they looked more like raiders from a prehistoric war. There wasn't any exposed skin. Some of them had rotten deer legs slung over their backs like foul guitars; all of them carried an axe or a machete in addition to firearms. She glimpsed poxy skulls wired all over the triple trees and hung like party lanterns along the flanks of the bikes. Her impression was brief, but enough to know these weren't some desperate outsiders trying to stay alive. These bikers had figured out how to make the end of the world into their finest hour.

Danny's bad hand was on the window side, so she hooked her finger over the steering wheel and rested the shotgun in the crook of that arm. Almost the moment she got onto the wide part of the road, she had a clean shot; she blew the nearest bike over with a load of old-fashioned buckshot and saw the passenger's face connect with the pavement. She'd hit the driver in the thigh, so he was out of action. Then the windshield frosted over on Kelley's side—they'd taken a bullet through the glass, but it didn't appear Kelley was hit. Danny rammed one of the motorcycles and the cable overrider cut deep into the gunman's waist as he was crushed between the vehicles.

Her course took her alongside the White Whale. She could only defend one flank of it, but she was on the side with the most doors. The gang wouldn't know the children were inside, but it still made a great target. If they figured out what the payload was, the fight was going to get extremely hot.

The vehicles were no longer moving. It was time to take the fight on foot.

The arsenal bag was locked in the trunk. Danny didn't think she could get to it without taking a bullet—the interceptor was drawing a lot of attention. The roof lights were coming to pieces as gunfire shattered the plastic.

"Get down!" she said to Kelley. When Kelley didn't move, Danny grabbed the bandages around her head and pulled her sister down. Then she kicked her door open. Pump shotgun and her sidearm and a knife if it got intimate. Time to go.

She dropped to the pavement and fired a load of shot underneath the interceptor, kicking the wheel out from under a bike on its way past. Then she came up on one knee and methodically fired into the densest part of the attack from behind her door. Fragments of window glass were raining down on her—not from the interceptor, but from the White Whale.

She saw Charity the scout race straight at a couple of the enemy bikes on her own hog, blasting away with a long-barreled .357; they collided, and once the bodies stopped rolling it was hand-to-hand. Conn ditched his own machine beside her and waded in, a Russian automatic in one hand and a crowbar in the other. *Time to move,* Danny thought. *Time to get bloody*.

Danny sprang into the open and a fresh round of gunfire heated the air around her, but the guns were rapidly turning useless because there were chooks, scouts, and bikers all over the place. It was a pitched battle, and the Tribe had a numbers advantage if every cowardly bastard among them manned up. Danny emptied the last shotgun shell into the crotch of a huge biker with an iron cross tattooed on his forehead, clubbed another over the head until the stock broke, and then she was beside Conn and Charity, still swinging hard.

Then a crowd of huge, wild-eyed men charged into them like football linebackers; Danny got sacked and hit the ground and was winded so badly she could only suck air, but the man who hit her had rolled off, so she forced her legs back under herself. She drew and shot him before he could bring the pickaxe in his hands to bear. He grabbed at his throat and vomited blood.

She didn't know where anybody else was. Conn, the White Whale, they were gone, replaced by shaggy monster-men draped in rotten skins. She was disoriented, in that dangerous place when confusion kills. Then she saw the interceptor through the fray. The passenger door stood open. Kelley was not inside.

Danny needed to get her back against something, so she made for the vehicle again. A tall, long-armed man with a chromed steel Nazi helmet collided with Danny, slamming her into the rear quarter of the interceptor. The wind barked out of her lungs, and she saw stars. One more hit like that and she was done.

She heard but did not see the man's boots scraping as he stepped back from her, and she sensed there was a blow coming in, even before her vision cleared. She threw herself toward the driver's side door, hoping it would deflect something; an instant later the whack of chain on the roof told her she'd saved her own ass for the millionth time. But the next blow whipped around her stump-hand and stung like fire. He was swinging a greasy drive chain at Danny, his lean face contorted with the desire to see her bleed.

Danny reached into the vehicle. There was a sawn-down shotgun concealed under the dash if she could get it. But hard fingers grabbed her hair and yanked her head back into the A pillar. There was a second biker, hauling her into the wedge of space between the door frame and the car. She was fully exposed for the next blow of the chain, her throat arched. She kicked, but the tall biker had gotten in close, his knee shoved into Danny's crotch so she couldn't twist away. Her eyes found the second biker, a big Samoan-looking dude with a greasy pyramid of hair pouring down his neck. She saw him upside down. Clawed for his face but couldn't reach. She felt her hair tearing out of her scalp.

Then the Samoan screamed, and there was a spidery shape wrapped around his throat—Kelley's arm. She was behind him, the bandages around her face unraveling as she opened her jaws and jammed her teeth deep into his flesh. He tried to pull her off and his hand met a fountain of blood. Danny's head fell free of his other fist. She dropped low and got one boot up and pushed the tall man away, taking the chain across her leg. His attention was off her completely; the screams of the second man were hideous to hear. Danny tore the concealed weapon out of its duct-tape moorings and fired it straight up at the man with the chain. The chromed helmet opened up like a flower and tumbled away with his head inside it.

Danny dragged herself back up, mastering the searing pain where she'd been slashed by the chain. If she could still move, she wasn't entitled to suffer yet. She saw Kelley clinging to the Samoan, who staggered backward past the wreckage, blood shooting out of his carotid artery. Kelley was glued to his back, her legs hooked around his waist. As Danny watched, her sister's head jerked back, and a huge chunk of meat pulled out of the Samoan, full of blood vessels and glands and yellow fat. Danny found Kelley's eyes, and saw a fire in them she'd never seen before, in life or death.

Danny's own eyes flickered to the White Whale alongside, and she saw small, pale faces up there. Some of the children were watching the slaughter.

Then a big biker with a lot of missing teeth was charging, machete raised high, and Danny's attention turned to him. She raised the shotgun and saw his face go white with fear; he tried to stop his momentum, but it was too late. Danny expected to see his guts, but the firing pin fell on an empty chamber. The biker kept coming, trying to turn his stumble back into a lunge. She stayed low; his center of gravity was a foot higher than her head. He took it for cowering and aimed a sloppy blow with his machete at Danny's hunched back as he covered the last meter between them.

Before the blade had made a quarter of its arc, she was inside his reach, thrusting with her thighs to jam the butt of the shotgun into his groin. She felt her shoulder crash into his pelvis, smelled the stink of piss and corrosion. He flipped and went over her head; the machete clanged on the pavement and he hit the interceptor door hard. Danny spun around, saw he was on his hands and knees, and sent her boot into his crotch with such force that she lost her footing and fell on her back. There was another biker coming. There were so many of them.

The next one had given her too much room to work. Danny grabbed the abandoned machete with her good hand, jumped behind the man she'd crippled, and when the next biker leaped over his buddy with a musical noise (his neck had something like five pounds of gold chains around it), Danny chopped his left knee with a long, raking blow that split his leather pants open at the knee and exposed a gristly mass of white and red anatomy that was going to hurt a whole lot when his weight came down on it.

She didn't bother waiting to see it happen, but ran toward Kelley. Two bikers in matching leathers had confronted the blood-soaked scarecrow crouched over the dead Samoan, maybe brothers, with their long black beards and bald heads. They carried pistols. One raised his weapon at Kelley; they had not yet registered Danny as a threat in the general background of violence and the horror of what they saw on the ground before them. The air was thick with screams and gunshots and crunching metal and the savage curses of people fighting for their lives.

Danny was too many strides away to stop the gunshot. It cracked the air. A black hole appeared in Kelley's side, dark matter spitting from the filthy muumuu. Danny saw that Kelley's right arm was missing below the elbow. It dribbled beads of black blood, but Kelley didn't seem to know it was gone.

Before the biker could fire his weapon again, Danny threw the machete at him. She didn't need it to connect; the idea was to divert their attention. She got lucky, however, and the long blade hit him on his sweat-shining head and split his ear open. He howled, fired into the air, and the second biker's gun was turning to cut down Danny when Kelley launched herself at his wrist and stripped it down to the tendons with her yellow teeth. More blood flew. The gun dropped from his fingers. Kelley struck like a cobra at his face and they both went down in a red, glistening heap.

Danny leaped over the hood of the interceptor and collided with the bald man with the bleeding ear, who couldn't figure out which threat he needed to address—the berserk living woman or the undead one ripping chunks out of his brother. Danny went to the ground with him, punching his meaty face with her gristle-hand, the hard stump a better fist than nature had given her. She didn't have the power to knock him out, but she needed to get him defending his face. Both of his hands came up, and there was his gun, held crosswise, not aimed at her; Danny hit the gun with her good hand, and it slapped into the biker's nose, crushing the cartilage. He kicked her off and she fell across Kelley's bony back, then tumbled and came up.

Beside her was the gun that the man underneath Kelley had dropped. Danny whipped it up at the same time the other biker recovered enough to aim. For a long second, they were staring at each other, bloody and panting, across the muzzles of their pistols. Like duelists. A Mexican standoff. The world slowed to a crawl and the only sound Danny could hear was the tide of blood rushing in her ears. She saw him like a photograph—the black beard matted with blood, a bubble of it at his nostril, his nose bent, a dark blue smear where the blood under the skin was flooding beneath the flesh. Wiry black brows and a creased forehead sparkling with sweat. The ragged edge of his ear where the machete had cut. The deep slit in his scalp. He must see her the same way: this battered, dirty redhead with her scars and hard, mottled green eyes. Time for one or both of them to die.

The difference might have been that Danny cared just a little bit less who died. She fired a nerve-twitch before he did, and his bullet went wide because by the time he yanked the trigger, his front teeth had made a tour of his brain from being shot in the mouth.

After that, it was a series of skirmishes; the hand-to-hand broke apart as the Tribespeople remembered their training for once and started forming groups, getting their backs up against vehicles, covering the compass. It was sloppy and chaotic, but the hard-learned lesson at the truck stop must have been recent enough for them to remember to fight back as units, not every man for himself like the bikers. Danny and Kelley fought together, or at least for the same ground at the same time. The results were the same. Danny snatched up bloody guns wherever she found them and emptied them at anybody she didn't know, wounding three; she found the machete again and used it to decapitate a dying man who was crawling along with his guts dragging behind him like a bunch of gray balloon animals.

She ran to the aid of some chooks who were clustered at the entry door of the White Whale and lost sight of Kelley. One of the civilians said there were bikers inside the RV, so Danny hurled herself up the steps inside and chopped the one at the steering wheel until he was puking blood and the other Tribespeople came up after her and threw him overboard through one of the empty window frames.

Then, through the windshield, Danny saw Kelley again: a dark, skeletal thing, hunched low like a hunter, soaked in blood, the tattered muumuu and sopping bandages clinging to her leathery frame. Kelley jumped with uncanny speed at a biker trying to get his machine upright to escape, and her teeth found his throat. Blood spewed out of the sides of her mouth like the wake of a speedboat. His tearing hands could do nothing against the bear trap power in her limbs, even one-armed.

Danny jumped down the steps of the White Whale and her chain-scorched leg buckled, but she got up and ran. Somebody was screaming "zeroes!" and she didn't see any others around. She covered the ten meters at a fast hobble and dragged Kelley off the dying biker by the scruff of her neck. Kelley spun around, hissing, her teeth ribboned with scraps of flesh, and those empty, blood-crazed eyes saw Danny and there was no recognition.

She immediately went for Danny's throat, but one-handed, couldn't drag Danny in close; Danny jammed her elbow under Kelley's jaw and locked it there.

"Kelley!" she shouted.

Her sister kept hissing, her throat gurgling with hot blood.

"I will destroy you," Danny said. But she didn't. She only strained to hold the writhing creature at bay.

They crouched like that for a long while as the Vandal Reapers' attack broke and they raced away past them and bullets whickered over their heads. The roar of engines drowned out the cries of the wounded. Danny wanted to take down the ones who came close, but she didn't dare let go of Kelley. That is, until she saw the kids.

They must have been in some of the other vehicles, probably thoughtlessly packed up in the Tribe's haste to get to the train depot; now they were running across the parking lot in a tight group. Danny recognized the eldest among them—Jimmy James, the boy who had been with her since Forest Peak. It looked like he was trying to get the younger ones to the huge derelict church at the back of the lot. Several Tribespeople were running after them, but there were Vandal Reapers riding up at far better speed.

Danny bellowed for somebody to get after them in a vehicle, but her voice couldn't be heard. She felt the iron claws of Kelley's one hand sinking into her own arm; she still couldn't let go. Maybe it was time to fire that shot she'd reserved long ago. But she no longer had a gun.

Her eyes followed the children running through the melee. The bikers were closing in. Then one of the kids broke from the pack, sprinting for a tangle of bushes at the margin of the church lawn. There was a small dog at his ankle. It was the Silent Kid. Of course. He was the only one who had a system. He couldn't know that this time, it was a better idea to stay with the rest.

The foremost motorcycle bore down on him, and Danny saw his little dog leap up, snapping uselessly at the bike as it thundered past—and then the Silent Kid was snatched up, flung across the gas tank of the motorcycle. The second biker tried to grab one of the kids, but crashed into the cluster and went down; before he could get the machine upright again, the Tribespeople were on him. Danny saw knives flash. Nobody cared what the children witnessed anymore. She had to do something. The other bike was escaping, taking up the rearmost position in what was left of the gang racing down the road.

Then Topper slewed up astride one of the Vandal's bikes, his face a bloody mask.

"The fuck happened here," he said, seeing Kelley's bloody, mutilated shape straining against Danny's arms.

"Kelley!" Danny shouted again. "Topper, back off."

In the next instant, Kelley's thin lips fell over the teeth and there was a blink of confusion; Danny held her at arm's length and felt the sharp fingers loosen.

This time there was recognition in the eyes.

Danny let go. Kelley stayed still, making no attempt to attack.

"Kelley, you need to get out of here. Get out now. Don't stop until you're fifty klicks away. Do you understand?"

"I'm not hungry anymore," Kelley said, tearing the bandages from her head. "I'm alive. I'm fucking *alive* again." Danny didn't know how to take that, so she pushed herself up on adrenaline-weak legs.

"The fuck we gonna do now," Topper said, seeing the corpses Kelley had ripped apart.

"Kelley's leaving us," Danny said.

"I'm okay now," Kelley objected. "I'm normal again." She discovered one of her arms was missing and clapped the remaining hand over the stump. "I swear I'm okay now."

Danny retrieved the black backpack from the back of the interceptor and climbed in. Kelley reached for the passenger door handle.

In that moment, the chaos of emotions in Danny's mind became clear. When she'd struggled with Kelley, they hadn't been sisters. She had been looking into the face of a zero. There wasn't anybody inside those cloudy eyes, any more than there was a personality behind the eyes of a shark. If Kelley had now come back—even if she was restored to her old self—it was because she'd torn living meat off a human body. Danny remembered the promise: If Kelley ever came to understand what she was, she intended to kill her sister and eat her heart.

It was over.

"No," Danny said. "We're done. You go your own way now. Get out of here. I need to go and I can't fuck around here trying to defend your ass."

Kelley looked around her. More and more bloodstained faces were turning their way. Eyes were on her. Everybody had a weapon in hand.

"Please let me come with you. Please."

"You tried to kill me," Danny said. "You're blooded now. Are you deaf? *Get out of here.*"

At last the message seemed to get through. Her sister took a halting step away, and then another, and finally turned around and moved with a speed Danny hadn't seen before, hustling away through the wrack of battle. It must have been the human flesh in her gut. She really did seem almost alive. None of the Tribe tried to stop her, but moved out of the way as she passed.

Danny waited until she was out of sight among the buildings of the slaughterhouse. A couple of tears fell from her eyes, but there wasn't any grief in them. Just pain.

She saw Wulf, up on top of the White Whale. He was raising his old Winchester. He alone could still see Kelley's retreating back.

"Let her go!" Danny shouted.

Wulf knew who she was talking to. A long beat went by, and then he let the barrel drift downward.

There was nothing more to wait for. Danny pulled onto the road and the pursuit team took off, roaring down the pavement after the pall of blue smoke rising from the gang's retreat.

The wind shrieked through the bullet holes in the police car's glass. Danny wasn't dressed for this. Her jacket was in tatters where it had been scored by the chain. She could feel the blood drying all over her, thick as old paint. She cranked up the heater and wondered how the bikers could take the cold. Topper and his fellow scouts opened up the throttles, and her thoughts narrowed to the chase. They were headed back the way they'd come, toward the interstate. There were more zeroes alongside the road than before; the human activity had attracted them. It wouldn't be long before the scene of the fight was overrun.

A Vandal wounded in the combat had ditched; he was lying on the shoulder of the road, almost bled out, his machine dumped against the crash rail. The pursuers didn't slow down for him. They could destroy him on the way back. He'd probably have turned by then; there was more blood on the outside of him than the inside.

Then the gang was jettisoning cargo: saddlebags and tools, anything that might slow down the pursuit. The scouts swerved and twisted; nothing went under the wheels. Danny just slammed over it. She hooked her bad hand through the wheel and began rummaging in the backpack for a suitable weapon. Moving at high speed, dizzy on adrenaline and starting to feel the pain of the fight, she wasn't sure she could do any damage when they caught up with the Vandals, but the Silent Kid wasn't going with them, whether they took him to the safe place or ate him or whatever the hell the plan was. She had to try. Her head was starting to hurt.

They reached the on-ramp to the interstate half a kilometer behind the Vandals; Danny couldn't tell which bike had the Silent Kid on it, but she could see there were several with children aboard, thrown across saddles or held under arms by the riders on the backs of the bikes. So they couldn't shoot their way through. She didn't know what they could do instead.

"Back off!" she shouted into the radio. "Scouts, back off!"

Several of the scouts did fall back, and the others soon saw the pattern and eased off as well. Not everyone had a radio, as they were riding commandeered machines. The Vandals gained ground, circulating up the inclined cloverleaf ramp onto the eastbound side of the highway. They were headed straight for the swarm. And Danny didn't think they'd have long to wait before it met them—there was a mass of the things all around the roadway, drifting westward with their heads tipped back, smelling the recently-departed Tribe's spoor. Topper dropped alongside Danny as they approached the foot of the ramp.

"What do we do?!" he shouted over the wind and engine noise.

"They fucked themselves!" Danny hollered back. "Keep back and when they hit the swarm we go in for the kids! Don't fight, you hear?! Don't fight! Just grab and run!"

They crested the on-ramp. The Vandal Reapers were opening up a good distance, but the road ahead was cloudy with dark figures. The swarm seemed to have turned around, attracted by human activity. Danny saw taillights flash on, chrome winking, engine smoke as they downshifted. There was gunfire. She and the scouts were moving at parking lot speed. Give the Vandals room to fuck up. One by one, the scouts rolled to a stop. They couldn't go any farther without tangling with the enemy gang.

Danny let the interceptor idle. There was a skirmish happening up ahead. The Vandals were going to have to come back at them; there was nowhere else to go.

"Do we get out of their way?" It was Charity, who was covered in blood like the rest. She was taking the opportunity to feed shells into a pump-action shotgun. Several of the others were arming themselves; the Vandals' bikes had weapons tucked away all over them.

Danny dragged her weary body out of the interceptor. She was armed with a pistol and a hand grenade. The latter was for zeroes. If they stayed where they were for five minutes, they'd be overrun. "When they come back this way, we gotta stop the ones with the kids," she said. "No guns. Knock the bikes down if you have to, but we got to get those kids back."

As it transpired, that wasn't the issue. In the distance, they saw the Vandals had stopped completely and were turning around. Then there were bundles being thrown off the machines. Bundles that got up and ran. *Jesus Christ, the kids.*

The bikes rumbled back into action and came racing straight toward Danny and the scouts. They'd left the kids at the leading edge of the swarm. Something to slow the zeroes down while they got away. And it was a damn good idea, because it meant Danny and the others didn't have time to fight the Vandals—not if they wanted to save the children. The fight wouldn't be much use anyway—the Vandals had scattered in several directions when the attack broke up, but even so, this group was some twenty strong, and Danny's side totaled eight.

Everything happened fast. Danny jumped back into her vehicle and hit the gas. The scouts were already moving. They aligned themselves in a flying vee straight down the center of the lanes, the Vandals heading straight for them like knights at a jousting tourney.

The distance closed between the sides. Danny was hindmost among the Tribespeople. Conn was up front. Then the racing bikes were flashing past each other—there was a chatter of gunfire, and Charity went down, along with two Vandals, their bikes scraping fat sparks down the pavement; a machete flashed and Ernie's machine wobbled, but didn't go over. Then the two sides had passed each other, the Vandals receding in Danny's rearview mirror. That would have been the end of it, except Danny had tossed the grenade out of her window a few seconds before. Two of the Vandals had the bad luck to be alongside it when it detonated. They were flung to the ground like dolls, and Danny had just enough time to hope they survived for the swarm's pleasure when she reached the first of the zeroes.

She rammed as many as she could. The Silent Kid was leading the other children over the concrete barrier alongside the road. A cluster of zeroes tearing at something on the ground told Danny that not all of the kids had made it. The scouts, Topper now in the lead, surrounded the young; they were terrified, but the familiar faces brought them back to sanity. All except the Silent Kid, who kept on going, pumping his thin legs across the gravel margin of the interstate, then dropped down into the drainage channel that ran alongside it.

As the scouts rolled out, each with a screaming child on his bike, Danny pulled a U-turn and stopped the interceptor, dodging a couple of emaciated zeroes. One of them had rootlike veins growing all over its skin, like a statue in some ancient Cambodian temple. Then she made her way on foot down the embankment, shouting after the Kid.

"You get over here *now*! I'm alone! Get over here!" He heard that— which part made him stop running, Danny didn't know. But he stopped. Danny reached down into the ditch and pulled him up with her good hand.

They raced for the interceptor, which already had a crowd of moaners nearby; they must have been able to smell Kelley on the vehicle, because they didn't come near. Danny threw the Kid in the back and drove away after the scouts. She hadn't gone far when she reached the place Charity had gone down. The scout was dead, a bullet through the neck. Conn must not have seen, or he'd probably be making a stand where she lay. Danny hated to leave her remains to the swarm, but she could at least send her off properly. She retrieved the dead woman's massive handgun and fired an arm-numbing round into her head, then drove onward.

The Tribe was scattered along the road where the fight had taken place; vehicles that had been abandoned in the early part of the fight stood with doors open and there were chooks wandering around alone, probably in shock. Discipline had completely broken down. Danny was still a minute's drive away when Wulf Gunnar stepped into the road and flagged her down. The scouts had already reached the parking lot in front of the church, so the return of the children was handled.

Danny stopped alongside the old man. Wulf leaned on his rifle like a cane, suddenly looking very old.

"What's up?" Danny asked. She didn't have any energy left, if he wanted to complain about something. Her head was thumping.

"Stay back here a while, Sheriff," Wulf said.

"Back where?"

"Just stay back. Give me fifteen minutes, okay?"

Danny had never seen Wulf look like he did now. There was defeat in his eyes. He appeared to have been hollowed out.

Then, through her fatigue-clouded mind, a terrible thought occurred to her. Her heart accelerated and her foot fell onto the gas pedal.

"Sheriff!" Wulf shouted, and slapped the roof of the interceptor. But it was too late.

Danny steered up to the church parking lot, rolling through puddles of blood and broken glass. Nobody looked directly at her. There were a lot of backs. The only ones who weren't ignoring her with great effort were the reunited families of the stolen kids, who were huddled in a ring, sobbing and hugging. Something told Danny that wasn't what was in store for her.

She saw Topper. He tried to wave her off, which told her where she needed to go. She stopped the interceptor, threw the door wide, and hurried on foot to the place Topper stood. His bike was parked in front of something. The other scouts stood nearby, hanging their heads. Danny was reminded of when she was young and her father's hunting dogs had torn up their new plaid sofa. Everybody looked like the dogs.

Conn reached out, tried to grab her sleeve.

"Sheriff, you seen Charity?"

Danny shook his hand off.

Ernie was next. Bleeding from the cheek, hands outstretched. Danny stepped around him.

Amy stepped in front of her.

"Danny, not now."

Danny pushed her aside.

She saw the muumuu first, the filthy fabric spread out on the asphalt. Then the narrow gray legs poking out from beneath it, and then the sprawling figure of her sister. There was a black halo around her head, and as Danny reached her side, she saw why. Someone had shot her. She was soaked in her own inky blood, except around the mouth where the gore of the living still shone red.

"She came back," Amy said in a voice that seemed to come from somewhere far distant. "She came back to wait for you."

Danny's body lost its coordinates; it had no weight or mass. The fear and anger that had earlier caused her to refuse to take Kelley was gone. She fell to her knees and scooped up the one hand still attached to the body, that skeletal claw with its tattered glove.

A crowd was gathering. She didn't give a damn. She pulled Kelley's corpse to her and cradled it in her arms, rocking, her mind broken into a million dull pieces. Amy was reaching for her, and Patrick held her back.

Danny knew nothing, but felt herself going over a cliff, falling forever into nothingness where the terrible world went sweeping past and there was only the cold sorrow of loss.

Voices were murmuring. Danny heard them now, and looked up into the faces. There was disgust in some, fear in others. The Tribe was looking at her and judging her: Her sister, the undead, had gone feral—and somebody had put the monster down. They all knew this day would come. She felt the fire rising in her face, and wanted more than anything to smash them all, these dull, complacent, lucky people who were still alive when Kelley was twice dead. What did they have? Why were they alive? They were a burden, stupid and selfish and helpless. They were nothing but sacks of meat to feed the legion of the undead, and Danny had never allowed Kelley to eat one of them when she was worth more than most of them even as a goddamn zombie.

She saw Wulf letting the Silent Kid out of the back of the interceptor. His little dog limped up to him and tried to hop into his arms, but the Kid didn't take his eyes off Danny. She wondered what he thought of her. He was alive. That was enough.

She couldn't endure another second. If the boy's confusion turned to horror, it would be more than she could bear. Then Amy Cutter was scooping the boy up and Danny couldn't see him anymore.

Danny lifted up her sister's corpse in aching arms and was shocked at how little it weighed. She stumbled to the interceptor, the back door of which still stood open, and tried to arrange the body on the seat, but the limp shape collapsed as if it hadn't any bones.

Hands were pulling at her, trying to stop her. She felt the time had come to be the dictator. It was time to kill somebody, make the Tribe pay for this.

"We had to do it," a man said. Crawford. Danny reached for her sidearm but the holster was empty.

"She turned savage," somebody else said. "You saw it."

Danny reached in through the driver's side window to retrieve Charity's gun. She was definitely going to kill somebody. There was a roaring sound in her ears and the world was dyed red with the blood pounding behind her eyes.

Then a shadow fell across them and Wulf was there, stinking, red-eyed, his voice raised. He had his rifle and there was spittle in his beard; he was shouting. Danny thought he was going to shoot her.

"Get in the fuckin' car," he said.

Maybe it was him Danny needed to kill. Maybe he was the one who shot Kelley. Her fingers touched the butt of the pistol. Kill him. Get some vengeance. Who cared if it was him who pulled the trigger? He'd do.

But Danny couldn't see herself doing it. Her rage was melting into sorrow. She looked at Kelley's remains in the back of the car. There was the only person Danny wanted to be with.

She climbed into the back of the vehicle with Kelley.

Wulf shut the door behind her, sealing them in. Then he turned to the crowd of Tribespeople standing around them.

"You fuckers were glad to have this here gal lead you, as long as you thought there wasn't any place safe. The minute you heard we were near the safe place, you all threw her overboard. Every last one of you chicken-shit fuckers let her down. And then you blown her sister's head off. So on behalf of the Danielle Adelman Welcoming Committee, fuck you. And you, and you, and you. Fuck every one of you fuckers!"

Then, unexpectedly, he slid into the driver's seat of the interceptor and started the engine. When the crowd didn't make way, he stomped on the gas and they scattered like ninepins, and after a few seconds there was only road ahead, no people.

Wulf drove Danny away. The last thing she saw when she looked back over her shoulder was the Silent Kid, his arms full of the little dog. They were both bug-eyed, staring after her.

18

Danny's mind began functioning again after they had traveled for fifteen minutes in the wrong direction.

"The kidnappers went east," she said. "We need to get to that train station."

"Right," Wulf said.

"We got to go after them."

"They're gone, Adelman. Hey! They're *gone*. What the fuck kind of heroic bullshit you think you're gonna achieve, I don't know. You always think you can just ride out and save the day, and for the fuckin' life of me I cannot figger out why. It's retarded."

"You can't just give up," Danny said. She felt like a prisoner in the back of the vehicle. She couldn't get out.

"I gave up years ago. And I'm still here." He spoke almost gently, with perfect knowledge, as if this was the essence of his entire philosophy. Which it may have been.

Danny forced herself to calm down. "I found Kelley, didn't I? We can still find those kids."

Wulf glanced over his shoulder at Danny to see if she was kidding. "*That's* your argument?"

"Fuck you."

"You wish. Okay: Listen up, Sheriff, because this is my party now. Them scouts we just left behind are perfectly capable of going after these here kidnappers. If any of them chooks want to join in, they can go, too. Hell, where are the parents? Why didn't they drive off after these shitheads themselves? Because they're scared pussies. They're more afraid of zeroes than they love their own fuckin' kids. So that leaves you, because you ain't scared of zeroes. So you want to go off and save those kids. *Bra*-fuckin'-*vo*. But here's the thing. Ain't gonna happen. They already got away, and them poor little ones gonna get ate alive, screaming for their mommies and daddies while some walking skeleton spoons out their guts. That's the way it is. The sooner you figure that shit out, the sooner you can give up. It'll be a lot easier after that."

Wulf drove in silence for a long time. Danny sat with Kelley's spider-light corpse in her lap, the broken head lolling against Danny's chest. The smell of decay was amplifying, a sick, gassy stink; whatever principle kept the animated corpse from putrefying as fast as simple dead matter, it had failed. Wulf rolled down his window, but still said nothing more. Danny did not weep. She sat in silence with the dead kindling limbs gathered close to her, and brooded about giving up.

She hadn't known Wulf could drive. It had never occurred to her. But of course he could. He had been an ordinary person once, too, with a job, car, wife, kids. Living indoors. He'd been a vagrant since before Danny was born. His filthy, tangled hair batted like half-deflated balloons in the wind that whistled through the bullet holes in the glass, and the stench of his armpits cut through the bilious reek of Kelley's remains. Danny only knew him as a big, stinking drunk who stumbled through the woods. Discovering he could drive was like seeing a bear picking up a guitar to play "Smoke on the Water."

They drove nowhere and nowhere again until the sun went down, and in the twilight Danny saw small fields from some family farm, a rare thing in the industrial-scaled crop monoculture of that region, deep in the un-beating heartland. Although the place was clearly abandoned and the coming winter had put the fields to sleep, they were matted with past growth. The headlights revealed a half-collapsed farm stand beside the road with a sign that read ORGANIC PRODUCE. So these were old-style plants that grew from healthy seed, while millions of acres of corn and wheat all around the little farm were sterile and could never reproduce, but only rot.

"Stop here," Danny said, and Wulf pulled over. It was the first time either of them had spoken in two hours. The old clapboard farmhouse was far distant, flanked by a couple of trees. He got out and opened the back door for Danny, then cleared his throat, and said:

"Bob G. Ingersoll said something about six score years ago," he began, and paused to gather the words. "The dead don't suffer." He didn't add anything else, so Danny nodded and began gathering up the limbs of her sister. That was his idea of an epitaph.

The moon rose bleary above the horizon as she carried the limp weight of her sister out into the fields. Wulf stayed with the interceptor. This wasn't his grief.

Danny waited beside Kelley all night in a field down the long farm road. It was cold, and she shivered and flexed her remaining fingers and suffered and hated. All the pent-up fury at the Tribe—and herself—was filling her mind, and she couldn't stop it.

She sat still and kept her vigil, kneeling beside the body, not knowing what she was supposed to do. The stars turned overhead, winking in a sky of darkest ultramarine blue. The Milky Way was a trail of frozen breath across it, the moon a bowl of snow. Danny looked into the night and blinked back tears, unable to let the sorrow loose. She hoped that Wulf would drive away and leave her. He did not. In fact, he was no longer in the interceptor. He had melted away into the night at some point, as he often did.

At some deep, silent hour, three moaners shuffled through the straw, attracted by Danny's scent. She reflexively drew her pistol, but did not shoot as they came nearer. By the moonlight she could see them: a naked girl, thirteen or fourteen years old, halfway through puberty forever, mottled and pale, missing a big scoop of flesh from one thigh. The crater was layered like a ragged onion inside. There was an older man who might have been the farmer, now missing his scalp and ears. The third was a bent old woman trailing ropes of rotten intestines.

They came within fifteen yards of Danny and stopped. They scented the air, making their soughing moans as they tested the stink of flesh. But they came no nearer. It had to be Kelley. Even inanimate, the thinkers must have possessed that warning smell moaners feared. For a time, the trio of zeroes stood and swayed and swallowed the cold air. Then they shuffled away, all in the same direction, like a family of ghosts.

Danny wondered if they knew each other in life. If they were relations. Or if the undead had simply found their way here coincidentally, all drawn by the same faint smell of humanity. She struggled with something, a thought she'd been suppressing all this time. The undead had lived once. They had been family. She remembered some survivors who had made the argument that the dead deserved respect, even kindness, despite their savage hunger. After all, there were people with repellent diseases who were loved. Danny might include herself among the unlovable living, scarred and mean and bitter as she was, and yet there were some who cared for her.

Was it possible that she was wrong? Did all the undead deserve something more than destruction, not just her sister? Was there some small observation that ought to be made when they were dispatched, the way cavemen had honored their kills in the ancient past? Danny didn't know; she didn't have that kind of philosophical mind. But she had to acknowledge that what made Kelley different from all the rest of her kind wasn't just the peculiar remembrance of self with which she had been endowed. It was Danny's own love. She had *chosen* to love Kelley, regardless of her condition. In that instant of reanimation it had somehow made the difference.

It seemed the thing that had kept Kelley from killing the living was the love of one living person. Danny had seen moaners slaughter their loved ones without hesitation. Maybe thinkers were closer to being alive. Maybe they were only sick. Danny had heard that drug addicts should be treated as people with a medical condition. Until she'd found herself relying on the bottle to get to sleep, she sneered at that idea. It could be that the thinkers were more like that, somehow.

With Kelley destroyed, she would probably never know.

She was numb, close to freezing. But Danny maintained her watch until dawn, shivering violently, hoping against hope that Kelley would come back one more time.

When the sky began to glow and Kelley's remains were rimed with frost, Danny knew it was over.

She wanted to bury her sister, but she didn't have a shovel and the ground was as hard as an iron pan. So she stirred her own aching limbs and arranged the corpse with legs and arms tidily straight, unwound the bandages around Kelley's face and neck, and then went to the trunk of the interceptor and collected every bottle she'd been keeping there. She bathed her sister in vodka and whiskey and Everclear, tequila and sochu and rum. The fumes made her eyes water and that was as close to tears as she would allow herself.

It took all the will she had to drag out the lighter. It seemed like some kind of prayer was in order, but if there had ever been a God, He had left this world behind. She stared at the wavering flame of the lighter, and couldn't touch it to the alcohol-soaked rags. To do this thing was to acknowledge it was truly the end. Even in her hungry, reanimated state, devoid of emotions or attachments, Kelley had been there, somehow.

Danny had kept that tiny essence going, her greatest failure remaining incomplete.

She stared at the flame, saw the way it glistened on the alcohol-wet corpse, and could not start the blaze.

"Forgive me," Danny whispered at last, and took out her hunting knife and rose up on her knees as if to pray beside the corpse.

19

Wulf returned ten minutes after sunrise, reeking of spirits; he emerged from a field of dried corn like a pagan mud effigy come to life. Danny was sitting in the driver's seat of the interceptor, so Wulf went around to the passenger side. Danny's weapons backpack was on the seat; he was going to drop it on the floor, but Danny snatched it away and put it in her lap instead.

Wulf settled himself into the vehicle, sighed a great gust of alcohol at the windshield, and said, "I'm outta liquor."

"Me, too," Danny said.

They drove onward toward nowhere in particular, looking for a place to refill. In the rearview mirrors, a column of smoke rose up to mark the place they had just left behind.

"That bonfire for her?" Wulf asked, after a while.

"I didn't want the crows to eat her," Danny said.

"They'll eat us all," Wulf said. He looked like a crow himself, a grizzled elder bird.

They found a town with one church, two streets, and three liquor stores. There was an overturned school bus on the main drag, and even as they rolled up near town, Danny and Wulf were counting the zeroes out loud.

"I got sixteen," Wulf said.

"They look like kids," Danny said.

"Zeroes all the same. Must have died in the bus wreck," he added, as if that made it okay somehow. "How do we want to handle this?"

"If we go down the main street, we're going to be at close quarters with a lot of wreckage," Danny observed. "I'd go in the back way. But we can't see what's there."

"We can take those things. They ain't much," Wulf said. Danny thought his judgment might be a little clouded by his thirst. But they probably could. Small zeroes were weaker and couldn't go for the head and neck as effectively. Besides, the presence of moaners meant there weren't any thinkers or hunters around.

Eventually they settled on a plan. It revolved around the unexpected fact that Wulf was a capable driver. There was a tow truck outside the town with a car rusting away on the hooks, its front end still suspended. They crouch-walked up to it, using abandoned vehicles for cover and a favorable breeze to keep their smell from reaching town. The tow driver was sprawled next to the cab; exposure and vermin had destroyed what was left of him, but the name MARTIN embroidered on his polyester shirt remained legible.

The elderly truck had a primitive ignition, which Danny quickly defeated with a screwdriver; she had a portable jumper battery of sufficient amperage to get the truck started, but worried the gas in the tanks might not be good anymore.

However, the truck started, belching smoke the color of five-o'clock shadow. Danny lowered the boom and disengaged the car from the hooks while Wulf laid down suppressing fire with his beloved rifle, popping the small zombies in the head as they emerged from town to see what the noise was about. Then Danny ran back to the interceptor and Wulf shoved himself up into the cab. The tow truck disappeared in twin plumes of choking blue smoke, then emerged at ramming speed, headed for the liquor store at the near end of town.

He drove the truck around the back of the store, across the few parking spaces, and crashed straight into the loading doors, exploding several cases of foul beer that had been weathering outside since the fall of mankind.

Danny, meanwhile, pulled the interceptor up at the rear corner of the building so she had a view down the back and side, and for five minutes she practiced shooting with a pistol. Any time a gray, leathery head emerged from cover, she punched a hole in it. Wulf had shot four earlier; Danny took down three of her own before Wulf emerged with his first armload of bottles, dumping them into a noisy-wheeled shopping cart.

He made three trips inside before there were too many zeroes to shoot; as soon as Danny shouted "Incoming!" he knew she couldn't take them all down, and he shoved the laden cart into motion. He made it to the trunk of the interceptor with half a minute to spare and transferred the bottles inside like there was a prize involved. Then he dashed around to the passenger door.

A zero that hadn't been more than three or four years old when it died followed him right up to the window. Its small, shrunken face was a caricature of human features, with cavernous eye sockets and tiny yellow teeth. A thin, rat-eaten hand scraped at the glass, finger-bones scratching clean tracks through the dried-on blood.

"Let's get the fuck out of here. I ain't any good with kids," Wulf said.

After that, the plan wrote itself. They had a 360 horsepower hemi-equipped vehicle, several gallons of hard liquor, five hundred rounds of mixed ammunition, and a couple of family-size bags of stale Funyuns. Danny drove until near midday, when they found a suitable location: a water tower atop a small hill, overlooking the entire landscape for miles in every direction. There wasn't much cover there should anything want to attack; there was a tall fence around the tower, which Danny locked behind them with one of the padlock-and-chain combinations she kept at hand in the trunk. If anything wanted to come up the ladder on the leg of the tower, it was going to make a lot of noise and present a perfect head exposure to do so.

The two of them climbed the tower: the old, bearlike man, stinking and weather-beaten, and the young woman with the scars and the ancient green eyes. Then they hauled their supplies up behind them on a rope.

Shortly thereafter, the drinking commenced.

20

Neither of them had directly said what they had in mind when they started their bender. It wasn't the sort of thing that bore speaking about.

Danny hadn't expected Wulf to break ranks with the Tribe, especially in support of anything to do with Kelley. Wulf hated the zeroes on a level that transcended the fact of them. They offended his sense of how the universe should operate. Danny regarded them as dangerous predators, for the most part; the exception was the thinkers, which she considered to be more like human beings than zeroes—meaning they were also more dangerous. No matter what, though, the real enemy in the world was still bad-hearted living humans.

But when the moment came, Wulf was the one who stepped forward and got Danny out of there, although he hated what Kelley was the most of all. He had left the Tribe, and in so doing probably forfeited his place in it. They had been natural enemies once, the vagrant and the cop; now they were two broke-down veterans of war, punching their way through an ugly world.

They drank the good stuff first: searing, smoke-flavored single malt washed down with an occasional swig of water. They each had their own bottles, and kept working until they drained them. Wulf could drink more than Danny, but she was the best competition he'd ever met.

Danny started to feel the booze after she'd drunk the first bottle down to the top of the label. It was the place she spent a lot of time—nursing a low-level buzz that took the edge off everything but didn't interfere with what she had to do. She tried to maintain that level of buzz as often as possible; it made her seem more agreeable to others, which was a benefit, but the chief effect was to make others seem more agreeable to her.

Wulf was a third of the way through his bottle. While Danny took small sips at short intervals, he favored massive chugs every ten minutes or so. Danny observed his technique with admiration. She watched the golden bubbles roiling up like jellyfish through the cruel, beautiful liquid, amber and hot to the eye. Six deep swallows and two fingers of the bottle emptied.

She tried that approach, and it damn near killed her. Which was fine. The end game, although neither of them had bothered to articulate it, could include death, if it came to that. Glorious drunken death. She took four massive pulls, filling her throat with whiskey, and it felt like molten lava. It hit her belly like a hammer, but that was secondary; the raw alcohol stripped the skin out of her gullet and set it on fire. The fumes punched the air out of her lungs. She retched and coughed until her eyes sparkled with purple and green fireworks and she was lying on her side. Her eyes streamed and there was snot hanging out of her nose.

Wulf observed this impassively. "You're doin' it wrong," he said, and proceeded to drink another two inches of whiskey out of his bottle with swallows that sounded like marching boots. Then he belched, and Danny thought she could see his whiskers turning to ash in the shock wave. Her head was starting to hurt.

"You in this all the way, Sheriff?" Wulf inquired, fixing her with a ham-colored eyeball. His nose had lit up like a stoplight.

"Cheers," Danny said, and set to drinking again. It was getting very chilly. Their breath made ostrich plumes around their heads. They shrugged sleeping bags over their shoulders, camo models from the trunk of the interceptor. She used them both for bedding; Kelley hadn't needed to sleep.

An hour into the binge, Danny was no longer altogether in command of herself. Gravity had ceased to operate on her nervous system; things weighed the same and moved the same, but they didn't *feel* the same. That was the tricky place where legions of high-school-aged kids got into trouble, back before the end of the world when drunk driving was a matter of concern. Danny's limbs were filled with what felt like a mixture of helium and elastic; it took skill and experience to move normally, to speak clearly.

The real, hardcore drunk—and Danny felt she could compete in that league—was aware of all the subtle ways that intoxication gave itself away. It was a point of pride not to reveal the effects of alcohol until they were absolutely impossible to ignore: Keep the motions steady, the hands moving accurately, the speech clear and articulate. But any quality drunk knew that *over*articulated speech was a sign of the influence. It had to look natural. You couldn't allow your movements to become too precise or careful, like a kid trying to operate a coin-operated claw over a heap of stuffed toys to impress his girlfriend.

"You know what the trick is?" Danny said.

"What is it?" Wulf asked, peering at her over the neck of his bottle.

"They jam those fucking stuffed toys in so tight that the claw can't pull 'em free. It's a bullshit trick."

"What in the name of blue-nutted monkey fuck are you speaking of, Sheriff?"

"You know," Danny said.

"I probably do," he said, philosophically, and drained his bottle almost to the bottom.

Wulf had now consumed enough alcohol to kill a nondrinker. Danny was about three-fifths of the way through her own bottle, and she knew her time was running out—the alcohol wasn't all metabolized yet, but when it hit, she would pass out. She needed a leaner mixture, like giving a carburetor more air so the engine didn't drown in gas. She drank a good measure of water, although her stomach recoiled in horror at the influx of cold liquid.

Wulf breached a bag of Funyuns and dumped them on the metal deck of the water tower; they ate them in greasy handfuls. Then Danny sat back and watched the horizon sway from side to side. The tower seemed to be three hundred kilometers tall. She had to cling to the railing. But it felt good. If she didn't puke, she was right in the sweet spot.

"Sheriff, you and me known each other a while. I used to think you were a cunt, but I changed my mind a long time back. You got the right stuff."

"That's right decent of you, Wolfman," Danny said, struggling to form the words. "I always thought you were a walking pile of ass. I was right."

They both laughed about this until Danny threw up in her mouth. She ate some more Funyuns and drank more water. "Got to pace myself," she remarked.

"Anyways," Wulf said, "I brung something special because I ain't going back to that pack of helpless assholes. So I brung it with me, and I want to raise a fuckin' toast to your sister, God rest her soul, if any. Viola," he concluded, and pulled a very special bottle out of his filthy jacket. It smelled like polecats, but the label said it was French.

"Wine?" Danny said. She didn't know a thing about wine. She drank for effect. Wine had too much water in it. Inefficient for her purposes.

"This ain't fuckin' *wine,* Sheriff. Found this particular artifact a couple months ago when we went through Utah. It's Château Lafite fuckin' Rothschild. This right here"—now he peered at the label, as if to verify it hadn't been swapped with an inferior bottle—"is a 1959 Pauillac, at the peak of its fuckin' powers. You will never set your heathen lips to anything as good as this. It ain't the '89, but this stuff tastes like a cherry orchard in a mountain forest on a warm summer day. Got a finish on it sixty feet long. I ain't a hunnerd percent sure you're worthy of this thing, but it's now or never. You suffered a grievous loss yesterday. I only wish we didn't have to drink it out of the goddamn bottle."

Wulf insisted they rinse their mouths out. They swished and spat water at the ground far below, in long glittering streams; Danny vomited and had to wash her mouth out again. The fanfare Wulf lavished on this bottle made her feel like she was on a first date. He examined the label gravely, speaking with reverence, like a lover, like a priest. He had to enunciate very slowly in order to be understood; his tongue was thick with the whiskey.

"This here bottle used to retail for about fifteen hundred bucks. You can pay more for wine, but it ain't easy to get more out of a bottle. It's about 90 percent cab-sauv with a little merlot, if I recall arightly. Them's the grape varietals. It don't fuckin' matter. Hell. You got a corkscrew?"

Danny did, as a matter of fact, have a corkscrew, on her utility belt. The cork was dry as leather at the top and crumbled like red velvet cake at the bottom, but Wulf took a whiff and declared the wine had survived the decades in perfect condition. He handed the bottle to her.

"First pull is yours, Sheriff."

Danny took the bottle, smelled the liquid inside. It had an intense aroma like evergreens, flowers, and fruit. There was something almost like a cigar to it. She regretted they hadn't started with this stuff, but what the hell. The old man probably hadn't intended to share it at all.

"Wolfman, how come you know about wine?"

"Used to have a life."

"I didn't even know you could drive."

"There's all kinds of shit you don't know about me, Sheriff. And I guess there's all kinds of shit I don't know about you. I know one thing, though. You finally lost that sister of yours for good."

Danny's fingers tightened around the neck of the bottle. This was the subject she was hoping to avoid.

"What do you think about that?" she said, after the silence had gotten too long.

"I think you lost her the one time and you kind of half got her back, and you tried to make that work on account of you were a shitty sister and a half-assed guardian when she was alive and you wasn't there when she needed you. That's why she run off. And now she's gone for good and you must have a hole in your heart about the size of a fuckin' elephant. Take a swig."

The wine tasted to Danny like sour milk and raisins, but she liked the velvety feeling of it on her tongue. They drank the entire bottle in short order, and spoke little.

After that, they drank whatever came to hand—vodka, tequila, rum. Danny lost touch with the world; the sun was starting to go down when consciousness fell away and she entered the universe of the profoundly drunk. She walked carefully around the perimeter of the water tower on legs made out of marshmallow, clinging to the railing as if there was a storm at sea and her on a small ship on the bosom of the water. She vomited again, more than once, spilling alcoholic bile over the side. Wulf was singing songs from his youth, the kind of stuff Danny considered oldies. His voice sounded like a hacksaw cutting through an anchor rope.

She remembered how she used to drink when she was in the service, hard like this, on leave with her buddies Harlan and the others in San Diego, drinking for nights on end, cheap tequila and beer, drinking dirty-sweet tamarindo when it wasn't time for beer, say, before 9:00 a.m. . . . she and the crew were so drunk for so long that at least twice on leave she never made it up to Forest Peak to see Kelley, who was living with people who were relative strangers to Danny. But now with the water tower at her back and the ruined world far below, she was so drunk that instead of feeling the sorrow of the memory, she saluted it on the way by, acknowledging the pain like a veteran at a parade, no longer a part of the machine, no longer invested, but intimate with it from indelible experience.

She and Wulf entered the holy state of drunkenness in which wisdom and nonsense become one, up and down ran forever sideways, and the motion of the planets and sun and universe could be detected merely by standing still. There was a roaring in Danny's ears like the ocean or a thousand-tongued laughing god, or the wind of cosmic wings; she felt no pain, no grief, nothing but drunk. The tortured self, whoever that was, she could see from above and below and knew it for what it was, a selfish illusion, the purpose of which was to keep her from savoring life. Life, which tasted like scotch and beer and wine, all the wet fire and dim light of it, burning, the fire that splashed and leaped, the liquid flame.

Danny slipped and fell but didn't drop off the tower; she lay where she landed on the catwalk, with one leg hanging in space, her body bound in the boneless mother of the sleeping bag. She watched the stars come out in a sky that rotated above her like a pierced tin lantern caught in the wind. The cold and the sorrow danced in the distance and she felt neither of them, but watched and felt nothing.

21

Danny awoke to a bitterly cold morning with the sun broken like an egg yolk on the horizon. Her head pounded intolerably. She couldn't tell if it was one of her increasingly mean headaches or just a savage hangover, and didn't know if it mattered. She had opened her gummy eyes to find herself in the fetal position, limbs pulled up under the sleeping bag in a stingy pocket of warm air. She struggled to the sitting position and her skull cried out as if it had been split in two.

Her first thought, which took a minute to generate, was to see how Wulf was doing. So Danny got to her knees and began to crawl along the walkway that surrounded the water tower. She was still quite drunk, she realized. The world was swaying and the height of the tower made her feel sick. She felt that falling sensation that came to her most often when disaster struck, but this disaster was internal: a hangover of the gods.

After what felt like three circuits around the entire tower, Danny found Wulf on the far side, snoring in a complex, syncopated pattern in the seated position with his head sunk between his knees and his sleeping bag pulled over his head like a monk's cowl. Danny suddenly understood why so many long-term homeless people wore heavy jackets all year: better to be too hot than too cold. And if you didn't have an indoors to retreat to, you didn't get to choose the middle. He looked relatively warm in his blackened layers, probably wearing six pairs of pants. Danny was shivering.

She needed to get down off the tower somehow and warm up. And if the sick feeling in her guts turned into the shits, she didn't want to be seventy feet in the air. There were no zeroes around that she could see. Down below her, she could see the police car, parked inside the perimeter fence around the base of the tower. It looked like a toy with its shot-up surfboard-shaped light bar and a big 213 painted on the roof. The view reminded her of the grain silo she'd climbed to view the Radiation Express. It made her think of Kelley, and a flood of guilt and sorrow rushed through her mind. She drowned in it for a minute. The headache was getting worse. If she was going to climb down off the tower, she'd better do it now. She might be incapacitated before long. The ladder up the silo had been caged in. This one was wide open to the world. Danny began the slow climb down, hooking the rungs in her elbows because her good hand didn't work much better than her bad one.

And so it went. Wulf and Danny drank steadily for days.

When a thin, icy wind began to slash down from the north, smelling of snow, they moved the operation down off the tower; there was a pump house at the foot of the structure that made a reasonable shelter for Danny, and Wulf preferred to sleep outdoors, so the subsequent couple of nights were passed without too much discomfort, except for the endless, increasingly drunken condition they were achieving and the bilious guts that came with it.

Night and day blended together. The cold snap seemed to be permanent. It was winter, after all. There was frost on the grass and the metal of the tower was so icy it burned. But the drinking companions warmed themselves with alcohol. They ate little and drank much. Sometimes Wulf wept; Danny didn't know what specific memory brought it on. For her part, she tried to shove the sadness down, building woozy compartments for all her woes and then drowning them one at a time.

Most of all, she avoided thoughts of the Tribe.

"I was the worst sister," Danny said, in a moment of drunken clarity. Wulf, who had been singing all the songs he could remember from the sound track to Jimmy Cliff's *The Harder They Come,* stopped and squinted at her.

"I never gave Kelley the time of day," she went on. "I blamed her for making me responsible for somebody." She had a tough time getting the word "responsible" to sound right, but Wulf understood.

"I handed her the anger I couldn't hand my goddamn parents for dying so young. I sucked, man. I was never there for her."

"You handed yourself the anger, Sheriff," Wulf said, pointing at the sky like an Old Testament prophet.

"This one time," Danny said, "Kelley had this good bra. I mean one of those ones cost real money with lace around the edges and foam padding and straps that don't twist up. It was like bucket seats for your tits. And I couldn't figure out how she got the money. I thought she must have stolen it." Here she paused to remember why she brought the subject up. "Anyways, she wears it like a week and finally I'm like 'you got to wash that thing' and so she does, and she puts it in the dryer. Well that fancy bra come out of the dryer looking like a rubber chicken with its neck broke. It was destroyed."

"What's your point, Sheriff?"

"I don't know, but it seems like a sad story to me now. I was just pissed off at the time."

Danny lost track of the days. They drank and passed out and woke up and drank again. At some point, there must have been a supply run; she couldn't remember where it had come from, but they'd ended up with six cases of Coca-Cola and thirty cans of Dinty Moore Beef Stew, and there was a massive new dent in the passenger side door of the interceptor. According to the shipping label on the cola, they had gotten it from Fossil Deep, Nebraska, so they might still be in Nebraska.

They shot up the water tower with Danny's sabot rounds and used the resulting waterfall to wash the zombie guts off the vehicle. It didn't make it much cleaner, but the stink was noteworthy.

This was no ordinary bender Danny had embarked upon.

There was a greater purpose down there, under it all. She wanted to die drinking, go out like a lord. She assumed Wulf was operating along the same lines. The Tribe must have moved on by now. It had probably gotten around the swarm and found the safe place, followed the train tracks to somewhere. Maybe chased down those damn kidnappers. *Those kids.* Guilt attacked her whenever she let herself get below a certain threshold of inebriation, so Danny wasn't sober for a single minute.

Something Kelley had said wandered around in her mind, repeating itself now and then, still meaning nothing at all.

One for you, twenty for me.

Another cold morning showed up despite their best efforts, and with it a light snow. They had stored their liquor supply inside the shed; Danny slept in the fetal position next to the pump housing alongside the bottles, jamming herself deep down in the sleeping bag. She awoke to discover they were almost out of drinkable liquor, her boots jingling among the empties. Even an alcoholic has standards; Danny did not intend to kill herself with Jägermeister or peppermint schnapps.

She'd been suffering from diarrhea and flaring headaches since the first morning, and she had vomited more than usual during the bender. Exhaustion had overtaken ambition: She simply couldn't keep on drinking anymore. Her attempt to drift painlessly away on a river of alcohol had not succeeded. Her biology was either too tough or too practiced. It was time to make a plan, if her head didn't explode. Her tongue felt and tasted like a roasted tarantula.

Danny crawled out of the shed. She was still plenty drunk from the previous night's festivities, but this was the trying-to-get-home part of the intoxication, when the fun has gone out of it and everything was a challenge. She looked out and saw clean white snow like a coat of paint on the world. Still not a single zero anywhere around. The local undead population might by now have gone into hibernation in one of their nests, buried in leaves in a cellar hole or burrowed into the refuse at the nearest dump. Not all that different from herself. Or it might be this was a place with so few people in it that the undead didn't even have a foothold.

She and Wulf had been trying to talk last night, and Danny remembered part of the conversation. It had seemed important. It probably was. Wulf had said something about how people didn't really forgive, but they did forget. Danny had pointed out, with the insight of the extremely drunk, that nobody ever asked for forgiveness anyway, so how would he know?

"You gotta forgive yourself first," Wulf had replied. "Afore anybody else can do it."

That seemed important in some way. Danny sought him out now in the sharp cold morning. Wulf was sleeping upright, as he often did, head between his knees, with his back against the interceptor. Danny could smell alcohol and concentrated urine from ten feet away. The old man was dusted with snow.

"Morning," she said.

Wulf didn't respond. She was about to try again when she realized something was different. He wasn't snoring.

She crouched in front of him, but her balance wasn't too good and she fell over backward. A lance of pain went through her head. She got to her knees and looked closely at her stinking friend. She shook him; he didn't stir. His eyes were open, but staring down at the snowy ground. His hair was frozen, his beard sparkling with ice.

No, Danny thought. She couldn't bear to lose another one so soon. And yet she found her sidearm was in her hand, unbidden, and the safety was down. Because the world said *yes.* She waited, wondering if he would reanimate. In the beginning, the contagion was airborne and spread like smoke across the world. More than half of all dead people rose again. Then the rules changed. Lately it took a wound to get infected, direct transmission. Not airborne any longer. Whatever the infection was, it changed all the time. Danny had herself seen those deformed and diseased zeroes recently, riddled with some mutation. She waited, wondering if the early form of the disease still lived in Wulf.

He never came back.

She waited an hour beside him, and he remained as he was, a frozen corpse, eyes downcast and his rumpled nose drooping. Somebody she once knew.

Danny remembered the last coherent words she had heard him speak the previous night: "I am the Ghost of Christmas Past." Maybe he had known he was dying.

Danny slipped her weapon back into its holster.

She drove the interceptor back the way they'd come, through all that blank, meaningless landscape of frozen grass and failed crops, prairie and cracked roads. The only break in the horizon was the distant smoke from Wulf's funeral pyre. She had a simple plan. It was like a gift that he had given her before he died in his sleep. She was going to go back to the Tribe, find them somehow, and forgive the fuckers if they would forgive her. Then maybe she could forgive herself. It was her only option left in this forsaken world.

22

During a map check to figure out where she was, Danny discovered a route that could take her around the swarm and the radioactive zone, south, east, then north. But she wanted to find out what the train depot was about, and see how the Tribe had disposed of things. They might still be sitting in the same place, or they might have caught a train, or could have scattered to the wind. So she took a more direct path, due north. It would run almost straight up the border of South Dakota and Wyoming.

Now that she'd stopped drinking, Danny was feeling the guilt she'd been avoiding. That wasn't all she felt: The headache seemed to be with her all the time, more than a hangover, like a wound. As if there were pins holding her brain in place inside her skull. And she thought she had a yeast infection coming on. It hurt to pee. She needed water. She cursed herself for shooting up the water tower, and they'd consumed all the water they'd brought. Kelley had scolded her years ago that drinking sugary stuff made hangovers worse, so Danny didn't touch the colas rolling around on the passenger side floor, bumping into the weapons backpack there.

The day warmed up, became mild enough so the snow melted away, except in the shadows. Eventually she found a cattle ranch, the feed lots studded with the shriveled carcasses of the herd that had been left behind the fences when the people went away. It reminded her of the place back where they'd found the half-eaten victims of the Chevelle driver. So much unfinished business.

The remorse beat at her; she'd left the idiots under her command to whatever fate the world decided to hand out. Her old friends, the Silent Kid, those still-missing kids. She'd abandoned her post. Nobody should be in a position of such responsibility they could fuck up so many lives just by falling prey to a little sentimentality for their own damn sister. It had happened before, when she thought her group was safe and she'd gone off on her own to seek out Kelley. Now she'd left them again, and again for Kelley. The results would probably be equally disastrous.

Danny siphoned gas out of a farm truck into the interceptor, ignoring the raging thirst that was turning her mouth into cigarette ash. Then she went in search of water.

There was a pump in the yard of the ranch house, an old-fashioned model with a long cast-iron handle. Danny considered seeing if the taps in the house worked, but she kept having visions of another charnel pit of blood and flies. She decided to see if the hand pump would work. She pushed and pulled at the resistant handle until there was stinking sweat pouring out of her, and at long last it barked, croaked, belched up rusty sludge, then jets of reddish water, and then the water ran clean and cold. Danny hadn't cleared the ranch house or barns for zeroes, but she didn't care right now. She'd see them coming across the yard. She sluiced the icy water over her skin, raising goose bumps. Gasped and blew and stuck her head under the stream. Then she pumped a couple of gallon jugs full, drank nearly half of one of them, refilled it, and turned to go back to the interceptor.

A zero was standing beside the vehicle.

It had been a tall black man once; now it was gunmetal-colored. The thing's clothing was stained and rotten. Wherever Danny could see exposed skin, it was covered in masses of tissue that looked like red grapes. They burst through the thing's rags and hung in heavy fist-sized bunches. For some reason, the zero didn't seem to be attracted to Danny. It just stared at the police car.

"Hey," Danny called, placing a jug at her feet and drawing her gun.

The zero turned its shrunken gray eyes toward her, then stumbled in her direction. Danny raised the weapon. Her hands shook terribly but it was an easy shot.

"Kiiiimuh," the zero moaned through its swollen face.

Danny hesitated. It was a thinker. Or almost a thinker.

"Kiii—muh," it said again, and fell to its knees. It was facing her, eyes fixed on hers. Then it lowered its head, offering its skull to her. Danny saw that the things growing out of its skin were translucent and had dark, wormlike filaments inside. Her stomach lurched. She tasted acid in her throat.

"Can you understand me?" Danny said.

The thing did not respond. Danny stood there a long time, squinting past her gun at the bowed head of the zero. The thing raised one blistered finger and pressed it to its own temple.

"Kiiii—muh."

Danny squeezed the trigger. The bullet entered the crown of the head, making a star-shaped hole, and black debris spurted out of its mouth; the zero fell on its side. She looked around the ranch and didn't see anything else coming for her. She was cold again. She holstered her weapon, picked up a jug of water, and got back into the interceptor.

Kill me. That's what it had been trying to say.

The White Whale looked like a mirage. Danny watched it through her binoculars.

Earlier, she had made a detour to the northeast, revisiting the radioactive train wreck. There was an iPhone Geiger counter—an accessory that had become popular on the West Coast when Japan had its meltdown—in the trunk of the interceptor, and she kept the thing charged. Lots of people had them now—the scouts all carried one. At the scene of the wreck, it had registered more radiation than the device could express. It was absurd, but she'd held her breath and run toward the derailed cars with one hand thrown up in front of her face as if the radiation was just heat from a fire.

Now she wasn't far from the place she had left the Tribe. The zeroes that had attacked the Vandals had returned to the swarm, apparently; on the interstate she saw some ravaged human remains and a few inanimate zeroes, but none moving. Taking the exit onto that minor road required more courage than it did to confront the seething invisible death inside the ruptured containment car.

She didn't expect the Tribe to be where she'd last seen it, between the slaughterhouse and the church; they would have gone east long before then. But she was still a couple of kilometers away when she saw the glitter of window glass far down the road. She pulled over and climbed unsteadily onto the hood of the vehicle and used her binoculars to see what lay ahead. She saw a boxy shape that had to be the White Whale, and many smaller vehicles before and behind it. It looked as if the entire Tribe was still sitting there, a week later (or however long it had been). She was too far away to be certain but she thought she saw human figures moving around.

So she rolled on up the road, heart pounding with fear that she would be rejected by the very people she had spent so long sneering at for their weakness.

She was going back to apologize to the people who had destroyed her sister.

But she couldn't gain access to the anger.

Somehow she'd always known Kelley's strange existence could not end well. Kelley herself had predicted she would murder Danny—what happened after that? A shot through the head, same as what actually did happen. She went out with a gut full of human flesh either way. That had always been the plan.

Danny *wanted* to blame the chooks. She wanted it all to be their fault. But she simply could not. Maybe it was the eternal hangover.

She spotted what she thought was a familiar face—one of the civilians from the Tribe, wandering around alone.

But as she drove closer, she saw it was a zero. Once a Tribesperson. A woman who had been wounded in the fighting. How had she come to this place? Why had she not been delivered out of the world on a bullet?

Danny was perplexed. Thinking about it made her head hurt even worse; tears were leaking out of her eyes. Not tears of grief, but of pain. Maybe both. Mostly pain. The thing was half a kilometer from the back of the convoy, and must have been wandering around aimlessly since the fight. Danny rolled to a halt beside it, rolled her window down. The zero hissed and opened its jaws. She shot it on the fifth try, her hand shaking although she rested it across the frame of the door. The noise of the gunshots set her ears ringing, and they didn't stop. Now she couldn't hear properly. She was going to have to be very careful with her senses as dull as they were.

Her thoughts kept uselessly returning to the matter of what she ought to have done, and what she would do next. Why hadn't she skipped the drinking game and just gone back and made amends? Two years back, it would have been pride. But this was something else. She figured it was something between shame and fear. It was her job to go back to the Tribe and seek forgiveness. She didn't expect to be nominated to lead them again, of course, and she didn't want the job. Maybe she wouldn't even be allowed to ride with them anymore. It didn't matter *how* they responded. She hoped only to be understood by anyone with enough sense to see what kind of a situation she'd been put in, and maybe for someone to say they understood. Maybe. She wanted some kind of absolution.

But she was afraid nobody would understand. She didn't know how to apologize. She might get it wrong. She might not find any words at all.

There were a lot of crows in the sky. That meant undead. Dread was settling over her heart as she approached the convoy. When she reached that fatal battleground, it shocked her to see how hastily the Tribe had abandoned the scene: There were Vandal corpses strewn where they fell, and empty vehicles scattered along the road at all angles. It was clear they'd packed up and left in a hurry. Danny saw one leather-clad zero, a biker in life, making its way across the slaughterhouse lot. A couple of hunters emerged from the bushes in front of the church—right where the Silent Kid had been trying to go. She'd known them in life, too, ordinary scared people, now hunched, vicious things, scuttling along the parking lot so as to remain alongside the interceptor, in case she stepped out. But they didn't come close. Smarter than the moaners. One was the driver of the shuttle bus, Sue Baxter.

Danny stopped the interceptor alongside the White Whale and opened the door. Put a foot on the ground. The hunters froze, their sunken eyes fixed on her position. She waited, and saw them begin to move. They slunk crabwise toward a motorcycle that lay crumpled on its side and crouched down behind it. She could still see them, but this was instinct. Like cats. The aching in her head was expanding with every heartbeat. She didn't want to wait—she wanted to gun the things down and be done with it, find out what happened to the Tribe. But she couldn't move around with hunters nearby. *Not without Kelley at my side*, she thought.

There was a noise off to her left. Danny searched around among the parked vehicles of the Tribe and saw a moaner working its way down the line. A Vandal with a wide cut in its throat. Again, Danny wondered where the mercy shots had been. She needed answers, and fast. As she scanned the area, she realized there were a lot of the undead around, attracted by her arrival, and if she wanted to solve anything, she had to work quickly, headache be damned.

She decided to take the risk. Hooked a fresh magazine from the backpack, checked the load in her pistol, and got all the way out of the car. The hunters were galvanized; one sprinted, low to the ground, toward the line of vehicles ahead; it wanted to get around behind her while the other stalked in front. She loosed several rounds at it and got lucky—its leg buckled, and the thing was left cackling incoherently on the ground, unable to get under cover. She ignored it, turning her attention to the RV instead. There was something written on the bullet-pocked windshield; she could see it backward through the open passenger door. She chanced leaving the cover of the interceptor's bulk, keeping one eye on the zero still hunkered down behind the motorcycle, and made her way around until she could read the message.

All down the convoy, there were more undead emerging from the shadows. They were looking for ways into the cars and trucks, probably attracted by the strong scent of humans that hung around them. Most were unknown; a few were once Tribespeople. They were pawing the windows, groping along the sides, looking for openings. Danny wondered briefly if the living humans were hidden inside their rides, heads down, but that was absurd. They would have fought back.

The convoy was deserted. She was the last living Tribesperson here.

Suddenly, the still-mobile hunter—the revenant of Sue Baxter—was far closer than Danny expected—a few yards away, sucking the air to get the smell of her, almost to the interceptor. She'd let her attention slide. She fired the pistol and the thing's jaw snapped sideways. A second shot brought it down. The ringing in her ears increased.

There were more of them, more than she had bullets, coming on as fast as they could move their clumsy limbs. No further hunters, at least. No thinkers in evidence. She looked up at the broad, flat face of the White Whale and read the message scrawled there in soap:

PROPERTY OF THE TRIBE
BRB

Danny went back and locked herself inside the interceptor, then drove along the file of vehicles, using the overrider on the bumper to shove the zeroes out of the way as they came on. Scaly hands clawed at the windows. One of the undead had a short length of pipe in its hand, but it lacked the coordination to strike effectively. There was a clank on the roof and that was all. She ran the wounded hunter over.

Now that she could see the entire convoy, she realized most of the high-capacity vehicles were missing—the shuttle bus and others like it were gone, although the White Whale remained behind, probably because several of its massive tires had been shot to pieces in the combat. It only carried one spare. So the living had gone away, packed together like sardines in the minimum number of machines, with hardly any luggage—most of the gear was still inside or on top of the vehicles they'd left behind.

She felt a vast loneliness rising up around her like the wings of a gigantic bird. She had again forsaken the people she knew in the world, and they had done their part and gone away themselves. Wulf was dead.

It was only her and the zeroes and thousands of square miles of empty landscape.

They must have hightailed it to the train depot, probably led by Topper, and caught a train or walked from there. Somewhere to the east, anyway. Where were the nearest living human beings? The guards watching the train line, probably. Maybe those anonymous travelers who had gotten off the courtesy shuttle when Mike the kidnapper showed up.

That's when Danny saw him.

It was sheer coincidence that Mike happened to be in her mind when she passed the foremost vehicle in the convoy and saw something dark and shapeless hanging from the slaughterhouse sign beside it. The sign stood on a massive arm of galvanized steel, tall enough to drive a tractor-trailer under it. Amalgamated Rendering, the big black letters proclaimed. Beef, Mutton. There was antipigeon wire along the top of the sign, like a bottle brush.

Beneath it hung a dead man. Danny would not have guessed it was Mike, except for his clothing and shoes. His hands were cuffed together behind him. His face was contorted, eggplant-colored, his neck twice as long as it should have been, a bundle of taut cords cinched in at the jaw by a noose.

"Holy fuck," Danny breathed, leaning forward as she drove past the effigy until her head touched the steering wheel. Then it was out of view behind the roof.

Whoever had hung Mike there must have climbed a ladder. Or they'd used the telephone line repair truck's extendable bucket.

In addition to stringing up the prisoner, someone had spray-painted a message over the lettering on the sign:

THIS IS WHAT HAPPENS TO KIDNAPERS

It didn't occur to Danny to cut him down. There were too many zeroes following her path down the convoy. He wasn't going to be any less dead. She'd burned Kelley's body and she'd burned Wulf's, as well, on a pyre of boards from the shed doused in sweet liqueurs. Mike would have to wait for the crows to release him from bondage.

Danny's repentant frame of mind was gone. Here was murder in cold blood. They had left their own dead behind to turn into monsters and hanged the prisoner while they were at it. Why? Because Danny wasn't around? What had Amy been doing? Patrick? Troy? Had they stood by or had they argued?

There was no coming back after this.

Danny wondered if anyone had left a note, besides the scrawl on the White Whale's windshield and the painted message on the sign over Mike's corpse. It didn't matter. She had gone back to apologize, only to discover the Tribe had murdered her prisoner. Whether it was retaliation for what she herself had done, or the assertion of new leadership, or merely an old-fashioned lynching, they were now even.

She'd be damned if she would ever apologize to them. In fact, she was a hell of a lot more likely to kill the bastards if she ever saw them again.

The headache that had been stalking her began to open up, to bloom like a time-lapse film of a rose blossom opening. But the petals were jagged, bloody claws, and the red flower was the tissue of her brain splitting apart. Her limbs stopped responding to commands. She was accelerating past Mike's gibbet when her nerveless foot slipped off the accelerator. The interceptor swung around of its own accord. Danny found the brake with a boot that seemed to weigh as much as her body. She came to a stop facing the front of the convoy, blinking back fireworks of white-hot light that rocketed through her eyeballs. Sizzling electric auras. Was she having a stroke?

Something was running out of her nose. She swiped at it: blood. There was a noise like machinery in her head. Danny's vision was turning red the way it did when she was very, very angry. But her heartbreak was bigger. And more than that, she was in agony. The redness before her eyes was laced with veins that flashed to the beating of her heart. She needed to get out of here before she passed out—there must have been thirty or forty zeroes coming up the road after her.

She saw a small zero, a hunter by the way it moved, running onto the pavement from a drainage culvert set alongside the edge of the church property. A child hunter. Where were the others? They worked in numbers.

Danny's thoughts were sliced apart by the pain, as if she had to think through a rank of slashing knives.

The thing ran straight at her. She groped around for her sidearm with useless fingers.

It was the Silent Kid, with his bat-eared little dog tucked under his arm like a football, running in her direction for dear life.

The mass of undead were now homing in on the child. Danny needed to get him out of there, if the boy made it as far as the interceptor. He wouldn't make it back to his drainpipe.

Half-blind, Danny fumbled for the door handle, hoping to get out and shoot the nearest zeroes. Popped the latch, but instead of standing up she fell helplessly to the pavement, facedown, her head churning with pain, filled with blood lightning that set her skull on fire. Her boots were still inside the vehicle. She couldn't use her legs, her arms.

The Silent Kid reached the interceptor half a minute ahead of the closest zeroes. Danny tried to speak to him, to tell him to get in, dump her feet out of the car, lock the doors. She was done for. She'd rather be torn apart than endure the pain in her head another instant. Instead of words, bile came out of her mouth. With an effort almost beyond her strength, Danny got to her knees, reached back into the interceptor, dragged the munitions backpack off the floor of the passenger side, and pulled it to her chest, struggling with the zippers.

The Kid was waving with his free hand now, leaping and gesturing at something behind Danny. She tried to struggle upright, but gravity had gone off-axis. She fell over backward and sprawled on the asphalt. She saw a wheelchair. *The medics are here at last,* she thought. But there was already somebody in it. She heard a strange *thwack*. And another, and another. Something whistling through the air. A meaty crunch.

"Get up," a female voice said, and Danny felt a handcuff snap onto her outstretched arm, heard the jingle of the chain. Then she was sliding across the pavement, and there were wheels arching up above her, someone between them, at the top of a cliff trying to pull her up. She blinked and the redness in the world turned green; she blinked again and a slab of red-stained darkness like a collapsing bridge came crashing down and the whole world snuffed out.

PART TWO

1

"If you die, I have to shoot you," a voice called from the end of a very long tunnel.

Danny blinked and saw what looked like the edges of a film strip, sprocket holes in the sky. She squinted. Not sprocket holes, but windows.

She was lying on her back inside a vehicle. Her head still hurt, but it was nothing. The savage torture that had visited her back at the abandoned convoy was gone, replaced by an ordinary headache. The dull throb of it was almost comforting, like having a doctor's note to stay home from school despite being only a little bit ill.

The woman who had spoken was the color of bittersweet chocolate, black-eyed, with a fleck of pigment in the white of her left eye. The hair on her head was carelessly buzzed short, all the way down to the scalp in some places. She had strong, lean arms. Her teeth looked luminous in her dark face.

"Where's the Kid?" Danny mumbled.

"Asleep underneath your bed," the woman said.

A shot of panic hit Danny's kidneys and burned through her bloodstream before she found the backpack she'd been lugging around was right by her side. The zipper lock was intact.

"You wouldn't let go of that thing," the woman said. "Coffee?" she added, opening a thermos.

Danny's mouth abruptly filled with water at the thought. The cab was filled with a long-forgotten aroma: good coffee, nutty, sharp, and strong, with a velvety depth like exotic wood smoke. Back at the Tribe they had all drunk freeze-dried instant dissolved in lukewarm water.

"Yes," Danny said. There was more to the exchange. She tried to think of the word. "Please," she added, as if saying "hello" in a language she hadn't used since high school.

"There's something wrong with your head," the woman said. She had an accent of some kind. Danny would have said Jamaican, and she was pretty sure she'd be wrong.

"It just happened," Danny said, and tried to sit up. A great chunk of pain collapsed into her skull and she had to lie down again, gasping involuntarily. She closed her eyes.

"And you think you can ignore it, am I right? Tough it out. You're tough, I see that," the woman said. "Bad-ass. I am also bad-ass, and I have bad legs as well. You can't ignore physical problems. I think you have a brain injury, unless you have a history of epilepsy or something."

"No. Just hung over, I guess," Danny mumbled, waiting for the lance in her head to withdraw. "Went on a massive bender the last few days. I don't even know what day it is." She opened her eyes to find the cup-lid of the thermos held just in front of them. She took it and propped herself up enough to sip it. It burned. Hot, acrid, and rich, black as ink.

"Fuck, that's good," she said.

"Creature comforts, Mama," her companion said. "I'm Vaxxine. That's with two exes, which is funny cos I have two exes in real life. It's Wednesday."

Danny's eyes were in focus now. She assessed her situation. They were inside the cab of a long-haul tractor-trailer truck. Danny lay on a bed in the little apartment behind the front seats. It was outfitted with ergonomic precision like the first-class cabin of a jumbo jet. There were pockets and compartments everywhere, a coffee machine and miniature microwave near her head, a tiny bathroom at her feet. It could have been the captain's berth of a submarine, shipshape and efficient.

Danny turned her attention to her host. Vaxxine was seated in the driver's position, twisted sideways so she could talk to Danny. Her jeans-clad legs were bone-thin, the knees knobby; they didn't match her strong, corded arms. Her pants were unzipped and a diaper poked out of the waistband. But then Danny remembered the wheelchair she'd seen before she lost consciousness. A paraplegic truck driver?

"So you know who I am, and I see you've sorted out my legs are just for show. Who are you in your raggedy police uniform with a gun and a corkscrew? You don't have any identifying papers or marks I could find, unless you count a relief map of Colorado on your back."

Danny involuntarily tried to sit up again, and again the hammer came down on her brain. She sloshed coffee over her hand.

"Sensitive about that? I won't mention it again," Vaxxine said. *"Me no maco,"* she added, turning her accent all the way up.

Danny *was* sensitive about her wildly scarred back, but at least she wasn't sitting in a diaper without the use of her legs. There was that. She had spent three months in a wheelchair after she'd been medevaced out of a combat zone with crushed legs and third-degree burns, and had nothing but sympathy for anyone stuck in one of the damnable things forever. So Danny swallowed her irritation and drank more coffee to chase it down.

"My name is Danny Adelman. I used to be a sheriff in Southern California." She didn't think much else was worth mentioning.

Danny had a view amidships forward to the driving compartment and the windshield, beyond which was an empty parking lot. Up above the cab, there was a deep space that was probably intended as further sleeping accommodation, but Vaxxine had used it for storage: Danny saw boxes of toilet paper, duct tape, ammunition, canned goods, adult diapers, and various other things it was good not to run out of. A helping-hand gripper on a pole hung on the bulkhead; her host could reach up from her chair.

"Anyway, we need to get your head examined, Danny. Nothing personal," Vaxxine said, and drank directly from the thermos.

"It's a headache, that's all," Danny said. She decided to expand her biography a little, in case Vaxxine knew anything about the Tribe's fate. "I was with a large group traveling around until recently. Just came back for a visit and they were all gone. Do you know what—"

"I only arrived a little before you showed up," Vaxxine said. "I was trying to figure out why all the vehicles were sitting there empty like that, when they'd obviously seen recent use. Then you came along and that boy and his dog came racing out to meet you, so I figured you were involved somehow. We barely got you out of there. The boy had to help me get you into the rig, with the zombies coming and all."

"I appreciate it," Danny said. "If you don't mind me resting up a couple hours, I'll take the Silent Kid and be out of your hair, unless you need help with anything."

"The Silent Kid," Vaxxine said. "That explains why he's so quiet. I thought he just didn't like me." She laughed at this, so apparently it was funny. Danny didn't bother to respond.

She must have fallen asleep again, because when she next opened her eyes, the sky outside the windows was purple with twilight and they were driving somewhere. The Kid was sitting in the passenger seat in front, with his snouted dog looking out the windshield with its front paws up on the dashboard and his tongue curling out like a pink wood shaving. Vaxxine was driving. Good enough. Danny threw an arm over the weapons backpack that rocked gently at her side and passed out again.

2

The hospital looked like a mirage. There wasn't anything around it except dead cornfields. It rose out of a dry ocean of leaves like the city of Oz, a modern building of green-tinted glass and bright steel. From a distance, it appeared that nothing was wrong with it, as if the disaster had passed it by. But as they drove closer, details revealed that the hospital had not escaped unscathed.

Danny was sitting in the passenger seat by now, having recovered sufficiently from the pain in her head, and she had been getting carsick lying in the back. The Silent Kid was on the bed now, playing tug of war with the Boston Terrier. Vaxxine drove the bobtail rig ably with customized hand controls that were bolted onto the foot pedals and rose up the steering column; Danny had seen similar units during her time at VA hospitals, but never on a machine this size. Vaxxine appeared completely comfortable with the ten-speed gearbox, and floated the gears as ably as any professional driver, using the clutch only to start and stop. It must have been doubly complicated when it all had to be done with hands alone.

Once Danny was upright and had some Advil in her, Vaxxine had started to talk. And she didn't stop until the hospital came into view. She was like a castaway on a desert island: Without companionship, it seemed all the conversations she might otherwise have had were stored up inside her head, and now she was getting them all out. She seemed to have an inexhaustible reservoir of trivia, observations, and theories about every subject. The topic of most interest to Danny was how Vaxxine came to survive at all.

"I used to be a dancer," she'd said, as they passed through a landscape of big hills swathed in brown grass. "Go-go and that. Then I had a skiing accident. Turns out it's true what they say. Colored folk can't ski. I broke my back. So I was all 'okay, note to self, need new life,' and I was pretty good at some things, I'm organized, get that from my mother's side of the family. So I got organized and found out all about how cripples fit in. And basically they don't. So I had to start coming up with work-arounds. 'Cause there wasn't anything good on TV.

"So I was doing that, and I got a job at the Circle Hotel in Hollywood at the pool bar, which was cool because the whole barback was just big enough for one person standing up, like an information booth. But I couldn't stand up. So I found this company made stand-up wheelchairs and that worked out pretty good, except it freaked a few people out 'cause they would come over for a drink and be all normal and then they'd see I was in this body brace and down there was this torture chamber looking thing with wheels. But I was making a living. Plus I got sympathy tips. 'Here's ten bucks, I'm going to dive off the board now,' I think was the feeling."

"I'm from outside Los Angeles myself," Danny interjected. "You're a long way from home."

"My theory is to keep moving," Vaxxine said. "Otherwise they find you. Plus, I got wheels. I'm made to keep rolling."

"So you're at the hotel bar—" Danny prompted.

"It was Fourth of July weekend, you remember the occasion. Hasn't been the same holiday since. I was in the booth serving up Red, White, and Blues—"

"Which are?"

"Grenadine, peach schnapps, and Blue Curaçao stripes on shaved ice."

"Fuuuuck." Danny's stomach lurched.

"Right? But they were a big hit. So it's crowded, beautiful people everywhere, sun shining down, celebrity sightings every ten minutes, all good. Then Emilio, he worked there, too, comes on over to my booth to see if I need a break, 'cause he can spot me a few minutes, he's one of our reserve bartenders. And he mentions there's some weird shit going around. I'm like, 'What?' and he's like, 'On the TV in the lobby bar, there's riots or whatnot happening left and right.' So I'm like, okay, I'll check this out, and I lower myself from stand to sit and wheel on out of there. The pool is behind the lobby on the ground level with a courtyard around it, so it was a quick roll.

"There was a big crowd of people watching the TV over the main bar, but it didn't have sound. Management thought sound on the TV was low-class. So we're just looking at these pictures of people in China and India and places running around in huge crowds, like riots only they were just running and screaming and falling down. Then they'd cut to some guys making a world-record barbecue or something for the Fourth."

"I remember that," Danny said. "The Internet, too. It was like a news blackout except it wasn't exactly a blackout." Despite herself she was caught up in the story, remembering that day. "It was like all the media companies decided the story was too much of a downer."

"And then they hit the Internet kill switch, I think," Vaxxine said. "But we don't need conspiracy theories anymore. I remember there was a live news feed out of Boston where they were supposed to be doing a parade, and all these brass marching bands were going along and suddenly these running people come tearing straight through the parade. Like streakers, only not naked. Just random people. I thought it was a flash mob thing. But more and more were running through, and I saw a guy with a tuba get knocked down by one of the runners, and then he got up like he was getting attacked by a swarm of bees, and started running. Still had the tuba, flashing in the sun. Everybody around me in the lobby was kind of freaked out. Even the valet parking guys had come in by now. Then of course the news cut over to some fluff story about a cornfield in Iowa mowed in the shape of a giant American flag.

"I was in my chair so people kept getting between me and the TV, and I didn't want to go up in the standing position because everybody always wants to talk about it and I kind of didn't want to discuss it right then. So I wheeled over to the doors. I don't know if you know the layout of the Circle, but it looks out on Hollywood and La Brea on the restaurant bar side and the lobby doors are on Marshfield. So it's a big intersection."

Danny nodded her familiarity with the area, although she didn't actually remember it at all. It hurt to nod.

Vaxxine went on: "I saw these people run across the intersection, and they were screaming. Going east-west. The screaming matched what we saw on the TV, so people didn't notice it at first. It was like the sound had come on. Then somebody said "Oh, my God," and now everybody turned around to look. I was right up against the lobby window at this point. Ringside seat. More and more people kept running through. A big fat guy got hit by a car. Horns were going. There was a four-car fender-bender a second later.

"People were running the other way to help the fat guy, because he flew up in the air, and he was on the ground, moving like he was still running. But then the people who went to help him freaked out and a couple of them started running, in whatever direction. There wasn't any sense they had somewhere they were trying to get to. I remember a lot of people in the hotel were looking down the streets trying to figure out if there was a fire or a terrorist attack or something.

"I was getting claustrophobic at this point because people were pushing me up against the glass. A lot of people went outside for a better look, and they blocked my view from there, too. Then one of the runners came straight at the windows. Just ran like crazy. I saw him coming. His eyes were rolled up and he had his hands in the air and he was screaming bloody hell. Everybody outside was like diving out of the way and then BAM he ran straight into the glass, right into the window I was at, and I saw his nose and mouth sort of explode against the window. It was horrible. Blood and snot and bits of teeth. He fell down, of course. Then the onlookers outside started running. A couple of people came into the hotel because it was obviously getting freaky-deaky in the street, more and more people running around screaming.

"This went on for a long time, I think. I don't know. It seemed like forever. Everybody wanted their car back all of a sudden and the valets were running around, people were checking out in a hurry or demanding to know what was going on. They wanted to speak to the manager, like that would make any difference. Then a fire truck came through the intersection at top speed headed for Hollywood and Highland, I think, because there was smoke rising up from down that way. It got slammed by a pickup truck doing fifty. It jackknifed and tipped over. Fell on about ten running people. Cars were piling up all over by now. People in the hotel just straight up panicked.

"Now, you don't know me, but you know I'm in a chair, and you can imagine what a panic in a crowded hotel lobby was like from my perspective. I jammed my way into one of the elevators, hacking ankles with my footrests left and right. They're designed for that, I think. Lot of people were going upstairs for a better view. I got off on some random floor. It was the eighth floor, as I eventually found out.

"So nobody was around at that level except some people trying to leave. They had a couple of small kids and their rollaway suitcases with them. I was glad to be out of the crowd, is all I knew. I was still worried about abandoning my post at the poolside bar, can you believe it? It had been about twenty minutes since Emilio told me I could take a break, and at that point, even with the fire truck tipping over, I still somehow thought this was just some kind of temporary freak-out. So I went to the service closet by the elevators, because there's a staff phone in there. But I couldn't get through. Not on any line. It was ringing, but nobody was picking up.

"I had the service closet door closed, because it's hotel policy. They don't want guests seeing the vomit cleanup gear and dirty mops. Especially when it's stored right next to the spare minibar soft drinks and snacks. But then I heard the same screaming like outside, except it was *inside* the hotel. I mean, it was this high-pitched screaming coming up the elevator shafts. It went on and on. I just sat there with the phone against my head like a dumbass for the longest time. I heard glass breaking. The whole building shook at one point.

"I wheeled myself out of the closet because I couldn't stand not knowing what was going on, and rolled over to the windows by the elevators. Floor to ceiling, so I had me a fine view. At this point I had the place to myself. Nobody was stopping at that level any longer, there was just screaming and chaos downstairs, coming up the elevators and fire stairs like somebody was watching a disaster movie on a TV somewhere. It didn't sound real.

"But it *looked* real. There was black smoke coming up past my window from down below; I couldn't see what was burning, but I thought it was part of the hotel, which as you can imagine scared the crap out of me. When you're a wheelie, there's no such thing as an emergency exit. Fire bells were ringing downstairs for the longest time, and then somebody must have switched them off.

"Past the smoke, there was the whole intersection and I could see up and down six or eight blocks of Hollywood fucking Boulevard, and it was pandemonium. Huge crowds of people running, other people trying to get out of the way, cars crashing, shit knocking over, fires—the fire truck had this huge pile of running people smashed up against it, like they just charged straight into it. I saw a couple of firemen up on top of it, which was the side, actually, and they couldn't do a thing except wave their arms to try to get people to stop. Didn't work.

"I sat there and watched forever. Just couldn't look away. I saw the shadow of the hotel stretch across the intersection, that's how long I was there. It was late afternoon when the running people started to thin out, and the screaming was kind of easing off somewhat from downstairs. I felt awful. I was scared to death, and it seemed like I should be doing something. When you're in the chair that kind of stuff drives you barmy. You see somebody drowning, you can yell 'help!' but you can't do a damn thing. You see an accident, you can call the police but you can't assist. I mean you can try but it's futile. So I sat there and felt awful . . . but I just didn't try to do anything.

"The one thing I did do was use my phone. I called my mother back home. It was everywhere, apparently. I mean like all around the world. My mother is in Trini, that's Trinidad, and it wasn't there, but like all over the mainland countries. If I'd known that was my last call, I'd have made it different."

"I don't remember the last call I made. It might have been trying to get hold of my sister," Danny said.

"Here I am, talking your ear off," Vaxxine chuckled. "Your head must be pounding. I'll stop talking, padna."

"No, keep telling me about it," Danny said. Aside from the warm, musical sound of her voice, Danny found Vaxxine's story interesting on its own merits. Survivors from the urban centers were rare. Most people who outlasted the first month of the crisis were from sparsely populated areas, or fled the cities immediately.

Her head wasn't hurting anymore, either. She felt much better—even hungry.

Vaxxine continued: "I haven't talked to a living soul in three weeks, and I shot the last one," she said. "Cheeky badjohn wanted my gear. I've been alone most of the time since spring. I'm not a loner, but it's the only thing that seems to work, survivalwise. You get into a group and the old saying about 'you don't have to outrun the bear, you only have to outrun your friend' kicks in real fast. I'm the one to outrun, see.

"Anyway, I'm there in the hotel, right? And by now I'd got the idea that whatever was happening, it was a chain reaction, like a relay race. Runners would crash into nonrunners, and then the nonrunners would start running. But most of all by late afternoon, they weren't running anymore. They were just falling down and staying that way, exactly like dead people. After a couple of hours of them not moving, I was pretty sure they *were* dead. It was quieter inside and outside, and the fire seemed to have gone out, although there were fires all over the city as far as I could see.

"I had to know what was happening, but the phones stopped working. My mobile, I mean. Probably all mobiles. I don't know if they cut the lines or what, but now all I had was the staff phone. So I rolled on over to the elevators and pressed the 'down' button but none of the cars came. I kept pressing the button again and again. Then I went back to the closet and finally got somebody on the phone, one of the laundry ladies from the basement. She was scared to death and didn't know what was happening either. I asked her if she could come up and see what was amiss with the elevators. She said she was too scared. She wanted me to come down. So I explained my situation. I guess that made her feel like she wasn't the most-screwed person at the hotel, because she said she'd come up.

"Half an hour later, she was good as her word. Rafaela was her name. She was a big lady and I thought she'd stroke out from climbing the stairs, but that's how she came. She told me the elevators were jammed with dead people. The whole of the ground floor was jammed with dead people. Living people, too, but they were just standing around the edges in shock or holding the dead if they knew somebody. No one paid attention to Rafaela. There was an automobile went straight through the restaurant. That's what the smoke was from, she told me. The whole place smelled of smoke, but thank God the fire sprinklers hadn't gone off, except in the restaurant. Blood all over the place. She said there were so many bodies floating in the swimming pool, she couldn't see the water.

Rafaela said she had to get back to her sister and nephews and nieces, which meant she was going to have to walk across town. The streets were impassable, right? I mean there were cars and junk all over the place. I begged her to help me get down to the ground level, and she didn't want to. But I said 'Just take my chair down and I'll make my own way.' So off she went with my fancy wheelchair, which was not lightweight. She went down the stairwell and I listened to make sure she didn't just drop it off after a couple of floors. It sounded like she took it all the way down.

"I was on the top step of the eighth-floor landing with a cardboard box flattened out like a toboggan. And I started down the stairs. It took me half the damn night, bumping down. Here's the nasty thing about legs like mine: They don't work, but they still hurt. I had bruises for the next month. I slid every step on the cardboard, hanging on with both arms to the railing to keep myself from sliding too far at once. But the railing is up here, right? So my arms kept going numb and my hands got so tired I'd have to stop all the time.

"My bam-bam was on fire. I don't have much padding there, so it was like tapping my tailbone with a hammer every twenty seconds for six hours. Oh, my God. Plus I had a catheter bag and diaper on and it wasn't going very well. Let's leave it at that. I even took a nap at one point. Another time, I lost my grip and slid down a whole flight and about broke my neck to go with my back.

"But I made it down by dawn. No windows in the stairwell, so I didn't even know what time it was except by my phone, and the battery died on that before I reached the fourth floor. But I got to the bottom, and there was my chair with a note on it. 'Good luck,' it said. And she'd left a bottle of water on the seat. I never saw Rafaela again, of course.

"I dragged my busted ass into the chair and went through the door into the lobby. Now, I hadn't seen anybody on the stairs, right? The door was closed and I guess nobody died there. So when I rolled out of the stair hall, I see everybody is walking around. I'm like 'What the fuck?' because Rafaela told me one out of two people was dead. But I saw only a couple of bodies.

"Then I realized there was something wrong with these people. They looked sick. There were people with godawful injuries, cuts and smashed faces and the like. All yellow and sick-looking. They were all wandering around. Then I saw not everybody was like that. There were regular people, too. A woman saw me and she was like 'Oh, God, what happened?' and I said, 'Ski accident three years ago,' which was supposed to be funny. But I guess she meant how did I get there. Anyway, I joined up with some people who were behind the main bar where the TV was, because the brain-dead people couldn't get back there. They couldn't *do* anything. You know, you must have seen it at the same time. One guy said, 'They're all retarded,' and the same woman jabbed him in the ribs and kind of tipped her head at me like I was retarded and he'd hurt my feelings. But he was right. They acted like they were mental.

"I don't know exactly when the killing started. I mean I can't remember it clearly. Something changed, and all of a sudden instead of just looking at us, some of the sick people started to go after us, not like they wanted to bite, but more like they needed a hug. I don't know how else to put it. Then somebody got bitten. It was a man, I think. Not sure. But a minute later, there was complete chaos. I mean, *pandemonium*. Being in the chair saved my narrow behind. People were struggling all over the place and the zombies came over the bar and started attacking and I fit right under the flip-up section of the bar you walk in and out of. I only had to duck. So I scooted out of there and straight to the supply closet next to the bar and hid myself. For ten days."

"Ten *days*?" Danny gasped.

"Ten days."

By now, there was a greenish cast to the night sky along the horizon; morning was coming. The predawn light revealed a bank of heavy clouds on the horizon. They were driving through relatively open road with the hills on either side getting lower and flatter.

"I hid in that closet like a baby," Vaxxine continued. "I had a key for those kind of areas, but the closets lock on the outside, not the inside. I jammed a stacking banquet chair under the handle and listened to those *obeah* freaks thump into the door and watched the handle wiggle for ages and ages that first day. The screams and shouting died out after a while, and then it was just the moaning. That awful *moaning*. If anybody else was alive, they'd gotten out of the hotel. So I took stock of what I had. I lived on fucking salt peanuts and Coca-Cola for ten days. Poured my piss down a floor drain. It was like the longest commuter airline flight in the history of the world."

3

The cracked parking lot of the hospital sprouted weeds, the landscape plantings were dead or run wild, and there was a scrum of abandoned cars, police vehicles, and ambulances jammed around the emergency room entrance. These had been attacked long ago. The glass of the vehicles was smashed out of the windows and most of their doors stood open, the interiors weather-stained and gnawed by vermin. The ground-floor glazing had been starred with bullets or stones; the safety glass didn't shatter, but it was damaged everywhere and in some places had been torn out of the frames. In one wing of the hospital there had been a fire, a couple of windows blown out and the structure blackened by smoke in a V-shaped plume that ran up the wall. But most of the place was intact, at least from the outside. Danny assumed the interior had been thoroughly ransacked.

Vaxxine didn't stop talking until it was a tactical necessity. She hadn't had human contact for more than a couple of minutes on end since the escape from Los Angeles. Danny let the words flow. She was listening for clues, for useful information. And she wasn't much of a talker herself, so Vaxxine was welcome to hold the floor. Now, with the hospital in front of them, the talk petered out.

The dawn sun finally crawled above the clouds gathering in the distance, and turned the upper stories of the building to molten gold that ran imperceptibly down the facade of the building. Vaxxine drove the truck cab in a wide circuit of the parking lot and access roads that surrounded the hospital. It wasn't just zeroes they needed to worry about, but humans. Hospitals were a critical resource. Medical and surgical supplies, drugs, syringes. These materials had replaced precious metals as the barter medium of choice. There were plenty of survivors who would kill rather than share. It was near full daylight when Vaxxine pulled up across from the front entrance.

"Some asshole parked in the handicap spot," she remarked.

"I'll just run in there and see what I can secure," Danny said, checking the clip on her sidearm.

Vaxxine shook her head. "You shouldn't run anywhere. There's something wrong with your brain, Sheriff."

"There's something wrong with your legs," Danny pointed out.

"You can ride shotgun," Vaxxine said.

She took a roll of duct tape out of the storage compartment in the driver's side door, tore off a strip a couple of feet long, and laid it sticky-side down on another length of the tape, turning it into a strap with adhesive ends. Then she bound her legs together just below the knees. The Silent Kid was watching with as much interest as Danny.

"Pass me the leather," Vaxxine said, indicating a top-of-the-line Schott Perfecto jacket in thick horsehide that hung on the bulkhead behind Danny. Danny passed it over and Vaxxine drew it under her legs and buttocks, the jacket oriented upside-down, so her ankles projected from the collar opening. She zipped it up over her knees. It formed a tough leather sheath over her limbs. She was already wearing a lightweight jacket on her arms and upper body. Next she pulled on work gloves and a knit balaclava to cover her neck and ears.

"Not bad," Danny said. She generally didn't wear anything more protective than a windbreaker or overshirt, and she had the bite marks to prove it. The one on her arm still itched.

It was the next stage of the operation Danny most wanted to see, however. The driver's door was a good forty-five inches off the ground. The wheelchair, a lightweight folding model, was strapped on the driver's side running board, as Danny had observed in the rearview mirror. She watched and waited.

Vaxxine flung her door open, checked fore and aft to make sure nothing had crept near while she leathered up, and then tossed a golf bag down from behind her seat to the ground. It made a hell of a noise, as if it was full of copper pipes. Then she popped the buckles that held the wheelchair in place and lowered it to the ground one-handed, the other hand firmly gripping the grab handle on the door frame. She shook the chair and it popped open like an awning. She dropped it and it rattled to the pavement, remaining upright.

Vaxxine swung her bound legs out using her free hand, and all in the same motion, like a gymnast, twisted her body and dropped out of the cab. She landed heavily but squarely on the seat of the chair, manually arranged her boots on the foot plate, then grabbed the golf bag and slung it over her shoulder and the back of the chair. Then she wheeled herself swiftly toward the hospital. She'd gone thirty meters before Danny shook off her astonishment and alighted behind her. Danny closed the cab door and pointed a warning finger at the Silent Kid as he pressed his nose to the glass: *stay*. Then she trotted to catch up to her unusual companion. They approached the hospital in silence, side by side. Thunder boomed out over the grassland.

There was one zero near the entrance, but it was almost immobile with decay. It lay on its side and raised a feeble arm, hissing, but no longer had the ability to approach them. They ignored it and went inside.

Vaxxine's wheels bumped over the fragments of glass and splinters of furniture that littered the floor. Potted ficus trees had been thrown around, and there were blood sprays on walls and ceilings, so old they'd turned to black varnish. Rat-eaten surgical dressings, gauze, and other field medical supplies lay where the treatment had been done, with dark slicks of dried blood here and there; a couple of hollowed-out corpses lay against the bullet-pocked walls like heaps of kindling. There were tarnished brass shell casings everywhere. A last-stand battle had been fought here a long time ago.

"Did you hear that?" Vaxxine whispered.

Danny found this intensely irritating. Yes, she had heard. And if people always talked right after there was a noise, they wouldn't hear anything else.

They listened, and after a short interval heard a second sound. Somewhere deep in the bowels of the hospital, someone or something was rummaging around.

They advanced down a dark central hallway. The hospital was intended to enjoy an uninterrupted supply of artificial light, and many of the corridors were windowless. Danny didn't use her penlight; better to allow their eyes to adjust to the faint glow that filtered in from the lobby end of the hall than to give themselves away with a flashlight. Except for the litter on the floor, the place looked as if it was only closed for the weekend. Like it could be put back to use the next day. But there was also a tang of mildew in the air, the sour stuffiness of disuse.

The noises were coming from downstairs. Elevators weren't working, as expected. They found fire stairs. Danny pointed at herself and then the stairs; then she pointed at Vaxxine, aimed two fingers at her eyes, and pointed up and down the hallway. *Going down. Keep me covered up here.* Vaxxine didn't object. Instead she withdrew a big hunting slingshot from the golf bag, fitted a fat steel ball bearing into the sling, and gave Danny the thumbs-up. Danny gently pressed the stairwell door open. It was silent. She eased into the pitch blackness on the other side.

Now she needed the flashlight. She tucked the butt end of the light into her watchband, stabilized it with her pinky, and used her thumb—the only other digit on that hand—to cover most of the lens, so that only a narrow crescent of light shone out.

The stairs were littered with acoustic ceiling tiles and medical supplies of various types, probably dropped by people in a big hurry carrying armloads of the stuff. She picked her steps with care to avoid crunching on anything; so far the noise from below continued intermittently. Whoever or whatever it was—probably the latter—hadn't heard Vaxxine's truck arrive.

Danny reached the basement level, where the door was jammed open by some kind of monitoring machine on an overturned stand. The air was stale and smelled of organic decay and more mildew. She stepped over the machine and her boot crunched on a drift of gritty blue pills.

The noises stopped.

Danny pressed her thumb over the entire lens of the flashlight and aimed it into her side. The darkness rushed in like a physical mass. All was silent.

After a minute, in which her mind filled the darkness with slinking hunters stealing toward her with scaly, distended jaws, the noises started again. Around a corner, somewhere ahead.

Then she saw a flicker of light. It had to be a human being.

Or a thinker.

She advanced down the corridor, sliding her feet so she wouldn't crunch anything else, as she was working without her own light; the activity was around a corner at the next intersection.

She doused her flashlight completely and kept the pistol gut-high, then dipped her head around the corner. Ducked back, processed what she'd seen.

It wasn't a thinker. She could hear the person breathing. It was a man in a one-piece leather motorcycle racing suit and no head protection. She saw that fairly often, usually on people who had lost an ear or had been bitten on the neck. They only protected the parts of themselves they could see. The man was of middle size, Asian.

He was utterly intent on what he was doing: filling a couple of ex-military duffel bags with medical supplies harvested from the rooms on either side of the corridor. Based on her brief inspection of the hallway, it looked like this was where the hospital staff stored most of the restricted materials; Danny had passed a nurse's station that would have overlooked the stair door, and there were key-card locks at various points, all of them unlocked because the power had failed. She took another glance and saw handfuls of sanitary-packed syringes and surgical dressings going into the bags. There were boxes stacked beside the man; she saw antibiotics and blood products, drugs, all sorts of things. The floor was thickly layered with similar stuff, but Danny guessed he hadn't made the mess—that would be scavenging groups blowing through fast and hard. This man seemed to have a specific inventory he was filling.

He stopped to listen again. Danny held her breath. The man started to turn, and she ducked out of sight, confident he hadn't seen her. He'd been working by the light of a big box flashlight that shone directly into his face half the time. His night vision would be terrible. Danny waited a few seconds. The man was silent. Then he began frantically shoving things into the bags again.

Danny dipped to one knee around the corner and raised her pistol. She switched on her penlight with her damaged hand held well away from her center mass in case he spun around shooting.

"Don't move!" she barked.

The man froze. His light began to quaver; he was shaking. But he stayed very still.

"I'm not a zero," Danny said. "I am alive, and I intend to stay that way and I know you want to stay that way, too. So turn to face me, slowly, and place your light on the floor pointing at the ceiling. Hands behind your head. Good. What do you have? I see a shotgun. Anything else?"

"Just the shotgun," the man said. "And a hammer. It's also on the floor."

"Where's your partner?"

"I'm alone," he said.

"That's so stupid I find it hard to believe. If you have a partner and your partner is right now planning anything, he or she should be aware that I will shoot you first and deal with them immediately afterward." She spoke the last of this in a loud voice intended to carry—not just down the hallways, but up the stairwell to Vaxxine.

"I'm police," Danny continued, in her best checkpoint-in-a-war-zone voice: clipped, professional, and toneless. "I am Sheriff Danny Adelman. I won't harm you, but we're going to maintain this situation as-is until I decide you're clear to move around. What's your name?"

"Joe Higashiyama."

"Why are you here?"

"I'm collecting medical supplies," the man said. "This is a hospital."

"For what purpose?"

"I'm a doctor. I mean, I'm a medical student, but I've been a doctor *pro tem* since . . . things happened."

"A doctor for who? You're taking a lot of materiel there."

"Have you heard of Happy Town?"

"Happy Town? What the fuck kind of bullshit is that?" Danny dropped her MP voice. She was getting irritated. Not for any specific reason. Post-adrenaline crash. She sensed this guy was mostly harmless.

"Happy Town. It's the safe place. But we need medical supplies like any-body else, and they don't deliver anymore. So I get sent out to do it."

Danny's thoughts streaked off in a thousand directions at once. *Happy Town.* The safe place had a name. It was real, if this guy was telling the truth. Why would he lie? But if Happy Town had its shit together enough to be safe, why were they sending out doctors on foraging expeditions? Didn't they have scouts or strike teams or anything? Were they understaffed? Besieged? Where was it, and who was in charge? She reeled her mind back in and sorted the questions into order.

"Why would they send a doctor? Don't you have people for this?" she asked.

"I know what we need. When we send the teams out, they come back with all the wrong stuff."

"Where's your backup?"

"He got bit yesterday."

"And you didn't return to base?"

"We need this stuff. We need it bad."

Danny had a lot more questions, but those were the top tier. If Joe was lying, he was very good at it. Yet she believed him. He was in too vulnerable a position to lie for the good of the group. And now that she could see what he'd been shoving into the bags, it was clear he wasn't just raiding the pill cabinet. He was stocking up on surgical supplies and sterile items, not tranquilizers.

Time for the big question, Danny thought. "Where is this Happy Town?"

"South Dakota badlands. Six hours northeast on a good day. Sometimes takes an overnight. Lot of people in Happy Town. We've picked over every medical facility closer than that. Can I put my hands down?"

Danny marched the young man back out of the basement to where Vaxxine waited. She couldn't believe he was working alone, especially as a forager for some town full of people. There had to be someone else with him. But there was no trace of anyone; Vaxxine hadn't heard or seen signs of an accomplice while she waited on the ground floor, and the young doctor didn't engage in the telltale behavior to warn someone, like knocking things over to make a loud noise, raising his voice, or narrating what was happening. Danny had seen all that before: "So why are we walking up these stairs to the lobby?" and similar lame-ass attempts at warning. The reverse was true: Joe was quiet and careful.

Vaxxine looked him over as if she was being introduced to a blind date. For Joe's part, he looked at Vaxxine, saw the wheelchair, and immediately turned to Danny: "This is your idea of working in teams?"

"She'd kick your ass one-handed," Danny said.

Vaxxine made a masturbating gesture. "Did you see any adult diapers or catheter bags down there? I'm running low."

"I wasn't looking for those," Joe replied. "Listen, I need to get in and out as fast as I can. Unless you're planning to arrest me for trespassing, Sheriff, I'd like to keep doing what I need to do."

"I'll help you carry things up if you'll locate what *she* needs," Danny said, after a few seconds of deliberation.

"And what *you* need," Vaxxine added, speaking to Danny. "I didn't come here for me, I came here for you." She turned her attention to Joe: "She's getting these splitting headaches, like for-real migraines. She passes out. And I think it's fairly serious. She's had some blows to the head, combat trauma, things like that."

"We have an MRI back at Happy Town," Joe said to Danny. "We could check you out there, if you'd like."

"Fuck you guys," Danny said. She was getting increasingly embarrassed, which made her angry, because all of her emotions eventually drained to the sea through the swamp of hostility. They were discussing her like a pair of VA doctors shooting the breeze at her bedside, unaware she was conscious.

Based upon his willingness to answer questions, Danny and Vaxxine decided Joe was okay, and after that they worked fast. He had a big pickup truck with a cap on the bed; it was already half-filled with carefully organized boxes and bags of assorted materials related to medicine, pharmacy, and wellness. Everything from vitamins and cough syrup to cylinders of nitrous oxide and oxygen. *Joe could start his own refugee camp,* Danny thought. Although she kept her hands on the work and her eyes on the hiding places, her mind was on Happy Town. She asked a few questions about it while they carried stuff up out of the hospital; there was no doubt that it was the same safe place the Tribe had been hearing rumors about. Joe's description of it sounded right.

Danny was sure of it when Joe saw the Silent Kid and his dog peering at them from the cab of the big rig.

"You've got a ticket to ride," Joe said. "That boy there. He'll get you in."

"In where?" Danny asked, although she knew.

"Happy Town isn't really there for adults. It's for kids. We're trying to get them out of harm's way, and to do that we need to entice adults into bringing them. So we offer safety to the adults, too."

"That's real generous of you," Danny said, and shoved a case of rolled surgical tubing into the pickup.

Joe didn't seem to catch the sarcasm. "We're losing so many kids out there to abandonment. People even use them for zero bait, did you know that? It's like the most basic human instincts have been given up."

"Kids don't mean shit in a crisis," Danny said. "To the parents, maybe. But you want to see how fast people give up on the little ones, fire a gun over their heads. The adults will scatter like cockroaches and leave the kids behind. I know. I've done it."

"Left kids behind?"

"Fired over their heads."

Joe clammed up for a while and worked in silence. If he hadn't had a clear opinion of Danny before, it was obvious he did now. But after a couple more trips up and down the stairs, while they were looking for unexposed X-ray films in the depths of the hospital basement, he spoke his thoughts aloud.

"We're trying to change all that," he said. "The cruelty to children. We decided to be the people who don't scatter and leave the kids behind the way you said."

"You turned them into barter instead," Danny replied. She'd been hoping he would reopen the topic. "You know people are kidnapping kids right and left to get in there, right? It's a total fuckup. You're making the situation ten times worse." She expected Joe to deny it. This was the kind of utopian social engineering bullshit that infuriated her about liberals, back when that kind of distinction mattered.

"That's been a real problem for us," Joe admitted, to her surprise. "People are bringing obviously stolen kids to us—they don't even know their names. We don't want that and we're trying to stop it. The Architect has a strict policy that you have to prove beyond a shadow of a doubt that you are the child's parent or sole legal guardian. But the benefit outweighs the drawbacks. The kids get a real chance at safe lives. You know we don't even keep them with the general population? They're literally housed on a resort island for security purposes. We travel them by train, because it's the most secure method. Trains, can you believe it? It's almost like normal sometimes."

"Your trains caused me a shitload of problems," Danny said. Joe shrugged. He wasn't interested in her war stories. So she changed tack. "Here's a question. What happens to the kids that you know were brought in by kidnappers?"

"That's the catch-22," Joe admitted. "We take them anyway. If their real folks show up, we prosecute whoever brought them in. It doesn't happen that often."

"That's because the real folks are usually dead by then," Danny said, and didn't elaborate.

They kept working until around nine in the morning, when Vaxxine shouted down the stairwell that they had company.

Danny and Joe clattered up the stairs. The sky had rapidly filled up with metallic clouds and there was a cold, wet wind coming in gusts. A couple of moaners were scuffing across the parking lot, both of them gray and sagging. They obviously hadn't fed in a long time. Danny didn't want to wake up the countryside with a gunshot, so she waited for them at the emergency room entrance, then took them out with Joe's hammer, crushing their heads with flailing roundhouse swings.

But across the parking lot, she could see another dozen of the things coming through the tall grass in the fields.

"Incoming," she said. For emphasis, she crushed the skull of the feeble zero lying by the doors.

Joe threw a last load of gear into the back of his truck and banged the tailgate shut. Then he recited, in a bad Scots accent:

> *"Comin thro the rye, poor body,*
> *Comin thro the rye,*
> *She draggled a'her petticoatie,*
> *Comin thro the rye!"*

"What?" Danny asked, not really wanting to know. She was hustling back toward the hospital, from which Vaxxine was just emerging.

"It's a poem by Robert Burns," Joe said. He threw the shotgun and flashlight on the front seat of his truck. "Seemed appropriate, but never mind.

I'm headed back to Happy Town. This was the last stop on my itinerary. You guys want to follow me there? You can't both get in, but it would solve half your problems."

"Hell, yes," Vaxxine said, as she rolled up fast with a couple of cardboard boxes balanced on her knees.

"No," Danny said.

"But we—"

Danny gave Vaxxine an unmistakable "shut up" look and interrupted: "We have some things to do, but if it's open call we might come along later. Is that how it works?"

"As long as it's daylight hours," Joe said, looking back and forth at the women, perplexed. "Take Route 334 north, exit on Jefferson Highway, get on the 15 east, and it's maybe fifteen miles past Winnehackett where the train tracks are."

"Danny—" Vaxxine began to protest.

"Then we'll see you again sometime," Danny said, again squashing Vaxxine's protest.

Joe shrugged, gave Danny a little salute off his eyebrow, and shut himself inside the truck. A few seconds later he was driving away, weaving between the undead.

Danny and Vaxxine hurried back to the big rig, where Danny observed as Vaxxine reversed the process of getting out of the truck to haul herself back in. She had true gymnast's arms: She lifted herself out of the chair and set herself on the running board, folded the chair and buckled it to the side of the truck, and then hauled her entire weight hand over hand up the handles on door and frame until she could swing her legs into the driver's seat like a sack of Purina Dog Chow. The entire operation took less than a minute.

"You're a crazy person," Vaxxine said, as Danny handed supplies up to her and she relayed the boxes into the back compartment of the cab.

Danny spat on the pavement. "He said we were welcome any time. I'm not following him there sight unseen. You have no idea how much trouble their so-called system has caused. What we do is ease up on the place quietly and scope it out, and then decide what to do. Recon."

That was true as far as it went, but Danny had another concern: The Tribe was probably there by now. That was a confrontation she wasn't prepared to have. And there was the matter of the Silent Kid. She wasn't handing him over to a bunch of strangers just because they claimed to have Disneyland open again.

While they were talking, Danny was keeping an eye on the nearest zeroes; as long as they were shambling toward the living, the situation was in control. But when she saw them scent the air like dogs and then scatter back toward the tall grass, she knew they were out of time.

"Hunters," she said. "Over there somewhere. Let's get buttoned up fast."

She tossed up the last of the boxes and climbed into the cab of the truck herself. A few seconds later the massive power plant roared into operation and they were rolling away from the lonely hospital out in the middle of the plains. She looked in the rearview mirror and saw three hunters, crouched like spiders, rush out of the fields after the rig. They didn't stand a chance of catching up, but the sight of the things always made Danny's flesh crawl. You could never relax. You could never let your guard down. She hoped the young doctor, Joe, knew what he was doing out there in this merciless world.

But there was a great deal of news to think over. Happy Town *was* a real place, apparently, somewhere in the badlands. The train line went there. Danny's theory was correct. And the motive behind all the kidnappings was confirmed. Vaxxine's thoughts were moving in the same direction, because they hadn't been driving for long when she said, "You're not stupid. We'll do it your way. We look the town over from a distance and suss it out, see if it's really as safe as all that. If it's cool, we go in. But we don't want to wait too long. Things have this way of changing."

"You can go in ahead if you want. Find yourself a spare kid, but you can't have mine."

"I'm not worried about me. But if they really do have a brain-scanning machine, you should get yourself checked out," Vaxxine said.

"Thanks, Mom. Listen. There's shit you don't know. I didn't bring it up with Dr. Joe there, but I have excellent reason to believe thinkers—the smart zombies—are kidnapping kids, too. But they're not eating them right away. So ask yourself: Why would thinkers do that? Why would they collect a bunch of kids they can't eat at once?"

"They're smart," Vaxxine said without hesitation. "They're storing food."

"Food they have to feed and keep warm? Doesn't make sense. They're better off letting the living do that. Then they can dive in and grab the young whenever they want."

"Maybe people got too good at defending themselves against those attacks."

Danny took that personally. The Tribe had suffered two devastating assaults within hours of each other. And it was supposed to have exceptionally good defenses, as traveling groups went. Yet they'd gotten their asses handed to them on a plate, one cheek at a time.

"I wish," was all she said.

An unhappy silence settled on the group. At length, Vaxxine looked behind her at the Silent Kid, who sat on the floor behind the seats with his dog in his lap, his face as grave as Buster Keaton's. "They prefer to eat kids who talk," Vaxxine said to him. "You're probably okay."

"I have two theories," Danny said, picking up where she'd left off. "First, the thinkers plan to use the kids for ransom somehow, and they need a lot of them to make it pay off. Second, they want to infiltrate this Happy Town. They can pass for living, you know. Sometimes."

"That's like . . . really paranoid," Vaxxine observed.

"There has to be a reason everybody is kidnapping children all of a sudden. The living and undead at the same time."

"Coincidence."

"Coincidence," Danny said, "is what a conspiracy looks like from the outside."

4

They drove for half of the day, slowed down by some bad sections of road Joe hadn't thought to mention. The storm clouds were stretched from one side of the sky to the other, and the daylight had turned to burnished silver. There was a sick, greenish cast to the clouds. The wind had died down entirely. Vaxxine stopped to fuel up alongside an abandoned big rig with a carload full of athletic shoes behind it; she had a system for that, too, but Danny jumped in without asking and took the process over, shoving a garden hose down into the tanks and pumping it out with a rotary pump that Vaxxine kept under her seat.

They were on an elevated section of road with a city three or four kilometers away; there was light industrial sprawl around their position, and Danny could see a couple of zeroes making their way in her direction, picking their way through the debris of a street that appeared to have been bombed. It would take them half an hour. The Silent Kid watched everything she did, moving from window to window of the truck, pressing his nose to the glass. His dog did the same, but looked mostly at the crows circling underneath the clouds, not at Danny.

Rain came down in fits. Danny got back into the cab a few seconds before the downpour began. It was icy-cold and the windows of the cab fogged up; Vaxxine started the engine and ran the air conditioner to clear the glass. The zeroes down below them among the warehouses were invisible, so dense was the rain; Danny had seen their kind take shelter before. Was that an instinct, or was it a practical matter? Did it accelerate decay? Did it ruin their sense of smell?

They decided to wait out the storm, or until it looked like the undead were getting too thick for safety. Elevated roadways were usually fairly secure, however, because there weren't many footpaths that led to them— only on-ramps and off-ramps, and miles of barricades at the sides. So they sat and listened to the thrumming of rain on the cab, watched the eels of water writhing down the window glass, and eventually the Silent Kid fell asleep with his dog tucked up against his chest. The rain seemed to be increasing in savagery, as if the sky intended to wash the vile world beneath it clean.

"How did you get out of that hotel?" Danny asked, after they had sat without speaking for a quarter of an hour.

"My God, you were listening to all that talk?"

"It's interesting. Most people didn't escape the cities if they didn't bug out in the first few minutes. And no offense, but you're not exactly set up for escapes."

"You underestimate the power of wheels, Baby Love. Ten days I was in that bloody closet. It had been dead quiet for three of those, but I was too scared to come out. But I felt like my kidneys were going to fail and the stink was something awful, so eventually I opened the door and peeked out. Oh, the stink was even worse out there! Corpses all around the place, some of them all blood with big pieces missing and some had black on them like ink, which I later sorted out was the difference between someone who died alive and someone who died after death, zombielike.

"It was no easy thing to get out of there with all the limbs and bodies on the floor, but I made my way, using a mop handle to push me a path. Then one of the things I thought was dead, it kind of twitched upright and looked right at me with those eyes like pieces of sushi meat. Zeroed in like a hawk. It was getting up and I just wheeled out the doors as fast as I could, and that's when I saw they were all about the place, the ones that weren't dead, or undead, or what you will, but had only been like resting while they waited for something to eat.

"I got out onto the street and pointed myself down the hill toward the Miracle Mile—you know how steep it is there, practically straight down—and rolled as fast as I could. Blistered my hands trying to brake so I wouldn't kill myself. I must have hit thirty miles an hour, and I was zigzagging all over trying to keep away from the monsters and not to hit any of the cars and the wreckage, it was everywhere you know. And right then when I thought for sure I was going to wipe out and die, be torn apart, this beautiful feeling came over me. Because it was the same as the last time I went down the mountain on my skis, this feeling like the wind was going straight through my body and I didn't weigh anything, I was flying, you know?

"I was so frightened, and at the same time I felt like God Himself was pushing me along, his hands on me. I don't remember if I was screaming or laughing, but for one minute I felt like I felt before, and this time I didn't break my back. I came to a stop down on Santa Monica Boulevard, I think it was, and I couldn't get the chair to slow down properly because my hands were so bloody they wouldn't grip. Now, this chair has a little motor, mostly to go up and down, but it will drive along real slow, so I motored until the battery died and there weren't so many zeroes there. But they surrounded me eventually. Came out of the shadows and oozing up out of cars and from piles of corpses. And I wanted to die somehow, but there wasn't any way I could think of before they got me.

"But that's when somebody came up in a van. I survived because somebody saved me. We made it out of the city, five of us, but then they right away left me because I'd just be a burden. They left me at an old folks' home in the desert, where I found this leg-free driving rig on a car, and a lot of my supplies came from there, too. But you know what? I wasn't hurt by their going and leaving me like that. You know what hurt?"

"Your hands?"

"What hurt was that somebody *saved* me. I wanted to survive all by myself, and now I do. But I'm tired. I'm alone and tired. Whatever I had to prove, there's no point proving it just to myself."

Danny thought about that. It reminded her of her own determination to go back to the Tribe. "I wouldn't give up what you got here," she said. "You might want a partner, but you don't need to get involved with a big group. I been doing that since the beginning and it was always a pain in my ass. This is better. Less is more."

"Are you volunteering?"

Danny shrugged. "No. Nothing personal. I gotta figure out what to do with this kid, and there's some unfinished business out there. But you're independent as fuck like you are now. Join up with some happy assholes in a big group, and you'll turn back into the handicapped gimp they don't want to deal with. You're kicking ass with both hands. Don't give that up."

Danny felt irritation bubbling up like hot tar inside her head. She wasn't accustomed to making long speeches and she didn't like to talk about abstractions like personal freedom. She dealt with concrete things, action. This conversation smelled like philosophy. And she didn't like how disappointed Vaxxine had looked when she said "no" to the idea of teaming up. But why the hell would anybody want to team up with Danny?

Of course, Vaxxine hadn't heard the story about Kelley, and Danny resolved never to mention it.

Vaxxine was about to respond, both of them now staring out their side windows in opposite directions, when the rain abruptly stopped. Now they made eye contact. It was weird: The sky turned the color of spoiled meat, an iridescent green, and the rain fell away as if a faucet had been turned off. They could feel the barometric pressure change inside their ears, as if aboard an aircraft descending rapidly. The Silent Kid woke up and looked around, blinking, and his pup stopped snoring, yawned, and pressed his stub of nose to the glass, staring out at the dripping gray world.

The clouds overhead looked strange, drooping in heavy globs like milk poured into a tank of water, knuckled and eerie. The air was absolutely still. Danny lowered her window and checked the flanks of the truck for any zeroes that might have crept up on them while they waited out the storm.

"Mind if I get out on the hood?" she asked.

"Don't scratch the paint," Vaxxine said, unconsciously placing a hand on the Silent Kid's head. There was a dense, airless feeling of foreboding that came not from inside them, but from the sky. Danny climbed out the window and onto the hood of the engine. The roof was too steep to stand on; she'd have preferred the extra few feet. But the nose of the truck was plenty high. She didn't have any of her best gear: no binoculars, only her sidearm and what had been in her belt and in her munitions backpack. But the air had become warm, oppressive, yet uncannily clear. She could see for miles. The rainstorm was like a seething curtain blowing rapidly away across the city, then trailing its tattered shrouds out across the distant plains; it moved faster than any front Danny had ever seen.

The strange clouds hung so low she felt she could rip them open with a stick held over her head.

Then there was a sound—it could have been whale song or the mourning of giants. Deep, bone-stirring sound. And several of the roots of the clouds began to descend. A million snakes were hissing in the air—nasty secrets being told by a multitude of voices all at once. Then a gust whipped past and nearly tossed Danny to the ground. She looked down below their elevated roadway and saw the grid below them was now crawling with zeroes, driven from hibernation by the storm. They squirmed like maggots.

"I think we got a twister," Danny said, slinging herself back inside the cab.

"Those come in the spring, don't they? The other half of the year."

"The fuck do you do in a tornado situation?" Danny couldn't remember. It was about the only natural disaster her high mountain hometown wasn't heir to. That and tsunamis.

"It can't be," Vaxxine said. And then: "I don't know. Shit. Get under something. Find an underpass."

"Not down there. We have a lot of company. Let's see what happens, and if it's coming this way we'll drive like a bat out of hell."

"Oh, my God," Vaxxine said.

Like a conjurer's trick, a genie, what had been a twist in the clouds descended until a corresponding vortex rose up to meet it. A pillar of smoky debris had joined cloud and land. They could see objects in it, whirling as if in slow motion—but that was an illusion created by distance. The thing leaned and warped but never broke, gaining girth and density as it approached the city, a titanic funnel sucking everything up and vomiting it out as wreckage.

There were several more of these, slithering along the landscape in the distance, all of them marching to war in the same direction. The nearest of them, the one approaching the urban area, was the largest, and its path was going to take it close to their position.

"It's heading up the goddamn road," Danny said. "We can't go that way. I think we'd better move, after all."

Vaxxine started the truck. The cyclone was behind them. Danny couldn't take her eyes off it. It struck the buildings at the fringe of the city and they exploded, roofs flying off, shingles lifting like bats off the plywood substrate and then the entire structures flailing into the air, skeletons of wood and steel contorting and breaking apart. The trailers of big rigs just like theirs were leaping into the sky, flying, coming down among apartment buildings and parking lots. Something detonated and the dirty red fire was wrung out by the blast of the wind. It was growing darker and darker, as if the storm was caused by the extinction of the sun.

Vaxxine sank the hand control for the gas as far as it would go and the truck's tires protested on the wet pavement, found purchase, and suddenly they were moving fast. Something rained down on them from above, chattering off the sheet metal; it was eyeball-sized hailstones. Vaxxine shunted the rig side-to-side, the light back end skittering on the road, bumping and crunching into abandoned cars. Up ahead, the roadway descended to grade. The local swarm had not been idle while they waited up above: A mass of zeroes was coming up the road. They were pale, rain-bloated things, so densely packed their reaching arms looked like the legs of some hideous millipede turned over on its back.

"You're going to have to ram them," Danny said.

"This thing will spin out," Vaxxine said. "We'll be overrun. Mother of Jesus."

"Then back up."

They both checked the mirrors, and then Danny stuck her head out to check whether she was reading the view wrong. Because all they could see was a wall of whirling debris. The entire world was being destroyed by a millstone.

"Get out and run for it," Vaxxine said. "Take the Kid and the dog. We have a couple minutes. Go over the side and you can get down into a storm drain or something."

"And leave you here?"

"I guess so. I'm not running anywhere."

"Fuck it," Danny said, and took the Silent Kid in her arms. He was crying, but soundlessly. He grabbed the whining little dog and wedged him between himself and Danny. She could feel the bony little creature shivering. Vaxxine's face was wet with tears, too. She slung one of her strong arms around Danny's neck and placed her closely-shaven head against Danny's and they sat like that, feeling the wind plucking at the truck, testing its weight.

They could not have been in a more exposed position, nor more helpless. Even with the windows up the roar of the tornado was deafening, all the devils in the universe screaming at once.

Something banged off the hood of the truck, and there was particulate matter chittering over the window glass like they were inside a sandblasting machine. The truck began to lean, rocking on its shocks, and then the back end became distinctly lighter and it began to turn. They would be airborne at any moment. Danny alone kept her eyes open, so she saw something vast and solid sail overhead, coming down a few hundred yards away, bursting apart on impact with a parking structure; it had been a suburban house. She saw an armchair fly out of a window frame. She discreetly pulled her precious backpack to her side and cradled it beneath her one free arm.

The zeroes were still coming on, their rudimentary minds unsuited to existential threats like this: They sensed prey and cared for nothing else.

"I wish you'd say something," Danny remarked to the Silent Kid.

Then the tornado was on top of them. The world went completely dark.

The noise was unbearable; they could have been rats trapped inside a pipe organ. The truck shuddered and bounced and there was a rapid, irregular tattoo of debris crashing all around them, metal bending and tearing, stone shattering, glass exploding. Danny raised her head because she had never failed to face an enemy down before and this was her last confrontation. So it was she who saw the churning skin of the tornado, a wild mass of darkness and destruction, an ancient god awakened to avenge itself on the sinful species that Armageddon had failed to extinguish.

And then it had passed, and they were still alive.

Three minutes after the traverse of the tornado, they dared to look around. Nothing big had fallen from the sky for sixty or seventy seconds. Light was returning to the world. In the distance, the tornadoes continued their march unopposed, destroying the abandoned city, hammering it to pieces on their way northwest. Where the funnels had dragged the earth, long, blackened paths had been scoured down to the soil, obliterating everything before them. To either side, debris was piled high, and nothing was entirely untouched—although strange acts of mercy were everywhere. A bathtub was perched in a tree. A church steeple stood firm and unruffled, except for an old-model Volkswagen that had been inserted through the belfry. On the hood of the rig in front of them there sat a frying pan filled with dirt.

The roadway ahead was completely clear, free of cars, zeroes, and wreckage. It had never been so clean.

Danny climbed down and cut away a long strap of barbed wire that had wrapped itself around the front of the vehicle; beneath the axle she found a severed arm, withered and rotten. She looked more closely at the ground and realized there were fragments of human remains everywhere—teeth, flesh, bones. The zeroes had been pulverized.

They drove on, and by late afternoon they were within ten kilometers of where Joe had said they would find Happy Town. Of the tornado, they spoke very little.

"Was that a miracle?" Vaxxine remarked, some twenty minutes after they'd left the city behind.

"If that was a miracle," Danny said, after some reflection, "it was a piss-poor example."

They didn't speak of it again, least of all the Silent Kid.

5

They found what looked like a relatively secure place to stop: an auto repair shop with a tall razor-wire fence around it and drainage canals along two sides. The shop was a low concrete block and there was a clapboard house on a rise behind it with a couple of old, leafless trees that probably threw nice shade in the summer. Rusting cars with no wheels were scattered around in the tall grass next to the house, an impromptu junkyard.

Although they were still distant from Happy Town, they kept lights to a minimum. Danny checked the house and looked inside several of the derelict cars. No zeroes present. They discussed staying in the house, but it had a lot of ground-floor windows and a wraparound porch, so they opted to stay inside the repair shop instead. There was a skylight and a ladder; they could get onto the roof if they had to, and by parking the rig alongside, they stood some chance of being able to effect an escape if it came to that. Vaxxine swore she could climb a ladder with her hands alone.

Danny covered the one window with a rolling tool chest, then pulled the shutter doors down behind them. It had gotten bitterly cold again, but they opted not to stay inside the truck, as comfortable as the accommodations were. Something about their close call of earlier in the day had made it seem more like a claustrophobic tomb than a rolling apartment.

The next day came with a sparkling dust of frost on the ground and a sky that was overcast, but smooth and low, with benign if gloomy clouds. Vaxxine made more of the real coffee and Danny made a detailed inventory of their supplies, filling a rucksack she'd found in the abandoned house with simple survival items. She'd need them on her Happy Town recon mission. Vaxxine had insisted she should come along, but it was physically impossible. Danny planned to approach Happy Town on foot and circle it at a distance to understand the lay of the land there.

It had been a long time since she needed woodcraft skills for a scouting sortie; the last occasion had been along the border of Iran, where she and a few other damn fools had spent the better part of a week crawling on their bellies toward a missile silo hidden in the desert. It turned out there was no silo. On the other hand, they hadn't been detected by any of the goatherds in the area. There had been two of them. Danny anticipated this was going to be a much trickier assignment.

Meanwhile, the Silent Kid and his dog were doing something peculiar. It looked pointless to Danny, until she realized they were playing. She hadn't seen that in a long time. The dog was hanging on the end of an old rope by his jaws and the boy was swinging him around in circles. Vaxxine was engaged in a lengthy personal hygiene ritual inside the truck. While Danny was rolling a sleeping bag of Vaxxine's into a thin, hard tube, so it would take up as little space as possible in the pack, a long-dormant part of Danny's mind turned over and she had a kind of vision. Someone less inclined to hard-nosed reality would have recognized it as a daydream.

It had to do with where they were. In the summer, it must be beautiful, a kind of forgotten corner of the world that hadn't changed much since the 1950s. There were the trees, and a stream ran past the place. There were split-rail fences here and there. The nearest town was too far to see; there were two other houses within sight, old-fashioned places like this one. The house behind the auto repair shop was a story and a half, with attic bedrooms, a parlor enclosed by the porch downstairs, a screened summer kitchen at the back, and a small but dry basement. Enough room for the three of them and the dog. Surround it with fences and accordion wire, maybe dig a moat. Something. Secure the place, grow some corn, live quietly.

Danny could see flickering images of stacking wood in the basement, welding herself combat gear in the auto shop, having an ordinary barbecue. The Kid climbing one of the trees. Sledding down the hill in winter. Picking off zeroes from the porch roof. Hell, they could find a trailer for the truck and park it next to the porch and fit it out as an escapemobile. If trouble came, everybody jumps in and they would drive away in their armored monster truck.

Less than a minute passed while the reverie drifted through her mind. The bag was as compressed as she could make it with her one-handed grip. She bound it with bungee cords and shook off the tranquil ideas she'd entertained. She felt strange in some way that was hard to define, but that had to do with the loss of Kelley, Wulf, and the entire Tribe.

She was alone now.

She could choose her friends. She missed the folks she'd traveled with all the way from Forest Peak, her fellow survivors of the first wave. Amy, Patrick, Maria, Troy. A few others. But she was always the hard bitch at the top, not a real friend to anyone. So much ugliness and suffering and history between them. These people she was with now didn't really know her—the mute boy, the cripple, the runt dog, they were safe. She had started fresh with them.

If she had been a more articulate person, Danny might have realized she was—for a fleeting moment—content. And that she liked the feeling.

The ground was frozen hard and Danny's boots chewed loudly at the hoarfrost as she crossed the last open ground before the forest that curved around Happy Town.

She hadn't seen woods in a couple of months, the Tribe having crisscrossed the Midwest and Great Plains, where ex-agricultural fields and grasslands dominated the landscape. She had grown up in the trees, and there was always a certain natural advantage she felt beneath their branches. She was still six kilometers from where Dr. Joe had said the town was, so she didn't think there would be any sentries or security systems in place this far out. But she adopted a tracker's stoop as she headed for the trees, keeping her head down. If they shot her for a zero, so be it.

According to the scrap of map she had duct-taped to the sleeve of her jacket, Happy Town used to be called Jordan. It enjoyed natural barriers on three sides: a river hooked around it on the east, with three bridges to the far shore, and there was a cliff-edged escarpment rising above the northern margin of town that a zero could step over, but it wouldn't be able to do much after it reached the bottom, where massive heaps of ragged boulders lay piled up. This was the border of the South Dakota badlands, Danny knew, but she no longer thought of the world in terms of states and political boundaries. Those things were gone. It must have been like this in past centuries, when there were frontiers. It was now a world of landmarks, not place names. Maybe that was why they had renamed their stronghold "Happy Town." "Jordan" didn't mean shit anymore.

The western end of town was wide open to a mixture of low, ravine-scored wilderness and serrated hills. This perplexed Danny. She had a crappy pair of bird-watching binoculars with a football team's logo on the side; these had been in a drawer in the living room of the house by the repair shop. Through them she could see the train line coming from the west, cutting straight across the flats, the same as on her map. So this was where the line went. If its people had indeed come this way, this is where the Tribe had ended its long journey. The railway entered the settlement close to the foot of the escarpment and exited on the far side across a trestle bridge that curved with the river there. Danny was approaching from the south, so she was going to have to skirt the shore to get close to town—but if she could go the long way around and get up on that escarpment, she could study the place from three hundred feet up, like it was a model train layout in a giant's basement. She had brought enough food to keep her for three days, so she thought that was the best plan.

The trouble, as always, was zeroes. There were a lot of them around. Even as she hustled across the field to the trees, she was taking a course equidistant between two of the things that were drifting in her direction, and there were several more almost at the edge of her sight in the distance. Of course, with a standing human population nearby, they would swarm in this direction. She expected the woods would be crawling with them.

Vaxxine had given her a slingshot lesson—she never missed—but Danny didn't have enough fingers to properly hold it. She was far better with a gun. They had a shotgun in the big rig, which Danny had brought but did not intend to use; she also had her pistol at her side. But the plan required stealth, so her primary weapon would be something she'd found over the fireplace of the abandoned house: a nice long-handled tomahawk, the steel inlaid with German silver. The stave was of hickory, and it had to be an antique, maybe hundreds of years old, because the wood was as hard as stone. There was a pipe bowl shaped like a hammerhead opposite the narrow cutting blade. Danny didn't intend to smoke with it, but she thought the pipe would punch a nice divot out of any skull it came near.

Despite the cold, Danny was sweating when she made the shadows under the trees. No sign of watchmen or scouts. There was a zero drifting directly ahead of her. It probed the gloom when it heard her coming, slack-faced, its lower lip torn away to reveal long yellow teeth in a shrunken black net of gums. She went straight at it and struck it in the temple next to its left eye before the thing could rally to attack. It collapsed in a spew of dark liquid. The tomahawk blade was designed to slip out of an entry wound without getting caught, Danny discovered. Those old-timers knew a few things about hand-to-hand combat.

She kept moving through the forest, bearing eastward until she reached the shore of the river. It was a carved-out sidewinder surrounded by rust-colored rock steeps, the brown water slightly wider and faster than she could swim and a lot colder than she could endure. She was going to have to pass under the bridges at night, or get on the other side of the river and circle around, then cross back again to get to the escarpment. She decided to risk a night crossing, and elected to go no farther that day, but settled herself between three massive boulders with a narrow space beneath the uppermost that would make a fair foxhole if she found herself under attack by zeroes—or humans. Even as she slid her legs into the cavity, a swollen corpse drifted past on the river, its stiff arms clawing at the sky.

Night took a long time to fall; the twilight lasted the better part of two hours. Then Danny felt it was safe to move around. Nothing had disturbed her hiding place, and although she couldn't bring herself to risk sleeping for a couple of hours, it had been good to rest after the long hike. She relaced her boots, settled the rucksack firmly on her shoulders, and took up the tomahawk and shotgun. Then she began stealing alongside the river until the first bridge came into view.

Danny had borrowed a dark balaclava of Vaxxine's. She pulled it down over her face now, and the itchy warmth felt good. It was needle-cold that night. Her hands were concealed in bulky black ski gloves she'd found at the house.

It was time. She'd already checked and rechecked her equipment and if she intended to get past the bridges, she would need every minute of dark-ness she could get. She moved forward into view of the bridge.

The first one was a high-span concrete structure with streetlights set along it; they were lit up, which seemed bizarre to Danny after so many months of living in a world that simply went dark when night fell. It seemed obscenely extravagant. As she crept closer, she saw there were men patrolling the bridge. Three or four of them, which wasn't enough to fight off a swarm, so there must be a garrison somewhere close by. She was moving through a band of eroded rock that followed the course of the river, overhanging slightly; keeping up against it she was able to avoid the loose piles of rock thrown up by the river and keep her silhouette from breaking with the general darkness around her. But it was slow going. After twenty minutes, the deck of the bridge was too high above her to see anymore, and she was out of view unless someone leaned over the side. This proved to be good luck.

She was almost to the foremost of the bridge piers that held up the span when a searchlight blazed on. Its beam was whiter and harsher than the sun. A figure was picked out of the darkness on the far shore, pure contrast of light and dark like the old movies of astronauts on the moon. Men were shouting up on the bridge. The small figure was at about the same elevation as Danny on the embankment opposite her, still a distance from the bridge. She tucked herself behind the poured concrete footing and debated whether to see what happened or use the diversion to try to make some time getting past the bridge.

A loudspeaker barked out an amplified voice:

"Okay, that's far enough. Raise your hands. Stand still. Are you alone?"

Danny couldn't hear what the man in the spotlight said, but she saw him raise his hands. A skinny little guy, a human, she could see that much. She decided to move on while attention was aimed elsewhere.

Another twenty minutes of sliding along with her back to the rock and she was around the next bend and the bridge was just a glare of reflected light on the water. The man back there hadn't been blacked up the way Danny was; they might have had night vision capability up there, but to see something it had to stand out, and Danny's drab clothing and concealed skin made her look more like a tree stump or a rock than anything else. The trick was to move with infinite patience.

The second bridge was the railway span, and there were men up there, too; one on each end of the bridge, looking bored even at a distance. Zeroes couldn't have made it across the span, as it didn't have a deck. The wooden trestles had nothing but empty space between them and there did not appear to be a catwalk alongside the tracks. Danny slipped beneath it without any difficulty. They clearly did not expect any trouble from that angle.

Danny's luck ended when a search party on foot swept along the bank above her head. She heard them coming—with dogs. She decided not to risk them catching her scent; a dog only needed a molecule or two to decide it smelled something. Not unlike the undead. She scooted away from the rock wall and got down on her belly as the noisy team came through the light woods about two hundred meters from her position, not far from the railroad bridge.

She slithered backward toward the river's edge, twisting herself like a lizard between the dark bulk of the boulders that strewed the shoreline. The dogs were baying and she could hear the men behind them shouting to be heard, but couldn't make out what they were saying. It was probable that this was just due diligence after they'd captured the man on the far bank, but if they'd detected her presence somehow, Danny wasn't going to let herself be caught. The noise of the river was close, drowning out dogs and men. And then her boots splashed in the water. She couldn't go any farther. The dogs were close—still up on the top of the bank, but nearly to the place she had been when she first heard them. She might have another couple of minutes while they found a way down to the shore, or she might not.

Danny was always working the problem in the back of her mind, formulating plans. *Observe, orient, decide, and act.* The results got passed up to her conscious mind while she was still trying to decide whether to stand up and call out to them as if she was simply lost, shoot the sons of bitches, or play dead; the frigid water was sucking the heat out of her feet but she didn't dare move them. A splash out of place and there would probably be another searchlight.

Then she saw what to do.

It was going to hurt, but it would get her out of trouble in seconds, if need be. She rearranged her burdens as quietly as she could. Then she sucked a deep breath through her teeth and slid backward into the black, icy water.

The search party stopped for about a minute near where Danny had last touched the bank, twenty meters from the water's edge and five or six above it. The dogs smelled something and they directed their attention in precisely Danny's direction. The men were discussing what to do. Several flashlight beams played around the shore, groping between boulders and cross-lighting deep shadows, but they found nothing out of place. Somebody lit a cigarette. Then they moved on upriver in the direction of the third bridge, hollering at the dogs and crashing through the undergrowth.

Danny waited through a count of twenty, then dragged herself back out of the water. She hadn't been completely immersed or she would not have had the strength to heave herself up; as it was she'd gotten soaked up to her nipples and halfway up her back. The rucksack was still dry, and she'd had the presence of mind to loop her gun belt around her shoulders, so the vital gear pouches were also dry. But it felt as if her skin had been peeled off—a sensation she had experienced in the burn ward—and there was no strength in her limbs. She'd been clinging to the back of a boulder that stood a little way out in the river, and if the men had not moved on, she was twenty seconds from losing her grip and being carried away in the vigorous current.

She got herself up against a tall chunk of concealing rock and immediately began to strip down despite the murderously cold air. Her teeth were jackhammering together and her hands were useless, pawing at the clinging, wet fabric. A headache was flaring up in her brain stem, pulsing until blue lights flickered in her vision. But she got her boots off, her pants off, shrugged out of the rucksack and dumped the belt beside it. It was a still night. If there had been a breeze, she didn't think she could have made it. But with all the vitality left in her, she took shelter behind a fallen tree, then yanked the rucksack open, pulled out the sleeping bag, dragged the bungees off it, and crawled inside headfirst. She was shivering so violently it made her bones hurt.

She pulled the rucksack in after her. She had earlier transferred some of the contents of her weapons backpack into it (and then relocked and hid the latter so no temptation would fall in the way of Vaxxine or the Silent Kid), so to get to the change of clothes in the bottom she had to dig through grenades, spare clips of ammunition, medical supplies, and Meals, Ready to Eat in their Mylar pouches.

She left her soaking-wet underwear on, but pulled thick socks onto her unfeeling feet, hauled on the Dickies work pants she'd found in the house, and pulled a fleece warm-up jacket over her head. She didn't need a shirt; she needed heat. These were all the clothes she had. The wet stuff she shoved into the trash bag she'd used as a liner inside the rucksack. There wasn't time to warm herself anymore—she was in a terrible position, and if the men came back the same way with their dogs, they could hardly miss the woman using her sleeping bag as a tent halfway up the shore of the river. If the bag had been camo, maybe she'd have stood a chance, but it was navy blue. Fine in the dark. Obvious under a spotlight.

She stowed the rest of her gear in the rucksack, transferring one grenade to the hand pocket of the fleece jacket, strapped on her stiff, half-frozen boots, then the rucksack and belt on her shoulders; finally she wrapped herself in the sleeping bag and started hiking back up the river, not too fast because she didn't want to catch up to the search party—and also because she could barely move. Her body simply would not warm up. It took fifteen minutes of stumbling along the riverbank before she had command of her extremities again; her solitary pinky finger on the left hand was so numb she wondered if she'd killed it, but she wrapped what fist she could make in a knot of sleeping bag and kept on going.

With her pounding head, she almost missed the third bridge—she was directly beneath it when she discovered chunks of shattered timbers lying all over the shore and looked up. No guards on that span, because the bridge wasn't there. It had been dynamited. She couldn't see the far side in the moon-dim overcast, but it must look much as the near side did: jagged stumps projecting out of the rockface.

"Nice try, idiots," Danny muttered.

For although the bridge was destroyed, there was a neat ascent made of undamaged iron rungs hammered into the rock that rose up alongside where the bridge had been, and at the top was the escarpment she intended to make camp on.

6

Dawn found Danny asleep on the topmost ridge overlooking Happy Town.

She could go for long periods without sleeping, as a rule. But the brush with freezing to death, the leg-burning hike, and the tension of near-capture had worn her out completely. She awoke at sunrise, closely wrapped in the sleeping bag with the rucksack under her head. The ridgeline was studded with tough cedars; she had bivouacked beneath one of these, sheltered by its low, contorted branches, which swept the stony ground. Her head had stopped throbbing, and she could feel all seventeen of her digits again.

Behind her position was a long, tapering slope of stone and debris, naked of vegetation, that led down to the rock drop-off and shoreline she'd traversed in the night. It had been a long, slow climb with her near-useless hands. The ridge was narrow and fairly flat, with the remnants of a forest along its summit; then the far side descended sharply in a series of cliffs and ledges scattered with rockfall and avalanche tailings, held more or less in place by further scrub brush and cedar woods.

Danny drank some of the mineral-tasting water she'd filled her bottle with at the river, ate an MRE that claimed without much justification to contain a cheese omelet with vegetables, and then crawled to the edge of the ridge for a look at Happy Town.

The place was located in a sort of natural harbor, the river cradling it like a bent arm around to the east and south, the escarpment rising up as a backstop against northerly winds; to the west the landscape was wide open, hills and badlands rolling away as far as the eye could reach. How the hell they kept that border secure, Danny could not guess.

Happy Town stood on level ground at the foot of the uplands and spread out to south and west—she estimated the town was built for seven thousand inhabitants or so, maybe more with the suburbs. It looked like the present population was higher than that. There seemed to be a fortified wall or fence of some kind extending around the entire settled area. The sunrise illuminated its top, which glittered like wire.

Within the fence and huddled against it on the outer perimeter was a city of tents and campers of every description, resembling a colorful mural of broken tile from Danny's elevated position. The town itself was mostly laid to a grid, with a broad central street forming the spine with the train depot at the skull end, and the ribs extending out to the fringes of town, where the streets became irregular, curving around to conform to the rocky landscape. There were big houses under the trees in the low parts of the slope, probably rich folks' houses. They always got the best views. Out in the flat areas were suburban developments with little square brown lawns and one tree per house.

The commercial center of town was a dozen blocks or so of uninteresting Old West–style structures with flat tarpaper roofs, false gables, and long, interconnected wooden porches; it reminded Danny of the studio backlot cowboy towns in Hollywood. She tried the binoculars. They lacked sufficient magnification to see anything more than antlike people moving around, but it appeared the place was bustling with activity, even at this early hour. Only a couple of vehicles were moving around—panel vans with something written on the sides in big, irregular letters—but the town was walkable in scale and plenty of folks were already on foot.

Church bells rang out, at this distance a small but clear sound. Danny realized most of the people she'd seen in the street were heading toward a big white-framed church that stood opposite some two-story brick buildings with white porches across the biggest intersection in town, where there was a little memorial square of some kind in the center with a statue on a plinth, ornamental shrubbery, and benches. The church was plain, with a tall, shingled steeple and high Gothic windows. It didn't look large enough to accommodate all the people heading toward it. Danny wondered at this: The end of the world had turned nonreligious folk superstitious, and religious folk into zealots, in her experience. These were probably the latter. Or it could be a requirement: You want to live in Happy Town, you go to services. The Tribe had run across a few enclaves like that.

Danny needed to get closer. She could see there were some pens built up around the train depot, which was almost directly below her position. There were several big warehouses, as well. The pens suggested this had once been a cattle transfer station, probably moving beef to cities on the coasts. A collection of industrial buildings and sheds indicated that this was where the real business in town took place, although whether they were in use anymore was impossible to tell from her altitude.

She scanned the steep slope below. It wouldn't be hard to get down from ledge to ledge without exposure by making long back-and-forth descents, and the tree cover was fairly good. It surprised her there weren't any lookout positions visible from where she was, but maybe they were exceptionally well hidden. She scanned the ledges below for evidence of a human presence. And found some.

Somebody had set up a hunting blind partway down the mountain. It was nicely camouflaged with branches and debris, but wasn't intended to conceal the occupant from eyes above, only below. It looked like a two-man shelter, probably about waist-high at its peak; she could see the rectangle of a camouflage-printed tarpaulin against the ledge rock, and there was a screen of rubble and sticks set up in front of it to break up the silhouette.

Even as she watched, a man emerged from the shelter on his hands and knees, looked carefully around but not up, and crouch-walked his way to the nearest stand of trees, probably to relieve himself. He emerged a few minutes later, looked at his watch, and then lay down in front of the shelter in much the same posture Danny was in. She thought she could see a telescope on a tripod, but it could have been a rifle. Again, she needed to get closer. She had all day for the recon, intending to return the following day to Vaxxine and the Silent Kid, and this looked like a place to start. Somehow she didn't think the man below here was on official Happy Town business. Otherwise, why was he concealed from there, and not her position?

She spread her wet clothing out on the ground; even the cold sun would still dry them eventually. If anyone found them, they could go ahead and wonder what it meant. Then she repacked the rucksack and rolled the sleeping bag tight. Tomahawk in hand, she began to make her painstaking way along the ridge, which sloped downhill to the west; in the trees there she could make a switchback and reach the ledge on which the watcher below was perched. The question uppermost in her mind was whether she could take him down with the tomahawk if it came to that. She hoped it wouldn't. But gunfire up there would be heard by every pair of ears in town.

Two hours of cautious going brought her obliquely down to the broad ledge on which the unknown man was watching.

It was a bright day with light overcast, but there were signs of bad weather coming. Danny hoped it wouldn't be another tornado. She had enough troubles without acts of God. She had seen no tripwires or cameras mounted in trees, no patrols had come her way, and in general she found Happy Town's security operations to be mostly show and very little substance. There must be some natural advantage there that kept the zeroes away. There were mine tunnels in the area; maybe there was uranium in the ground or something like that. It sure as hell wasn't the crackerjack armed response teams.

She reached a position from which she could see the man hunched over his telescope. There *was* a rifle, but it was on the ground at his side. He was dressed for invisibility like herself, but his outfit was quality hunting gear, insulated woodland camouflage. Dirty but new-looking. Danny considered throwing a rock at his head—sportsmanship was of no interest to her in a world with so many perils—but she was sure he was unaffiliated with the town, and in that case he might know something she didn't. So she stole from cover to cover, getting around behind him by degrees, moving not much faster than the shadows.

At last she was directly behind his shelter.

"Don't touch the rifle," Danny said, in a low but commanding voice.

"Fuck," the man muttered. He didn't move, but his entire body radiated tension.

Danny thought he seemed familiar. "Topper?" she said.

At this, he turned fully around. There he was, with leaves in his beard and a big stupid grin on his face. "I'll be fucked in the ass," he said. "You are a sore for sighted eyes, Sheriff. Stay where you are."

He scooted back from his position at the margin of the ledge, only standing up when he was next to Danny, far enough back so they weren't visible from below. Danny had lowered the shotgun right away, but it was the tomahawk that caught his eye.

"You were gonna scalp me," he said, and threw his arms around Danny and kissed her full on the mouth. She threw her arms around him, too, and kissed him back. She didn't care how he smelled or how hairy his face was; she had seldom been so glad to see another human being as she was to see him.

Once the initial delight had passed, it got awkward pretty fast. They drew apart at arm's length, still hanging on to each other's shoulders. They were both laughing, although Danny's laugh sounded more like a saw going through bone.

"So what the fuck brings you here?" Topper asked, when they were done grinning.

"Same as you, I figure," Danny said. "Recon. Do you know if the Tribe is down there?"

"Most of 'em. Some run off. Sheriff—Danny—there's somethin' you need to know. After you left—"

"I know already."

"Oh. Well then you understand why some folk lit out. Me and the scouts, we did, too. There was a big old fight, bunch of raised voices. Then some took off in the direction of the station, me and the scouts took off for the interstate, and others just plain took off. I figure sixty-seventy ended up going this way. Assumin' they all made it."

"It's really over."

"The Tribe? Yeah."

"Now what?" The news made Danny nostalgic. She remembered the campfires and the common kitchen, the gifts of prize liquor people sometimes brought. Bartering for a hundred pounds of jerky with some intrepid settlers. She remembered sitting with Amy one night in lawn chairs outside the White Whale. Inside, Patrick had organized a movie night and a bunch of people were watching a DVD of *My Fair Lady.* Amy had been talking about the first human baby she'd ever seen into the world, about three months before.

It was a squalling baby now, the fattest person in the Tribe. Everyone saw the little girl as a token of future prosperity, as if she was a new apple tree growing from the stump of an old one long gone. Danny had complained about the smell of babies and told a story about her time in Iraq when she'd been in a yard with her squad, firing back at some rebel yahoos across the street, and a goat had given birth to its kid right in the middle of the firefight. Mother and child both made it through the fight just fine, because the enemy had been mostly fourteen-year-old boys who couldn't have shot a camel if they were sewn up inside it. Danny thought this was a hilarious story, and Amy didn't.

"Maybe I shouldn't bring it up, but I'm sorry as fuck about what happened with your sister," Topper said, and at that moment Danny tuned back in. He'd been talking and she had been remembering the quiet times with the Tribe. Topper's words cut through her reverie. Fury instantly took over. She stepped back two paces and her knuckles went white—one fist and one finger, all squeezing the anger back.

Topper let his hands drop to his sides, speaking without rancor: "Take it easy. You want to know what happened?"

"I know what happened, you asshole. They shot her."

"I mean do you want to know why."

"No, I fucking don't want to know why," Danny snapped.

They were silent for a while, tasting the cold air and hearing the occasional sound from down in Happy Town, distant as a radio through an open window.

Then Danny spoke, all her anger having dissipated into the cold air. "So why are you here?"

"Recon, like you," Topper bluffed.

"Are you working with the Tribe again? I don't care, I just want to know."

"Nah. Just us scouts, parked about fifteen miles east of here far side of the river," he said. "But we couldn't just ride away like it weren't nothing.

It's the kids, you know? We don't give a rat's cunt about the adults; as far as I'm concerned the Tribe did its bit and it don't exist anymore. But all the little ones got stowed away in some kind of holding facility they got down there. And apparently once a week they send all the kids they collected around the backside of the mountain on that train of theirs. Ernie went off to check it out. He's been up here with me."

"He went last night?" Danny had a terrible foreboding.

"Yeah. Must have been on his way down when you was on your way up," Topper acknowledged.

"They caught him," Danny said. "Chaser patrol took him on the river-bank. Dammit, if I'd known it was him, I'd have—"

Topper cursed and punched the air. "You fuckin' shithead, Ernie. God-damn."

"I should have—"

"—Don't start blaming yourself again," Topper cut in. "You ain't the boss of Ernie. You're a free agent. He took his chances, that four-eyed dumbass." Then he added, without any conviction, "Anyhows, he's probably all warm and well-fed right now."

"You don't believe that."

"No, I don't."

"Do we go after him?"

"Us scouts agreed there weren't gonna be any of that bullshit. Not enough of us. He's on his own." It clearly pained him to say this, but he was right, of course. Danny thought he might cry, so she changed the subject.

"Do you think the kids are in danger?"

"Not right away," Topper said. "Least we ain't seen any little kid bodies yet."

"We talked to a guy from Happy Town couple days ago. He said they're even taking in the kidnapped ones. So that explains all those assholes chasing the Tribe around."

Topper's eyebrows crawled up. "Who's 'we'? You got a new team already?"

"Me and the Silent Kid and this lone survivalist," Danny said. She didn't want to elaborate, not least because she didn't want to admit Vaxxine had saved her from certain death. But Topper's thoughts had gone a different way.

"We went off after you, Danny. When you and the Wolfman split. After shit got ugly with the prisoner. We rode out all over the place, but there weren't no sign of you nowhere. Where's Wulf, anyways?"

"He's dead."

"Ah, hell."

Topper did something Danny had never seen in real life before—he pulled the knit cap off his head and held it over his heart. Then he picked at loose threads sticking out of it, saying, "He was a good one. How—"

"Died in his sleep," Danny said.

"I'll be damned."

"We're losing daylight," Danny said. "We can discuss this shit later."

They got down on hands and knees and crawled back to Topper's overlook position. Danny put her eye to the telescope's optics and was amazed at the magnification. She could see people's faces, although not well enough to distinguish individuals. Topper scratched his chin while she panned the lens around town, taking in details.

"Me and Ernie," Topper went on, unconsciously lowering his voice as if they might be heard now that they were within line-of-sight, "we started off trying to figure out if we can come down the mountain and get to the kids from here, because this cliff kind of butts right up to the train station down there. Not as defended. But it don't look real good, so we was thinking maybe we could spring 'em out of that summer camp thing they got going upriver. I guess with Ernie out of the picture it's time to report back to the others. Get an expedition set up."

"You're sure we shouldn't be trying to rescue Ernie?"

"Well, I didn't see any corpses go on the pile yet today—so far, so good."

"Corpses?"

"They got a lot of rules down there and they behead a fucker every couple days. Usually at sunup. I weren't kidding about the bodies."

"Shit."

"I think they keep it a secret from the Happy Town chooks. Don't make a ceremony out of it or nothing. You can't see it from down there; it's behind a wall. But there's a yard by the station where they take care of business. They pile the bodies on a truck, cover them with garbage, and take 'em away early in the morning. No heads. We seen it twice in two days."

"Goddamn. You thought *I* was a hard-ass."

Danny gave Topper the binoculars and spent an hour with the telescope, studying the town. She paid special attention to the area around the train depot—there was a lot of activity centered on a couple of the warehouses, with men in orange safety vests coming and going. There was also a shed with a locomotive engine underneath its sheet metal awning; it looked like they were overhauling the big diesels aboard it, with showers of welding sparks spraying down and men wrestling huge machine parts in and out. She saw a gang of a dozen men carrying an immense cast-iron connecting rod of some kind, like zookeepers holding a record-size python out straight for the photograph. There were several cattle cars on a siding, as well. It looked like somebody was planning a mass migration down there—either that, or they planned to start a circus.

The panel vans cruised around town. Danny could read the writing on them with the telescope: HAPPY TOWN SAFETY PATROL, it said. Hand-painted with a spray can. More of the men in safety vests inside the vans—the vests seemed to be the official uniform.

Church got out about an hour and a half after the bells rang, and Danny watched the outflow of citizens. She didn't recognize anybody.

"They do services morning and afternoon," Topper noted. "God ain't fuckin' dead, apparently."

While she watched the town, Topper filled her in on further details of the past few days: The scouting team was down to eight individuals. They stayed in touch with Patrick, Amy, and some others inside the fence because there was a whole town set up outside the wire, and you could talk freely through it. Get lost in the crowds if security came poking around. Connor was in charge of the scouts' encampment while Topper was away.

This put her in mind of her own situation. Danny was on a schedule. Vaxxine and the Kid would be waiting for her back at the house, and if they ran into any major trouble, she still wasn't confident that the wheelchair-bound woman would be up to dealing with it—if only because she couldn't run across the fields. Danny's return time was tomorrow afternoon. She'd need to head out before dawn to make it there on schedule.

"So how safe is it?" she asked, while she and Topper were eating what passed for lunch. Hers was a Chicken Breast with Cavatelli MRE, essentially identical to the omelet she'd eaten last; Topper ate venison jerky and what appeared to be cat shit, which he claimed was freeze-dried bananas he'd found on the floor of a ransacked sporting goods store. They drank river water.

"From zeroes? I ain't seen but a handful the whole time I been here, and they're on the other side of the river. That big swarm to the west is like the end of the zeroes. Out this way it's real peaceful. Whatever gimmick they figured out, it's working."

"I meant do you think these Happy Town fuckers know what they're doing."

Topper noisily scratched his neck. "I don't know, be honest with you. I mean, there's maybe a couple hundred in charge, mostly guards. Thousands of chook-ass civilians. They could overrun the joint in five minutes if people rose the fuck up. On the other hand, they got harsh discipline like I said, and people are scared to rock the boat. Those vans stay busy. Most of all I think people keep their heads down because of the little ones. The kids are like instant hostages. I'd call that a pretty good security strategy."

There were more questions, but Danny didn't think Topper could answer them. It occurred to her he might know something about the big picture.

"One other thing. Did you guys check out what's keeping the zeroes back to the west?"

"You found that radiation train yourself. It's keeping the swarm way the fuck back."

"Only to a point. Why doesn't the swarm come north, hook around the hot zone, and nail this place? Those fences down there aren't shit."

"We was wondering the same thing. So far we can't make it out. There's land mines on this little road leads to where the kids are at around the far side of the mountain, which is why they take the train this way instead. Weirdest thing is this: They got a perimeter of scouts scattered around all over the place, kind of in rings around here as far out as five, six miles. But they don't do shit, they just stand around and none of the zeroes come close."

"Could they be thinkers?"

"Not real fuckin' likely. Why would thinkers stand around in the desert like assholes when they could be eating fresh meat back here?"

"I can't think of any other explanation for the swarm staying put."

"Could be more radiation, too. I guess you should know this: We killed one of them. Practically drove over him on our way to scout this place out a few days back. He told us to 'halt' like some German asshole from *The Dirty Dozen*. Conn got off his hog, they didn't agree on much, and next thing you know the guy's dead with a broke neck. He wasn't no thinker. He was one of us. But he looked real ill, and we thought maybe he had radiation poisoning or like that. Or cancer. Pale as fuck, and he smelled weird. Anyways a search party must of come around after that but we were long-gone. The body weren't there next day, so they probably picked him up. We got his radio, but they don't say much."

"The whole thing stinks," Danny said. "But I can't figure out where the smell is coming from."

7

There was another tolling of church bells and gathering of the faithful in the early evening, but not much else happened that day in Happy Town.

It grew colder as the shadows lengthened. A mean-spirited wind swept over the ridge and poured down on them as the sun went down. Danny and Topper retreated into the shelter, which was stale as a clothes hamper, but kept the chill out; when the light failed, they were in darkness. It was too risky to use even the dim red key-chain light Danny kept on her tool belt.

"You're all right," she said to Topper, after they had sat in silence for a while.

"I wish we had something to fuckin' drink," Topper said. "Take the edge off."

"I quit the stuff," Danny said, surprising herself. And it occurred to her this might actually be true, especially after the epic bender with Wulf. She'd been tormented by thirst lately, but since that blinding headache, she hadn't touched the booze. Her body didn't care what the real diagnosis was: It thought that crisis was a hangover, and it revolted at the thought of alcohol.

"No shit," Topper said. "For real?"

"Yeah. At least for the time being," Danny said. She was starting to feel defensive, like quitting the alcohol was something shameful. Maybe an admission that she had a problem before. Which it probably was. They were lying inside the dark shelter staring up at the tarpaulin overhead, seeing nothing. The wind made the shelter expand and contract, rustling.

"Let's check out the lights," Topper said. "It's something to see."

They crawled out and stood on the rim of the ledge looking down at Happy Town. No need to conceal themselves now. Even night vision goggles couldn't penetrate this far into the darkness. The entire town was lit up: rooftop searchlights, streetlights, windows with lamps in them, even shop signs and some Christmas lights strung up here and there. It looked so out of place in the dark world, and yet this would once have been an unremarkable sight. There was so much light flooding the town that Danny could see Topper in the reflected glow.

"Looks like old times," Topper observed.

"Where the fuck is the power coming from?"

"Near as we can tell," Topper said, "they're sending it down the power lines alongside the railroad. From upriver. Might be a generator up there."

Danny couldn't stop staring at all the lights. "I don't know what they're up to, but you gotta hand it to them. This is one major operation with its shit stowed secure."

"There's even a whorehouse," Topper said, apropos of nothing.

"Not a surprise. The church doesn't mind?"

"Hail Mary and lie down with Jezebel, as my old man used to say."

"Who's Jezebel?"

"Some chick from the Bible."

"That's why I went into law enforcement instead of prostitution," Danny said, watching the glittering lights of the town below. "After my combat barbecue, I couldn't get laid with a million-dollar bill up my twat."

"Aw, hell," Topper said, laughing quietly. "At this point I'd fuck a saguaro cactus if it agreed to throw in a handjob."

They both laughed at that.

"Let's go," he said, and to Danny's surprise, kissed her. It was the right move.

Unexpectedly, her mouth flooded with desire. She found she was grabbing his neck with all seven of her fingers, and there wasn't enough air in the world. She groped in the shadows and found the hot weight of his balls inside his jeans. Danny was suddenly, almost painfully turned on like she hadn't been in years. There was a hot pink wire running straight through the middle of her, and she wanted this man to pluck it till it broke.

Halfway through their lovemaking, all the lights of town went out except for the sweep lights on the roofs; it was midnight, at which time they shut off the grid every night.

Afterward, neither of them knew what to say, so they didn't. Danny picked a hair out of her mouth and they sat in the darkness with the tarpaulin against their heads, panting for breath. Then they slept for a while. Danny awoke around 0400 hours and shook Topper awake. He was snoring, which for some reason filled her with affection.

"Get your clothes on. I've got a new plan," she said, lacing on her boots. An idea had come to her while she slept.

"Honeymoon's over," Topper grunted.

"I'll tell you where to find the Silent Kid and the woman I told you about. Name's Vaxxine, like the shots. She's in a wheelchair, but she's hard as nails. You'll like her. Anyway, soon as you can, rendezvous with them. Make sure you tell her I sent you, or she'll kill you with a slingshot. I'll give you their coordinates."

"You're not going back?"

"I'm going to follow that railway line to its source and see just what the fuck these assholes are up to. Find out where they're taking these kids. I think it's a concentration camp or something. If I'm not back in three days, figure me dead, you got that?"

"You're gonna end up like Ernie, for chrissakes."

"Come on, man. The fuck else are we supposed to do? There's nothing to learn from up here. And there's no other way into town, unless we do some Rambo commando shit and sneak around. That's stupid."

"Your whole idea is stupid," Topper said. He took a risk and switched on a button flashlight, cupping it in his hands. He wanted to make eye contact. "You go off and get killed, that's step one. We hook up with a cripple and a kid who don't talk, step two. That's it. That's the plan."

"You got a better idea?"

"Yeah. Let's round up everybody we got left and get out of fuckin' Dodge. Keep on looking for a safe place somewhere else. Or maybe we could take a chance down there. I don't know. At least there ain't no zeroes in the area. I'd rather deal with a human enemy than a undead one, personally."

"What about Ernie?"

"Aw, they'll probably just throw him out—he weren't armed," Topper said, and there was deep pain in his voice. He didn't believe it.

Danny's head was throbbing again. She didn't want to argue about this. Her irritation was swelling up like a balloon, pressurizing her skull. It was a long, treacherous drive eastward through some of the most infested regions on the continent, according to rumors. But she couldn't rest easy again if she didn't know what was happening to the children.

She didn't like the look of those boxcars.

8

Danny was on her way out when the situation changed for the worse. Topper had helped her fill her pack for the multiple-day extension on her recon mission; he had some camping gear that would make things more pleasant, including electric socks and spare batteries. He reminded Danny of her long-gone mother preparing a bag lunch for school—turning chores into gestures of affection. He had disassembled the blind and left the tarpaulin under a tree, erasing any signs that there had been a lookout; now they were almost down to the river again. But then Danny's headache came back. It was getting worse, fast.

She saw pulsing auras around everything, as if some weird light in the invisible spectrum had revealed itself to her. They stumbled through the darkness. At first she tried to ignore the pain, but it was becoming all she could think about. It reminded her of having to pee as a child and knowing Dad wasn't going to stop the car. Holding it and holding it until she was writhing and sweating. Except this wasn't the bellyache of a full bladder, it was knives jabbing her in the brain.

They were near the largest bridge by now, if her reckoning was correct. She went down on one knee.

"You okay?" Topper said, whispering.

"Been having these headaches," Danny said.

"I can't understand you," Topper said. He was a dim outline against the false dawn in the sky, but Danny thought she could see him flashing in blue luminescent streaks.

"I said 'you keep going and I'll catch up,'" she wheezed.

"I still can't understand. Are you sick or something? You ain't talking right."

"Go," Danny barked. "Go now."

There were voices up high somewhere. She must have shouted. The watchers had heard her. Topper threw her arm over his shoulder and began to half-carry Danny down the riverside, lurching over rocks and driftwood in the dark. The shouting was distant, but not distant enough. Then there were dogs barking. Danny shook herself out of Topper's grip. She collapsed and vomited on the stones. Her head hurt so badly that the onrush of every wave of pain frightened her. She spat and hated that Topper's hand was rubbing her back like a concerned preschool teacher. Just because they fucked didn't make them responsible for each other. She cleared her throat and tried again.

"Can you understand me?"

"Now I can. What the fuck is happening to you?"

She spoke in short bursts, forcing each one out through clenched teeth. "Head's fucked up. Keeps happening. You go. Find out where they're taking the kids. Keep Vaxxine and the Silent Kid safe. I'll get Ernie out. You got ten seconds."

Topper stood there like a fool for five of them. Then he said, "I'm coming back for you," and ran down the riprap shore of the river. Danny waited until the crash of his boots sounded distant enough, and then she drew the deepest breath she was capable of and shouted, *"Over here!"* at the full reach of her voice. A blazing white searchlight flamed on, plunging lances into her skull. The baying of dogs and shouts of men, the cackling of the mad, dark river, became the din of a tornado filled with lightning.

She pitched forward into darkness.

PART THREE

1

Kelley was alive again, laughing about something. For once, Danny didn't think Kelley was laughing at *her*, so she wasn't irritated. Their laughs were so different. Kelley's was musical, pitched high. It reminded Danny of a ringtone. She looked around: The two of them were sitting in an apple orchard in Tehachapi, California. September, probably. Cloudless plate-blue sky overhead, cool shadows, warm sun. They were sitting at a picnic table eating steamed hot dogs with relish and mustard; Danny had diced onions on hers, as well. They were drinking lime Jarritos.

Kelley was around thirteen years old, wearing hand-me-down jeans and a checked shirt that had been Danny's, some years earlier. They sat under the broken shade of an apple tree and watched people pick fruit and drop it into wicker bushel baskets—tourists, not farm laborers, enjoying a ritual return to the soil for an afternoon.

"You laugh, but I'm not kidding," Danny said. "Like five years from now, you're going to get bit by a zombie and turn into one yourself."

"That's crazy," Kelley said. "Zombies aren't even real."

"Not yet," Danny said. The hot dog was so tasty—fresh factory flavor, nothing spoiled or stale or scary-old. They weren't planning to pick apples, but they'd seen the menu sign from the road and it was lunchtime, so they spontaneously stopped to eat. Exactly the kind of thing Danny never, ever did. Maybe they could pick some apples after all. Danny couldn't quite remember where they were going that put them in Tehachapi. Something fun. Something just for Kelley. Because Danny was missing so much of her sister's childhood with her military career.

Kelley had mustard on the side of her mouth. She was looking out at the rolling slope with the apple trees on it, one leg tucked underneath her. Danny felt relaxed for the first time in ages. Not cold or sore or beat-up. No migraine. Nothing to worry about. The dead lay firmly in their graves and the living walked free among the apple trees. Then a voice called across the parking lot behind them. It was Amy Cutter, fresh out of veterinary school. In fact, it looked like she had only just graduated. She was still wearing the burgundy suit jacket from the graduation photo.

"Hey, Danny!" she called. "Tell Diggler to do a number two!"

Danny looked around at her feet. There was Diggler, the famous potbellied pig who could shit on command. What the hell was he doing here? He seemed to be deep in conversation with a bug-eyed little dog with a flat face, rooting around under the table. That was the Silent Kid's dog, she realized. It was like a big family reunion all of a sudden. She looked around. The Kid himself ought to be somewhere nearby.

She saw him standing under a tree, peering out from around the trunk. He looked worried. Not that it was unusual. But he looked like something was wrong. Danny wondered if he'd eaten too many apples. But then he pointed—Danny thought he was pointing at her, but then she saw it was Kelley. She turned to see what was the matter.

Kelley looked sad, all of a sudden. She was staring down at her half-eaten hot dog with an expression of regret.

"What's the matter?" Danny asked. She seldom inquired after Kelley's well-being, but this looked serious. Kelley shook her head and didn't say. She was at that age when she stopped communicating, so that much made sense. But then Diggler and the little terrier bolted out from under the table and ran for the road. Amy wasn't there anymore. In fact, Danny realized, there wasn't anybody around. The Silent Kid, the dog, the pig, the tourists and farmers had all vanished. It was just her and Kelley. The leaves were falling from the trees and a breeze was blowing all the warm out of the air. Felt like fall coming in.

"Kelley?"

A black tear ran out of Kelley's right eye.

"Are you sick?"

"I'm dead," Kelley said, in a quiet voice. Danny saw that the tear-track had left a groove in her sister's face, and now the skin around it was turning gray. The dab of mustard on her lip stood out vivid yellow against it. She became ash-pale, her eyes sunk in dark pools, her lips blue and flaking. Then a slab of her cheek fell away, and Danny could see teeth through the bloodless hole. Kelley raised her hand to inspect the crater and the fingers that explored it were rotten, the nails peeling off.

"Please don't go," Danny said. She didn't know what to do next, except watch Kelley fall to pieces.

Kelley slumped forward, coming apart like waterlogged bread by now, the picnic table slimy with globs of her flesh. Bones poked out of her shirt in places. She was trying to say something to Danny, struggling to get the words out. Danny leaned in close, although she was afraid.

"One for you, twenty for me," Kelley croaked, black foam spilling between her teeth.

And then her head fell off her neck.

Danny opened her eyes, and immediately closed them again.

She was in a hospital. It didn't look like one—the room she was in appeared to have been part of a grade school, originally, complete with cloud-glazed green chalkboards and U.S. presidents marching around the cornice in chronological order—but she was in a hospital bed and the smell of a hospital was heavy in the air. Sickness and strong cleaning fluid, mostly. She closed her eyes as soon as she opened them because there were three people in the doorway to the room. Two men were talking in low voices to Joe Higashiyama, the doctor. The men were guards of some kind, with black military-style uniforms, blaze orange safety vests, and masses of weapons and gear. They could have been SWAT, or mercenaries of the type the government used to hire to keep overseas troop levels attractively low for voters back home. Like those guys Danny faced off against in the California desert when everything first went to hell.

None of the three had been looking in her direction, so she pretended sleep and listened to their conversation.

"Rules is rules," one of the guards said. "One child, one adult."

"We also have a rule that we don't turn injured people away," Joe said. "Until recovered."

"We were told she just has a headache. That's not injured."

"Her brain is damaged," Joe replied. "We did a CT scan and there's subarachnoid bleeding, which corresponds with her symptoms. It could kill her. She's well-known to a number of people here in town, and according to them, she's taken some major hits to the head since the crisis began. Do you need to see the pictures?"

"Okay," the second guard broke in. "So she *is* injured. We still only got one kid for the pair of them. So either she's out of here or the gimp is out of here. That means we send the wheelchair on her way."

The acoustics of Joe's voice changed; Danny guessed he'd stepped into the hallway beyond the room. "Gentlemen," he said, which Danny thought was probably an exaggeration. "I think we can keep them both here for a couple more nights. I need to examine the young lady in the wheelchair for skin rash, urethra lesions, and so forth—it's extremely difficult to remain healthy in confinement like that. And this woman here isn't going anywhere until she's conscious, at the very least. So if we can table the discussion for at least twenty-four hours, I'll be very grateful."

The three of them were walking down the hall now, voices breaking up into echoes, their footsteps clattering. They'd gone to the left, Danny noted. Exit that way. She opened only the eye farthest from the door, in case anyone was looking into the room, and glanced around. It was indeed a classroom. Dusty light came through the blinds in hot white strips, falling across a second bed nearer the windows. There was a teenager in that bed, a boy, with his head and arms wrapped in bandages. His eyes were open but nobody was inside looking out. Danny could hear voices elsewhere, and squeaking shoes. There must be several rooms with patients in them.

While she lay there trying to decide what to do, she fell asleep again.

When she awoke, it was dark outside. Danny didn't like sleeping in proper buildings anymore. They didn't offer real safety, unless devoid of windows and doors, and they couldn't be started up and driven away in an emergency. Sheds and barns were okay. Nowhere to hide and few ways in and out, simple to defend. But this place sounded like a lot of rooms, hallways, stairs. Glass everywhere. No good. But from the conversation she'd overheard, she must be in Happy Town proper. The guards had spoken of the one-child rule. She cursed Vaxxine's stupidity. Who else could it have been they were talking about, and the one child must be the Silent Kid.

That jolted her fully awake. She sat up, despite the pain that zipped through her skull like a coarse rope through tender hands. The Kid. He might already have been sent to the summer camp place Joe had described.

in one of those cattle cars. Topper hadn't said what day of the week they took the kids away on. How long had she been in this place? She listened for activity in the hallway and heard nothing. There was only a small night-light to illuminate the room, so it must be quite late.

As far as she was concerned, she had been captured by the enemy. Now, while they still thought she was incapacitated, was her chance to reconnoi-ter the area and develop a game plan. Simple escape was out of the ques-tion. Not while the Silent Kid's welfare hung in the balance. She had memorized the layout of Happy Town; the school, if it was the one she'd seen from the ridge, was on the western side of town, with a suburban neighborhood between it and downtown.

Danny swung her feet over the side of the bed, slipping into stealth mode despite the thumping in her head. This was it: time to do the stupid Rambo commando shit and sneak around after all. There weren't any moni-tors attached to her, nor any IV tubes (unlike her fellow-patient in the room). She spared a glance at the other bed. No response. He had the brain-dead look that Danny had grown familiar with when she used to visit her wounded friend Harlan at the VA hospital. She took a brief inventory of her situation: loose pink drawstring pajama pants and a short-sleeved shirt of the kind nurses wore, with little teddy bears all over it on a jolly blue back-ground.

None of her gear was in the room—utility belt and uniform were else-where, along with her boots. But someone had left a tray on a table by the door with various commonplace medical items on it. Danny saw there was a pile of clothing on a chair next to the comatose teenager, and under the chair a pair of black Converse All-Stars. Several sizes too large for her. She pulled on his socks and laced the shoes as tight as she could, feeling like a clown because the toes were two inches longer than her feet; bending to tie them, it felt like someone was hitting her in the back of the skull with a frying pan. She saw sparkling lights and almost blacked out.

Once the burning feathers had cleared from behind her eyes, she care-fully stood up, took the boy's hooded sweatshirt, and crept to the door. She examined the contents of the tray table and selected a disposable scalpel, held it in her good hand so the blade was concealed against her arm, and draped the sweatshirt over that. Then she cracked the door slightly and checked the hallway beyond.

The floor was smooth and clean and the sneakers made no sound, so she had the advantage of silence as she stole through the hospital. It had definitely been a grade school before; most of the bulletin boards still wore the last few days of crayon drawings, homework assignments, and notices that had been there when the dead rose up. The only light came from red emergency exit signs and floodlights outside the windows here and there. They had a good supply of electricity in Happy Town, but they didn't waste it at night. Danny took a left, the direction she'd heard Joe and the guards go, and after a couple of minutes reached a stair hall full of steel lockers that must have been the central hub of the school.

There were offices off to the right, and a classroom to the left, with BURN UNIT taped to the glass in the door. Somebody was crying the night away in there. Danny had done the same, long ago and far away. The stairs downward led to the old nurse's station, shop class, and athletic lockers; upstairs was WARDS, according to the notice written with Magic Marker directly on the plaster. If most of the patients were up there, Danny thought her level, the ground floor, could be for special cases. So she might not have a lot of time to look around. *Fuck it*, she decided. She wasn't a prisoner yet. There was an exterior door on the stair landing. She crossed to it and looked out through the wire-reinforced glass. Guards outside. Not the same ones she'd seen earlier, but three equally well-armed men, stamping and slapping their sides in the cold.

Danny went down the basement stairs. Beneath the school, the concrete walls radiated damp cold. She realized why the school had been chosen for their temporary hospital—they didn't need a school because there weren't any children. They were all hidden away upriver. She wondered why she didn't see any medical staff in the halls. She'd seen a clock in the stairwell that claimed it was 2:00 a.m., but hospitals didn't keep business hours. They must have been understaffed, or it could be some kind of security thing. She'd encountered that in Pakistan—civilian hospitals closed at night by the military, as if they were cafeterias. In the morning, the staff was allowed back in to clean up the mess and remove anyone who had died overnight. But she had to remain vigilant. She hadn't seen any security cameras, but it didn't mean there wasn't surveillance.

She kept on moving, ready to defend or attack.

Less than fifteen minutes after Danny had gotten out of bed, she was outside the school. She'd emerged through a narrow tilting window over the sinks in the boys' locker room into a light well set in the school yard, like a foxhole; even as she took stock of her situation, two additional guards strolled past, talking in low voices, and went around the corner of the school to Danny's left. There were several portable classrooms and storage containers down that way. The icy winter air had shocked Danny's system enough that she realized what she was doing didn't make any sense. She wasn't going to find the Silent Kid in an unfamiliar town in the middle of the night. But neither could she lie quietly in bed until some asshole decided whether to throw her out or not. She needed to get in front of her situation. Recon was a good start. See the lay of the land.

Danny pulled the sweatshirt on and followed the guards—the safest place to be was behind the most recent patrol; otherwise you'd be in front of the next one.

She reached a Dumpster at the wire fence that surrounded the playground and crouched down against it. She was freezing. It was a cold night, and her hospital clothes were tissue-thin; her breath smoked in the air and lingered, frozen. Her feet were already numb. The Dumpster was warm to the touch, probably because it was seething with microbial activity on the inside. Danny pressed her seven digits against it to get some feeling back, then took up the scalpel again and slunk along the fence at a low crouch until she came to a place where a vehicle had crashed through it at some point in the past. Nobody had repaired the damage; someone had stood a sheet of plywood against the torn wire. Security in Happy Town was absolutely terrible. It reminded her of the TSA—security theater to reassure the people on the inside, not to discourage threats on the outside.

Five minutes later, Danny was moving as swiftly as her cold-struck feet would carry her through the deserted suburbs of Happy Town, with downtown directly ahead.

2

The first thing Danny needed was warmth, or she wasn't going to be able to accomplish anything else. Besides, her outfit was impossibly conspicuous, the sweatshirt light gray and her pants flashing in the dark like a whitetail deer's ass. Danny crossed the lawn of the nearest house. The grass was overgrown and matted down with frost, but the house appeared to be intact. As she approached, Danny discovered the house was occupied. There wasn't any electricity, but a ceramic oil lamp shaped like a lighthouse was burning in the living room. She could see someone asleep on the couch. There was an automatic rifle propped up against the wall. They must have quartered people in these houses. She had to assume that nowhere was vacant until proven so.

Luck was with her, however. There was a Jeep with a soft top in the driveway of the house, and in the backseat someone had left a dark-colored insulated jacket. Danny slashed the top with the scalpel, extracted the jacket, and zipped it on over the sweatshirt. It was also far too large, the sleeves hanging down past her fingertips. She was still cold, but it wasn't unbearable now. And she was slightly less visible. She searched the pockets for anything useful, then continued toward downtown, not on the sidewalk as before, but behind a shaggy hedge that ran alongside it in front of the row of houses. A van with several silhouetted people inside drove past; she got down behind the bushes. The engine noise provided cover. Danny hurried along as soon as the van passed, less stealthily than before. A big dog barked at her from inside a house, but whoever shouted at it must have assumed the dog was barking at the van.

The core of Happy Town looked quite ordinary from street level, much as it did from above. Although there were no lights at this hour except for floodlights mounted on rooftops, washing back and forth across intersections, the buildings seemed to be in good condition, with not too many broken windows or burned-out facades. The abandoned vehicles and wrecks were absent from the streets. There wasn't much trash in the gutters or broken glass glittering across the sidewalks. She could see the railway station at the far end of the street, and the big white church wasn't far from her position.

It reminded her a little of Potter, California, a town that had figured prominently in her initial search for Kelley a lifetime ago, where she had fought a savage battle against rogue paramilitary elements and zeroes alike. The layout was nothing like the same, and the style of buildings was different, but the presence of a railroad passing through town recalled those desperate hours to her mind. It made sense: The rails were probably the means by which America would someday be stitched back together, as if the clock had been turned back to 1869.

The Wild West was everywhere now. But this town was inhabited by the living, not the undead. She could sense the presence of many people, but saw nobody. There was a curfew in effect; during their mountainside vigil she and Topper had heard the siren wail and watched the citizens scuttle indoors, precisely at 2300 hours. She heard an engine approaching and slipped around behind the church when she saw the van coming back. Getting shot on sight wasn't going to advance the Silent Kid's cause.

As she shivered in the deep shadow behind the church, watching the van drive away into the suburbs, Danny saw a couple of people slip into view from between what had once been a drugstore and a skateboarding shop. They were trying not to be seen, that was immediately clear; they were wrapped in dark blankets and hunched down low. She watched as they hustled across the wide street, zigzagging around the spotlit areas. It wasn't clear where they were heading. Halfway down the street, a *crack* snapped through the crisp night air, and the foremost of the people cried out and fell to the ground. A woman. Whistles blew, and several doorways were flung open; a dozen armed men raced into the street. They wore the blaze orange vests.

The two fugitives were surrounded. A minute later, the security van returned. The prisoners were thrown into the back; the guards were indifferent to the cries of pain from the woman. The other chook was a man, and he argued loudly until someone punched him in the teeth. The doors of the truck slammed shut.

Danny observed dozens of faces hovering in upstairs windows along the street, pale ghosts keeping out of the light. The whole town was inhabited, but there were no lights inside and nobody wanted to show themselves. Now the blaze orange security team spread out, looking for additional fugitives. Danny could hear the leader barking orders.

She cursed behind her teeth—bad luck. Now she had to get indoors or find some other way to vanish. She moved along the flank of the church and ducked into a vestibule, her back to the door.

There was a shadow black as paint there. A couple of men ran past the end of the church, conducting the most half-assed sweep Danny had ever witnessed, and were gone. She forced herself to breathe again. Then she felt the door move against her back, and warm, stale air eddied out through the gap. Danny gripped the scalpel firmly in her fist and slipped inside the church.

3

Although it was dark outside, it was darker in the church, and Danny was glad of it. She could hear someone moving around in front of her somewhere in another room; she had entered near the back of the building, which was divided up into small spaces. This one appeared to be a mudroom, with linoleum on the floor and coatracks all around the walls. A patch of searchlight crawled through a small window, revealing an electric space heater on the floor, but it wasn't working. Still, it was warmer inside than out. Danny was struck by a fit of shivering that convulsed her entire frame, and she crouched with her knees against her chin while waiting for it to pass. The headache that took her down seemed to have gone away entirely. Sensation was returning to her feet, which was a mixed blessing—now they stung fiercely inside the cheap sneakers. She saw a heavy peacoat on a hook, and some rubber boots, but left them where they were. She was better off with unrestricted movement and silent steps, at least indoors.

She crossed to a doorway and pushed on the door, which was ajar; it croaked, so she lifted up on the knob to reduce the weight on the hinges and it swung open silently. She listened.

Someone was definitely here with her in the church, making a regular hissing sound. Sweeping, she thought, or mopping. Danny dipped low through the doorway into a second room utterly dark except for a pale square of doorway in the right-hand wall that let into the public part of the church. She crossed the room one careful, sliding step at a time, ready to stop if she met anything that could knock over in the darkness.

Now she could see into the main space of the church, the thorax or whatever it was called; she hadn't gotten much religious training. There were big stained-glass windows all around, and the floodlights outside cast gaunt rags of color across pews and aisles. The place was full of folding chairs, as well; hardly any floor space was left bare. There was a balcony across the opposite end of the church with organ pipes at the back and the vaulted ceiling above. The main doors were beneath the balcony and presumably led directly outside.

A man in a hood was indeed sweeping his way down the center aisle with a wide push broom. Danny glanced around her end of the space: She could see the back of an altar and a raised platform beneath it, and against the wall up above her to the left, centered on the gable end, was a gory, life-sized crucifixion, Christ's arms outstretched, head sagging on his chest. She hadn't been in churches very often, and couldn't guess if this was a Catholic, Protestant, or other kind of operation. She associated such places with funerals, and they made her nervous.

This one made her more nervous.

She determined to slip back into the mudroom, grab the boots and peacoat, and make her way back to the hospital, rather than risk being discovered; this wasn't getting her any closer to locating the Silent Kid. She'd seen from the incident outside that the downtown area was more or less impassable.

As she started to move back through the doorway, a voice barked, "Who goes there?"

It echoed around the big, hollow space. Danny crouched low to the ground, scalpel ready to strike. She expected the lights to come on, but it remained dark. The man in the hood, however, seemed to know exactly where she was. He rushed directly at her with the broom in both hands. He made no outcry, to Danny's surprise; the only sound was the whack of his boots on the tile floor. Danny waited in the doorway taut as a snare while he closed the distance; as the man swung the broom-head like a sledgehammer, she jerked back, the broom striking the door frame, and the handle broke in half. Unfortunately the hooded man didn't lose his grip, so he was now holding what amounted to a four-foot spear. He was about a head taller than Danny, and his reach was a foot or more longer than hers.

He thrust the jagged length of wood at Danny, grunting with the effort; she twisted past the thrust and grabbed the broom handle with the thumb and palm of her mutilated hand, pulling it past her in a single motion. The man overbalanced and tumbled into the dark room, knocking things over. It sounded like cartons of books. Danny ducked out through the doorway and danced backward into the big church space like a boxer. She didn't want to fight in a pitch-black, confined area. A couple of seconds later, the man came surging out of the room and Danny understood why he'd been able to locate her so quickly—his hood had fallen back, revealing night vision goggles.

The man launched an all-out assault now, whipping the broom handle back and forth like a sword with one hand; he clipped her on the elbow with it and it hurt like fury, but didn't disable her arm. Then she saw him draw something from his belt and heard the pinging power-up sound of a Taser. If it was a pistol-style unit she was in trouble. She decided not to wait to find out.

Danny grabbed a steel folding chair and bowled it at the man. He swiped it out of the air with his forearm, which knocked the goggles on his face askew. Danny leaped into the gap between them at this moment and struck down against the wrist holding the Taser with the heel of her fingerless hand; he didn't drop the weapon, but he forgot about the broom handle, which gave Danny an opportunity to grab it and twist it around so that his arm was extended backward. He could either let go or break his wrist. He let go, and attempted to grab Danny instead. She caught his outstretched arm and pulled him toward her. His Taser hand was flailing.

Now the hooded man had forward momentum and nowhere to send it, which gave Danny the advantage. She couldn't do the kind of grips they taught in boot camp, not with so few fingers, but she didn't need much. As he crashed into her, she brought her leg around his and drove his knee downward until it was bent double, hurling him to the floorboards. All of this happened in a single, fluid motion. He might be hard, he might be big, but Danny could tell this man wasn't experienced in dealing with a motivated opponent. She caught a glimpse of his face as he crashed to the floor. He was scared out of his wits. The goggles flew up off his head.

Until this moment, Danny hadn't considered what kind of fight this was. But the terror in the man's face told her. As far as he was concerned, this was a fight to the death. She wasn't going to get away from Happy Town if this man was alive. He had seen *her* face. He would raise the alarm. And there was another, bigger problem: She wasn't a hundred percent certain it was he who had shouted "Who goes there." The voice hadn't come from his direction, although she couldn't be sure with all the echoes.

But Danny didn't want to kill. She hated it. Too many had died already. For the living to slaughter the living in these times was the worst thing of all. It didn't matter: The man made the decision for her. He was on his back and saw her hesitation; while she paused, he got the Taser up and fired it at her head.

Police training had taught Danny the best place to fire electrode-based weapons wasn't center mass, as with a firearm, but at the belt. One electrode in the lower abdomen and another in the thigh was the perfect shot. Such a hit would buckle the leg and fold up the torso so the target was completely helpless. Her attacker had not been trained. He fired the electrodes at her like a handgun, aiming for her face; she felt the coiled wires whip past her neck, but the electrodes didn't catch her skin or her clothing. By that time, she was already diving straight at her attacker. He tried to get his feet up to kick her away, and Danny brought the scalpel into play.

He was okay for a moment, attempting to get back on his feet while Danny shoulder-rolled across the floor to the base of the altar, and then the pain reached his skull. She'd slashed the tendons holding his left knee-cap in place. He made a gurgling cry—trying to suppress the scream, for some reason—and pitched sideways into the folding chairs. The fight was out of him.

Danny wasn't in this merely to defeat him, or she could have stopped there. But the Taser wires singing past her ear had unlocked the killer inside her. Before the man could untangle himself from the chairs, she drove forward, slashing, ripping through his fingers as he threw his hands up to defend his face. His palms split open and the tip of his thumb came off and then she got him hard in the throat. Danny kept hacking until the handle of the scalpel broke, and now the man started to scream at last, but he didn't have time for a single unbroken cry before his voice was drowned in a fountain of foaming, foul-smelling blood.

Danny was soaked in gore. Tasted it in her mouth. It stank like vomit. She was so adrenaline-hot she felt like there ought to be smoke rising off her skin. She backed away from the twisting body of the dying man and scanned the church to see if the noise had attracted any of the guards patrolling outside.

The place was still and empty.

The man bled out, gagging, his heels sliding in his own blood, and then it was quiet. Danny panted for breath and watched the lights of a patrol vehicle wing across the windows, casting beautiful colored projections of the biblical scenes in the glass onto the walls. But it continued past and drove away. Nobody was coming from the street.

Then she heard a voice, hoarse and wheezing: "Bravo."

Danny spun around. Someone else in there with her after all. She couldn't see anyone.

"No need to be frightened," the voice said, from somewhere above her. "As you can see, I'm unarmed."

Danny looked up, her mind short-circuiting. *It couldn't be.*

The voice was coming from Jesus on the cross, now looking down at her with pale, wet eyes.

"Did—did you just make a *joke*?" Danny said, when she found her voice.

"Why, was it funny?"

"No."

The thing on the crucifix was a zero.

A thinker, its hands and feet securely nailed to the cross, a dim sketch in the shadows. Danny saw the outlines of an emaciated male body, almost naked and much abused. It spoke with a southern accent, and right now it was out of air.

It filled its lungs and said, "On to business, then. I saw what you did there. If I was one of your kind, I'd say it was impressive."

"Your kind doesn't use a knife," Danny said, and realized she was still holding the broken handle of the scalpel in her hand. She looked around for the blade and didn't see it.

"You don't like me," the thing on the cross said. When it spoke, its sparse beard wagged.

"No, I don't."

"Plain-spoken. I'd like that, if I gave a damn about anything."

"Why are you here?" Danny asked, grasping at her sanity as her lizard brain shouted for her to run, to get the fuck out of there. She was trying to think of what to do instead: The thing was up too high to destroy it easily, but it was a witness to the fight. It knew she had killed the hooded man. No matter the bizarre situation, it had to be silenced. Her heart was racing and she saw green blossoms behind her eyes, the coils of panic grabbing at her mind. She needed a ladder, or a fifteen-foot pole with a point on the end. Get at the monster's head.

"I have the best gig in town," the zero was saying. "I rest up here safe and sound, and my followers feed me pieces of their own living flesh."

"And children?" Danny said, a ghastly suspicion revealing itself in her mind. "Do they feed you kids? Is that what's going on?"

"I wish I was as lucky as that," the thing said, and again Danny thought she detected amusement in its voice. "I see you are missing some fingers yourself," it added.

"I didn't feed them to one of you fuckers," Danny said, and started looking around her for something she could use to get up there and bash the creature's skull in.

"Wait just a minute, Sugar. You're that sheriff everybody talks about," the zero said. "I recognize you now. Sister of the Dead." Danny stopped moving. The thick burn scars on her back tried to shiver; tendrils of ice trickled along the courses of her nerves. *Sister of the Dead.*

"Got your attention?" the zero went on, drawing another breath. "Thought it would. You're known to us here, you see. Others from your so-called 'Tribe' came here a few days ago, bearing strange tales. My acolytes tell me all kinds of things. You just killed one of them, in fact. I suppose I ought to be very . . . cross. Was that funny?"

"I don't have much of a sense of humor these days," Danny said, wanting to keep the thing talking now. "So you heard who I traveled with? My sister?"

"Yes," the zero said, and took a long, wheezing breath. "And we *thinkers,* as you hot-bloods call us, we have heard of you from our *own* kind, as well. Your *exploits.* We've been trying to get you on your own for some time now, kill you . . . isolate you. It appears we have succeeded in that, at least."

That fuck in the Chevelle, she thought. Trying to get her away from the Tribe. Score one for the undead.

"Okay. You've got me isolated. Now what?" Danny said. She'd been gone from the hospital for at least an hour. They were probably already looking for her. When the alarm went up she'd be discovered here, covered in blood, with a mutilated corpse at her feet.

"Do you know how Happy Town works?" the zero asked. "Of course not, or you wouldn't be here. I'm what you would call the 'spiritual leader,' for lack of a better phrase. I am the way and the truth and the light, you understand? Thousands follow me and worship me and feed me of themselves, because I am the Risen Flesh incarnate. Beats working. I play stupid, of course. First got here about six months ago—I'll tell you that story another time. But here's the important thing, Sister of the Dead: I'm not the only of the Risen here in town."

He drew another breath. She was desperate to escape this place—she needed to get the hell out of town entirely, right now, and see about rescuing the Silent Kid from outside, somehow. Otherwise they'd hang her for sure. But this creature was telling her things that might be useful. She ignored the staccato bursts of panic that kept fluttering through her hair like bats at twilight. *Keep talking,* she thought. *But talk faster.*

"There's another of my kind," the zero said, when its lungs were filled again. "And he's oh-so terribly wicked you would not believe. He hides what he is. Only one or two of you hot-bloods know his secret. Unlike me, he plays at being a living human. So far, he has gotten away with it. You mortals know him only as 'the Architect.' I don't know if he's really an architect, of course." The Risen Flesh breathed again, but Danny thought he was pausing more for effect than for air. She was right.

"The Architect and I don't see eye to eye, and not just because I'm up here. That's another joke. Was it funny?"

"No."

"It doesn't matter. His headquarters are in the bank across the street. The brick building with a white porch. Even now, at the end of the world, the real governing is still done inside banks. But you're impatient, I can tell. So here's why I'm so glad to have this chat with you. A large number of people in town are extremely unhappy to see their children sent away . . . their fragrant, juicy children. It is only a matter of time before there's a revolution. There is another shipment of recently-arrived children supposed to travel up to the resort in five days. Something has to be done before then, or there will be riots. This place will *burn.* When that happens, the unbelievers won't spare this church, or me, unless someone carries me away in time. But I don't want it to come to that. I have the perfect strategy for survival right here, if only the Architect didn't overplay his hand."

It stared at Danny with its cloudy eyes and she thought it was smiling through its lank beard. It inhaled and said, "That's where you come in. It pains me to say that I need your help. My acolytes are useless, as you just demonstrated. But I can't confide in any of the other locals. I need someone to take the Architect down, before he takes *me* down, in the most literal sense."

Danny was past the point of bewilderment, unsure how to react. She said nothing, and the Risen Flesh took this as an indication that she was waiting to hear his proposition.

"I want you to get through to the Architect. And then I want you to kill him, Sister of the Dead."

The adrenaline from the fight had worn off; Danny felt sick and cold and afraid. She wanted to escape. But they needed to close the deal.

"What's in it for me?" she asked.

"Anonymity. You were never here. I'll tell my acolytes someone else did this killing, someone from the Architect's side of town. I can lie, you know. I'm practically human."

"So I kill the big bad dead dude, the kids stay here, and you and me never met, is that right?"

"You have my word."

"I guess we can't shake hands," Danny said, and slipped out the back of the church.

4

Danny fled back through the darkness, stinking of blood and sweat. The rasping voice of the Risen Flesh was in her ears, and her mind whirled with the things he had told her.

There was little time.

She'd been gone from the hospital an hour and a half at least, but so far there were no search parties rushing around, no whistles. Now that she had survived the lethal combat in the church, she sure as hell didn't want to get caught and beheaded by a bunch of volunteer cops.

She shed the blood-stinking sneakers, sweatshirt, and jacket, and stuffed them deep in the Dumpster she'd found on the way out of the hospital grounds. Then she entered the same way she'd left, through the basement locker room window. Still no guards. In the locker room there were sinks and showers; she didn't dare run a shower at full strength, lest it be overheard, but she let the hot water trickle down on her, lathered herself with grainy industrial soap, and by the dim light of the exit sign she eventually determined the water was running clear. She was clean enough. She dried herself off with coarse paper towels, stuffed the bloodstained pants and shirt up inside a plumbing access hatch, and ventured naked into the basement hallway. No one. Dead quiet.

Six minutes later, she let herself into the room she had awakened in and hurried toward the bed. If the zero on the cross was lying to her, she was about to climb into her deathbed. Literal-minded as the zero thinkers were, it didn't seem possible the thing could lie—but then again, they weren't supposed to tell jokes, either. So their weird bargain might well have been a set-up to get her out of the church without destroying the monster inside. In that case, she had been outsmarted by a corpse.

"Welcome back," a voice said, and Danny involuntarily jumped as if the Taser had hit her at last. She spun around and saw a shape in the shadows: Dr. Joe Higashiyama was sitting in a chair by the door, his left ankle propped on his right knee.

"I went to take a shower," Danny said, and felt it was possibly the worst excuse any human being had ever invented.

Joe stood up, nodding. "I see that. Did you soil yourself?"

"Yes," Danny said. "I threw away my clothes."

"There's more under your bed," Joe said. "You helped me get them, in fact. Back when we met at that hospital down south. But listen, the next time you want to take a shower, keep it under an hour. Otherwise you'll catch cold and have to stay in bed all day. And then I can't give permission to move you out of here, and they can't throw you out of Happy Town or arrest you or anything. Do you understand?"

Danny couldn't believe her luck. "Yes, I do," she said. "Thank you."

Joe stood at the door, leaning on the handle. "In the morning, I'll let your friend Vaxxine know you're not feeling well. Apparently somebody on the outside told her you had an episode and got taken in here. She came rushing right to town along with that quiet boy. She must think you're pretty cool to take a risk like that."

He closed the door behind him. Danny's mind was reeling. She found another loose shirt and drawstring pants under her bed and dragged them on with trembling fingers. Then she crawled into the bed, the mattress fooshing air through its plastic cover, and pulled the blankets up to her chin. The comatose kid in the other bed lay unmoving, eyes half-open, mouth agape. That monster in the church knew Danny would never give away its secret intelligence—she had more to lose than it did. But it might very well intend to have a proxy accuse her of the killing.

She intended to lie awake until she heard the inevitable outcry go up when the corpse in the church was discovered, or when Joe betrayed her and they came to sever her head, but the silence of the predawn hours was absolute, and in two minutes, despite her best efforts, she was asleep.

5

Vaxxine was staring at her, head tilted, mouth slightly pursed. She was so lost in thought that it took her a moment to realize Danny had opened her eyes. She blinked and smiled.

"Danny. You look terrible," she said, affectionately.

"You sound like my friend Amy," Danny replied. Her voice was hoarse, but she didn't feel ill. It was the freezing air of last night, that was all. Amy. Where the hell was she now?

Danny tried to sit up; Vaxxine touched a button on the side of the bed and it motored into a lounge chair position. It was daylight now, with a bleachy overcast that made it impossible to tell the time without a clock.

"They gave me a new wheelchair," Vaxxine said. "I didn't need it, but I took it anyway. Joe says you're not well enough to leave town."

"Yes. Are we alone?"

"Except for him," Vaxxine said, tipping her chin at the boy in the other bed. "Why so paranoid? You're always paranoid, Danny."

"You would be, too, if you knew what I knew."

"Well you don't know what I know, do you?"

"Jesus, it tastes like a rat had babies in my mouth. What is it? You go first," Danny said. She wasn't sure whether she should tell anyone about her encounter of the previous night, even in an edited form. But if Danny decided to act on what she knew, Vaxxine would surely end up in jeopardy. Danny would have to warn her before things went down. Whatever that was going to be. Danny had no idea how to handle this.

Vaxxine reached around into the big canvas bag hung on the back of her chair and fished out a grubby can of Tab. "All I could find," she said, and handed it to Danny. Danny drank the entire can in a series of greedy chugs.

Vaxxine continued with her voice pitched down to a husky whisper: "So Danny, while you were in here with the headache, I was all around town today. Hard to believe but it's a proper town with shops and everything, but you can't buy anything unless you have what they want to barter, and it's a different thing for every shop. So the butcher man has fresh meat, and my mouth is watering like a rain cloud because I haven't seen fresh meat in a year and a half. But he's only taking gasoline today, not gold, canned food, or ammunition like a regular person. So those who have gasoline get the fresh meat.

"So I go to the laundry, because my clothes smell like an extinct volcano, and what do they say: 'We're only taking nails, screws, and lumber today.' They don't take anything else in trade. So what do I do? I go to the clothes shop. All the latest fashions since before the zeroes. And I ask the lady, 'What do you take in trade?' And she says, it doesn't matter, we only serve Americans here.'

"Anyway I obviously didn't like *that* much. It reminded me that you didn't like the sound of the place. I thought, 'Maybe's she's right. The crazy sheriff,' so I went down by the train station to see what's doing. That was interesting. There's an engine on the siding, almost done with the overhaul, with one passenger car behind it. Men working on it like they have a tight schedule. And there's barbed wire and fences all around the place, fit to keep out a lion.

"You were right about something, by the way: The main track is as shiny as water going east, so it gets plenty of use, but more rusty going west. Apparently they rarely travel that direction. I could be a detective, you know. And there's notices with all these names on them, pages and pages up on the boards there at the station, all the names of the children who have gone to their safe place. Hundreds of them. Name, age, and the names of their parents or guardians. And a departure date for each group of children. There's always some parents hanging around looking at it or arguing with the guards."

"Does the list say who's going next?" Danny asked.

"Only the ones who went before. I saw some other odd things, too, like there's a bank building in the middle of town that's guarded like it's got the crown jewels inside. But anyway the whole day was like that, finding out Happy Town isn't all that happy. There's a place down one street like a brothel, I didn't even go near. And there's a part of town nobody can go into out past the station, like with warehouses in it—could be that's where they keep the food, or could be the children. I didn't see a single child all day. There isn't a one in the whole place."

Danny didn't want another conflict right now, but it had to be asked:

"The Silent Kid is back there?"

"I didn't know what else to do, Danny. I couldn't care for him on my own, and those scouts of yours—nothing personal but I didn't like the look of them. They showed up in the morning on their great big motorbikes and told me all about you from outside while I covered them with a bang-bang from inside. It took me a while to believe them. Some of them are still at the house with the cute little dog. Big fellows, the ones got beat with the ugly stick, they took off on their motorbikes. Said they had some scouting to do."

"Bless your fucking heart, Topper," Danny said to the ceiling. Then she turned her attention back to Vaxxine. "I knew this place sucked," she went on. "I knew it the first time I even heard about it. There *is* no safe place. You know why? Because as soon as a single live human being shows up somewhere, that place isn't safe anymore. We're worse than the fucking zeroes."

"You are a very bitter woman, Sheriff. Me, I have the racists tell me I can't shop and there's no law to say I can anymore. Half the places I can't go at all, because wheelchair access doesn't exist, so there's no ramps or lifts, and plenty of stairs. I could go on and on. But I don't. People are bad doings, you're right. But they're also the best angels in the world. Who keeps looking out for you? Me. And I'm as human as they come. Even you"—here she lowered her voice until it was almost inaudible—"risking your ass for kids you don't even know. You're an angel, too. So just you remember that. The only safe place is with a friend, and that means there's a live human."

Danny wanted to change the subject. "Did you . . . hear anything weird happened last night?"

Vaxxine's face went serious again; she even looked behind her at the door and past Danny at the boy in the coma, making sure they weren't overheard, before she whispered:

"Funny you should ask that. Early this morning, I left the disgusting flophouse they stuck me in to come check up on you, and halfway here I rolled past this big old church downtown, and there was crazy business in there, I can tell you. There must have been a hundred people arguing and shoving each other, and other ones wailing like babies, and then they carried out a dead man in a hoodie. He was cut to pieces and covered all in blood. People were afraid in the street. I got away from there myself just as fast as my wheels would take me, because all the deputies or whatever they are down that way were pointing their guns at anybody who dared walk by. You'd think they were looking for a confession.

"And they found a bloody coat and shoes right outside in the hospital trash, can you believe it? Looks like a big man did the killing. That's what they're saying."

Danny didn't respond to this, but examined Vaxxine's face. She was so dark, her skin so lustrous, that she appeared to be made of some polished wood or stone. There were fine lines like cat whiskers around her eyes, but otherwise her face was smooth. They were close in age, maybe five years apart, and yet Danny knew her own face was weathered like barnboard.

There wasn't a damned thing she could do about her companion's suspicions, but she didn't like the feeling she had that Vaxxine guessed more than she said. She didn't like that Joe guessed even more.

As if cued by her thoughts, Joe knocked at the door and let himself in. Danny glimpsed a new armed guard in blaze orange vest in the hallway, getting in the way of the nursing staff as they went back and forth.

"So you're not feeling any better," Joe said, and pulled up a chair. "What a pity."

"I'm not?" Danny said, failing to catch on. Then, when Joe and Vaxxine had both stared at her for a while, she stated, "Yeah, no, I'm not."

"That's too bad," said Vaxxine.

"Why are you doing this?" Danny asked Joe, watching his face carefully.

"I'm a doctor," Joe said, fanning himself with the clipboard he held in his hand. "You are my patient, and you have bleeding in your brain. That's why you're having the headaches."

"Okay," Danny said. She'd known this since the conversation she'd eavesdropped on the previous day. She didn't bother trying to fake a reaction.

"We can talk about that later, if you're not in the mood," Joe said, nonplussed. He had clearly been expecting a bigger response. But he had something else to say: "Also, there's something I feel personally responsible for. That boy of yours is in our custody, and you didn't get to choose what happened to him. Miss Vaxxine here was dealing with you and they sent him off with the other children. He was only supposed to be here for a few hours, but they put him in the system and would not listen to me or Vaxxine when I said he hadn't been released by you. He's waiting for the train with the other children. I hold myself personally responsible for that."

"Don't stick your neck out too far," Danny said. "I'm a big girl. I came here with a migraine, you lost my kid, I took a long shower last night, and now I don't feel good. That's it. *I'll* deal with the boy. *You don't fucking touch him.*" The calm she'd started speaking with had boiled off and rage had replaced it.

"I wasn't offering to," Joe said, taken aback by Danny's sudden anger. He held his hands up in front of his shoulders like he wanted to push the fury away from him. "I just want to help. Jesus."

Danny felt helpless and it made her anger worse. Vaxxine dragging the kid here while she was out cold, and now sitting there wide-eyed like she didn't get it. This amateur doctor with his stolen medical supplies and his smug conspiratorial manner. That damn kid with his big worried eyes, expecting her to save his ass. She felt the fury spit, sizzle, and turn to steam, drying up like the calm that had preceded it.

Then she said, "Listen. We can't operate as a team. I don't know how far either of you dare to go. You've gone too far already, I think. I can't count on you. There's a guard outside this door and they're looking all over town for a murderer and there's a trainload of kids waiting to get shipped off, and my kid is not supposed to be there. This is a sick, fucked-up town. The less you're involved in my business, the better."

That was a long speech for Danny. She had to suck in air at the end of it and was reminded of the crucified one, the Risen Flesh. Vaxxine looked hurt; the good-guy enthusiasm had gone out of Joe's face. Danny looked defiantly at them both.

"I see why you're alone," Vaxxine said, presently, and wheeled herself to the door. She knocked, and the guard held the door open, his arm extended out awkwardly against the hinge side.

"I'm out. Leaving town," she said. "They don't need my kind here, and apparently neither do you."

Vaxxine rolled away.

"Well," Joe said, after he'd run out of rhythms to tap out on his clipboard, then spent a while examining the papers on it as if he'd written anything there, "anyway, you'll need to stay another night for observation. And I think you're going to have visitors soon, so you'll want to be prepared for that."

He gave her a doctorly look as if peering over the top of a pair of bifocals, although he wasn't wearing any, and then stood decisively and strode out of the room, nodding curtly at the guard. The guard took a brief look at Danny with an expression so blank it felt like an accusation, then swung the door shut.

Danny hardly had time to sort through what had just transpired when she heard boots and voices in the hallway. She feigned sleep, one eyelid parted slightly so she could see watery globs of shadow moving beyond her eyelashes. In case anyone rushed her. Two large men, not dressed like the guards, but unmistakably paramilitary, entered the room without fanfare; the orange-vested guard on her door remained outside in the hall. Another man stepped between them and approached her bedside.

Danny opened her eyes. He was clad in a button-down shirt under a safari jacket and his graying hair was discreetly rinsed to give it a little color. He was about fifty, and slightly overweight, which was something Danny hadn't seen in a long time. He wore gloves and tinted glasses.

"Cad Broker," he said, and at first Danny thought he was telling her his job.

Then she understood. "Danny Adelman. What's going on?"

She sat up, feigning feebleness, and tried not to look like she was ready to attack them if anyone made a fast move. Her new hospital shirt had zebras printed all over it.

"Well," said Cad, in a way that made Danny think he was going to add "I'm glad you asked!" Instead he paused, collecting the words in his head. Then he said, "My employer—the mayor, if you will, of Happy Town—wishes to speak with you, and he thought tomorrow might be too late, given how things are speeding up around here. If you're fit enough to be moved, he wants to see you now."

"He's coming here?" *He has balls,* Danny thought. *Dead balls.*

"No, your doctor has agreed you're well enough for a short visit. Come with us to the bank."

Danny didn't have a choice, of course. The hallway guard joined the others in formation behind her, and she knew there was no way she could do them enough damage to escape. It had been more than three-quarters luck that she'd been able to kill the acolyte in the church before he killed her. He had been a poor fighter, slow and uncoordinated. These men appeared to be seasoned and hard, even the guard with the goofy orange vest.

But her spirits improved when the group reached the stair hall she had crept through the previous night, and they were stopped by a brisk-looking suntanned woman with tan hair. She was carrying a grocery bag.

"You'll catch your death in those things," the woman said, rocking her head back and forth like a music teacher keeping time. "Here are some clothes."

Danny emptied the bag and pulled the garments on over her hospital pajamas, right there in the hallway—partly to show she didn't care how she looked, and partly because one more layer would help keep her warm if she did make a break for freedom once they were outside. Jeans four inches too long, a baggy red turtleneck, a brown hooded sweatshirt with a pink sequined unicorn on the chest. She took her sweet time putting on the provided socks and shoes—cheap drugstore sneakers a little too narrow, but a hell of a lot better than hospital slippers. She double-knotted the laces. The woman handed her a musty quilted parka with duct tape patches—a worn-out discard from someone. Danny didn't mind. With shoes and clothes, she had two of the three keys to any escape: distance and time. The shoes would carry her far, and the warm jacket would stave off hypothermia as long as she kept moving. The third key to escape was opportunity. She was going to have to improvise that part, if it became necessary.

She didn't see Joe or any of the hospital staff as they left; she suspected the way had been cleared on purpose. There was a big late-model American sedan idling in the school yard. They got in, with Cad in the passenger seat, Danny in the middle of the backseat next to the tan woman (whose name was Nancy), a guard crushed in on either side, and the third guard driving. Despite the cramped quarters, Danny made a show of cuffing her jeans so they didn't get caught under her heels. In fact she was also leaning forward to take an inventory of the guards' equipment. If anybody had an unsecured knife sheath or a boot pistol, she might be able to take control of the situation. They hadn't handcuffed her or put a gun against her neck. She certainly would have.

But they drove through the suburb and got onto the main street (Galveston Avenue, Danny saw it was called), and drove halfway down to the train station past the memorial statue. Several guards were stationed along the route, watching the civilians who moved around the streets. Then the sedan pulled up to the curb in front of the bank opposite the church. It was a typical small-town establishment designed to look reliable and permanent, with granite steps and windowsills and clean white trim, the kind of bank where old people looked at their jewelry in the vault.

Everyone got out of the car. Danny didn't feel any violence emanating from the men. It didn't mean a thing, but at least they weren't trying to menace her. They were strictly at work. She followed Cad and Nancy into the bank with the three guards in a wedge behind her; they were as watchful as the security detail on a Mexican district attorney.

Inside, they crossed the marble-armored lobby to an elevator hall. The car was already open to the ground floor. The guard in the vest stayed in the lobby, probably not cleared for the inner sanctum; the other two accompanied Danny, Nancy, and Cad up to the third floor. The ascent of the car felt bizarre to Danny—it had been a long time since she rode in an elevator, since before the evacuation of San Francisco. The doors opened on a big wood-framed mirror and a hallway extending to either side. Danny saw her reflection as they got out of the car and turned right: a gaunt, green-eyed face, florid and chapped like a bricklayer's hands, surmounted by an owl's nest of red hair. She didn't look like anything much. Not a warrior. Not the Sister of the Dead.

There was an office at the end of the wood-paneled hall. The glass in the door was frosted, and on the glass was written MANAGER in gold paint. Cad knocked on the door with one knuckle.

"Mr. Vormann?"

"Come in," said a voice behind the door.

They went in.

The office looked like the set of a western movie musical: Everything was brown and heavily ornamented, and the opal glass shades on the brass lamps were green as a gambler's eyeshade. It was dark in there, the velvet window curtains drawn shut. The air stank of cigar smoke, which wasn't a surprise—the man seated in a fat red leather chair by the unlit gas fireplace was smoking one. He sat in the angle of the darkest shadow in the room. The only light cast back by his figure was a reflection from his dark-tinted spectacles. Danny immediately understood why he smoked filthy cigars and sat in the dark—if this was the Architect, he was a zero. Mask the smell and hide the face.

"Sit," he said, and aimed the glowing ash of the cigar at a chair beneath a bright pendant lamp. That put her in the best-lit corner of the room—a disadvantage. She sat in the chair next to it, partly in shadow. One of the guards stepped outside into the hall; the other stood by the door, rocking his heels on the thick green carpet. Nancy and Cad remained standing to Danny's left, like nervous parents at a school interview. She waited, unwilling to start the conversation.

"I trust you're not too unwell for this conversation," he said. "I've heard a great deal about you."

Danny didn't respond. She was here. Get on with it.

"I'm Martin Vormann," he said. "I am the provisional head of operations here at Happy Town, and helped found the place. The Architect, they call me, because I am the architect of the system. I don't know how much you know about our situation here, Miss Adelman, but to be blunt it isn't good."

He paused to take a drag on his cigar. Danny noted that he didn't take a breath after his speech: He inhaled directly through the cigar, inflating his chest. Nobody alive could suck down a lungful of acrid cigar smoke that large. She said nothing.

"You see," the Architect continued, smoke puffing out with each syllable like frozen winter breath, "we have so many parents here who sent their children down the line and now regret it. It breaks our hearts. But this place isn't safe. There's an immense swarm not a half-day's walk from here. We hold the line, but these out-of-control people rioting and making demands and trying to get their children back, it's taking far too many of our brave guards off the front. We've had to triple security and enforce a curfew, can you imagine? If this keeps up, one of these days that swarm is going to spill over our defenses and this town will be overrun. Are you aware of our program for securing America's future?"

"Government bonds?" Danny said.

"I assume that's a witticism. The program to which I refer is the Children's Security and Wellbeing Initiative. Once a child is brought here, we check him or her for illness. The sick go to the hospital in which you have sadly languished; the others are sent once a week to our secure facility."

"That's great," Danny said, so without feeling she might as well have been undead herself.

"You must be curious about that," the Architect said. "Everyone is. We send the children five miles upstream to a defended island position. It's a resort, in fact, once a luxury spa retreat for wealthy Victorians taking the train to the West Coast. The place is in the middle of a deep reservoir, connected to the land only by a bridge, and it's entirely secure. There is also a hydroelectric station at the dam. That's where we get our electricity from."

"Excellent," Danny said. She tried to look like this was all news to her.

"Now you may think I'm joking about the resort, but I am not. The children are fed, bathed, even given a little education. There's a heated swimming pool. How about that? Children playing in a heated swimming pool, in this day and age!"

He'd taken a further two cigar-breaths by this time; watching the amount of smoke he consumed made Danny's guts squirm. Even if he couldn't feel it, Danny could. His lungs must have been as dry as stale bread. She didn't know why he was spinning a tale for her. Did he want her to believe what he was saying? Or was he compelled to talk to his victims before he killed them, like the villain in a spy movie?

The Architect went on: "Things were going quite well until recently. Our authority was respected and the system honored, if not loved, because it was best for the little ones. But then the Preacher moved into the church across the street. He brought with him an object extraordinarily disgusting to behold. Cad? Nancy? Would you step outside for a minute? The guard, too," he added, when the guard showed no sign of leaving.

"Do you think that's wise?" Nancy asked, from the doorway.

"Ms. Adelman is very weak with a serious brain injury. And she wouldn't harm me. I'm the only individual here who can make a bargain he can keep."

So it was going to be a bargaining session. There was something he wanted her to do.

The door closed behind Danny and she did for a moment consider springing across the room and hacking the Architect to pieces with the big scissors she'd seen on the console table by the door. She didn't move, however.

First, hear the offer.

"Ah, that's better," the Architect said. "Would you like a drink? I heard you enjoy a taste now and again. I have some excellent whiskey, although I can't touch the stuff myself. Bad for my health."

"I quit," Danny said. In fact, she wanted a drink right now with every cell of her being. "Anyway, how do you know what I like?"

"You're the Sister of the Dead. Practically famous in some circles."

"Don't call me that," Danny replied.

"Why not? You should embrace it," the Architect said. "It's your ticket to the future."

At last, a cloud of smoke spilled out of his mouth.

"Now listen," he continued. "No games. You know what I am. I know what you are. Your sister wasn't quite as isolated from our kind as you may have thought. Those long walks she used to take. The feeding expeditions. Hard not to bump into one of us now and then."

Danny remembered the figure that she'd glimpsed during Kelley's last feeding trip. What else had Kelley not thought fit to tell her about?

"The attack with the hunters. Truck plaza. Was that yours?"

"It was not, and I am deeply sorry it occurred. I feel responsible because the perpetrator was seeking to collect children for entrance to Happy Town."

For the first time, the Architect rose to his feet. He began to pace, very slowly, across his end of the room.

"This is a world in which mother may devour her child, brother may slaughter sister—we don't care how the children get here. We don't want to know. We just want to get them out of that godforsaken wasteland and into the safe, clean environment we have created. Where they can get medical treatment, nutrition, education, and untroubled sleep. It was a terrible compromise we had to make, taking in children whom we knew to have been taken by stealth or force. But it worked, and now we have threefold the number of admissions. We may open a second facility soon, as our first is near capacity."

Having delivered this statement, which sounded rehearsed, he lowered himself into his chair again. Then he did something almost human: He drew a handkerchief from his pocket, as if to dab the sweat from his brow. But he must have remembered he would never sweat again, because instead he refolded the linen and put it back inside his jacket.

"So what's your pitch?" Danny asked. Nothing he'd said mattered to her so far.

"Let me tell you a little more about our situation. Otherwise you'll never understand why we do what we do."

"It's your fucking town. Talk all you want."

He nodded, taking no offense. "You must be wondering how we secure our perimeter. It's a wonderful secret in a way, but humanity isn't quite ready for it yet. Have you encountered anyone who seemed to be half-alive and half-dead?"

"Like Kelley?"

"This will interest you. Mr. Broker, whom you have met, is a very special, new kind of person. The acolytes at that damned church across the street are the same sort, although terribly misguided. You see, the condition—I hesitate to call it a disease—that first created my kind is mutating, refining itself. In fact my kind is the result of such a mutation; had I turned a few months earlier, I'd have been one of those brainless things that wander the land."

"Lucky you."

"There's a new infection going around. The lucky victim becomes one of us very slowly, a sort of metamorphosis. Those infected retain their human character and personality for the most part, but lose the absurdly inefficient metabolism. And they become immortal, of course, like me. As I'm sure you guessed."

"Is that why Broker's wearing the makeup?"

"Yes, exactly. He's a little too far along in the transformation to pass for living without a little added color. Soon, he will have to join the sentinels at the perimeter and allow the last of the life to seep out of him. It's the sentinels that keep the town safe, you see. They're unliving, but thinkers like me, completely intact in the mind. The stupid ones can't abide the scent of us. They stay back. After a few months on the perimeter, the fully transformed unliving joins a lottery to determine if he or she will travel up the line, where we maintain the secure facility for children between the ages of two and twelve."

Danny had heard enough. The acolyte she'd killed was half-zombie. These fuckers were collecting the kids to eat, she was almost certain. The only thing she didn't understand was why this evil creature was telling her all about it, knowing that she *must* do something to stop him.

"I see aggression in your face," the Architect observed. "Don't attempt anything, please. Hear me out. We're not eating the children, you understand? Heavens, no. We are raising them as if they were our own, so that there will be unliving and living in a new, tolerant world, side by side, putting away their differences to forge a new future of unity and understanding."

"Bullshit," Danny said.

"I'd send you over there for a look tomorrow, if I could. You'd see how well we keep them. But it isn't practical. The town is about to come apart, and all because that monstrous cretin with the nails in him thinks he can snack his way through eternity."

"So recap for me," Danny said. "What you're telling me is you have how many—a hundred, two hundred, three hundred smart zeroes—"

"I'll have you know I consider that an offensive, racist term."

"—Zombies, like that better? You've got less than a company's strength of your buddies out there keeping the moaners off the living. That's right neighborly. But what are you eating? Kelley lived on rats. You fuckers don't look like you eat rats to me."

"We subsist on criminals, outlaws, and scavengers, primarily. Consumed methodically, a single body can provide a dozen of us with enough sustenance to last a week."

"So you admit you're eating people."

"If I told you otherwise, you wouldn't believe it. Our relationship must rest upon complete honesty."

"So how did you find out who I was?" She already knew something based on what the Risen Flesh had told her, but she was pretending that conversation never happened. The Architect might not treat her so well if he knew she was taking offers from both sides.

"From time to time, your sister would make contact. Oh, nothing *bad,*" he said, off Danny's scowl. "Very discreet. She was one of the deadpan, as we affectionately call them. No emotions, really. An earlier form of the condition, of which one might immodestly say I'm the flower. But of all of us, she is the only one ever to have retained a personal human connection. She spoke of you with admiration, you know. Even without emotions, she knew you were a giant among the living, a fighting queen."

"Don't blow smoke up my ass," Danny said. Thinking of smoke, she observed that the cigar had gone out, the Architect forgetting it in his zeal to suck his lungs full of air so he could make long, impassioned speeches. "I left her to be destroyed."

"We never could get through to her. In the dozen or so times one of our kind made contact with her, she was always defiant. *There's more,* she would say. *There's more than we know.* I think she was talking about existence, or the difference between living and unliving. We would have treated her so well if she'd escaped your primitive followers. It's terrible."

Here the Architect hung his head and pantomimed a tear rolling down his cheek with his finger. The interview so far had lasted half an hour. Danny decided she'd probably learned everything he had to tell her; it was time to get to business.

"There's a boy under my protection here. I want him back. He was never supposed to be processed here."

"The quiet one. Well that's the thing, isn't it," the Architect said, relighting the stub of the cigar with a match. Danny noticed he held the match by the very end, as far from the flame as possible. Unfeeling, unhealing flesh.

He had to be careful. After another scorching drag, he continued: "The boy is scheduled for the next train to the resort. That's four days from now."

He leaned forward until Danny could see the cloudy eyes behind the dark lenses. "I'll be frank with you, Sheriff. From what I've heard about you, there's only one person in this town ruthless and violent enough to have killed an acolyte in his own church."

Danny opened her mouth to speak, to make noises of denial.

The Architect raised a hand to cut her off, palm outward. "Don't bother. I don't want to know. The point is, if I could find the person who was able to accomplish that task, I would want that person to finish the job for me. I would want that person to kill the blasphemous effigy hanging in the church and expose it as an abomination to all, before that damnable preacher delivers another of his rabble-rousing sermons and this whole place comes apart."

"And if that person delivered, you'd hand over the Kid."

"For starters. I might also be able to arrange safe passage all around the countryside for such a person. Almost as far south as the Alabama border and east to Albany, New York."

"You don't have that kind of reach," Danny said, not trying to hide the contempt in her voice. "There are assholes like you stalking all the roads, grabbing kids and eating them, collecting them like fucking frogs in a bucket. You can't arrange safe *shit*."

The Architect tried to laugh, but only made a sound like a broom on a concrete floor. "I was told you were quite intelligent. Do you imagine we don't recruit from our side of the life-death divide?"

One for you, twenty for me.

Suddenly it all came together in Danny's head.

The entry fee for the living was one child. For the undead, it was twenty.

The Chevelle driver had been collecting the toll. The mutilated things hanging in the ranch house had been older, maybe thirteen or fourteen years old. The driver must have been eating the ones that were too old while he gathered enough younger children for entry into the secret, undead side of Happy Town.

"Did one of your kind show up a few days back with kids he got off the Tribe? Maybe bragging about his trained pack of hunters? The truck stop attack. You probably heard."

"Why yes. You'd come after him so relentlessly he was practically frightened. Brought lots of children to us in terrible condition. We were appalled. He has been disciplined. The children are recuperating; they will be making the trip to the safe place with the others."

"Disciplined?"

"We treat our own just as harshly as the living, ma'am. We are scrupulously fair."

With that, the Architect leaned back, reaching out to a mini-fridge behind his desk. He opened the door and light flooded out. Inside there was a plastic deli container; inside the container was a human jaw—the bony mandible, with teeth, chin, and lips. Danny saw fillings in several of the teeth. Bloodless meat, resembling pork, hung in gobs from the severed parts of the jaw.

"He left this with us. We let him go back into the wilderness, of course. He'll starve. Before we removed that from him, he confessed you almost caught him on two separate occasions. That's the spirit I'd like to see applied to my own enemy across the way."

Danny swallowed the bile that gurgled up out of her belly.

"So I wipe out the wall hanger and you let me leave town with the child, the woman in the wheelchair, a little guy named Ernie that your people captured up a couple days back, and anybody else I choose?"

"I didn't say that," the Architect said, sucking in air through his teeth.

"No, I just said it. Those are my conditions. Anybody I used to travel with who wants out of here can go. And you allow a tour of inspection of that so-called resort of yours. If you got nothing to hide, you got no reason to keep these people out of contact with their fucking kids."

"It's not so simple. You clearly don't understand human nature the way we do. Because we're objective. You living, your whole worldview is tainted because you came from women, from mothers. We transcend that. You see, we come from *death*. Your world ends when you die, and ours is merely beginning. We see you for what you are, Sheriff. If we allow your kind to do whatever you want, you'll poison the minds of the children against us, make more and more irrational demands, and ruin our mutual chances of survival in an uncertain world. The living can't go on without us, don't you see that? And we need the living."

"Then I guess it's a hearty 'fuck you,'" Danny said, and stood up. She kept one hand on the arm of her chair. She could kill this son of a bitch dead with it before his people could even get the door open.

"Not so hasty," the Architect replied, hastily. "I'll grant you everything except the last condition. If you *alone* wish to go down the line, you are welcome. Be an emissary to the undead, report back, make people understand. But nobody else. And this task I've set for you is a *secret.* As for the rest, you can have the child and your friends, although you're cursing them to a terrible world. There's no coming back. If you *remain* with us, we could make you a very influential and important person. But if you leave, you return only as an enemy. Are we understanding each other?"

"It's pretty fucking clear. But listen, I'm not fit for a couple days, maybe a week. There's some shit wrong with my head. And before I do anything, I'll need some things," Danny said. "And no more guards."

"Agreed, agreed, and agreed. And one more thing," the Architect added. Danny waited. She could almost hear the sound of his skull caving in under the blow from the chair. She wanted to *do* it.

"You must have made a deal with the thing in the church, am I right? Otherwise you would have destroyed him. Whatever it was, that deal is now null and void. Are we clear?"

6

Ten minutes later, Danny was on her way back to the school-hospital. It had begun to snow. Nancy and Cad Broker flanked her in the backseat, with the guards up front. Danny found herself shrinking away from Cad, something she hadn't done with Kelley. But the idea of a half-man, half-zero was somehow even more repulsive to Danny than an animated corpse. Like it might be contagious to the touch. And she knew nothing about the man, except he was probably insane, to willingly relinquish his life like that. He could still bite.

It was still relatively early in the day, the streets not as busy as usual, people staying in because of the precipitation. There wasn't a rush hour here. People didn't have jobs in the old-fashioned sense. Let it snow. Danny noticed there was a pair of hooded acolytes standing on the church steps, watching them leave; she wondered how differently the fight would have gone if she'd known the thing she was fighting was only half-human. It explained the foul stench of the acolyte's blood. Somehow it was changing, and whatever death was occurring there, it made his blood stink like puke.

Her mind returned to Cad sitting beside her, a sour sack of vomit blood, half-dead, half-living, and she felt her own gorge rising.

Back at the hospital, Danny found herself left unguarded.

Nancy had let her keep the clothes she'd been given. Apparently, Danny was no longer considered a security risk. It made sense—she'd been authorized to kill. Let her have the room to operate. She felt sick in her guts and spent a long time with her head hanging over a toilet in the girls' room. When she didn't throw up after twenty minutes, she returned to her bed, weary and ill, her thoughts worn out.

Right now she didn't have a plan. She'd need one very soon, however. But there was a lot to process: "There are more of us than you think, and we're everywhere," the Architect had said, as Danny was leaving his smoke-stale office. She, of all people, was having long conversations with living corpses who ate human flesh to maintain themselves. It was wolves talking to an unusually violent sheep. But she was still on the menu, and they'd eventually kill her, if not eat her. There was no way these things would risk having a proven zero-killer like Danny around.

So she knew there were two plans to make: The first was how to destroy one or both of the monsters running Happy Town. The second was to escape the place before they destroyed her right back, with as many kids in tow as possible.

The comatose teenager watched eternity go by in the gloom of the classroom. Danny watched the presidents. None of them had known what would happen, or that there would one day be a *last* president. She eventually slept a little, drifting in and out, waking with a start every time her dreams stuffed the doorway with rotten undead. At some point in the early afternoon the snow stopped falling.

7

The bed wasn't particularly comfortable by ordinary standards, but to a body accustomed to sleeping in the front seats of cars, the simple fact of being fully prone in a warm room was luxury beyond compare. When

Danny awoke, it was because lunch had arrived; another male nurse was backing a cart into the room. He turned around, and she cried out:

"Patrick!"

He put a finger to his lips, tipping his eyes at the door by way of caution, and rolled the food to her bedside. "Let's get you upright," he said, operating the bed motors to get her into the full sitting position. "Today we have shepherd's pie, creamy whole milk from an actual cow that Amy just gave a checkup to, coffee, bread, and jam. Fuck a duck, you're skinny. You've completely let yourself go."

"What are you doing here?" Danny asked, stupid with surprise. Her mind was whirling. She thought she had no allies in the Tribe, and yet here was Patrick, chattering along like a jaybird just as cheerful as could be.

"I'm Amy's official nurse. They let me work here while they figure out the Tribe. It's the largest group they've had in quite a while; most are still outside the wall in this kind of shantytown. Anybody with useful skills the town keeps, that's how it really works. If they like me, they'll say I brought in child X; meanwhile if they don't like child X's father, they'll throw him out. The system here is completely corrupt."

"I figured that much. God, It's good to see you, Patrick."

"Me, too," he said. "To see you, I mean. Not me, I can see myself any time. Don't judge me for coming here. I wasn't going to participate except for two things: First, things totally imploded as soon as you left and I'm pretty sure I'd have got killed sometime soon . . . and second, if you turned up anywhere, I figured you would turn up here. Where's Wulf?"

"Died in his sleep," Danny said.

"I'm sorry. Amy thought that was going to happen pretty soon. She said the way his nose was turning blue meant his heart was congested."

"Amy," Danny muttered, and her eyes went to the window.

"We don't hate you, Danny," Patrick said, his voice low and soft, the way people spoke at funerals back when there were such things. "Some people do, but they're assholes. What hurts is *you* hating *us*."

"But I don't—" Danny began.

"Even after what happened?"

"You didn't start that."

"Oh, eat your food," Patrick said. "I can't deal with it when you're being reasonable. I'm going to check on your roommate. We can talk once you're sedated by carbohydrates."

As it happened, they didn't resume their conversation until noon. Patrick came in with a cart laden with sheets, towels, hospital gowns, and washing materials; he started by changing Danny's bed linens, and chatted with her in low tones. Danny stood by the window and mostly listened. Patrick told her that the administrators of Happy Town (which was the worst name imaginable—*underpromise and overdeliver*, he often used to say on his television show; "Happy Town" just screamed hubris) were taking a special interest in the Tribe. And their interest seemed to focus especially on the banty sheriff who led them. He didn't know why.

"There are bureaucrats here, can you believe it? The end of the world happened and we still have bureaucrats. They test everybody before you're allowed into town. And we are not in Kansas anymore, by the way. They asked me if I was gay, what my political orientation was, and whether I believed the zombie outbreak was caused by Islamic militants. They wanted to know if I was religious! Like, 'Hey, are you interested in religion? Separation of church and state? Would you consider converting to a new religion if asked about it?'"

"They Scientologists?" Danny interrupted. She knew the answer, but she wanted to hear more about this question. Patrick was sponge-bathing the comatose youth in the other bed.

"They're looking for converts, I guess. A lot of people feel like their faith doesn't work anymore, these days. You know. They think it's End Times because Walmart is out of business. But—I guess you don't know this yet—there's a religion here in town, and it's pretty twisted. There's a church downtown where they have this crucified zero standing in for Jesus. I think the bureaucrats are worried about it."

"Huh," Danny grunted.

"Then they asked a ton of questions about the Tribe. We're better known than I thought. They know a lot of inside stuff. Who the players are, first of all. A lot of questions about you. I tried not to sound like I knew you personally, right? Because I didn't want to give them any details. Especially about . . . somebody you used to know really well. They were very interested in these rumors that we traveled with a thinker, and I played dumb about it."

"Good idea," Danny said. She could see Patrick was extremely cautious around that subject; it showed her how much of a wall she had erected between herself and the others to keep Kelley safe. She wondered why he was speaking in a near-whisper. The hall guard had been pulled off her room, but they might have had listening devices in place, she supposed.

"Anyhoodles," he went on, flipping the patient on his side, "they wanted to know how many members were permanent to the Tribe, how many vehicles, how much fuel we used per day for how many miles of travel. What hours did we travel per day? And did we know any good places to get medical supplies, food, and weapons? I didn't know anything detailed about all that stuff, but they tried anyway. I wanted to seem real reasonable because I think it was a strike against me that I admitted I was queer."

"So basically they're stuck here and they need eyes and ears out on the road. That's what I'm getting out of this," Danny said. She wondered how the bureaucrats came to know as much as they did, but Patrick wouldn't have been their first interview. They probably talked to that bastard Crawford first. He'd have told them everything he could think of, and more.

"But here's the part I thought you ought to know about," Patrick said, finishing up the sponge bath. He lowered his voice so Danny could hardly hear him. "They asked me about you in some detail. 'The leader of your organization recently departed. Do you know where she went? . . . Is she on good terms with others in the organization? . . . How is she equipped? . . . Does she have traveling companions? . . . Have you communicated with her recently?' The woman asking the questions didn't say *why* she was asking these things, but the *shape* of the questions was telling. You know what it felt like?" he concluded. "It felt like they were thinking of hiring you for a job, and I was one of the references on your résumé."

Patrick turned his attention to Danny, making a noisy show of getting her washed up. He showed her the sponge at one point during the cleanup: It was red with reconstituted blood.

"Don't ask," Danny said. He didn't, but kept on talking, wringing the sponge out and pouring the bloody water out the window.

"Somebody killed a guy at the church last night," he remarked.

"That's too bad," Danny said. She waited, but Patrick seemed to have taken the hint.

"You missed an awful scene back on the road," he continued. "I mean not just the—the thing that happened. But after that, after you went. There were all these arguments. Guns got pointed at people. The chooks went crazy. I thought for sure somebody else was going to die. A bunch of people drove off to find this train station of yours. I went with them because me and Maria were watching all these kids and most of the parents wanted to go that way. We got to this little depot place and there were guards and another big argument broke out. People started throwing punches. Some wanted to go and some wanted to wait and see.

"Then we heard the train whistle, and that was that. A day later we were all in the processing center behind the train station, waiting to be admitted into Happy Town. And now, here you are. One big happy family again," Patrick concluded. "Of people who mostly refuse to speak to each other."

He came for his late-afternoon round and arrived just as Danny was getting out of bed.

"I have to take a dump," she said. "I'm not doing that in a bedpan."

"Try to look ill," Patrick said, and when she didn't: "Perfect."

She allowed Patrick to escort her into the hallway, past a couple of people dressed like surgeons who were struggling to interpret an X-ray print, and down to the girls' room. Those two might have been yoga instructors or massage therapists, Danny thought. There were so few doctors left in the world—or cops, for that matter. The very first people to be attacked and eaten had all been first responders.

On the way back to the room, she announced she was hungry again.

The relatively good rest and the multiple doses of nutritious food seemed to have filled Danny's cells with energy, as if she was made of billions of microscopic batteries all charged up. But this revitalization only served to increase her feeling of being trapped in the schoolroom—and more so, Happy Town in general. It might only be a matter of time before someone figured out she'd already made a move in the church—the Architect guessed as much, but had given her a pass, and Patrick and Dr. Joe certainly had their suspicions. Nor had her unexpected interview with the Architect gone unnoticed by the Risen Flesh and his minions, she was certain. This was no time to lie around. She'd only forced herself to stay idle the last few hours because Dr. Joe was right: The more people thought she was ill, the more room she'd have to maneuver. It didn't occur to her that she *was* ill.

But enough time had passed so that it was clear that she had not been identified by the general population as the killer inside the church, which meant the crucified monster hung up inside it was true to his word. At least so far. He might claim infinite patience, stuck in place as he was, but Danny suspected if she didn't make some move in the Architect's direction very soon, he might decide to reveal her, just to get things moving along. She tried to focus her mind not on her own uncertain fate, but on the plan.

Dr. Joe Higashiyama came by in midafternoon to find Danny getting dressed to go out.

"What are you doing?"

"I'm going for a walk," she said. "Maybe do some shopping. Do you need anything?"

"I don't think you understand," he said. He had a clipboard in his hand and kept looking at it as if his lines were written on it. "Your brain is bleeding. This isn't a joke."

"I didn't say it was funny, Doctor," Danny said. She finished knotting her laces and stood up. If he had something to say, now was the time.

"We need to discuss your condition."

"I don't want to," Danny said.

"I have to because I'm your doctor." When Danny folded her arms together and leaned against the wall, he continued, "I'll keep it brief. I told you your brain is bleeding, way down inside beneath the two big lobes, near the stem. If it doesn't get worse, you could remain functional, except for the headaches and the blackouts. If it gets better, you might still experience the occasional headache, but probably not. I've been reading up on this. I'm not an expert."

"If it gets worse?"

"You have a stroke and you're paralyzed, or die. Short form. A lot of ways that can happen, but it's not good."

"So what does anybody do about that?"

"Don't hit your head. Like not even a little bit, ever again. Don't drink a lot of alcohol, hang upside down, get into fights, or use speed. Basically retire and live somewhere quiet and you should be okay."

"Is that it?"

"There's a lot of stuff happening here," he said. "People are freaking out. You turned up at a time when I think things are changing kind of fast . . . And from what I hear, that's where you're at your best. Don't go for it, okay? Whatever happens, keep out of it."

"I'm not interested in your town or your politics or any of that. I want the Silent Kid back. You can have this shithole all to yourself. Can I ask you a personal question?"

He was taken aback by this change of subject, but nodded. "I guess."

"Which one is worse: the Architect, or the Risen Flesh?"

As she spoke, the church bells began to ring for the afternoon service.

Dr. Joe tipped his head in the direction of the bells.

"Why don't you make that call yourself?"

8

Danny's heart was kicking as she approached the church. The overnight snow still survived in the angles of buildings and against the curbs, a rime of dust left in the corners by an indifferent housekeeper, and it looked and felt like another snowstorm was on its way. Danny found she was one of hundreds walking up the street; the shuffle of the worshippers reminded her uncomfortably of the undead. Now she found herself wondering how many of them were infected with this new poison, half-dead, half-living. Was that the future? Or was it something so rare all the infected had already been isolated from the general population?

She saw that many women had covered their heads beyond the purpose of warmth—a measure to ensure modesty or an attempt to conceal their identities, maybe, so their neighbors wouldn't judge them for joining a cult that in another time would have been considered blasphemous, unthinkable. It occurred to Danny to pull the brown sweatshirt's hood up over her own distinctive head; her notoriety was going to be a problem when it came time to act. Anonymity was always an asset. For the first time in her life, Danny considered dyeing her hair.

By the time she made it in past the big, sullen-looking ushers on the steps, the place was packed. She saw the Risen Flesh down at the far end of the nave, rolling his cloudy eyes and moaning like a common zero. The sight of the thing was even more hideous by daylight; she could see the permanent bruises, the peeling skin, the ragged apertures where the nails pierced its limbs. It was standing room only on the ground floor, so Danny allowed herself to be pushed along with the rest of the latecomers into the upper gallery where the organ pipes were. She struggled to a point near the railing of the balcony, determined to see what kind of system they had going, how many acolytes there were, and whether the crowd seemed convinced by what they were doing or not.

The Risen Flesh's followers were crammed into the pews, chairs, and benches of the church; they filled the aisles and the balcony and the stairs. There were others massed at the windows outside, their silhouettes visible through the stained glass, and still more stood beyond the front doors, massed on the steps, stretching their necks for a glimpse within. Except for the grotesque centerpiece of the scene, it reminded Danny of the refugee food distribution centers she'd done security on in Pakistan, Iraq, and Afghanistan: countless hungry, unwashed faces all turned to the same spot, bodies pressed together, united by desperation.

But where the deuce-and-a-half truck laden with bags of rice ought to have been, there was an altar. Danny hadn't been able to see much during her nocturnal visit, so the fixtures were new to her eyes. The altar was older than the church, battered and blackened; it had probably been one of the props used by the preacher when he was still on the move with his sideshow religion. Behind the altar stood four of the acolytes, presumably half-living infected, as the Architect claimed; they were costumed in hooded sweatshirts after the fashion of monks, heads bowed, hands clasped in front of their groins. Behind them, overspreading the scene, was a tall wooden cross made of thick timbers with gilded edges. A ladder was set against the right-hand crosspiece; atop the ladder waited a fifth hooded acolyte.

It was the Risen Flesh from which Danny could not take her eyes. In daylight the thing was so hideous as to invoke pity, mouth working without words, beard wagging. Its milky eyes roamed hungrily over the crowd below. The thing had been nailed firmly to the cross, hands and feet, and upon its head was set a crown of rusting barbed wire that had scraped the flesh down to the skull. In its side was a wound; black fluid had run from the gaping cut all the way to the zero's feet, and spattered the wood of the upright beneath. The zombie writhed against the nails. Danny saw there had been more than one set of nails—a couple of secondary holes in feet and wrists must have been from earlier attempts to keep the thing in place.

All eyes were upon the inhuman effigy. And then their heads turned in near unison, in the way a flock of birds will change course in midflight, as a new actor walked upon the stage at the front of the church. A pale-skinned man with dark eyes, a narrow beard, and long hair parted carefully in the center. He looked like Rasputin, Danny thought. One of those Russian mystics. He was dressed all in black leather, except for a white silk scarf at his throat; on the back of his jacket was painted a crimson X with a white cross over the top of it, in rough strokes like Japanese calligraphy. It was the Preacher, come at last to minister to his flock.

He took his place in front of the crucifixion, his fists thrust against the altar. There was a massive leather-bound book on the altar that might have been a Bible, or it could have been the register of an old hotel. To Danny's suspicious eyes, the entire thing was pure theater; there was no question that everything had been composed for maximum dramatic effect. She wondered who had first conceived of this obscene ritual: the Preacher or the Risen Flesh?

"Children," the Preacher said.

"We are all but children," chanted the monks and a number of the most fervent worshippers at the front. "O Lord, save me!" someone shouted.

"God visited his wrath upon us again, as he always does, for these are the times beyond the end. One of our very own, murdered here at the foot of the Risen!" Here he thrust his finger at the spot where Danny had slain the acolyte; a dark stain still marbled the floorboards.

"And although our humble church was spared, yet it has been wounded, as was the Son of our Lord. Yet look you upon the Reborn: He was untouched. He was untouched. He was untouched."

As the Preacher chanted these words, he shook his open hands up at the creature transfixed above him.

"This was no miracle," the Preacher continued, turning suddenly on the congregation. "No no. We used the word 'miracle' too easily before the end. We cheapened it. No, this one of all the millions of reborn was chosen to guide us, but he is not God. He is not Christ. He is *nobody*. We know not even his name. He could have been you, or you, or you"—here he stabbed his fingers at people in the crowd—"or anyone here. He is reborn. That is the only thing which matters, can't you understand? And that is why he hangs there still, when the murderer who came among us, who slew one of our own brethren right here on this spot, could have destroyed the Risen Flesh as well. Why did the killer stay his hand? Why did he not cast our Savior to this bloodstained floor?"

People actually looked at the floor when the Preacher said this, as if trying to identify the spot upon which the crucified thing would have fallen. Danny couldn't believe their stupidity. They were emptying their minds and letting this man fill them back up again with—what? She remembered a word Harlan had used back in the war before he got his own brains knocked out. He'd been speaking of a camel spider at the time, but it was a good word and Danny remembered it. *Abomination*. This preacher was filling his congregation's heads with abominations. Danny wasn't versed in the Bible, but she had a feeling this wouldn't go over very well with God. She expected there should be lightning blowing the steeple off.

"This animated clay that hangs above you is the living flesh of the departed soul, as predicted in every book of religious wisdom ever written in every religion there ever was. On this they all agree. There shall come an end to the world, but not an end to suffering, not yet! Not at the same time. Only in this time after time shall we determine whether our suffering shall end. If we yet struggle against the will of God, he will give us the gift of suffering. And there hangs proof. Proof! Our mortal frames continue while our souls burn in hell, so we may suffer here on earth and in the fires of Hades at the one and very same time."

Danny looked at the crowd, searching for familiar faces. There were a few Tribespeople there. Not many. Maybe a dozen. There would be others who didn't follow this weird cult, but latched on to something else—whatever allowed them to fit into the group. Some would mold their very minds to conform. Give them time, and most of them would eventually believe the hideous effigy gnashing the air above their heads was a sacred being resurrected for their salvation, if they had to.

"But there are sinners among us," the Preacher went on, his eyes coincidentally sweeping over Danny's position, "among the citizens of this blessed town. They are the enemy. They would destroy the Risen Flesh, if they could. But they could not. They are outside these doors, the Architect and his minions, his killers, his whores to Mammon. They did this thing. They sought and failed to destroy the Risen Flesh. They could succeed, brothers and sisters. They could yet succeed. Vigilance! Vigilance. Watch them, and know that they rule by force of violence when the only true strength in this world that is left to us miserable sinning shitheads is *faith*. Vigilance, and a hard right hand, will save your souls when the time fucking cometh."

As grotesque as it all seemed to her, Danny had to fit in, or seem to, until she knew what was going on. Nobody appeared to have recognized her in her civilian clothes—her "chook costume," as she thought of it—and with the pendulous sweatshirt hood pulled down low, she was fairly sure to remain anonymous. Besides, nobody was looking in her direction, up in the gallery. All eyes were on the Preacher and the moaning autopsy above him.

"Come all ye faithful," the Preacher cried. "Those of you who see the evidence of the world and the world beyond with your own eyes, who have felt the pain of suffering and the agony of the spirit which has outlived the very plan for which God intended it, O you poor suffering bastards, come ye on up here and get yourselves anointed and let the unbelievers marvel and the undecided think back on the moaning and the howling of their dead and *repent*. It's none too soon, sinners. None too soon. But God has given ye one more chance and any minute now he might revoke the offer and there you are, doubly unrepentant. The hottest fires and the sharpest teeth and the worst death forever, that's your reward for doubting. Step on up."

The first few rows of congregants all but climbed over each other to get up to the front; they formed a rough line two across up the aisle of the church, shoved into position by the four monks, who had stepped forward at a gesture from the Preacher. People were already pulling their shirts up over their heads; apparently this was part of the ritual. Danny saw that most of the exposed backs were striped with scabby wounds, roughly parallel lines carved into the flesh across their shoulders. This must be part of the feeding rites. It was alien to her to stand mutely at the edge of the action like this; she felt a growing sense of urgency, the familiar instinct that something was wrong and she ought to stop it. But she'd learned a great deal of circumspection in her last year of survival. She stood impassively and watched.

The ritual was obscene.

"You miserable worthless bag of meat!" the Preacher bellowed at the first of the congregants in line, a middle-aged woman with scraggly gray hair. "Is this enough to save you?"

"No!" cried the congregant, almost collapsing to her knees, bent double, her sweater flung over her head to expose a wound-striped back.

"Have you suffered enough?"

"No!" she pleaded.

"In a world of horrors, have you suffered enough to join the bosom of God?"

"No!" the congregant shrieked.

"So you're fucked, unless you go the full distance. Unless you eat the flesh of the Son of man, and drink his blood, you have no life in you. Whoever eats his flesh, and drinks his blood, has eternal life; and he will raise him up even now, *after* the last day. For his flesh is meat indeed, and his blood is drink indeed. Like the man said, 'He that eats my flesh, and drinks my blood, dwells in me, and I in him. As the living Father has sent me, and I live by the Father: so he that eats me, even he shall live by me. This is that bread which came down from heaven: not as your fathers did eat manna, and are dead: he that eats of this bread shall live forever, undead or alive."

At this moment, the Preacher's arm snaked out and struck at the cowering woman and a strap of bright blood appeared on her back, spilling down over her shiny white flesh. The congregant's knees buckled, and in that moment the foremost monk caught her up; the second dashed something from a bottle onto the wound and applied a scrap of cotton to it, then roughly yanked the sweater back down over the woman's skin. She stumbled to the foot of the crucifixion behind the Preacher. Already the next true believer was receiving the wound.

Now Danny could see what the Preacher had in his hand—it was some kind of woodworking tool, like a draw chisel. It must have been scalpel sharp. He was slicing short strips out of his parishioners' skins. *Chicharrones*, Danny thought. Pork rinds. But why?

The next act in the ceremony answered her question. She felt hot bile stinging the back of her throat. It felt like she did nothing but puke anymore. Danny swore she'd keep it down this time.

The woman in the sweater stood below the crucified zombie, and that thing looked down at her, teeth bared, pale eyes rolling. The third monk was stationed at the monster's feet, his hood at about the same level as the rail spike that transfixed both insteps of the Risen Flesh. He held a long pole, probably a length of old-style iron sprinkler pipe; on the end was a leaf-shaped spearhead. The monk dipped the spearhead into a dish on the altar.

Danny didn't catch this detail until the third wound had been inflicted: The Preacher tapped his slicing tool against the edge of the dish on the altar, and a worm of bloody flesh fell into it. The monk with the spear caught up the first of these bits of skin on the tip of the spear and raised it up—hundreds of eyes followed its course from the congregation—and there was a collective sigh of relief or awe or horror as the flesh was transferred into the snapping jaws of the zero on the cross. The creature was *feeding* on the flock. A spurt of vomit flew into Danny's mouth. She swallowed it, grasping her belly in her hands. Everyone on the balcony around here was watching the rites; none of them seemed disgusted by what they witnessed.

But the worst was yet to come.

The first of the worshippers had been processed in a matter of seconds, from the incantation to the cutting, bandaging, and taking up of her position beneath the blasphemous effigy. Now there were three congregants crowded behind the altar, as the call-and-response went on:

"Have you suffered enough?"

"No!"

"In a world of horrors, have you suffered enough to join the bosom of God?"

"No!"

And another worm of flesh was stripped away. Danny couldn't understand what they were waiting for. Only one of the monks seemed to be standing by at this point, on the side of the cross opposite the spear-handler; the thing on the cross wasn't doing anything but sucking down pieces of human flesh. Otherwise everyone was busy. Then the zero raised its barbed-wire-wreathed skull and moaned to the rafters, and a moment later a dark stream spilled from its side.

There must have been a puncture there, all the way into the creature's entrails. It was *digesting*. The monster had begun to process the feast. Whether this filthy stew was yesterday's feeding or the bleeding scraps now being thrust between its yellow fangs, Danny couldn't tell and didn't care. She felt she was suffocating. It might have been her imagination, but she thought she could smell the ichor spilling out of the belly of the monster. Her skin was cold, but sweat was pouring down her own back, a cold evocation of the mutilations being done to the congregants below. Now there were a dozen people in the line, already processed, blood dappled through their clothing, faces raised to the undead.

The fourth monk raised his hands. All of them, Danny now realized, were wearing surgical gloves. Even the Preacher. The monk pressed a finger into the bubbling slime that ran from the monster's wound, then drew a cross on the forehead of the first congregant, the woman with the sweater. Then he dabbed the slime on her outstretched tongue.

The woman clasped her hands in a gesture of passionate thanks and rushed past the crucifixion behind the altar and circulated back down into the crowd, where she was lost to view among the swirl of congregants pressing forward to donate their gram of flesh.

The monk carried on with the next congregant and the next, anointing them with zero filth made out of their own flesh.

Without warning, Danny vomited. She threw her hands in front of her mouth, but didn't have enough fingers to stop the stream. The men and women on either side of her made noises of revulsion—as if *she* was the disgusting one here—and stepped apart, their shoes spattered with thin bile. Danny shoved her way to the back of the balcony, hands pressed over her face as much to conceal her features as to suppress the waves of nausea that threatened to overtake her at every step. She stumbled down the creaking scaffold stairs that led down from the upstairs window, stumbled outside, and heaved out her guts on the littered ground beside the church, ignoring the sneers of the people crowded outside the windows watching the ceremony within. The smell reminded her of the acolyte's blood and brought on a fresh wave of retching.

Empty, dripping with puke, Danny made her way to an old garden faucet on the brick foundation of the church and washed herself off. She still could not believe what she'd seen.

These insane people were feeding themselves to the undead—and taking infected tissue into their mouths.

The entire new religion was centered on making more infected half-zombies out of gullible, scared fools, as far as Danny could tell. These people believed they had to become part of the feast to atone for mankind's sins. Where did it end? Would there be a splinter cult that hacked off their own limbs and fed them to the zeroes? Or would they capture victims and make them into sacrifices?

This had all happened in the past. Such violent religions had flourished for thousands of years. It seemed impossible that it could be happening again in the fresh ruins of a once-civilized place like America. But Danny had seen it with her own eyes. And already there were Tribespeople involved. The message was convincing to them. More than *her* message, whatever that had been. Why not a wrathful god demanding flesh?

Perhaps she should have given them something to believe. Now, unbelievably, they were joining up with the undead.

Danny's own back, with its thick web of scar tissue, would never make a suitable sacrifice for the Risen Flesh. She had already given that part of herself to another cause.

She drank some of the frigid water directly from the flow at the faucet, crouching low, and with her head at an angle, she surreptitiously observed the bank building across the intersection. She saw the curtains of the Architect's office twitch, thought she could see the wink of spectacles in the shadows of the room behind them.

The Architect was an evil son of a bitch, collecting children for his feasts, or making them into followers, or whatever he had in mind. The Risen Flesh was equally evil, stripping tidbits off the living backs of his followers, selling them fear, exposing them to zombiism. Which one should she attempt to destroy? She'd only get one shot, and time was running low. But Danny knew the answer to the question, now.

They both needed to go.

9

After the service was over and the crowd had spread out, milling around in the town center, Danny walked back up the steps of the church, ignoring the ushers who remained standing beside the doors. Were they half-living? She didn't think so. They were too easily examined in the daylight. Their exhalations smoked in the cold like warm-blooded breath ought to do. The mood in the street was ugly—the place was split down the middle between church and state, and many of the people who had been outside during the service weren't just overflow, but hecklers. She thought things were going to get rough no matter what she chose to do. Maybe not today, but soon.

The church seemed darker within, now that the congregation was gone. She stood in the doorway and let her eyes adjust, at the same time locating the acolytes; she could see three of them. One was on the ladder pressing a bandage to the wound in the Risen Flesh's side; two of them were clearing up the altar, ragging off stray droplets of blood and tissue.

The crucified zero saw her (or smelled her, she didn't know which) as she advanced up the aisle. The acolytes, seeing her, immediately formed a defensive rank in front of the crucifix—which was absurd, because the only way to get at their mascot would be with a gun, and they weren't going to reach up and grab the bullets out of the air.

"Close the door," she called over her shoulder.

One of the guards looked in, eyebrows raised.

The closest of the acolytes glanced up at the crucified zero, and there must have been some subtle signal between them, because the acolyte turned to the door and said, "Do it."

The doors banged shut behind Danny and it was darker in the church, making the sunlit windows look like multicolored fire by contrast.

"I hope you enjoyed the show," the Risen Flesh wheezed, once the guards were sealed off outside. "But I'm told you spoke with my rival across the street."

"He made me a damn good offer," Danny said. "You didn't."

"You got the best I could give," the thing said, and ran out of air. It drew a long, hoarse breath and continued, "I let you go free and didn't give you away. My bargain was to absolve you of sin, so to speak, not to enrich your life—besides: My acolytes here, they're very upset about the death in the family. We're all *avoiding* death, you understand. We are coming from it, not going to it. Dying isn't our thing."

At this moment the last of the acolytes and the Preacher stepped out of the back room from which Danny had emerged in the dark only hours before.

"Has she come to confess her sins?" the Preacher asked, and laughed a little.

"Fuck off," Danny explained. "This has nothing to do with you."

"She's charming, you have to admit," the Risen Flesh said. "Duncan, meet the Sister of the Dead."

"An honor," the Preacher said. He looked like a commercial rock star, Danny thought. A decorative bad-ass exterior wrapped around the core of a corporate lawyer. The Preacher turned and looked up at his accomplice on the cross: "Pardon the interruption, but it's official. We're running out of places to strip the skin off the true believers. We need a bigger flock, you need a diet, or we're going to have to find somewhere else to get the flesh from."

"The shoulders is a deliberate choice, of course," the zero said, looking at the Preacher but speaking to Danny. "Because Christ was flogged. It sounds right. What else can we do? We need more people, that's all. Unless we can claim the Romans flogged their victims on their tender, blood-warm buttocks, of course."

"If people can't sit down without discomfort, they won't come to church," the Preacher said. He kept glancing at Danny, clearly uncomfortable with having such a practical conversation in front of an outsider—especially this one.

"I'm on a schedule," Danny cut in, uncomfortable herself. "You fucking psychopaths can work this out later."

"If anyone needs me, I'll be in the back, crying because the famous sister-sheriff was so mean to me," the Preacher said, and left the main room of the church, deliberately swaggering, radiating insolence and power.

"Listen up," Danny said to the Risen Flesh. "The Architect made me a nice little deal and I can close it right here and right now. *Don't move,*" she added, slipping her good hand under her sweatshirt when the acolytes all stepped toward her at once.

"She must be in possession of a firearm," the crucified thinker said. "How clever of her. So original."

"What have you got?" Danny barked.

"You've made me terribly cross," the zombie said, and tried unsuccessfully to laugh. "Come on, that was funny. Well it was funny to me . . . Be that way."

When Danny failed to respond, it took another long breath and said, "With that terrible fellow across the street out of the way, we reduce the bureaucratic component of this society and gain a larger role for faith. There are other, less *modern* churches operating within the population here, throwbacks from the old days. They aren't the competition. The trouble is that secular man-eater in the bank, with his pretend-living nonsense. Be honest, I say. I'm honest. Look at how honest I am. The Architect is unliving a lie."

"Here's what I want," Danny said. "If I take him out, the kids go free. *All* of them. The living take over operation of the trains, the electricity-generating operation, and the running of the town. Any of you fucking half-dead assholes"—here she addressed the acolytes—"who want to stick around, you guard the perimeter against the hunters and moaners. How you eat, I don't know. Eat rats, like my sister. But you don't eat *here*. That's a special deal for this freak show alone."

"That's a fairly broad bargain, Sister dear," the Risen Flesh said, the amusement gone from his voice. "Things might not work out that way."

"I might not keep you from destruction, for that matter," Danny said, and sank her hand deeper under the sweatshirt, as if she had something to advance her position in it.

"Well then, let's say I'll take that deal," the Risen Flesh replied. "We can call it a miracle and the goodness of the church. And in return . . . *you* destroy the Architect. Within the next two days. That's what *I* want."

10

It was cold, but not the bitter cold of the night hours. Her breath formed long white scarves. Although she'd attracted some attention by puking during the ceremonies, Danny thought her civilian costume would probably help her avoid being recognized, as long as she stuck to the side streets; in any case, the most interesting action was to be found off the main drag, which was apparently the "respectable" part of Happy Town. She left the milling crowd in the town square behind. Nobody paid her any attention; there were quite a few people around, most of them clearly filling the days with nothing much. Some had errands and moved briskly. Once in a while the security vans would circulate.

She took a side street westward, a block below the Civil War statue. This took her through a neighborhood of small apartment buildings with between two and six units in each; a lot more people lived in them now. Then she turned northward again and approached the heart of town from the westward margin, so she reached the low-rent commercial area that surrounded the better buildings: residential upstairs, shop fronts below. There were a lot more people here, mostly wandering aimlessly around and shooting the breeze. She pulled the hood closer around her face. There were some Tribespeople here. None observed her, that she could tell. They were chooks, folks she hardly ever interacted with before. She found herself wondering if anyone within her immediate area was one of the semi-undead, still passing for normal. It could be almost anyone.

She passed a row of little shops—once a blacksmith, a saddlery, and a surveyor's office, according to the mock–Olde West signs up above the porches; now they contained a bunch of individuals selling all manner of stuff off the top of milk crates and boxes. Feeling exposed on the street, she ducked inside the first of them, and that's when she understood how crowded the town really was. There were vendors on the porches, inside the doors, in the back rooms, crammed anywhere they could seize a scrap of floor space. The customers were shoved together like subway riders, everyone haggling and coughing and knocking things over. It reminded Danny of the Asian import marts in Los Angeles' Chinatown, in which subsistence-level shopkeepers and entrepreneurs vied for customers with their elbows almost touching. There was also a strong whiff of the junktique shops such as Forest Peak had supported, too, in which every imaginable bit of rubbish was worth attempting to sell: an early Budweiser can, a broken fishing pole, some spent shotgun shells. It looked like when business hours ended, everybody just lay down where they were, among their stock: She saw bedrolls, pots and pans, camp stoves, old grocery sacks full of laundry. And nobody took cash, of course. The favorite medium of exchange seemed to be food.

Danny watched as a couple of tins of baked beans were exchanged, after much back-and-forth, for a dozen syringes still in their wrappers. Someone else traded a sack full of belt buckles for half a package of teething bread. There wasn't any fruit or fresh meat available in this part of town, but she didn't expect it. If Danny had been running the place, she'd have controlled access to perishable stuff, and she assumed the Architect did the same. It just made sense. Keep the merchants from gaining power.

She pushed through the shop floor to the back rooms, which once would have been the shopkeeper's residence; now it was more vendors crammed in all the way to the back door. People were living, it appeared, with less than a dozen square feet of floor to call their own. It reminded Danny of San Francisco before the city fell, with the refugees jammed into every building until the very streets smelled like bad breath and dirty feet. She'd seen people there who were living on a single stair step, standing on it when awake and lying on it when asleep. This was much the same. In a vast country nearly empty of living people, the living still ended up crammed together like pickles in a jar.

Danny stepped out the back door of what had been the kitchen. There was a narrow yard with a garage at the end; several tents had been pitched on the dirt where the lawn should have been. She stepped through these and followed a gravel-topped alley for another block until it terminated in the perimeter fence of Happy Town. The fence, ordinary wire cloth on metal poles, topped with barbed wire and a couple of electrified strands stood off on insulators, was about twelve feet tall. It wrapped all the way around town, at least on this exposed side, and cut straight through the neighborhood. So there were houses on the fortified side of the fence and identical houses on the outside.

The main difference was more tents. Danny could not imagine living up against the fence on the outside, waiting for that seething horde of zeroes out to the west to figure out a way through the town's mysterious defenses. Although it was a good, long march away through radiation-poisoned country, the idea of half a million undead moaning and yearning for blood just over the horizon would have been enough to drive her crazy. Sleep in a tent? Might as well be a burrito skin. In any case, it looked to her like as much as half the population was stuck outside the fence. And there was a lot of activity against the wire.

Guards were patrolling the fence, guns across their chests, and always in pairs; there was a van down the next block with several of the orange vests standing around beside it. Danny couldn't quite understand why they were there, until she got close enough to see how the commerce in town made its first step: Anything small enough to fit through the mesh of the fence could be exchanged right there, and people were constantly doing it. Many of the links in the mesh had been enlarged into round or square holes, but only by stretching, never by cutting the wire. People pushed things through these openings: cans of food, clothes, shoes, clocks, almost anything. Even building supplies. A 2x4 would just barely fit endwise through a fully-expanded gap in the fence.

The scavengers outside the fence were relaying things to their confederates on the inside, who were conveying them to crowded markets like the one Danny had seen. When the undead inevitably came, the people outside the wire would be no less doomed, of course. They wouldn't be allowed inside for being good trading partners. But it filled the days, and from the looks of things this might be the only way a lot of people on the inside were able to afford to stay alive—they had diligent foragers working for them in the badlands. If it was true that people were thrown out fairly frequently, it might be a big advantage having good friends on the outside willing to risk their asses to collect cans of soup for you. It might guarantee you a little scrap of floor space behind the wire when there was a cull going on.

The trouble was, as Danny could see from her first cursory glance, that the fence itself was useless, except for containing living people. It was too lightly built for its height; a swarm mass would push it over. And the single layer of wire would rip wide open if a tree fell on it or someone drove a vehicle through it. So whatever was keeping the swarm away, out there in the badlands, it wasn't a fence like this one. And the Architect and whoever else had fortified this place must know it. Again, Danny wondered what their system was. The Architect said it was the semi-undead, standing around smelling bad to the moaners. But that would take hundreds of them, or thousands; otherwise the swarm would pass between them. Their numbers weren't that great. If they had been, then they, too, would probably have turned on the fully living and eaten them like cattle.

She was feeling tired again. Her head fluttered a little, as if there was a headache in the area, but it hadn't decided to settle in. She needed to drink more water. What she wanted more than that was a few good hard pulls of bourbon, but since Wulf's demise she had kept away from the stuff and it seemed like a waste of the DTs to start into it again. Running her mind without alcohol was like running an engine without oil. But so be it. She could destroy herself some other way.

She started back toward the center of town, planning to find a spot from which she could observe the two institutions of church and government and decide what to do. She had permission from both sides to kill the opposing leader; if she played her cards just right, it might be possible to get them to do it to each other. That would be the best thing, she thought. Get rid of the Architect and make a new deal with the half-living sentries out in the wilderness to keep them in place; get rid of the false god in the church and make a new deal with the folks who wanted religion to go back to the old-fashioned wooden effigies.

Her thoughts were circling like this, the low afternoon sun sinking to the top of the fence behind her, when she heard shouting.

At first she thought there must be a zero attack, but the voices were raised in anger, not fear. She hastened toward the main street through town, where a crowd was already gathering. She saw a knot of people pushing up the street past the monument. They gathered in front of the bank; a mass of others filled in behind them, reaching as far as the church steps and the sidewalk on Danny's side of the street, which was opposite the bank. Three or four hundred people. They stood there looking on, with more and more excitement-seekers filling the cross-streets and upper-story windows. The smaller group at the front of the protest kept chanting and shouting; some of the larger crowd took up the chants, and it seemed most folks at least shared in the mood of discontent.

After fifteen minutes, during which time the upstairs balcony of the bank and the rooftops of the nearest structures filled up with armed men in safety vests, Cad Broker emerged. He was on the balcony among the orange vests, and he looked worse than when Danny had last seen him, his makeup more obvious.

"We're busy trying to save the world!" he shouted. "What do you folks want?"

A man at the front of the crowd, taller and broader than most, stood up on something, so he was now visible from the back of the crowd. Even Danny could catch a glimpse of him.

"I'm Darren Williams," he said. "You brung me and my wife in here with my two daughters about two months back."

"I hope you've been safe and well," Cad said, pitching his voice for the crowd, not the individual. "Do you want for anything?"

"We want our kids back is what we want, Broker," Darren said. "We didn't fill out adoption papers. We handed our children over to you on the condition that you'd keep them safe."

"And they are," Broker said.

"You said *we'd* be safe, too," Darren interrupted. "But this whole place is a cult."

"Sir, there is a strict separation of church and state here," Cad said. "If you have a problem with the true believers, that's none of my business."

"I mean this whole damn thing is a cult. We want our kids back."

A dozen people took up this cry. The spokesman Broker waved them to silence.

"That wasn't the deal."

"If this is the safe zone for us, I can only imagine what the hell you're doing with the kids. You got them in pens? Jail cells? I don't think it's any damn country club. Not if this is your idea of a town. Damn head-busting thugs everywhere. Curfew. Never enough food."

A general shout went up at this. Danny wondered why they didn't allow visiting hours or something. It seemed obvious. Maybe they'd tried it and it didn't work. But even prisons had visiting hours. Even West Point. The Architect was making a mistake here. Unless it was all part of the plan. That seemed more likely.

"Sir, the children are cared for as our most precious resource," Cad said. "The line here is effectively one-way. That's how it works. That's how we keep the children from further trauma, from accidental exposure to disease.

We have a crisis on our hands. We can't undo what we've done or we lose the war on the undead."

"That's bullshit. That's just words. This isn't a crisis, it's the new normal. We live in a zero-infested world, end of story. You don't call alligators a crisis."

"It's the new normal in the sense that the crisis is ongoing and there's no end in sight. So we're agreed on that. And the last thing—the *last* thing—that anybody needs is to introduce the children back into this chaos before we've got a handle on it. You're right. Things here in town are kind of wild. We're working on it. That's what the so-called 'thugs' are doing. Do you really think this is a fit place for children?"

"Wait a minute. You take both sides of every damn argument and somehow the answer always comes out the same. I'm not falling for that." More shouts of agreement from the crowd.

"I don't care what you think, sir," Cad said, dabbing his face with a handkerchief. Danny wondered if it was a theatrical gesture—he might already be so far gone in his condition that he didn't perspire anymore.

He continued: "Here's why I don't care: because you're not thinking, you're just reacting. The kids are safe beyond the mountain, and we're here. It's *working* for the kids. Not one of them has died. If you decide to be selfish and insist on having *your* way when the whole system is set up to go the *other* way, you're just creating a nightmare for everybody. The kids most of all."

"Everybody?" A man not far from Danny shouted. "Everybody wants their kids back."

"I see about thirty to fifty people here," the spokesman replied. "That's not everybody."

"I see five hundred people here. And there's a lot more where we came from."

"We'll have to agree to disagree on the math. The point is we can't have mob rule. We can't allow a momentary failure of courage on your part to turn into an endless nightmare for everybody else."

"You said this nightmare was *already* endless."

There was a lot more shouting. Danny saw something arc through the air—a shoe or a piece of wood or something. It clattered off the facade of the bank. She decided she didn't want to be there if crowd control became an issue. She didn't need a riot, she needed a ninja. So she turned her back on the scene just as one of the guards started shouting through a megaphone and the vans pushed into the throng. She was a block away when the gunfire started—into the air, by the sound of it, but a moment later she heard the stampeding feet and screams of a panicked mob.

She had a good lead on them, so she trotted easily, heading in the general direction of the hospital. The exercise warmed her up. She entered the school grounds without difficulty; her interview with the Architect had apparently squared her with all the guards. She was one of them, now. Then she strode around for a while up and down the halls until she ran into Dr. Joe, who was emerging from what appeared to be a ward for flu cases, once a science classroom. Danny heard a lot of wheezing and coughing in there.

"Ah, Sheriff," he said, when he saw her. He stank of alcohol. Danny wondered if he was a secret drinker until she realized he was rubbing sanitary gel all over his hands. "How's the head?"

"Good," Danny said. "I'm fine. Listen, can we talk?"

"We can talk here," he said, seeing nobody in the hall but them. Danny got up close.

"I need a favor," she said.

"I'm all done with favors," he said. "I'll be lucky if they don't take me down right along with you, at this point. I don't know what the Architect and you have in mind, but I am only here to take care of people."

Danny ignored the protest. She didn't have a choice, so as far as she was concerned, neither did he. "I'm going to give you directions to a farmhouse not too far from here. There will be some buddies of mine there. Tell them I need my backpack. Black one with a lock, weighs about fifty pounds. I'll let you know where it's hidden, and that's how they'll know you're legit."

Dr. Joe shook his head.

"I can't do this for you," he began, but Danny held up her fingerless hand to silence him.

"The Architect wants me to do something. Lives are at stake. I need that backpack. Sixteen hundred hours tomorrow, no later."

Joe opened and closed his mouth, but nothing came out. At last he turned around and went down the hall.

"I'll be in my room," Danny said. She meant it. She needed a nap.

Amy visited Danny in the night. Her old friend was asleep, and she decided not to wake her. The hospital-school was quiet, except for the heating system kicking on now and then. Amy was deeply tired. The drama of the last couple of weeks had caught up with her, and along with it the grief. The Tribe had fallen apart, Danny had finally, irretrievably lost Kelley, a prisoner had been murdered, and if the kidnapped children were here in town, nobody was lifting a finger to reunite them with their proper guardians. She knew this was catnip for Danny. A windmill to joust at.

Amy sat in the chair by the door, looking across the room at Danny's bed. It was rare to see her at peace. She might even be awake, and only pretending. Danny did that sometimes when they were girls.

"You're a good egg," Amy said, in a voice neither quiet nor loud. "It's been a hard time and you made some good from it. I wish Kelley didn't end up like she did, but she did. So there you go. Did and done. I'm sick of you being Mrs. Angry Pants all the time, and I'm sick of you being a drunken drunkard. But I don't care about that. I heard from the nice Japanese doctor about your brain problem. It's serious. I love you and I want you to get better. So don't do stupid stuff, please. Me and Patrick and some others are leaving town in the morning, so we probably won't see you again. I guess that's it. The end."

Amy sat for a while, hoping to see some sign Danny had heard what she said. But the eyes remained shut, the face slack. It might be that Danny was having a proper sleep for once. Amy wasn't going to wake her for that. She wanted to express her love of her battered friend somehow, but there wasn't a way.

"Good night," she said, in the same soft tones, and left the room.

Danny walked into town the following morning with a light snow swirling down around her. It stopped before she reached the town center. She strode to the cadence of the church bells, like any of the worshippers around her, but didn't turn to go into the church. Instead she positioned herself beside the war memorial in the middle of the square and looked up at the bank. To her surprise, the Architect himself was on the upstairs balcony of the bank, outside his office door. In the daylight, she could see he was wearing heavy makeup, painted like an old nearsighted showgirl. His head turned toward her and froze for a few seconds; despite the sunglasses he wore, she could feel his eyes on her. She showed no recognition, and neither did he. But he made a point of looking at his watch.

Danny observed an unusual number of blaze orange vests in the area, and the outlines of men crouched at the rooftop parapets. A crowd of worshippers had assembled around the statue in the middle of the intersection, making a show of force before they went inside the church; there was a crowd of onlookers lurking around the perimeter. It was similar in atmosphere to the confrontation of yesterday. It wasn't clear which way the general population's sympathies lay. With whoever looked to win, Danny assumed. She was reminded uncomfortably of the finale to *Butch Cassidy and the Sundance Kid,* or possibly *The Wild Bunch,* movies she would never see again.

She saw Nancy emerge from the bank. A ripple of ill-tempered remarks spread out among the churchgoers, who recognized her as one of the Architect's close advisors. She was flanked by security men with automatic weapons; despite the firepower they walked in a broad arc around the hostile part of the crowd. Danny realized they were heading in her direction.

As the woman approached, Danny studied her condition. Not as far along as Cad, maybe. Not as dead as the Architect. But committed.

"Good morning," Nancy said, as she reached Danny's position in the shadow of the bronze warrior. Danny said nothing.

"So," Nancy continued. "We noticed you were at church yesterday. Did you find it interesting?"

"It made me puke," Danny said.

"So we saw. But you went in for a talk."

Danny didn't reply. Let the silence do the work.

"My employer has already said he will equip you as needed for your mission, whatever you want. A prerequisite he failed to mention, and he so seldom makes even a small error that it's an inspiration to us all, but a condition he failed to mention is that you have no further discourse with his ah, um, opponent, or *rival* if you will."

"It's kind of too bad he didn't bring that up," Danny said. She saw motion in the tail of her eye and glanced back at the church. The acolytes were filing out through the doors, lining up on the steps as if there might be a rumble; there was a renewed noise from the crowd. The cordon of guards around the intersection closed in a few paces. "Because my buddy in there did make me a counteroffer."

"Then you've broken our agreement," Nancy said, her voice flat.

"Not if your boss up there is still on his feet, I haven't. Tell you what, if you all want to fight it out right here and now, go ahead. You don't need me. Kill that thing on the cross and burn down the church. I'm sure his followers will return the favor to your little bank. Me? I'll be on the road a hundred miles away, laughing my ass off."

The crowd had spread out, people forming sides, until it was divided across the intersection. Danny's anonymity had ended. She was now a player. Even the onlookers appeared to be choosing teams: They wanted a fight, and didn't care what it was about. Danny didn't know which side was stronger. It didn't matter. The important thing was that the balance of power was thrown off: The authorities were evenly matched with the civilians. That's when things got done. Nancy must still have had her human emotions intact, because she looked plenty rattled.

Danny observed an earbud tucked in Nancy's left ear: She must be in communication with the Architect by radio. The Architect, his balcony sufficiently distant from the onlookers so he could pass for human, appeared to be chewing; Danny now guessed he was speaking, probably into a lapel microphone. Such technology was available for free wherever looting could be done in the post-technological age they'd entered, but it had fallen out of use. Why rely on something that could never again be replaced?

Nancy was listening, but watching Danny. Then she spoke. "You're trying to play both sides against the middle," she said.

"In case you haven't gotten too stupid, I am the middle, you dumb half-rotten fuck," Danny said.

"How dare you!" Nancy gasped.

"You gonna eat some of those tasty little kids, Nancy?" Danny asked, stepping closer to the woman, keeping her voice down. "You gonna go around the mountain and visit those kids—"

"Shut up!" Nancy hissed, her voice low but urgent. "If these people hear you there will be absolute pandemonium."

"I'd call this a standoff, then."

"You ruthless b—"

"—Was that you talking, or did you just quote the Architect?"

Nancy pursed her lips, seething, and listened to the earpiece again. Then she said, "He wants to show you something. Follow me."

Danny swept her eyes around the town square, taking in the guards, the civilians, the acolytes, the Architect, the bronze Civil War veteran on his pedestal above her. Beyond the train station at the end of the street, she could see the mountains shelving up beyond the rooftops, and thought she could tell on which ledge she and Topper had spent their brief time together. Her situation had become so strange she almost felt as if she must still be up there, watching all this through the telescope.

"Why the hell not?" Danny said, and looked provocatively back at the church. The Preacher was standing inside the doors, now, surrounded by true believers. His arms were folded across his chest and his face was sour. Danny winked at him: Let him take it how he would. Then she sauntered on up the street after Nancy, swaggering much the way that sonofabitch did inside the church.

The arrival of Dr. Joe Higashiyama created a brief sensation at the farmhouse. He showed up in a pickup truck, alone, driving in that slow, brake-tapping way that had once been associated with deliverymen in unfamiliar territory, back when there were deliverymen. The Boston Terrier had become alert to his approach first, snarling at the glass of the front window in the living room; Conn went upstairs and spotted the truck with binoculars, and within a couple of minutes there were armed scouts hidden all around the front of the property, waiting for the truck to arrive.

Dr. Joe nearly got himself killed by climbing out of the truck with a rifle in his hands, but he placed the weapon on the roof of the truck, stepped away from it, and hollered, "Anybody here?"

"The hell are you?" a gravelly voice called from an upstairs window.

"I'm from Happy Town," he said. "Sheriff Adelman asked me to show up here and ask for something."

The scouts emerged from their various hiding places, and Dr. Joe went pale; Danny hadn't mentioned how rough-looking they were. But he explained to the tall one (who introduced himself as Topper) what he was looking for, and where it could be found; this cemented his credentials and it was insisted that he have a drink with them. The scouts wanted to hear how the sheriff was doing. The last time Topper had seen her she was incapacitated.

"Her brain is damaged," Dr. Joe explained, holding a coffee mug full of tequila in his hands, seated in the living room on a shabby floral couch. "She's totally fine, I mean she can do anything, but if there's another shock to her head I don't know if she'll survive it."

"Are you a good doctor or a shitty one?" Topper inquired.

"I'm pretty good, I think," Dr. Joe replied. He wasn't offended by the question; he knew what Topper meant. How qualified was he? "I'm not a brain specialist, but it's unmistakable. Subarachnoid lesions and stuff. What's amazing is how well she's doing *despite* it. I guess I can tell you guys she's been in at least one fight since her episode, and it didn't seem to have any negative effect on her."

"That's the sheriff," Ricardo said. He was a little guy with a huge mustache. "How long has she got?"

"I don't know," Dr. Joe admitted. "But she has a deathwish, that's for sure. What's in this backpack she wants so bad?"

"Nobody knows," Topper said. "Weapons, anyway. Any time she needs a little extra firepower, it's usually in there. Maybe grenades, maybe a flamethrower."

"Maybe we should look in it," Conn said.

"I'll tell her it was your idea," Topper said.

"Maybe not," Conn reflected. "Anyway, whatever she got in mind it's her fuckin' business."

"You Oriental cats can keep secrets, right?" Topper said, addressing Dr. Joe. He was taken aback, but nodded as if agreeing. "Okay, I'm gonna take this pack back myself. Ain't leaving it to you, nothin' personal. But I don't know you from a fuckin' serial killer. Thing is, though, if the sheriff wants out of there, she's gonna need inside help. I want you to be that help."

"I'm prepared for that, as long as it's nonviolent," Dr. Joe said. "Showing up here is a hanging offense, I have a feeling. Might as well go all-in."

"We might not need nothing from you, but an inside man is always a good thing."

They didn't have any specific role they'd need him for; Topper's real goal was simply to get Dr. Joe feeling like he was in too deep to cause them any trouble. Like if he snitched, he would be implicated. This wasn't the kind of work any of them were good at. It was like spycraft. Most of all, he knew he was going to drop the backpack off in a specific location; that meant he would be right where an informant said he'd be, and holding a backpack that could be full of sarin gas, for all he knew. The sheriff liked the dangerous toys. It occurred to him Conn might be right: Maybe he should see what was in there. But he was still going to drop the pack off, because Danny wanted it. No point looking at its contents, even if it meant getting caught by the Happy Town police and thrown into the clink like Ernie. Fuck it.

Nancy was chatting with manic brightness as she, Danny, and their escort of guards walked the five blocks from the town center. Danny didn't say a word, but cut her eyes back and forth, taking in every window, every doorway, every means of escape or attack the length of the street. They were surrounded by orange vests, and beyond that the civilians lurked in every corner, down every alley, watching. Nancy had been talking the entire walk, but it was only when they got closer to the train station that Danny tuned in.

Nancy was saying, ". . . best possible care, of course. We have the MRI machine, superb surgical facilities, a burn care ward, a dialysis center, and we even have a cancer center in another building with complete chemotherapy and radiation treatments available."

"Radiation?" Danny muttered, half-aware she said it. By now they were at the gate; the bored-looking man waved them through, Nancy being well-known to him.

"Yes," Nancy said, and looked suspiciously at Danny. "Is that so odd? The rate of cancers has skyrocketed in the last few decades, and these days of course it's going untreated. Why, going forward, it could kill more people than those nasty moaners out there."

The first security perimeter was a chain-link fence about five feet high, not too heavy, no barbed wire; just a kennel fence for keeping people organized. There was a gate in the fence with a man in winter clothes sitting on a stool, opening and closing his hands to keep them warm. He had a clipboard tucked into the throat of his jacket.

There was a blaze-vested guard standing nearby, but he was making a show of boredom, and if he carried a firearm, it was concealed. Even the casual distance between him and the gate seemed calculated to project how relaxed they were, how mild the security was. The guard's studied nonchalance was particularly ridiculous in light of the fact that fifty or more people had followed Danny and Nancy up the street and were now standing in an angry knot in the middle of the pavement, complaining loudly and trying to provoke the guard. From a safe distance.

"I'm just surprised you'd bring radioactive material into town. Radiation kills zer—the undead," Danny said, correcting herself, remembering that "zero" was apparently a pejorative with this bunch. She didn't want to antagonize the woman; she wanted to destroy her. Be polite until then.

"There are no undead here," Nancy said, lamely. "I mean except that nasty thing in the church, God forgive me." She was just repeating what she'd been told to say to the ordinary, ignorant people she met. Her slowly dying mind wasn't equipped with a response for an outsider who *knew*.

"Right," Danny said. "Anyway I bet you keep real close tabs on those radium pellets or whatever they are. Are you at the point where it would kill you instantly, or are you still human that way?"

"You disgust me," Nancy said, when she had thought it over for a few paces.

They had arrived at the next security perimeter. This one was considerably more serious: Three men in combat gear stood there, no vests, lots of guns. The gate stood in a twelve-foot fence with razor wire along the top, but only a short section of the fence was visible from beyond the station; it crossed an access road over the tracks between the station house and the next building, a luggage storage shed. Danny saw a forklift go past, its arms laden with crates of canned food; she caught a glimpse inside the building and saw stacks of crates up to the rafters.

There were men working in this secure inner sanctum who had a frontier look to them, the kind of men who would drop their tools and pick up a rifle at the first sign of trouble. It reminded Danny of forward posts she'd been to in the deserts of the Middle East. She wondered if the workers could all be infected semi-living people like Nancy and Cad, and decided it was impossible: Zeroes, even part-zeroes, wouldn't be able to heal or build muscle the way the living could. They needed living hands for the hard work. So these men (it was all men) must have some kind of special status here, some privilege others didn't.

Nancy explained their business to one of the guards, who looked frankly skeptical and picked up an all-weather telephone to call someone. He listened for a while, nodded, then hung up and indicated his colleagues should pat Danny down. Danny spread her arms out and allowed the inspection to occur. They groped her thoroughly; as had happened before, she felt the probing fingers hesitate when they encountered the geography of her back through her shirt. But they moved on. Of course, none of the men had thought to feel the fingers in her gloves, or there might have been a delay at the gate.

They passed through, and now one of the guards accompanied them as they turned left and moved down the tracks westward, the station behind them and the warehouses and train-repair sheds ahead. Danny estimated there were fifty or sixty men working here. In combination with the various security men around town, the Architect probably commanded a private army 250 strong. Not enough to stop a rebellion but sufficient to fight a decent rearguard action. These were definitely fully human, not the half-dead or unliving. She wondered what they had been promised in return for their service.

Although she rejected the idea with every impulse in her being, she understood what Nancy, Cad, and the acolytes were in it for: immortality, of a kind. Stockholm Syndrome taken to the next level. They were like Dracula's groupies. But what was in it for these other men with their unsmiling faces and heads-down labor? Did they get free whores? Better food? Maybe they got the nice bungalow houses in the suburbs, like the one from which Danny had stolen the jacket on her first night in town. Or it could be that they'd simply been given a little authority. That went far with some people. A little stamp of approval from the VIPs: *You'll make the grade. You're better than the chooks. We need these pallets moved by noon.*

They walked past the train engine project, on which a crew was working at speed. There were showers of sparks and clouds of smoke and steam, all to the beat and clang of hammers and steel. The engine was mechanically finished, it appeared; there were men bolting cover plates on over the massive power plant, and all the drive wheels were in place. But they were adding a huge, hand-built plow of steel at the front, and armored baffles along the entire fuselage. It was becoming a war-wagon.

Nancy didn't look too pleased to be allowing Danny to see any of this, but she had her orders. Behind the special engine stood three old-fashioned passenger cars, these also armored, the windows barred and shuttered, roofs laden with supplies. Once coupled to the engine, they would allow about two hundred passengers to get somewhere the easy way. Danny didn't think these would include the men outfitting them.

The third and final barrier was formidable. This one wasn't for show. A fence made of tall sheets of iron, topped with accordion wire and welded-on spikes of bent rebar. There was a deep hum of electricity. A crudely painted lightning bolt flashed on the sheet metal, which Danny now saw was crisscrossed with cattle wire stood off on insulators. She wondered what the voltage was. It must be lethal, of course. There were no guards in front of this gate, but two men atop the wall, which crossed the western end of the tracks and appeared to stay shut. End of the line. The trains that came from the west must stop outside town, going back and forth like a shuttle. This wall kept men in and trains out.

The wall extended across the tracks, over the sulfur-stinking clinker rubble on either side, and up to a natural rock formation on the north side (the lowest foot of the mountain) and a concrete block warehouse on the south. This building Danny remembered from her survey up on the mountain—it was the largest structure behind the barriers. A door in it opened, and four men in combat fatigues issued from within.

"Stay here," Nancy said to Danny.

Danny stood looking around her, ignoring the guard who remained at her side and the hard stares from the men who'd emerged from the warehouse. "No guards," she'd stipulated. So far, so bad.

Nancy crossed to the warehouse men and discussed her mission at some length. One of them eventually went inside, returning several minutes later, by which time Danny was starting to feel the cold. She pressed her gloved hands over her mouth, breathing through them to warm her fingers. She could feel the pocket knife and cigarette lighter she'd concealed inside two of the empty fingers of the left-hand glove. She had liberated both items from the jacket she'd stolen. They might not be a great deal of use, but she wasn't entirely unarmed. If nothing else, a punch from that hand was going to hurt.

Eventually three of the armed men advanced on Danny and fanned out around her, marching her into the warehouse. Danny could feel warm air coming at her through the open doorway. It smelled familiar, a sort of yeasty, sweet-salt smell like fresh bread dough and dirty laundry all at once.

It was the smell of a lot of children.

The guards were fools, in Danny's estimation, for all their scowling and bravado. They formed a delta around her, one in front and two behind; the doorway was a standard opening just wide enough for one. So she could hypothetically knock the man in front of her down, slam the door on the others, and raise hell before they could do much to stop her. She passed through the door with a tingle of adrenaline, but made no move, did nothing but take in the interior with quick, darting eyes.

High roof with bow truss frame, insulated with fiberglass batting. Walls of concrete painted in sanitary green. Space partitioned up to an eight-foot height with enclosed cubicles and offices at this end, with the far end walled off but open to the rafters. Plumbing recently added over the surface of the walls. The thing that most caught her attention was the noise of children, of small high voices and squeaking rubber-soled shoes and many bodies moving around. There wasn't any laughter or sounds of play; it was a zoo sound, animals pent up and restless. So far Danny couldn't see any of them, but the warmth and stink and noise brought out some instinct in her that could almost be described as maternal. It was sympathy, at least.

She had found the children.

"I need you to understand only the best behavior will do in here," Nancy said.

They were signed in at a desk by an intensely bored-looking man with a side holster. Then he rose, pistol in hand, and they walked behind him across the concrete floor to a padlocked door. The man unlocked it and they entered a hallway, the three guards trailing along behind. The man relocked the door behind them. Nancy continued her spiel.

"This is the transfer hotel, as we call it. As you can see, we take every possible precaution to keep the children safe and secure after the long nightmare of uncertainty they have endured out there in the unforgiving world. Once you have seen how we handle things, there's something additional my employer would like you to do, besides the work you discussed with him the other day, whatever *that* was."

Nancy's implied question caught Danny's ear: Did she genuinely not know what had been agreed upon? Was the Architect that opaque with his people? *Minions,* Danny thought. *That's what you fuckers are: minions.*

"What did you say?" Nancy asked, one eyebrow cocked at Danny.

"I said 'What's your opinion?'" Danny didn't have any idea what she meant by that; it simply sounded like "minion," which she must have muttered aloud.

"My opinion of what?"

"This setup for the kids," Danny said, still covering. But it turned out to be a good question.

"Oh," said Nancy, suddenly enthusiastic. "I think it's brilliant. Not one single child has died after arriving here. You can almost feel them relaxing. Gentlemen, we're all set here. I'll meet you outside in ten minutes."

This last statement was directed at the guards, who seemed to be slow to comprehend. Nancy waited, straining her smile at them, and at length they turned around and went back down the hallway. Before Danny and Nancy was a door with a window in it, but someone had painted a rainbow on the reverse side of the glass, so they couldn't see through. There were child-height shadows moving behind it. Danny willed herself to be patient and calm and not to betray the burning urgency she felt.

Nancy waited while the guards were allowed back through the previous door by the desk man. Then she turned to Danny and pitched her voice to a whisper, which made her sound like a child herself, a saccharine peep.

"I can see that you avoid coming near me," she said. "You've clearly been told that I am managing an infection right now, as are a goodly number of folks in town; it's not something we like to discuss, of course, because there is such stigma associated with it."

"Did you volunteer for it?"

"I got scratched before I came here and it didn't take me away like what you usually see. I thought I might be immune, at first."

Nancy was warming to the subject, which surprised Danny. But she must feel incredibly isolated, unable to speak to anyone who could possibly be sympathetic. Kind of like at the VA when they encouraged vets with PTSD to talk about their experiences with others. Except not.

"Not everyone understands," Nancy continued, almost babbling. "But we are slowly changing in our bodies and becoming more like those individuals who have suffered and died and returned intact. Not all the way, of course. I still have my soul, heaven forbid I should lose that! But still. I feel judged when you look at me that way."

"Your poor feelings," Danny said. She thought it might be useful to express some kindness, but she didn't remember how.

"I guess I wasn't expecting sympathy," Nancy said.

"Show me the kid," Danny said, becoming irritated. "I'm not here for the scenery. I don't give a shit about you, your diseased ass, or any of this bullshit. You want sympathy? Go loot a Hallmark store."

Nancy's mouth opened and closed like a fish in the bottom of a boat. Whatever she wanted to say, it never happened. Because a few seconds after Danny spoke, the door opened.

There was a glimpse of many children in a small place, swarming like zeroes. They didn't look happy, but they didn't look emaciated or abused, either. Then a woman with gray hair and a badly-ripped mauve pullover emerged with the Silent Kid's shoulders in her hands. She propelled him to the doorway. When he saw Danny, he didn't need any urging: He sprang toward her and threw his arms around her waist.

"It's good to see you, too," Danny said, her voice hoarse with unexpected emotion.

The child squeezed her around the hips, hanging on the same way Danny had clung to the rock in the icy river. Then, as if an urgent message had just come through, he leaped back a pace and made a puppet mouth-snapping motion with his hand, then pointed at the ground, then made goggles out of his fingers and stuck them around his eyes.

"Your dog's safe outside town," Danny said. "Friends of mine have him. They're tough, don't worry."

The Kid was more worried about his runt dog than himself. Danny thought that was a good sign. "He's gained a little weight," Danny said.

Nancy had regained her composure. "Oh, we take great care of them. Plump children, can you imagine?"

"I bet they're delicious," Danny said.

"Don't be disgusting," Nancy said, recoiling.

"Don't act like some kind of innocent here," Danny said, carefully pulling her gloves off. She didn't want to drop anything on the floor. She stuffed them in her jacket pockets and ran her fingers, such as they were, through the Kid's hair. "If you didn't have some kind of crazy bullshit planned, you'd leave the kids here, not run them around the other side of the mountain."

"You've seen what those survivors out there do. You've seen it. They discriminate against people of color, handicappeds, you name it. How do you think they'll respond to a whole new kind of person such as myself and the many others living with infection? We need to get these kids isolated and educated from that kind of ignorance and cruelty or the future belongs to none of us."

"You said there was something else you needed from me," Danny said, cutting through the insanity. "A part of the deal."

"We should discuss that in private."

"The Kid doesn't talk."

"If you give satisfactory results in the matter you've already been asked to undertake, we might like you to take over security operations."

"I'll think about it. But I'm not doing a single fucking thing for anybody unless this boy walks out of here today, right now, with me."

"I got an idea," Topper said, and took a swallow of the doctor's untasted tequila. They were watching Dr. Joe's truck roll away into the distance, having first enriched the young doctor with a couple of bottles of vodka for his personal medical use. The backpack was at Topper's feet. It was a lot heavier than he expected; maybe Danny had a tactical nuke in there, or something.

"Check it. Me and the sheriff were up top of that mountain behind the town. We was there a while and got a good sense of the . . . lay of the land, so to speak. Down the bottom of the hill there's the town, and it's open on the west end like a funnel. If fuckin' zeroes break through the defensive line in the badlands, ain't nowhere to go but straight at the town, all the way to the river. They could bust in by the river, too—there's even a town beach. Now, speaking of the river, that leads up a few miles to the fuckin' resort place where they keep the kids. You can just about see it from the mountain. Water all around, train goes by, damn good defensible position. Zero can't swim.

"But 'cause of that they ain't guarding it for shit. So if we could cause some kind of a situation at the island where the kids are at, my guess is those fuckholes would fire up the train and send all their best boys up to deal with it. Then we could maybe hit town and spring everybody who wants to get out."

"So we just go around the land way and set up a diversion at the island? Hell, let's get started," said Ginny, one of the female scouts. But Topper shook his head.

"You can't get to the island real easy because first you gotta get by the town, if you're going upriver. They blocked the fuck out of the access road that goes the long away round the mountain, and for all we know there's mines in the woods up there, too."

"You could hike the long way through the badlands in a couple hours," Conn rumbled. "Fuck the road."

"Yeah," Topper said. "That's what I was thinking. But when you get there, there's only this bridge to the island from the shore. You make it that far, sure, and then they strafe the shoreline with a .50 cal and that's that. They blow the bridge up like they did the other one across the river. I mean it ain't rocket science. Only other thing is to get some boats and raid it at night from the far end of the reservoir. But I don't want to put all them fuckin' kids at risk, neither."

He was sweating by now, his mind working with unaccustomed vigor and the tequila working as it always did.

"But the basic idea is good," Ginny said. "Make a diversion involvin' where the kids are, somehow, then crash the main gates of town. If we got word to the people inside, they could be waiting for us there. Right now there's only eight of us but there must be a few hundred on the inside who would join us in a heartbeat. Get Ernie back, too."

11

Ultimately, Danny walked out alone, without the Silent Kid.

It took two hours of negotiation, first in the hallway and then, when raised voices were disturbing the children, at the desk. The Architect himself eventually showed up. Had he been capable of much emotion, he would have been furious; as it was, he was as irritated as Danny imagined one of the so-called unliving could become.

A timetable was established. Danny had to make her move tonight or it was all over; the Kid was collateral to ensure she performed.

"We give you the boy now, you won't follow through," the Architect said. "We're done negotiating."

"And if I put that church out of operation and kill the thing on the cross, you'll make me head of security."

"Yes. I'll also guarantee you a seat on the escape train if things go amiss."

The escape train. Danny had been right about that.

"All these people working for you, did you make them that promise? Is Nancy here expecting a seat on the train? Seems like it doesn't have that many seats."

"It's a moot point, is it not? With us keeping the so-called moaners out, and you keeping the locals under control, we won't require it."

"Twenty-four hours, starting now," Danny said. "And the first thing I do is take a walk in the countryside."

"What?"

"You just offered me a permanent job. I want to review the perimeter and see how good the security really is around here before I commit."

In the end, they had a plan. Topper shaped it and everyone else contributed; after a certain point there weren't any devil's advocates telling the others it was a crazy idea. Consensus was that they had to do *something*. Even if Danny had a scheme of her own, it couldn't hurt. The essentials were to create a situation at the island that would draw security resources away from town, toward the reservoir. Then they would hit the main gates of town, maybe drive an expendable vehicle through them. It wouldn't compromise safety much, because the gates were not there to keep zeroes out. That was handled at the outer perimeter in the badlands.

This plan required that someone get word to Danny—which they hadn't dared use Dr. Joe for, as convenient as it would have been. Ginny contributed the excellent idea of tucking a note in the grab handle of the backpack explaining what they planned to do.

"I hate like a motherfucker to say this, but I think it's me needs to do the mission alone," Topper said. "I'm the only one been up there. I can get up the river to that reservoir there and make enough noise."

"You know what's wrong with this plan?" Conn asked.

"It's a piece of shit," Topper said.

"It relies on a bunch of chook assholes on the inside doing something on their own."

"Nah. The place is tense. On the fuckin' edge. They're beheading people. First taste of freedom, they'll join us. We form up a fuckin' army and we parlay with those cocksuckers running the place. That makes sense."

"It's better than sitting on our asses," Conn said.

"I'm heading out solo to drop this pack off," Topper said, when the silence had gotten old. "Then I wait. I'll make my move after dark. You fuckers stand by. The action will be early morning, if this shit goes right. If not, fuck it. I'm probably dead. In that case get good and fucking drunk. And forget all about it."

It looked like snow outside. Any minute now.

Danny walked through the badlands and saw nothing but wildlife. It was empty and cold and lonely, but she liked it. Stray snowflakes fell from the gallows sky, but didn't add up to anything. There were no zeroes. It was a strange feeling, as if the world had been reset to a long-ago time. Animals everywhere, unafraid of her. They had a new enemy; the living posed no special danger to them. She strode among deer, saw coyote and foxes slipping low and straight-backed through the scrub and bracken. Long-footed jackrabbits flashed from cover as she passed, then stopped and eyed her over their shoulders. Birds cried from every tree, and the crows settled thickly on telephone wires that were already sagging without men to keep them firm.

For an hour, she was left alone. The temptation to check the spot she'd selected for the backpack delivery was almost overwhelming; it was a cairn of rocks with a rude cross stuck in the top, the funeral mound of somebody with the good fortune to be buried, about fifty meters from the road. Danny had chosen it because there was a deep erosion wash nearby and a lot of dense bushes all around it; easy to approach, and the floor of the wash was hard-packed silt, and therefore easy for a person with wheels to negotiate. The road dipped down to it, which protected that particular spot from view of the town.

She wanted to look right away, but it wasn't directly on her route, and it might yet be too early. She hoped Dr. Joe had delivered the message. She hoped the scouts were still with her. If the black backpack wasn't there, she'd need to improvise on a level that didn't promise much success.

She headed away at right angles to the drop location. Early in her walk, she saw a distant figure almost beyond sight, lying atop a kopje of big rocks, elbows up at the shoulders; he must have been watching her with binoculars. One of the half-living, she guessed. He probably didn't think she could see him, and she made no indication she could. But she'd been a man-hunter too long to miss a human silhouette.

The unliving wouldn't do anything to hinder her, she expected, not with the public relations value of this visit. She would bring back a glowing safety report that might defuse the tension in town for the Architect and his underlings. None of them would interfere. Unless all of them attacked her at once, which was a distinct possibility if the Architect didn't think she *would* bring back a glowing report after all. Danny's mind was working every facet of the problem at once, her thoughts crowding and shouting for attention. This quiet interlude helped. She was starting to organize the data. A plan would follow. Now that there was a time limit, she had to take decisive action.

She made a great show of walking in a beeline toward where she'd been told to find the outpost. She knew the playbook well: They would have wired ahead to the sentinels there. Clean everything up, conceal anything unpleasant that didn't suit their story. Danny had encountered this a hundred times in the war zones of the world. Politicians thought the illusion of compliance mattered far more than actually performing according to treaties and human rights standards; Danny knew that it didn't matter much to boots on the ground, either. Just make a good presentation and let everybody get back to their strongholds. But this was different. She wasn't interested in a show; she knew better. So she walked along upright and swiftly without deviating from her course until she was sure she'd been seen by another couple of spotters.

Then she found what she'd been hoping for: The badlands were scored by erosion channels that twisted like veins over the coarse ground. They ranged from a couple of meters deep to near-canyon gulfs with walls of ancient, striped stone. At last she encountered one that ran northward, which would take her well off the direct course to the outpost. It was deep and broad. She marched down below the horizon, bearing along her direct course, until her head was invisible to any onlookers beneath the rim of the wash. Then, when her boots found hard stone that wouldn't leave any tracks, she ran.

She kept up a good pace, following the northward windings of the ravine, for about a kilometer. Then she scrambled up the steep western bank and crawled into the open again on her belly. Plenty of brush to conceal her. She took a few moments to search for another watcher, and saw none. This redoubled her suspicion that someone was keeping an eye on her.

She crawled through the frozen dirt for the length of two football fields, reached some dense shoulder-height scrub, and hustled through it in a half-crouch, like a hunter zero stalking its prey. She was following the same course as before, now, but almost a kilometer north of the expected route, behind what she guessed would be the observers' line. Her stealth was rewarded: As she moved along below a low ridge of black stone, she crossed a gap. In that gap she saw a figure, certainly one of the sentinels, with his back to her; he was positioned in such a way that he would have enjoyed a good view of her passing by along her original course. He was only a hundred meters to the south of her position. He heard nothing, but stood leaning against a rock, shading his eyes with a hand, staring southward. Danny moved on, angling to the north to increase the distance between herself and the sentinels.

Then she came to the defensive line, the perimeter where the infected waited out the last months of their mortal lives keeping Happy Town safe. She could see a couple of them, standing motionless, eyes fixed on the western horizon. They were supposed to be harmless around the living, like the ones in town, but they gave her the creeps. She was too acquainted with the hunger they felt to reveal herself unexpectedly to them. Far from the eyes of town, bored and ravenous, they could attack her and claim she'd never arrived. Danny continued to move cautiously, although she had very little time to lose; any moment now they would realize she had disappeared, and they would be following her intended route back to find her.

As she drew closer, bent double so that her chest was parallel to the ground, she saw that there were moaners out beyond these infected few; more and more the closer she got. They drifted parallel to the line formed by these sentinels, and now and then a sigh of hunger would punctuate their wandering, like the groan of rigging on abandoned ships. The terrain became grassland to the west, which represented the easternmost fringe of the plains where Danny had discovered the radioactive train wreck and where she had left the Tribe. Here was scrub and short, tough trees. She was almost upon the line by now, and saw that there was a physical border between the land of the undead and the land of the unliving.

Buckets—white five-gallon paint buckets, black plastic nursery pots originally for rosebushes, trash bins, anything that would hold liquid—had been set down in a ragged bow-shaped line running north to south, curving toward the east at each extreme, forming an immense hoop with its center somewhere near Happy Town. Did they shit in the buckets? Fill them with thinker laundry? It had to be scent-based, whatever their system for deterring the moaners.

Danny crawled the last of the distance with her chin in the grass, desperate not to be seen but equally determined to see what the sentinels used to keep the zeroes at bay. Whatever it was, she intended to use the same system in the future. This was the secret of Happy Town. Break that formula, and every place could become a refuge.

The nearest bucket was an ornamental planting pot made of terra-cotta, stamped with swags and cherubs. Probably from someone's front porch. The one to the south about thirty meters distant was a drywall Spackle bucket, the one equidistant to the north a rusty steel drum that had once contained deep-frying oil. All around the five-gallon size. She could see one of the sentinels with his back to her, close enough so she could see the emblem stenciled on the back of his insulated vest. Slightly too far to read the lettering. From here she moved like a cold snake, lazily slithering toward the terra-cotta pot, moving with as little sound as she could.

There was a terrible stink near the pot. She suspected she'd been correct about the deterrent; probably these things crapped in the buckets, one after another, keeping the stench fresh. She wriggled around until the bulk of the pot was between her and the sentinel, then got her knees under her and gingerly raised her eyes to the top of the container, keeping them fixed on the sentinel's back. He continued to stand casually, relaxed, shifting his weight from foot to foot. The picture of boredom. Danny's nose was almost over the rim of the pot by now, and she risked breaking visual contact with the sentinel to glance down into the pot.

Cloudy eyes stared up at her, skinless teeth snapping; the head floated in a pool of rotten blood and gutted vermin, boiling with maggots even in the freezing air. Steam rose from the cadaver-broth.

She almost cried out, but stifled the shock with her good hand and flung herself back on the ground, flat and shaking.

"Who's there?" a voice cried, hoarse from long disuse.

Danny lay in the dirt, choking back a flush of acid in her throat. She waited. No footfalls approaching, nothing but some warring songbirds in the tall grass. The pot stood between her and the sentinel; she doubted he could see any part of her. But precious time was slipping away, and she might be stuck here indefinitely.

Then she heard a radio line crackle open, and there was a brief conversation. Moments later the sentinel scurried away. She waited for another thirty seconds and cautiously raised her head. The sentinel was almost gone from view, hurrying along down the line of pots southward. Her absence from the appointed route must have been noted. Her time was now extremely limited.

She scrambled to the next pot, and the next, keeping as low as she could, watchful in case another sentinel was answering the call. But none came.

In each pot there was a severed head, usually with the entire neck and throat attached. Each head was half-submerged in obscene ichor of guts and dead animals, probably by way of a nutrient solution, to keep the things animated. She hurried down the line and peered into another dozen containers. From each a pair of sunken, sightless eyes rolled up at her, accompanied by sneering, champing jaws.

She looked up and down the line and guessed there must be a thousand such containers. Only a few of the sentinels were volunteers. The rest had little choice, deprived of their bodies as they were. She wondered if any of the things were conscious.

At least she now knew the secret to the key defense of Happy Town.

Thirty minutes later, the sentinels found Danny sitting at the bottom of a ravine in more or less the correct path, one boot off, massaging her ankle.

"Where the fuck have you been?" she said harshly, as soon as the first of them appeared atop the edge of the ravine. "I damn near broke my leg."

It took a while, limping as she was, and unwilling to accept any assistance from the unliving; they walked along beside her, and she had time to see what they really looked like without makeup and fresh clothes. They appeared more or less like thinkers, except there was a livid purple stain around their eyes and their lips were swollen and congested and black. Their hearts must still be forcing some blood around inside them. Their skin was metallic and gray, with an almost gelatinous transparency. Their clothes were as rotten as those of the moaners wandering along the western horizon, but kept in some sort of order, and some of the items—boots and jackets, mostly—were recent additions. The things must still be susceptible to cold. Still human in that way.

She hobbled along between six of them, and others came near to look at her before returning to their posts. All of them looked like ghosts, sallow and emaciated and with incalculably sad, hungry eyes that watched her with something near to yearning. Danny was reminded of *Oliver Twist,* one of the eight or nine books she had ever finished in her life. She'd read it in high school. The descriptions of abject poverty had fascinated her, because until she read that old book she hadn't understood that she herself was poor. These things looked at her the way the children in that book watched the feasting of their superiors, swallowing their own saliva and dreaming of something more substantial to fill their bellies. There was only a shred of humanity left to them.

She saw something else in their eyes, but couldn't name it. Had she thought about what these creatures knew of her, or had heard the stories they had been told, she would have known it was awe.

They were afraid of her.

After a fifteen-minute interval of limping along that would otherwise have been five, they reached the outpost. It was a tin shed with sods of dead grass on the roof, probably to keep it from blowing away. There was a radio aerial towering up over the shed and a single power line strung up on ten-foot poles that ran away to the east. A couple of pickup trucks stood in the hard-packed dirt of the yard. Down the access road a little way was an Asplundh wood-chipping truck with a Dumpster next to it.

An unliving in whom the infection wasn't quite as advanced as it was in the others emerged from the shed. She was missing a lot of hair, and her face was marked with opalescent boils that looked to Danny like the mutations she'd been seeing more and more of among the undead; it was probably this affliction that had caused her to be sent away from Happy Town prematurely. No makeup could cover these growths, which resembled eyeballs bulging from crusty red lids. But she had the vulnerabilities of the living, still, and breathed and coughed and covered her pustulant face with her hand when Danny came close, like a geisha concealing laughter.

"We thought we'd lost you," the woman said. "You'll pardon me if I won't shake your hand. I'm Lashawna. Are you hurt?"

"Took a fall down one of those gullies," Danny said. "I should have let somebody drive me out here."

"I'll drive you back," Lashawna said. "God it's good to see another liv—I mean, somebody who can talk and stuff. These guys are so quiet. I've been out here for a month getting colder and colder and there's just nothing going on except those things out there and these guys over here and a whole lot of smelly buckets."

"What happened to your face?" Danny said. She didn't want to chat.

"It's a symptom."

"It sure is," Danny said. That took care of Lashawna's desperate desire to talk. "Tell me about these buckets," Danny went on, when she realized Lashawna might start crying.

"We . . . Okay. We put remains in the buckets. Any undead that get destroyed, they go in the buckets. We, um, relieve ourselves in them, too."

She didn't mention the still-animated heads. The best lie is almost true.

"The buckets are just part of it," Lashawna continued. "The main thing is *we're* here. The moaners won't attack us because of our condition, which I guess you know about, but there aren't enough of us to make a solid wall. So the buckets make sort of halfway-stops to keep those things away."

"You just crap in the buckets and chop up moaners and put them in the buckets?" Danny said.

"That's it."

"Like hamburger?"

"I can show you," Lashawna said.

Danny made a limping inspection of a dozen of the buckets nearest the outpost, which had been filled just as Lashawna described. There were no severed heads gnashing their teeth in these ones, of course, but a slurry of purple-brown, unidentifiable mush. They stank the same, but lacked that crucial ingredient, the thing that *really* kept the moaners at bay. Still, the subterfuge was convincing, and Danny allowed herself to be convinced. An especially effective flourish occurred toward the end of her visit, when a pickup with a couple of moaner corpses in the back arrived at the outpost.

Danny and Lashawna watched from the doorway of the shed as a pair of sentinels climbed out of the pickup; another emerged from the cab of the wood-chipping truck, which was of the commercial type, like a big orange-painted garbage truck. The three of them off-loaded the corpses; then the one from the cab returned and started the chipping mechanism, which roared and coughed smoke. Then the three of them unceremoniously tossed the corpses into the chipper. The steady rattle of the motor went shrill and staccato as the bodies were torn to pulp. Once the unit was powered down, the sentinels rolled the Dumpster to the back of the truck; then the operator tipped the entire cargo bed back on its hydraulics and a slurry of black muck slurped into the Dumpster.

"That's the system," Lashawna said. "It's obviously pretty nasty, but it works."

"And this would work anywhere? To keep the moaners out?"

"Oh, sure, I guess," Lashawna said, sounding entirely unsure.

"Amazing," Danny said. There was nothing more to learn here. She'd politely (or impolitely) watched the show put on for the visiting dignitary; none of them suspected, as far as she could tell, that she'd discovered how they *really* kept the perimeter zero-proofed. Everything was going according to the Architect's plan. And Danny had gotten what she needed to know: On her walk from town she'd seen the barricaded turn-off road that led around the mountain to the resort. She'd seen how big the safe zone around town was. She'd seen how close to the perimeter the moaners came, and that there were a lot of them out there waiting for a breach in the line.

Happy Town was one small fuck-up from disaster, and there were fifty fuck-ups waiting to happen.

Maybe the Risen Flesh didn't know it, but the Architect certainly did, or he wouldn't be rushing to get the escape train ready: This little safe place was almost out of borrowed time.

It was getting dark, later than she'd intended, when Danny got into a truck with Lashawna, with one of the sentinels riding in back; the sentinel got down a kilometer outside Happy Town, and Lashawna stopped a couple of hundred meters from the front gates.

"I can't come any closer, because of . . . you know," she said.

"Yeah, I sure do," Danny said, cruelly. Her mean streak was getting worse, she thought. But she could not hide her contempt for these creatures who had given up their humanity so cheaply, who had allied themselves with their mortal enemies. Lashawna was a vulnerable, very sick, terribly deformed woman whose future was even bleaker than that of the living who were doomed to be devoured alive. But she was also a collaborator, a traitor not just to her species, but to everything with a pulse in its veins. If Danny had found an opportunity, she would have destroyed her companion without hesitation.

"I gotta piss," she said, by way of farewell, and left Lashawna to her unhappy fate. Then she limped toward the nearby burial cairn and out of sight of the town gate. The truck drove away into the badlands.

Danny glanced back to make sure she wasn't observed, then crouched down and circled the pile of stones, her heart accelerating into her throat. If the pack wasn't there—but it was. She saw it propped among the stones at the base of the pile, the black nylon camouflaged with a few handfuls of dirt. She opened the combination lock and checked the contents. All there. She almost missed the note tucked into the handle, as it had slipped to the ground, but paper litter was rare in those days. It caught her eye. She read the note twice.

Then she headed back up the wash, backpack slung over her shoulder as if she'd had it with her the entire time. The feigned limp was gone, no longer required. She passed through the gates as they were laboriously shoved open by the guards. Nobody spared the pack a glance.

Her course of action was perfectly clear, now. Her resolve was set. She might have remained undecided, except for the contents of the last bucket she'd looked into during the unauthorized part of her reconnaissance. It was just another severed head with its bare teeth and rolling eyeballs, except Danny knew the face, because it was fresh and the features were unmarked by decay. It had once belonged to one of her finest scouts. Ernie—who was also Topper's best friend. Even then, she might have found some way to reconcile herself to the savage frontier justice of these people.

Except there was no question in her mind that Ernie's still-animated eyes had looked up into her face—and recognized her.

The twilight was rearing up under the snow-pregnant sky, darkening the world. Danny was planning her next move, watching the light die. A couple of guards regarded her from their shed next to the gate; a light came on inside and Danny got a glimpse of a cook stove and a couple of cots before one of the men closed the door. Then headlights winked through the gloaming up near the center of town and a security van came tearing down the street toward her. It scraped to a halt and Cad Broker jumped out, scooping his arms at her:

"We have a situation. Get in the van. Now."

Danny heard a distant roil of voices that she had previously thought were crows. There was gunfire that echoed and clattered against the mountain. She sprinted forward and jumped into the van after Cad.

"There's a fight," Cad said. He was out of breath, and his wheezing for air sounded like the Architect or the Risen Flesh. Danny clung to the grab handle in the ceiling as the van rocked around corners. There were three guards with them, and they weren't there to keep an eye on Danny. They were looking through the windows, fingers hooked around the triggers of their weapons. Amateurs. One good speed bump and they'd shoot up the van.

A couple of blocks into Main Street they stopped and the guards piled out.

"Somebody give me a sidearm," Danny said, and nobody did. So she opened the van driver's door and held out her good hand. The driver looked at Cad, who nodded, and then he slapped an automatic into her palm.

There was smoke rising up from the area around the Civil War statue. Searchlights roamed over the gathered heads, but didn't know what target they sought. It had the look of a rock concert. A mob of people blocked the view down the street; fists and sticks and bottles raised overhead reminded Danny of all the riots she'd seen in the war zones before the fall of civilization. She dropped the clip and counted the rounds. Nine. The ammo was mismatched, from three different manufacturers. There was a muffled *bang* and a puff of black smoke rose over the crowd. People screamed.

The asphalt and the sky were the same color. It was dark now. Felt like snow. These thoughts flitted through Danny's head as they always did when there was a battle ahead. Occupy the mind, distract it with trivia, keep it away from the fear and anger that would come when the fight was on. As the seconds ticked past she expected the fight to break up. But it appeared to be escalating.

Glass broke. There was another *bang*.

"I'm going to see what's happening," Danny said. "This entire fucking town is on the edge of collapse. You know that, right?"

Cad nodded. He was scared shitless, Danny saw. He must know how short his remaining days would be if the Architect fell out of power. People must have known there was something alien about him. Some must know about the infection. Word would travel. He'd find himself in one of those stinking buckets out there in the badlands.

She thought of all the people crammed into their little shops and apartments cowering in the dark, and the kids in the warehouse hearing all the noise, probably descending into terror. It was time. The Architect was right: She needed to act immediately. But after what she'd seen out in the badlands, he wasn't going to like what she'd decided to do. He was going first.

Danny strode toward the back of the crowd, then when she was among the most timid of the rear guard, she got up on a wrought-iron bench and looked over the heads in front of her. There on the ground by the statue was an acolyte, dark blood flowing out of his head. He was dead for real, not only half-dead. A couple of the blaze-vested guards were carrying one of their fellows to the back through the crowd on that side of the street. He didn't show any outward injuries, but his face was fish-belly white. He didn't look good. Then a brick sailed through the air and clipped one of the men carrying him. He tumbled to the ground and the stunned guard fell across the wounded man.

A syncopated refrain of gunfire crackled out, and now people were running. The shots had been fired into the air, Danny thought, but she still jumped down off her perch. People were stampeding. Then a second wave of gunfire broke out, and now several panes of glass in the Architect's upstairs office shattered. There were gunmen inside the church, shooting across the square. Several young men with rags tied around their lower faces rushed out of a building on the third side of the square—the same building Danny had seen the refugees running from on her first fateful night in Happy Town. They were carrying Molotov cocktails, several each. The one in front used a lighter to set fire to an old flannel shirt, dropping it on the pavement, and the others dipped their improvised missiles into the red flames. Now the crowd was panicking two ways—gunfire and fire itself sent them in all directions. The silhouettes of the people in the crowd looked like shadow puppets. A path was opening up in the direction of the bank building.

The military training that ran Danny's waking life kicked in and she found herself drawing a bead on the young man who had set the shirt on fire. She could knock him down with a single easy shot. She hesitated. Take him out for the safety of the people around him, sure. And then she would have publicly chosen sides. She'd be in the fight, and whatever happened after that she could not shape events to achieve her goals. The Silent Kid wasn't going to jump into her arms again just because she shot some asshole with a Fanta bottle full of gasoline. She lowered the weapon and waited as he threw the blazing vessel in a high arc at the bank. It didn't even come close. One of the guards had to beat the flames out of his pants leg; otherwise all that was accomplished was a sooty fire in the middle of the road.

Danny moved. She got low and hustled toward the bank in a zigzag that would take her to the side farthest from the main street, where the vestigial ATM machine was. Her course of action was simple: use her VIP status to claim she was joining the defense of the bank, get upstairs, destroy the Architect. She'd have to wing that part, because they couldn't know it was her who did it—not until she'd used the ensuing excitement as cover to get to the Risen Flesh. This whole thing could be over inside half an hour.

As Danny hustled toward the bank, another guard shot the bomb-thrower. He went down heavily, strings cut. A hail of flaming bottles followed a second later from his companions, and then they were scattering into the crowd with the rest, covered by the blooming garden of flames leaping up in the town square. A couple of bystanders didn't move fast enough and were engulfed in flames. Danny got to the porch of the bank and immediately found two automatic rifles pressed into her face. She tucked her pistol in her waistband and showed them her hands, identified herself. The guards were so wound up she felt the real possibility of getting her head blown off. She hadn't expected it, but these men were not as panicked by the action in the street as typical civilians would be. They could be ex-military, or mercenaries from an outfit like Blackstone or Xie. She calculated the odds of killing the Architect were still pretty good; she could argue her way up to him, at least.

But there was no chance she'd get away alive once the job was done.

And that was an important part of the plan. It was no good destroying one of these things if the other one was still around.

The crowd dispersed once the guards built up a solid cordon around the town center. A van pulled up and the wounded cocktail-thrower was dragged aboard. Half a dozen civilians had been injured badly enough so they had to be carried, but no others were picked up by the guards; the rest were borne away by their allies, leaving pools of blood to jelly up on the cold ground. The burn victims left under their own power, although Danny knew it was only shock. Once the blackened flesh started to crack off and reveal the white fat beneath, they wouldn't be moving around. Not for a few months. The gasoline fires in the street went out on their own once the fuel ran out, leaving carbon scars and bubbling asphalt and darkness behind.

By then, Danny had herself dispersed; Cad had told the guards she was on their side, the guns had been lowered, and Danny had taken the opportunity to do her best "pissed-off superior officer" face at them. But her thoughts were on something else: the scouts. They would probably meet heavy armed resistance to their feint at the Happy Town gates. It wasn't going to be as straightforward as it would have been only a few hours earlier. But that kind of diversion was ideal for Danny's purpose. Draw the firepower away from the church and the bank. Get security's backs turned, then use her apparent insider status to slip inside and do the dirty work.

Topper's plan, as outlined in his note, was exactly what she needed.

13

Topper moved through the darkness and wondered if he was in love with the sheriff or just a dumb asshole. She had some kind of hold over him. It wasn't her complete lack of charm, her croaking voice, or the fact that she ran like a man. It wasn't the scars or the broken nose or the stumps of her gnawed-off fingers. There was just something about her, like down underneath it all, if life had gone another, better way, she would have been the friend he'd want to go hunting with. Ride across the deserts and camp under the stars and get drunk at the Double Down in Vegas.

He'd heard gunfire a few minutes earlier, but that wasn't unusual in Happy Town. So he let his thoughts go where they would. If anything, the action in town would keep him safer from detection. He might even be able to get inside the perimeter.

He still had trouble believing they'd gotten naked together. Topper had a standing bet with the other scouts that Danny did *not* have a penis. He knew he would never collect, even though it turned out he was right. Why was that? Because he respected her, maybe. But more than that. He didn't want to betray her. They had a secret and it was worth more than he could express.

Happy Town cast a tea-colored glow behind the bulk of the ridge across the river, against the low clouds. Topper moved quickly by flashlight for the first few miles, and then switched to night vision goggles. Good military-grade gear. He reached the blasted-out bridge piers. Above him were guards on the intact bridge, and up in the trees on the far side of the river there was a patrol crashing around. He moved with deliberation, watching for trip wires. At one point, he saw an incongruous pool of greenish light ahead, and had gotten considerably closer before he realized it was a fixed infrared camera's light source shining across a small path along the river's edge. He skirted around behind it, his route taking him partway up a cliff.

After a couple of hours of slow-motion creeping along, he was feeling the cold through his layers. But up ahead he could see with his naked eyes a glimmer of light that must be the dam holding the reservoir in place. The authorities in Happy Town focused on the bridges, of course. The dam would be heavily watched. He didn't think they'd be looking at the steep cliff walls on either side, however. An avalanche would get their attention. He settled the night vision goggles on his face and began the tricky ascent up the rock, taking a long, angled route that should end up with him directly above the end of the dam.

He was about two hundred feet above the gurgling black river on a sharp ledge, easing his way toward a slim pine tree that sprouted from the cliff, when a spotlight blazed on. The night goggles seared his eyes for a second; he tore them off and they whirled out of the light into the water below. There was a crackle of amplified static, and then a voice boomed out, "*We are lowering a rope to you. Don't move, or you* will *be shot.*" Pebbles chattered down from above.

"Sorry, Sheriff," he muttered to himself. "You're on your own."

14

Danny went back to the hospital. She had never expected to see it again; she could hardly claim she was bedridden at this stage, and if her brain was bleeding, it didn't change much. She could bleed out there where the action was just as easily. No headaches that entire day, despite all the activity and excitement. But she went back because she had a feeling her adventures might be drawing to a close, and she wanted to see Amy and Patrick one more time. She promised herself she wouldn't get maudlin and talk about death, weep on their shoulders, or any of that horseshit. She just wanted to look at them again, say something that wasn't mean, and slip on out while everybody was feeling good.

But she didn't see them, as it turned out. The hospital was busy, even at the late hour when she returned; the wounded were crying in pain somewhere on the second floor, there were extra guards patrolling the halls, and when she inquired, nobody knew where her friends were. She thought of leaving a note, or waiting around to see if one of them came by. It didn't seem like the right thing, somehow. In the end she stopped a female nurse heading up the main stairway and asked her to convey her thanks to Dr. Joe—thanks for everything.

Then she went out past the guards and into the cold night.

15

Topper expected to end up at the bank building, which seemed to be the new town hall; instead, he was marched through the woods to a gate in the perimeter fence at the foot of the mountain, then straight through a series of security barricades near the train tracks. His captors had this down to a science. He didn't try to escape. With his wrists zip-tied together and the darkness and uneven ground he wouldn't get far. They took him across the tracks, where a bunch of men were outfitting a sort of war-wagon train, and then he was taken into what had once been the station. It was blessedly warm. He hadn't been warm in days, not even at the little farmhouse. His greatest fear was that they would behead him; so far, he seemed to be heading in the right direction for that. He imagined his headless corpse flung atop the garbage as he'd seen done to others. If luck was with him, maybe they'd just stick him in a cell and he'd see Ernie again.

He wasn't made to wait long.

A man wearing dark glasses despite the night hour arrived. He was wearing so much makeup he looked like Liberace, and he chewed an enormous cigar. Topper would have loved a cigar. They found them sometimes, but usually rat-eaten or as stale as mummies. This one looked fresh. The new arrival looked strange, somehow, like he had a sickness. Topper puzzled over this. The man must have been important, because he had half a dozen guards flanking him with guns at port arms. They filed into the station and took up positions a couple of yards away from Topper; it reminded him of the scene in Hong Kong gangster movies when the villain and his minions met the hero face-to-face. In the movies, the hero always bluffed his way through the meeting, relying on sheer balls. Topper wasn't sure it would work in real life, so he waited silently.

"I am the Architect," the man said.

"Hi," Topper said.

"You came at a perfect time. We were just going around the mountain. Are you fresh as a daisy?"

"Am I what?"

"Never mind. Why were you at the river?"

"Recon," Topper said. Tell enough of the truth and they might leave him be.

"For what? Were you going to break in?"

"Friend of mine got picked up here. I was looking for him."

"Not her?"

"Him. Name of Ernie." Topper had a feeling this guy knew there was a connection between himself and Danny, and he wondered what she'd been up to. In the thick of things, probably. That being how she rolled. He decided he would deny knowing her, no matter what. Give her room to operate.

"Well enough," the Architect said. "Bring him along."

Then he went back outside, and Topper's guards shoved him into motion. He followed, and they descended to the tracks. There, a pickup truck was waiting. It had ordinary tires, but they were mounted on special wheels that allowed the vehicle to travel on train tracks or roads. Very stylish, Topper thought. He loved vehicles of any kind, especially if they were specialized in some way. This thing would make an awesome touring car— travel on the tracks wherever they ran, avoiding the messy, disintegrating roads. And if the tracks were busted somewhere, drive off the rails and travel as if it were an ordinary truck.

His thoughts were interrupted when a gun stock was jammed between his shoulder blades and he was half-hoisted into the bed of the pickup. Six men got in with him, all of them keeping their eyes on his face. The Architect and a driver got up in the cab. Then they started the journey along the tracks. They rolled through the sheds behind the station, and a big gate was hauled open by men waiting at the edge of town; the truck drove through, the gates swung shut, and they were moving through the night.

The train tracks clung to the cliff's edge for a while, skirting the foot of the mountain with the forest overhanging the rails. Then the route took a sickening turn out over the river, with a long drop into the darkness on both sides. This was the one bridge they hadn't blown up. Then they were running along the foot of the cliff opposite, traveling north along the route of the river. Topper's flesh was crawling. He could not imagine what they had in store for him. But if they tried to execute him in cold blood he was going to take at least two of them with him.

The canyon opened up ahead. He saw lights twinkling in the distance, and identical lights rippling below: water. They must be near the reservoir. Then the tracks crossed a broad concrete surface—the dam, Topper assumed—and even over the noise of the truck's engine he could hear the rumble of big turbines. So those sheds on the deck of the dam must be where they generated the power. These observations passed through his mind in a jumble; at the same time, he was thinking about whether he'd survive a jump into the water, and what a beautiful night it was, and wondering how long it would take the snow to start falling. It was as if his mind was eager to stock up on mundane observations while it still could. He had a terrible feeling his head was going to part ways with the rest of him, and soon.

The truck rolled to a stop at a jetty built up next to the tracks. There was a boat waiting there, a party barge on big pontoons: stable, safe, and slow. Probably something the resort kept around for guests. He was dumped without ceremony out of the truck, then manhandled down the wooden jetty and onto the boat. It seemed weirdly normal here, somehow. There were electric lights burning over the jetty, and here and there on top of the dam, and the resort island itself looked like Christmas. Lights everywhere. The barge's engine started up, the Architect got on last and sat primly near the stern rail, and they puttered out across the still, black water. Topper saw there was a lot of ice on the lake, but it had been broken up to make way for the boat. The island itself looked welcoming—bright lights, windows glowing, lawns with light coats of snow throwing the window light back. There were winding paths through the landscaping with tiny lights planted every few feet.

They landed on an identical jetty on the island, and the Architect went a different way with his entourage. Topper was marched along the less-scenic route, a paved road that ran along the water's edge, with paddleboats under tarpaulins lining the way. He still had four men holding guns on him. He might have tried something if his hands were free, but it was suicide as he was. So he allowed himself to be led, although keeping his eyes open for any avenue of escape. He could at least delay whatever they had in mind.

They circled a low hill that made up the bulk of the island. The biggest building, what must have been the resort hotel itself, stood on top of the hill and spread out in wings and additions down its flanks. It reminded Topper uncomfortably of the hotel in that old movie *The Shining,* like the carcass of a giant dinosaur punched full of windows. They came to a place where the hill had been cut away and the hotel came down to the same grade as the road. This was the service entrance where delivery trucks would have come. Big double doors, a concrete loading dock. The guards led Topper through an ordinary door set beside these, and all at once he was bathed in heat and light.

They walked down linoleum-floored halls. The lack of ornamental trim suggested this was the employee level; then Topper smelled food and heard the clatter of big pots and it was confirmed. The kitchens ran off underneath an entire wing of the place, and he caught a glimpse of several people scrubbing down industrial-sized cookware in big stainless sinks. They didn't glance up as he went by with his guards. It must have been a common sight. Or maybe they didn't want to see. Again, the fear took a firmer grasp on him, driving the warmth off his skin. They took a couple of turns, the hallways getting narrower at each branching, and then there was a flight of stairs.

"After you," one of the guards said. Topper could hear children's voices coming down the stairwell. He didn't move.

"I said get the fuck going," the guard added.

"I'm listening to the kids, man," Topper said. "They sound . . . happy."

The guard shrugged. Another gave Topper a shove. He ascended the stairs.

At the second landing, there was a door with a diamond-shaped window cut into it. The noise of children was coming through the door. Topper hesitated.

"You want a look?" the guard said.

Topper didn't respond, but ducked his head so he could look through the pane. He was seeing the dining hall. It was a big room with decorative columns and a carpet patterned with roses and vines, white walls and ceiling, chandeliers blazing with light. Long tables were set up in rows all through the space; a vast stone fireplace at the far end contained a log fire that leaped and danced. At the tables, or sitting cross-legged near the fire, or skylarking around the room because they were done eating, were hundreds of kids. They looked happy and well-fed; Topper saw some hadn't finished their meals. Mashed potatoes, some kind of meat, peas. Real food, it looked like. Topper's stomach wrung itself against his backbone. He could do with a plateful of that. He didn't see any kids from the Tribe in there, but they probably hadn't been processed yet. What he saw was laughter and play and an absence of fear and hunger.

Something tickled his face. He realized it was tears. He stood up.

"Thanks," he said to the guard. There wasn't anything else to say.

They walked along a hallway that ran the entire length of the dining hall. At the end was a freight elevator. Topper assumed they were going up, but the guard nearest the panel thumbed the button labeled B2. So they were descending to the waterline, or below. The elevator rumbled and Topper felt the long-forgotten tug of gravity as they dropped deep into the building.

He noticed the guards weren't looking him in the face any longer. They weren't answering his occasional remarks. The fear that had taken root in him began to branch out. The mood had changed. He wasn't with these men anymore, just among them. And he noticed the guns, which had relaxed their vigilance, were now concentrated on him again. He tested the bonds on his wrists and thought about how he was going to escape. The elevator doors opened, and they stepped into a concrete room with a couple of doors let into it to the right and left. Straight ahead was a corridor with stone walls. They were inside the hill.

Topper allowed himself to be led as before, but he found he was walking more and more slowly. The guards had to prod him to keep up. Being underground was driving home the desperation of his situation. The rock of the walls radiated cold and the concrete ceiling was dappled with mildew.

"Where are we going?" he asked, although he would rather have acted tough. He couldn't stop his mouth from forming the question.

"Debriefing," the guard said.

They reached a metal-clad door marked COLD STORAGE at the end of the corridor. One of the guards rapped on it with the heel of his hand, and it was opened from within by a man not dressed like the guards, but more after the fashion of a medic. Topper's heart sped up.

"When is the last time you had a meal?" the medic asked.

"Eight hours ago," Topper said. "Why?"

"Do you need to move your bowels?"

"Uh—no. Dude, what is this?"

"We like to keep things clean," the medic said. Then he swung the metal door wide, and Topper's guards half-wrestled him through into the space beyond, a low, concrete room with some peculiar equipment in it—frames and tables and plumbing he didn't recognize. A lance of panic cut through the fear. Topper gave no warning, but swung around and kicked the guard to his right as hard as he could. He caught the man on the hip; he fell heavily, shouting with pain, and Topper head-butted the man to his left in the temple as he reached down to pick up his comrade. An instant later, fists and knees flew into action, and more men came from behind somewhere. Now there were eight, and although Topper struggled and swore and kicked, he was immobilized within a couple of minutes.

The men dragged him into the room. In the middle of it was an upright X-shaped frame with straps dangling from it at intervals. There was a sort of skeletal table beneath this, and it appeared to be hinged. Topper went wild at the sight of this thing, he roared his threats and struggled against the men who dragged him to the cross. Then he pleaded with them, promised to help them fight back, even offered to join them. They were polite but disinterested. They simply did not care, any more than a slaughterman cares what the cows are thinking. Despite his struggles, they got his legs strapped to the lower half of the X, and three men held each of his arms while the others guided them into the straps and attached him to the upper half.

"Easier to tranquilize you," said the medic. "But we don't want to poison the meat."

The entire world blinked out for a second, then returned, but it was different now. Topper knew how he was going out. Then one of the guards operated a crank and the frame went from vertical to horizontal, so that Topper was staring up at the light fixtures on the ceiling. Then the guards passed scissors and box cutters around, and among them they were able to cut off all of Topper's clothing.

He lay there naked, spread-eagled, arms stretched out to the sides, and writhed against the Velcro straps that held him down. The tubing of the frame was narrow and cold, so it quickly became unbearably painful to lie on, digging into his spine and limbs.

Now his imagination had caught up to events. It was going to happen. There was nobody but him, and he wasn't going to get rescued or bust out. Topper wondered if he could swallow his tongue or stop breathing, kill himself somehow. Anything but what was coming. Hope was extinguished.

Poisoned meat, he thought. *Maybe I don't taste good.*

It was the living who had broken his spirit. They were human beings like himself, working for the undead in this godforsaken place like servants. Not slaves. These were people who went home at night, commuted to work. They didn't live in cages with leather collars around their necks and suffer floggings for impertinence. They were maids, butlers, and footmen. Mere subservient employees. He saw it when the guards brought him into the presence of the weird guy in makeup before. *The Architect,* they'd called him. They'd treated the Architect like he was rich and powerful.

Then he saw the Architect was in the room with him, looking on with a blank expression, as if deciding which lobster in the tank would be his dinner. But there was only one lobster. Topper had no allies. He was already dead, but had yet to die.

Now he wept. He could not recall having done so before. He must have cried as a child, but his memory didn't go that far back. And with his father being such a hard case, he might not have cried at all. This was different. He was blinded by tears. They ran down his upturned face and collected in his ears, spilling down the back of his head and falling to the concrete floor.

It was sorrow he felt for himself, not quite pity. All that life he'd had, all that surviving he'd done, and it came to this. He had to die the hardest way a man could in this ugly world. His destruction would go unrecorded. He was already nothing. The Architect looked silently on while the guards and the medic filed out of the room. Then he, too, walked out, and for a long time Topper was alone, the pain in his limbs gathering strength.

An hour later, three undead filed into the room. He could hear them forcing their lungs to inhale, sniffing the air with their sunken noses as they entered. But with his neck strapped down, he couldn't see them until they stood around him, their slack faces devoid of hunger, of interest, even of malice. There was nothing inside to animate them. Just skulls clothed in flesh. Their stained eyes gazed on him unblinking. Cold hands touched his skin. Their shoes squeaked on the polished concrete.

Then another entered, and the rest stepped back. Topper twisted his eyes to see. It was the Architect, and with him he had two people who had an undead look to them, but who were sweating and nervous. So not undead—but almost as if they were halfway there. From Topper's perspective, they were upside-down. He felt the blood racing under his own skin, the heat and sweat of himself, and knew it was about to be taken from him.

The Architect took the cigar from his mouth and drew a long, rough breath. Then he began to speak.

"We are gathered here to feast upon man. We shall feast according to the just law. We are not monsters. We are not barbarians. Are not we civilized?"

"We are civilized," the others breathed, in a chorus like a prayer.

"You fuckers," Topper spat out. All eyes turned to him, not with interest, but as human eyes would turn at the sound of a window slamming. He thought he saw a little sympathy in the face of the female who wasn't quite undead. "You fucking monsters call yourselves civilized? You're cannibals."

"We have risen from the dead," a female corpse said. "We are no longer creatures made of sex and desire. We have come from death and go to eternity."

"Fuck you," Topper said. He had no gift of speech. If they couldn't be reasoned with, he wished they possessed feelings he could hurt, or that it was possible to make them take offense. But they cared for nothing. All he knew was he wouldn't beg for mercy, no matter what happened. He was going to go out the way he lived: no prisoners.

A door opened and the medic circulated around the room, studiously ignoring Topper, and handed out cushions. Each of the undead took one.

"They'll eat you, too," Topper snarled at the medic. There was no response. He went out and shut the door. Once again, Topper was the only entirely living thing in the room.

"Tonight is a special evening," the Architect said. These two"—here he indicated the man and woman who looked ill, but not undead—"are new to the taste of man-flesh. They are becoming immortal. They are transforming. Tonight they release their fears and taboos and learn to be one with the eternal, unmoved by the feast. He is Cad and she is Nancy. Human names, a legacy of their fading humanity. Let's begin."

The Architect lowered his knees onto the cushion he'd been given. Mustn't harm the knees. Topper looked down past his body and could see the desiccated head with its cloudy eyes now hovering between his thighs. He felt his genitals shrinking, cold sweat running through the hair on his legs. His heart was smashing against his ribs and he wished it would explode. He made another furious attempt to escape his bonds, twisting his body, pumping his limbs. But there were straps around his ankles, knees, thighs, belly, and on up his body so that he could only shift his weight a little. He couldn't even bang his head against the bar that held him aloft.

"Watch and learn," the Architect said, glancing over his shoulder at the trembling inductees.

And with that he bared his long, dry teeth, and ate Topper's testicles.

The undead formed a vague line after that, in order of rank; they each chose a favorite part. One of the others held a basin beneath the mutilations to catch the blood, which was passed around to the half-undead. Cad and Nancy sipped timidly from it. Topper saw the hunger in their faces after the first taste, but he didn't make anything of it. The pain was too great. As the Architect had opened his jaws, Topper promised himself that he would not scream, but with the first agonies of teeth crushing and slicing through his living flesh, he shrieked at the top of his lungs, and continued to scream until no sound came out except a hoarse whistle. The pain was a flower of fire that bloomed new and bright every time his heart beat, always increasing until it seemed impossible that he could survive another moment of it.

When they began working with knives, Topped begged for mercy.

Gauze was stuffed in his wounds to keep him from losing consciousness; they slit open the skin of his chest and excavated one muscle at a time, cold fingers tugging at the meat, blades carving away the anchors and tendons that held the muscles in. First they mined out his pectoral muscles, the cuts bisecting his nipples; then they skinned and ate his calves. His buttocks were next, the blood flowing so freely they had to interrupt the feast to have the medic enter the room and bind the larger blood vessels with hemostats. Topper heard the knives grating against the exposed bones of his pelvis.

He was insane with agony, but he did not fail to see the living man working on his injuries, and the emptiness in his deliberately blank face and averted eyes. Topper wanted to beg for a cut throat or a thrust to his heart, but no coherent sound emerged from his mouth. He was an animal now, capable only of experiencing pain.

He lost consciousness only after they had greedily pulled out his intestines and the two new recruits were struggling to pull out his hot, heavy liver.

When Topper awoke, there was no pain, only hunger. A feeling of cold—not quite the sensation, but the sense of it—pervaded his mind, like a frozen landscape viewed through the window of a chilly room. He knew who he had been before, but that memory was all that remained of himself.

He was not an individual, but a bland consciousness devoted to its hunger. The world was filled with objects he could not consume, but there were living men present as well, and they stank with richness. He wanted to feast on them.

He saw with poorly-focused eyes that his remains were lying on the floor of the concrete room, the X-shaped frame above him, straps hanging down empty, glistening with blood. His head was tipped on its side so that he could see a mass of bloody driftwoodlike sticks festooned with glistening white and red tissue. Those must be the bones of his limbs, and the shapeless, empty barrel his body, all sloshing in a pool of clotted blood.

He felt no remorse, no horror. Only hunger.

There were others standing around him.

He rolled sluggish eyes up to look. It was the creatures that had eaten him, their clothes and faces stained with blood, rags of meat hanging from their teeth. One of them reached down and lifted him into a plastic bucket. He was staring up at the ceiling. A shape moved into view.

"Welcome to forever," the Architect said.

16

Danny forced herself to wait. She was sitting inside a tiny toolshed tacked on to the side of a house a couple of blocks west of downtown; the house itself had been extensively burned, so nobody lived inside it, and few windows overlooked the lot. It was cold in the shed, but not intolerable; there was so little space her body heat warmed it up.

She spent the time organizing the backpack and examining its contents; in combination, she had enough materiel in there to start a war or finish a small city. It scared her a little. She had got hold of something that was well above her pay grade. Letting other people handle the pack had taken a lot out of her, but there had been no alternative. At least nobody had tampered with the lock or tried to get into the bag; there were no signs of it, at least. The scouts were reliable people. Danny thought she ought to be nicer to them in the future. She often thought that.

She should have added a blaze orange vest to her demands. As it was, when she started moving around in the dark, she was going to have to rely on stealth, or if she was spotted by a patrol, she'd have to hope the Architect had sent word down to the troops not to apprehend or kill her. If they saw what she had in the pack she didn't think they would bother to ask for advice. It was a moot point, anyway: She couldn't ask the Architect for special dispensations, because then people would know he was complicit when things went down. He'd deny it.

When she couldn't stand to wait any longer, she forced herself to hold out for another half-hour. Then she stole out of the shed, oozing from shadow to shadow, still refusing to act upon the urgency that was trying to burst out of her. Everybody in town was on alert. This was going to take absolute caution.

After crossing through several yards and traversing the main street between searchlight sweeps, Danny reached the shadow of one of the buildings behind the church. She had decided, during the long wait in the shed, to attack the Risen Flesh first. The Architect commanded too many guns; she'd never make it out of the bank alive. So the church had to be first.

The door through which she had first entered the building was ten meters away. She thought it was probably locked, these days. But the Victorian hardware wouldn't stand up to much abuse. The Preacher and acolytes lived elsewhere, maybe in the very house she was hiding behind right now. Once she was inside, there would probably be at least two acolytes on guard, however. Maybe the entire contingent. She'd made her present task harder when she destroyed the first of them.

But her mission didn't require finesse. She had a dozen baseball-style hand grenades, some NATO and some U.S. Army. She thought two of them would take care of business. One to take down whichever guards were in there, and the second more or less shoved up the Risen Flesh's asshole. That was phase one of her plan. Phase two involved the bank across the street.

She took several deep breaths to get oxygen into her tissues and stuffed four grenades into her jacket pockets. Then she shrugged into the back-pack—it was heavy and cumbersome, but she couldn't afford to end up parted from it again. She even latched the chest straps around herself. If a stray bullet hit the pack or it caught fire or any of myriad other mishaps, she would be feeling no pain. Then she slipped the gloves from her hands. Absolute dexterity was required, and she was already at a disadvantage there. In ten seconds she was going to kick the door down.

"One," she whispered. "Two."

On three, the church exploded.

17

Danny was thrown off her feet.

The stained-glass windows all lit up at once, then turned into a million glittering butterflies, and then they were gone in a blast of smoke and debris. The entire structure of the church seemed to leap into the air. Its walls bowed outward and clapboards burst apart and flew whickering over Danny's head. With a great and mournful note, the bell in the church tower broke free of its moorings and sang its way through the air, then smote the Civil War statue, shearing the head off the bronze soldier and clanging to the ground. Thick mats of smoke belched out of the gaping windows and turned the now-crooked tower into a chimney.

Danny's ears were ringing and the backpack stuck jagged fingers into the coarse flesh of her back. She was covered with debris and bright fragments of colored glass. There were voices now, distant shouts and cries. A siren wound up to full voice and the spotlights wheeled around, glowing through the smoke. For the better part of a minute, she couldn't get up. Danny's head was blazing with pain again. She'd been told to avoid this kind of thing. Then self-preservation took over and she scrambled back away from the church, along the side of the house that had mostly sheltered her from the explosion. A storm door was flung open just in front of her; it led out onto a raised porch with three steps. Danny dived under the porch, jamming herself into the cobwebs and dead leaves underneath it as heavy footfalls banged on the boards overhead.

She'd been right: One acolyte came down the porch steps and ran for the church. They must be quartered in the house. She waited, although the cramped space was suffocating her. Where were the others? Had they come out the front door? After another half-minute she was rewarded by more cautious steps coming out onto the porch. She saw the Preacher's cowboy boots on the stairs, then watched as he walked down the side of the house. He stood a long while surveying the destruction of the church—the smoke was already clearing, and it appeared the place wasn't on fire. He stood there immobile, a crow-black shape framed by the ruination of his little empire. Then he spat on the ground next to his left toe and walked rapidly back the way he had come. He didn't go back inside the house. He just kept on walking. Somehow, Danny didn't think anybody would ever see him again.

She emerged from her hiding place and brushed herself off as best she could, then circled around the house so she could emerge at a distance from the action. The central square of town was pandemonium. Hundreds of people were spilling out of houses and businesses all up and down the streets, rushing to see what had happened. Some were wailing with terror, others whooping with excitement. Most were simply shouting, confused and alarmed. The guns on the rooftops were silent. They couldn't shoot this situation down.

"What happened?" Danny asked a woman running past in nightgown and ski parka.

"Oh, my God," she said, and kept on going.

So Danny joined the throng, and nobody seemed to take note that she was fully dressed, filthy, and wearing a heavy military-style pack on her back. The church was still standing, but it was an empty shell now. The doors had been blown off and the interior, while dark, was revealed in glimpses by the spotlights that roamed over the window holes. A great wreckage of pews and folding chairs was scattered across the floor. Lengths of broken timber spilled out of the window frames. Where the Risen Flesh had once hung, now there was only the upright post; she thought she saw a single foot, upside-down, still hanging from one of the holy nails.

Danny turned her attention to the bank, which the crowd was entirely ignoring in all the excitement across the street. The Architect was outside on his balcony, Cad on his right, Nancy on his left, with a dozen fully armed guards on the downstairs porch beneath their feet. But all of the interior lights were off. They didn't want anyone to notice them. None of the unliving saw her, as far as Danny could tell. But she now understood the game.

The Architect had set her up. He didn't know exactly when Danny would strike, or even if she would do so at all. But he knew she would be somewhere she wasn't supposed to be, and his minions could kill or capture her and that would be that. She was the scapegoat. Capture the terrorist, probably execute her, and he would win the sympathies not only of his own followers, but of the churchgoers who had lost their rotting god.

She'd seen it coming, of course. But she hadn't expected anything quite this spectacular.

She needed to get the hell out of there.

As Danny retreated through the backyard shadows of the suburbs, aiming vaguely for the school-hospital that was her temporary home, she saw gangs of men running down the streets, waving flashlights and guns around. She saw bewildered civilians beaten to the ground, mostly women. She had a feeling the setup theory was correct. A group of people were herded out of their house and forced to lie on the icy pavement in their underwear, guns pressed against their necks. Danny remembered there had been something like this in Nazi Germany, the Night of the Broken Glass. A witch hunt. If they found her, she wasn't going to make it as far as the show trial.

The hospital looked like a beehive stirred with a stick. There were guards patrolling the grounds and the streets around it. She wasn't going back there. Danny caught a glimpse of the medical staff being marched down the front steps; Dr. Joe Higashiyama had his hands laced together behind his head like the others. She wondered if they would kill him just for being her doctor. She wondered how many patients they would lose because the staff wasn't able to attend to them. Then she kept on moving. She needed to get through the perimeter fence.

The gates that controlled access to and from Happy Town stood open. There was a guard on the ground, facedown, and in the little guard shack where Danny had seen the stove and cots there was another guard lying faceup, his throat cut. She looked up the long axis of the main street and in the distance there were searchlights and smoke and noise, but here it was eerily silent. It could be a trap, but she decided to find out the easy way. Danny crawled out of the bushes of the last house beside the fence and walked up to the road. She paused. No voices rang out to challenge her. She approached the gates, which stood slightly ajar. Still there came no warning, no shots, no sudden glare of searchlights.

She stood in the opening, irresolute. Should she flee into the badlands and rejoin her companions at the abandoned house? Should she pay the Architect a personal visit by some devious route through town? Her ability to develop a plan seemed to have deserted her. Now her head was throbbing with pain, as well. If she had another of her blackouts, she wasn't going to find out how this thing ended.

She looked back into town and saw it was snowing again. Starting to come down hard, in fact. There was some gunfire and tiny screams reached her ears. The moaning of the wind was a sad commentary on the state of humanity. She watched the fat snowflakes spiral down, already dusting the road from black to gray.

Then Danny realized there was something impossible about the scene. She analyzed the feeling, because it was important somehow. She took each factor one at a time: the attack on the church, clearly coordinated by the Architect. The search for women. That much she understood. Then there were the open gates and slain guards. Something was wrong. She listened to the faraway noise of the mob, the howling wind, and watched the snow falling.

Then she understood.

The snow was falling straight down. But the wind was moaning, getting louder.

There was no wind.

Danny turned back to face the badlands, and saw the swarm approaching.

18

Adrenaline hit her veins like somebody was packing her entire body with ice. The area lights around the gate were nothing special, just outdoor fixtures of the type people put up over their garage doors. Several of them were motion-activated. Now they began to click on, casting light on the foremost of the undead.

Security around the gates had always been nominal, just for show; the real security was out in the badlands. Danny understood now where the acolytes had gone. They were out there in the wastes, breaking the thin line of defense. Now the moaners and hunters were on their way to the biggest human buffet this side of North America.

Danny shoved the gates closed. The locks had been cut open with bolt cutters, which lay on the pavement beside the nearest dead guard. Danny slung the broken chain around the frame of the two gates and jammed the cutters through the chain like a kind of steel clothespin. It would hold for a couple of minutes, no more. The entire road was filled with the undead, and their moans now drowned out the noise from downtown. As far as Danny's eyes could see, extending out into the darkness on either side, there were thousands of zombies, rotten and damaged and hungry, many of them grotesquely diseased with knobs and filaments and warts bursting through their putrid skin. She could already smell them with fifty meters to spare.

Danny knelt beside the corpse of the guard. He had a walkie-talkie on his belt. She had to make a decision. Call in the situation and risk capture or summary execution, or let things happen as they would, resulting in the destruction of every living soul in town. It wasn't a fair choice.

"Come in, somebody," she said. "I'm at the town gates."

"Who is this?" a male voice barked in response, fuzzy with static.

"This is the sheriff," she said. "You're looking for me. But you have a bigger problem. I'd deploy your entire force, right now, with everything you've got, to these gates. You have about ten thousand zeroes coming up the road."

She dropped the radio on the ground. Snow immediately began to accumulate on it. It was going to be a serious storm.

The first of the zeroes reached the fence, a small male she took for a child at first, but it was an adult. It hissed at her, fingers hooked through the mesh of the fence. Another joined it, and then another, and she saw the wire bulge and ripple as they threw themselves at the barrier, driven by hunger. Already the headlights of one of the security vans were bouncing down the road—they had taken her warning seriously. Or they wanted to capture her while she was still there. She was sure they wouldn't worry about her any longer once they saw what was coming.

But still, she ran alongside the fence and into the undergrowth. There was no point in getting shot along with the zeroes. No matter how far she ran, the undead were crashing into the fence. A pack of hunters, wizened and lean, were already halfway up the fence, the uppermost one of them tangled in the barbed wire at the top. It caught at the electrified strand and a spit of blue sparks followed it to the ground. The others snarled and snapped their jaws at Danny as she fleeted past.

She realized with a heavy certainty that whatever defense was to be made of Happy Town, she was going to be a part of it. The Silent Kid might be behind several near-impregnable barriers, but near wasn't good enough. The sheer weight of the undead would take down every obstacle. She was going to have to defend the children until the flesh was torn from her bones.

The return through Happy Town was easy. Everyone with a firearm was heading toward the gates as further reports of the swarm began to spread. Danny simply kept to the side streets and made the distance unopposed as far as the central intersection in town. There she paused only to see what was happening; the Architect and his immediate staff were nowhere to be seen, but the lights were on inside the bank. Panic had gripped the chooks as word got around. Most of the civilians, as had been Danny's experience throughout the crisis, fled at the first sign of trouble. So the streets were emptying out. Danny could not imagine how they thought a man-eating horde of the undead could be stopped by hiding under their beds. She spared a moment to think of her old friends. Patrick, Amy, Maria, so many others trapped in this shithole. She hadn't seen some of them in a while. Maybe at least Patrick and Amy were out there in the world already, far from the swarm. But there were other swarms. Other places like Happy Town trading the illusion of safety for the certainty of imprisonment.

Good fucking luck, Danny thought. That was as close to a prayer as she could manage.

Then she broke cover and sprinted up the street, heading straight for the fortified train station.

19

The guards had not left their posts. Danny was moving in the opposite direction of the tide—most people were fleeing into the suburbs or heading to the defense of the barrier. Word hadn't spread far enough so that there was a mob at the station, but there would be, soon. It was going to make the evacuation of Saigon look like a bus queue.

She was counting on these guards not being a part of the teams that had been looking for her earlier; if she was proven wrong, she'd shoot them where they stood. She let her hand rest on her hip, casual to look at but only inches from the gun in her waistband.

"They need you at the perimeter fence," Danny said to the foremost of the guards. There was snow settling on his shoulders.

"My orders—"

"There hasn't been time for new orders," Danny barked. "You got thousands of zeroes at the wire right the fuck now, soldier! Do you hear them?"

The uncanny sound of the swarm reached all the way to the mountain. She saw recognition and disbelief in his face. The guard looked to his fellows on the other side of the first, lowest barrier to the station. They didn't give him any clues.

"I'll go see," he said, and trotted down the street.

Danny wasted no time. The rest of the guards wouldn't be so easy. There were six men at the second barrier, and she couldn't see how many beyond that. They had fully automatic weapons and they were nervous. Danny didn't have any authority here, and they could even discover she'd been the enemy a few minutes earlier.

"We need to mount a solid defense," she said, her voice hard and loud, in order-delivering mode. "You're going to have every civilian in town trying to get on this train within ten minutes, when those gates go down.

I'm talking about ten fucking battalions of the ugliest zeroes you have ever seen, and they are *hungry*. Moaners and hunters. There are two things going to keep them from overrunning this town. Firepower and thinkers. There are thinkers here, but not enough. *Do you understand me?"*

Several of the men nodded; one even said, "Yes, ma'am." But none of them moved. She had to feed them every damn thing, apparently. Already there was screaming from the far end of town, muffled by the heavy snow-fall, but still unmistakable. Raw terror. The zeroes must have gotten through.

"You hear that? I want every one of you to take up a defensive position above arm's reach, you copy? Get up out of reach. Bring all the ammo, food, and water you can get your hands on, because that may be all you ever fucking get. We are going to mount a defense of this station. There are two enemies: panicked civilians and zeroes. You want the civilians on this side of the third fence, no matter what, because if they overrun the train, the children die. Are we clear?"

Nobody spoke. They were probably still trying to decide whether to shoot her.

"Are we clear?"

There was an explosion off in the distance. The snow falling from the sky lit up. That did the trick. The men scrambled from their positions, running to collect their gear. Danny only hoped they weren't running away entirely. She wanted one of those rifles.

She knew it was the perfect storm. Panic spreads asymmetrically. It's driven by what people can see and hear, not by information. People would freeze if they *heard* something like marching feet or engines approaching, losing precious seconds while they listened to determine which way the sound was traveling and ascertain what made it. They would run immediately if they *saw* something happen, always directly away from the thing they feared. People who hadn't seen or heard would often run in the direction of danger, to witness it for themselves. Others would join the panic and run, but in a random direction because they didn't know the source of the threat.

Danny wanted to get through the barriers and find the children, extract the Silent Kid from among the rest, and have him at her side while she did what she could to defend him. But it wouldn't work. In practice, you couldn't pick one kid and abandon the rest. So instead she scaled the quaint railroad props left on the station deck, barrels and crates stacked up almost to the eaves. She hooked a leg over the wooden gutter and almost fell—the snow and ice made the shingles as slick as soap, and the heavy pack overbalanced her. But she clung to the gutter and shifted her weight by main force. She was on the roof. Already the first of the guards were coming back, laden with gear. And they had men and women with them. The laborers, Danny guessed, who were quartered behind the barriers. People with strong arms. They would have to do.

She risked getting to her feet, her boots shuddering on the snow. They still didn't realize she had no authority here.

"Okay, listen up!" she shouted, and thirty or forty faces looked up. "Anybody who doesn't have a firearm, get one. If you can't get a firearm, find a weapon. Shovels, hammers, axes. Anything. You don't have to take the zeroes down, do you hear me?"

"Who the fuck are you?" one man shouted.

"I am the person who stands between you assholes and death," Danny said, and continued without missing another beat: "You don't have to take them down. You only have to break their jaws. If they can't bite, they can't kill. Are you hearing me?"

"What's happening?" a woman shouted.

Danny was glad she was on the roof, now. She had command of the situation. But more than that, she had a hell of a view down the main street.

"The town is about to be overrun by zeroes," Danny replied. "That's it. That's the situation."

"What happened at the church?" a man called, from the back of the group. As he spoke, another dozen workers appeared, coming through the heaviest of the fences. Danny observed they left the fortified gate open behind them.

"Unrelated incident," Danny said. She had every reason not to get into that subject. "We have five minutes to set up these perimeters for defense. No more. Pile up anything you can get your hands on across this gap. I want the doors and windows of this building barricaded with enough shit to keep a tyrannosaur out. Those of you with guns, get up top of something so you have a field of fire. The rest of you man the barricades and bust the head of any motherfucker that comes near."

"What about the noncombatants?" one of the guards said. He was among those Danny had seen when she arrived.

"Tell them to head for the river. Anything as long as they don't overrun this position."

In fact, Danny had no idea what to do about the civilians. They were going to hit the barriers faster than the undead. And now that they could hear the moaning of the undead coming up the main street, they were on their way.

Danny's vantage point on the station roof gave her an axial view down the entire length of town. She could see the back of the bank, with the crooked church and the headless bronze soldier beyond it. A flood of terrified people was coming straight up the road. They might not have thought of the train as a means of escape yet; so far they were simply running away from the danger. But the moment the train turbines started up, there was going to be a riot.

A ladder clattered against the eaves of the roof; a window opened in the charming cupola of the station. Men and women swarmed onto the roof, dragging all kinds of materiel behind them. Danny saw several rocket launchers and bristling armloads of guns. Cases of ammunition. One of the men, sixtyish with a salt-and-pepper mustache, slipped his way along the ridgeline of the roof and shook Danny's hand.

"I don't know who the hell you are," he said, "but welcome aboard."

His name was Mickey Orlando, he was ex-Navy, and he knew a Marine when he saw one. That was all the conversation they had time for. Then Danny was shouting orders down at the people on the ground and Mickey was organizing the defenses on the roof. Somebody slipped and fell over the edge and broke something, but otherwise they were working with the desperate calm of people with no alternative.

Then the civilians arrived.

Fifty people became a hundred, and a hundred became two hundred, shouting in fear and demanding to know what was being done to secure their safety and the safety of the children. Somebody handed Danny a bullhorn. She slid down to the edge of the roof, wet slush clinging to her boots, and clicked it on.

"You need to remain calm," she began, and nobody heard her amplified voice. She reached out to Mickey, indicating his AR-15. He handed it to her. She fired a burst of five rounds into the sky, and the crowd settled down enough so she could hear the brass jingling to the ground below.

"I will tell you what you need to do," Danny tried again, shouting into the horn. The people were still making a lot of noise, but they could hear her. "Head for the river. Go east to the river. You will not be opposed. Tear down the fence there if you have to, but get down to the waterline and follow the shore south. The quicker you go, the fewer casualties. Now!"

She handed the bullhorn to Mickey. He got the idea, repeating Danny's message as the crowd swelled to three hundred, then five hundred, the street black with people. They were beginning to flow along the edge of the fence that protected the railway tracks, moving east. There could be an army of zeroes moving up the river shores. The chooks might be running to their deaths. It was a shitty idea, Danny knew, but the only alternative was to lose control of the station, the train, and the kids.

She had hoped to hold the line until morning; if they could get the kids out by train, the surviving defenders might be able to get up the steeps of the mountain and escape that way once there was enough light to see by.

As it transpired, the line held for another ten minutes.

At first she thought there was another wave of civilians rushing up out of the suburbs behind those who already crowded the street in front of the station. But they were zeroes. The things formed a solid, lurching mass as far as she could see, like a tide of cockroaches. The panicked civilians began to pour over the barriers at the station, and soon the defenders down there were overwhelmed.

When the first zeroes reached their perimeter, many of the living were fighting each other.

There was a different kind of scream that came with the teeth. The bite of a zero made the cries shrill, almost too high to believe they came from a human throat. Suddenly the swirling snow was crowded with such awful sounds, and beneath the cries there was the coronach of the undead, the ceaseless, bitter lament of hunger that rose up when prey was close.

Someone threw a grenade and rotten meat spewed into the air. Now people on the ground were fighting with their bare hands. The rooftop defenders opened fire, mostly hitting the solid mass of the undead as they surged over the first barrier.

The thunder of small arms was punctuated by the rush and bang of anti-tank rockets. Shovels, iron bars, axes, and wrenches rose and fell, black with the blood of monsters. Red blood illuminated by spotlights and fire jetted into the air and the snowy ground became a foul soup of guts and corpses.

Danny lost any sense of time. She fired the gun until the barrel was red hot and it jammed, then threw it into the melee and picked up another and emptied every clip she could get her remaining fingers on.

The defenders on the roof were a brave bunch, and doomed. Danny saw a woman slip over the side and two men tried to pull her back up; claws from below hooked into her legs, but the men would not let go. They hung on even after the woman's leg was peeled down to the bones. Then one of the men pitched off the roof along with the woman, and they disappeared headfirst into the swarm. A man who had been swinging a sledgehammer hesitated, dumbstruck by horror when confronted by a zero completely covered in bulging veins that rose out of its flesh like tree roots; in the moment he hesitated, three others attacked him and he went down.

Fire broke out as someone threw a torch into the undead and it found rotten fabric. The blazing zeroes looked like skeletal puppets, wreathed in flame. Buboes exploded and the frothy whitebeard filaments curled up like roasting hair. Yet still the undead attacked the living, tearing out throats with their burning jaws. The fire spread, turning the dark chaos into a tableau out of hell.

"Diesel fuel!" Danny shouted. "You have shitloads of diesel here, right?"

"Yes we do," Mickey said, scrambling to her position.

They both paused to shoot a burst into the undead. Then Danny said, "Get some drums up here. Fuckers can't eat if they're cooked."

"What about the civilians?"

"What civilians," Danny said. Anybody left alive below them was already done for. Workers were scrambling through the cupola onto the roof now. The zeroes filled the narrow yards between the fences, ripping at anything with blood in it. Danny spared a few seconds to examine the most massive of the fences, the one between the station building and the concrete warehouse inside which the children were housed. She didn't think it would collapse, but the zeroes had built up to such great numbers they might yet find a breach in some adjacent structure and get through. Even the station itself, although built of heavy timber, could not stand forever. They would get through the downstairs walls.

"Mickey," Danny said. "You know the score. Get back down there behind the final barrier and make sure all the kids are loaded on that train. I don't know who the fuck is in charge of that, but if the engineer is still alive, get him in there, too. Get the train running. We got one shot at this. Get those kids out of here."

Mickey grabbed her arm by way of response. His eyes were wet. He nodded, then skidded his way across the roof and dropped down through the cupola.

"We're done here!" Danny shouted over the gunfire of the other defenders on the roof. "Fall back! We can't take them all down. We need to fortify the station and keep the tracks clear!" The snow was blinding them by now; it fell so thickly that the civilians fleeing eastward seemed to disappear, the zeroes coming after them like wolves. There wasn't much else to be done. Soon the remaining defenders would have to fight hand-to-hand. If they were lucky they would choke the entrance into the children's building with so many corpses the zeroes couldn't dig their way through. She felt a cold inside her, a dread. She knew her future, what was left of it.

The pain in her head had come back, too, and it was getting worse. She had a feeling her time was running out, one way or another.

Then the swarm of the undead parted from the back, as if some cosmic zipper was being pulled through them. As if they were the Red Sea and Moses was cleaving the waves. Danny couldn't put it into words, but she had never seen anything like it. She squinted through the snow but couldn't see what was causing the phenomenon. There was someone in the middle of it, scattering the undead like a bull shark moving through a school of vile dark ragged fish.

The Architect.

He was at the head of a small wedge of followers; they must have been the half-dead infected. They passed through the swarm and it split apart, leaving a red carpet of steaming blood and flesh for the Architect to tread. A weird calm seemed to radiate out from the Architect's position: The moaners and hunters stopped attacking where he came, and instead took on the shrinking, craven look of whipped dogs. Those nearest would have fled, but there was nowhere to go. The zeroes were packed in so densely they couldn't get away from the only thing such creatures feared. The screams and fighting continued unabated out in the dimness of the storm, but where the Architect went, a dreadful quiet fell.

Guns went up: Danny's fellow-defenders saw only the threat of the uncanny.

"Don't shoot!" Danny barked. "It's your Architect. If he goes down, we all go down."

To underline her words, she placed her hand over the hot muzzle of the nearest rifle and pressed it downward until it pointed at the roof.

"The Architect?" the gunman whispered.

"That's him," Danny said. "And he's not what you thought."

She felt the pressure on the gun barrel as the guard struggled to raise it again.

"You shoot him, there's nothing to stop the swarm," Danny barked. She pushed the weapon down and wondered how many other trigger fingers were a foot-pound of pressure away from blowing the Architect's head off.

"Look who it is," the Architect said. He was within earshot now, standing where the first of the barrier fences had once stood. It was flattened now, mashed into the gory snow. Danny realized he was speaking to her. She didn't reply. Nancy and Cad were with him, among others.

"You let me down," he said. "I had to take the initiative, and look what happened. Those zealots blamed *me*. You know, this all could have been avoided."

"I was on my way," Danny said. The others were looking at her now. They were soaked in adrenaline and sweat and fear, their own master turned out to be some kind of enemy they hadn't seen before, and Danny had a relationship with him. She could well be the next one to die, unless things went precisely right.

"Are you suggesting the unliving lack patience?"

"I'm telling you that fucking church blew up in my face. *You* brought this place down."

"We had a deal," the Architect said to the others on the roof. "She was going to rid us of that meddlesome priest. She didn't. Now I'll have to start all over again. Are the children safe?"

"So far," one of the other defenders said. "You're not going to find out."

"Yes, he is," Danny said.

"She's no fool," the Architect added. "Either we take the train out of here, or nobody does. If you surrender, I'll allow every one of you to leave town. If you do not, we set fire to that old wooden building of yours."

The stupid, burned, broken zeroes all around him were beginning to straighten up, to cease their groveling; it was as if they had found some quietus in total submission. Danny noticed all the moaners that still had faces were turning to look up at the survivors. Danny felt the world tipping away from her. It was that cliff, the endless fall into oblivion that seemed to wait for her in her worst moments. Nothing felt real. Then she recognized a weight against her belly: hand grenades. And a weight on her shoulders. She had the pack on her back and the grenades in her pockets.

"So we let you take the kids, we walk out of here."

"That's right," the Architect said.

Danny looked across the roof at the defenders. They were all spent, shaking, covered in snow and soot. If the battle continued, they could hold the zeroes off another ten minutes. Then the kids would die, or the Architect would take them away. If they took the Architect down, the kids would only die.

"He can't eat them all," Danny said, her voice low so only those on the roof would hear. "Let them go and we'll regroup. The tracks only go one way."

"It's a fucking trap," the man next to her said.

"We're already in the trap," Danny said. She saw a couple of blaze orange vests among the undead below—bloody guards who had already reanimated, although half-eaten. "Which way do we go? It's your call, people."

"Whose side are you really on?"

It was Mickey. He was standing by the cupola, and his face had taken on a new hardness.

"I'm on the side of the kids," Danny said, and knew it wasn't enough.

"You said you made a deal with that cocksucker. What were you supposed to do? Take out the zombie Jesus?"

"That's right."

"And what did you get in return?"

"They have a kid of mine."

"What about the rest of them?"

Danny didn't know what to say. She reached for the right answer and it wasn't there. She looked helplessly down at the Architect, and his bland face with the dark glasses seemed perfectly neutral. It infuriated her: He looked *reasonable*. A geyser of rage that had been building inside Danny's chest rose into her throat. She felt daggers of pain in her skull and it was nothing to the hot fury that threatened to blow her head clean off her shoulders.

She looked over at Mickey and the faces of the other defenders. They didn't know what to think, but there was something like disappointment there. Something like the death of hope. She felt it, too.

"That's enough talk," the Architect said. "Are you dead or alive?"

"I don't know," Danny said. "How about you?"

And with that, she tossed a grenade at the Architect's feet.

20

The blast threw the Architect backward over the heads of his companions. Danny distinctly saw Nancy's legs disappear below the knees; she pitched to the ground screaming. A dozen of the moaners came apart in the explosion, and whatever spell the Architect had cast over the rest was broken.

The sunken, clotted eyes that had been bent on the survivors seemed to kindle with renewed energy, and then the swarm attacked.

Things happened fast, in stuttering bursts of frenetic motion. The gunfire opened up again. Rockets leaped into the swarm. A drum of fuel came up through the cupola and tumbled down into the writhing attackers; in a fusillade of gunfire it ignited. Now there were flames devouring the station walls. The heat consumed the snow as it came down and black smoke unfurled around the defenders. They fell back, spilling down through the cupola into the station, where a rough wooden ladder gave access to the main floor.

Heaps of sheet metal and supplies had been shoved up against the windows and doors on the exposed side of the station, but there were rat-eaten fingers thrusting through the very walls. Smoke and flame spurted out of every crack and fissure in the facade. As Danny reached the floor, a hand fell heavily on her shoulder; she reflexively brought up her fist, but braked it in midair. It was Mickey.

"I was about to do the same fucking thing," he said. "I'm sorry I doubted you."

That was all the vindication Danny was going to get. She and the others bashed through the back doors of the station that led out onto the platform and ran down alongside the massive wall between station and warehouse. It was booming and vibrating with the struggling undead on the far side. The stink of them penetrated the iron plates, it seemed; the narrow space between this fortification and the rock wall at the foot of the mountain was hot and smelled like a sewer. The train was directly ahead, and as Danny ran with the others, she experienced a rush of pure relief: The children were being handed up into the boxcars by a crew of workers who hadn't joined the combat.

"Are they through?" the foreman of the workers shouted.

"Five minutes," Danny hollered back. Then she was among them, trying to help lift the children into the cars, but she didn't have the right hands for the job. She dropped a screaming, snot-webbed toddler.

"Which one's yours?" Mickey called to her. He was up in the doorway to the second car, packing the kids in as they were lifted into his arms.

"The one that doesn't talk," Danny said. The entire scene got brighter; she glanced over her shoulder and saw the station was now fully involved, the fire pouring like liquid through all the windows and doors and leaping up out of the cupola.

A woman leaned out of the warehouse door through which the kids were being led in weeping groups. "Are you with the quiet one? He won't come with us!" she called.

Danny sidled through the terrified children—some of the older ones were carrying the infants, others clinging to each other as if there was a high wind blowing through. All of them were wet-faced with tears, their mouths bent in wobbly Os of despair.

Inside the warehouse it stank of the children, not of the undead. The hanging fluorescent lamps seemed alien; the whole world outside was lit by fire, and here was steady, bland light. But the walls were booming: The undead were hurling themselves at the obstruction outside. Danny saw most of the young had already been evacuated, but there were two women struggling in an area full of bunk beds. Danny headed for them.

There was the Silent Kid. He had locked his arms through the wooden upright of one of the bunks. The desperate, sweating women turned at the sound of Danny's voice:

"I got him," she said.

And she was right. The Kid instantly released the post and ran to her, winding his fingers into her jacket. "Get out of here, there's no time."

The women's faces were masks of relief. They rushed for the back door, where the last couple of children were just then disappearing into the box-cars. Already the door of the foremost was rattling shut on its rails.

"You want to go with them," Danny said. "Go with them, okay?"

The Silent Kid shook his head. Danny knelt in front of him, eye to eye. They were the last people in the building. The lights flickered. Power lines were probably burning.

"If you stick with me, you *will* be eaten by the zombies," Danny explained, in her most reasonable voice. It came out as a harsh growl. "One hundred percent certain. You will be eaten."

The Kid shook his head.

"Do you want to die?"

He shook his head again.

"Then you gotta go, right now." They could hear the doors of the second boxcar clattering shut.

The Kid pointed to Danny's pistol, now stuck in the front of her waistband, and then pointed to his temple.

"You and me, then," Danny said. She stood up, her knees protesting, and marched over to the warehouse door. The smoke coming down the tracks was choking by now, and over the roar of the flames she could hear the moans of the undead. But the train engine was powering up, its diesel smoke mingling with that of the structure fire. Sparks rained down along with the snow. Mickey was there, walking down the short row of cars, checking everything was ready for the trip. Danny waved him over. They stood in the light of the warehouse door, lit greenish on one side and red on the other.

"Take the train up to the resort. You'll probably meet some resistance there, but try to get the rest of the kids out of there," Danny said. "Then go as far as the line will take you."

"That's the plan," Mickey said. "I got a dozen men say they'll fight rearguard, slow down the swarm."

"I been saving some goodies in my pack," Danny said. "We might be able to do some damage."

"You're staying? What about the kid?"

"He stays, too."

"You're a shitty parent," Mickey said.

"He's not my kid," Danny said, and clapped Mickey on the shoulder. "Get the fuck out of here."

Mickey gestured a half-salute and turned back to the train. Danny let her own hand fall on the Kid's shoulder. Then she saw something strange: Mickey was almost up to the engine when he turned toward the high iron wall, his face distorted with shock; then a bulb of flesh sprang out of the back of his skull and he fell to the tracks.

The Architect stepped into view. Now Danny could see there was a door in the wall, as heavily fortified as the rest of it. The Architect had a gun in his right hand; he had no left hand. His arm was missing at the shoulder, and the upper side of his face had also been blown off. His eye socket was a black crater through which Danny could see his sinuses.

Cad Broker stepped through, and then a couple of the other infected un living, including Lashawna from the badlands with her onionlike boils. The Architect struggled to make his lips work; much of his breath escaped through the holes in his cheek.

"I have a key."

21

Danny reached for another hand grenade, but the Architect raised his pistol hand in a gesture of dismissal.

"You want to blow things up with all these precious children?"

Danny didn't think the blast would get through the boxcar walls, but she hesitated.

"Anyway," the Architect continued, "kill us and the swarm comes in. You can't get to this door before they do. You've ruined my looks," he added, when Danny didn't reply. "You've spoiled my eternal life."

"So kill me," Danny croaked. She was all out of ideas.

"Oh, no," the Architect said, his tattered cheeks puffing out. Danny could see a couple of his upper teeth. It reminded her of the nightmare she'd had. "I want you to live. If nobody else, you. Get her out of here," he said, turning to Cad. Cad had escaped most of the explosion, Danny saw. He was only missing his nose, and dark red blood poured out of the wound.

"Fuck you," Danny said, and drew her pistol.

Cad took the bullet, his forehead splitting open. Then the Architect was gone behind a mass of undead that rushed through the doorway in the wall, as if at a prearranged signal. Defenders leaped down out of the train. There was more gunfire, and screams, and Danny could hear the screaming of the children inside the boxcars. She thrust the Silent Kid between the wheels of the train and attacked the swarm.

She emptied the pistol and drew her knife and slashed at the undead until she was blinded by their black blood. She went down under their weight. But no teeth found her. None of the screams of agony, none of the crackling bones and ripping ligaments were hers. She fought until she was drowning in rotten guts, until she could not move for the weight of the dead piled atop

her. She was buried alive in corpses. A diseased thing with mushroom erup-
tions all over its rotten flesh lay directly atop her, its mucus-drooling eyes
fixed on hers, jaws hanging slack, until the light was blotted out by the bodies
above. Danny struggled to roll over, to press her face into the mire.

The muffled sounds of combat and pain were already tapering off. Then
there was silence except for the moaning of hungry ghouls, those that
couldn't feast on the remains of the defenders. Danny didn't hear the shrill
cries of children anymore. She heard nothing. Her ears were stuffed with
dead flesh.

The blood-soaked gravel against which Danny's face was pressed started to
vibrate. The train was moving.

The mass of dead things shifted as the car beside Danny rolled forward.
No coherent thoughts penetrated her mind, but she wanted the Kid to be
dead now, to die under the wheels if he hadn't already been devoured. It
was a shapeless wish.

Then she found she could move one of her feeble arms. She dragged
herself forward and a rush of icy air entered the fetid tomb in which she
was buried.

Danny emerged from the human ruins to find the train had simply advanced down the tracks far enough to get it away from the burning station.
A hundred meters or so past the platform, which by now was a mass of red
embers and black staves feeding the yellow flames. The Silent Kid stood on
the opposite side of the tracks, unharmed, although several dozen of the
moaners stood around him, ropes of yellow saliva dangling from their jaws.

"You're the only living adult left in Happy Town," the Architect said. He
was standing at the back of the train, surrounded by his army of zeroes.
"The children live. That's our policy. I told you that. But they come with
me. Including that one," he said, and gestured at the Silent Kid.

"No way," Danny tried to say, but the foul liquor of rot in her mouth
made it impossible to form words. She hooked her hand at the Kid and he
scrambled through the dead to her side.

"No child left behind, that's my motto," the Architect said.

Danny grabbed the Silent Kid's hand and they ran for the doorway in
the wall.

They ran down the main street, although Danny was so weary and her head
ached so much that she lurched along hardly faster than she could normally

walk. The undead all around them moaned and reached out, but whatever power the Architect had, it still held. At least until they'd made a couple of blocks from the conflagration at the tracks. Then she saw the zeroes were closing in, showing signs of their native hunger. Their master's influence had limits. Something reached for her leg and she sidestepped it—then saw it was the half-living Nancy, her face gray, the remains of her legs trailing behind her like butchered snakes as she elbowed her way through the snow on her belly.

"Save me," Nancy said.

Danny ignored her, shoving the Silent Kid back into motion as the undead circled closer. They were halfway to the bank building before a pack of hunters broke from the rest and began loping along behind them. By the time Danny was limping past the headless bronze soldier, the moaners had joined the chase.

The Architect was too far away. It was her and a few thousand zeroes, closing fast.

There was no way they could get out of town on foot. Everywhere there were corpses, the dead and undead alike heaped on the ground, now blanketed with snow. Danny looked around them. She had explosives—grenades in her pockets and more in her pack. She lobbed a couple of them among the hunters.

"When those blow up, run for the church," Danny said to the Kid.

It might just have been the violence of the noise, but when the grenades exploded and threw fistfuls of hunter-zero into the sky, the Silent Kid broke and ran for the church, weaving among the zeroes that stood between him and the gutted front doors.

Rotten fingers brushed Danny's face. She had almost passed out. Several seconds had gone by, and she was just standing there like a fool while the undead closed in. She broke into as much of a run as she could muster, following the Silent Kid, and seconds later was inside the church.

The stairs up into the steeple ended ten feet from the floor. Right away Danny saw there was a way up. One of the stringers still clung to the landing above, like a big wooden saw; everything else was gone.

"Use that thing like a ladder," she said to the Kid, and picked up a baluster that had once been part of the stair railing. A zero was coming out of the darkness inside the church, where the firelight could not penetrate. She clubbed it down and stomped its head until the rigid skull went soft. But the Silent Kid didn't move.

"Get the fuck up there or I swear to God I'm going to bash your fucking brains out next," Danny elaborated. The Kid started climbing.

Danny didn't think she was going to have time to get out of arm's reach herself—the zeroes from inside the church were nearly upon them, although they were hampered by the tangle of broken wood and plaster underfoot. Others were coming through the outer doors. She swung the baluster at the nearest of the undead, an emaciated creature with half its scalp missing. The blow only turned its head. She thrust the baluster straight at its eyes and managed to jab one of them out, but it didn't reach the brain. She didn't have any strength. Scaly hands slid over her arm, found a purchase, gripped with that nerveless power the things got when prey was near. They grabbed at her backpack. They couldn't have that.

Danny hacked the club blindly at the confluence of the grasping hands, felt them drop away, and then she sprang after the Silent Kid, who had reached the landing above. There were twenty or more of the undead now, clawing and falling over each other in their haste to reach the living flesh they craved. Danny was halfway up the stringer, balancing with her backpack pressed against the steeple wall and her boot heels on the notched lumber that had held the stairs up, when the nails at the top gave way.

She toppled and fell full-length among the undead.

Three of them collapsed when she hit. A splinter of wood penetrated the flesh of her upper arm. Danny kicked and pushed, knocking the things away, and in a matter of seconds was on her feet, but one of the things had bitten her, down low on her right leg. She didn't know how badly.

The Silent Kid had disappeared from Danny's field of view and she hoped he was on his way to the roof or wherever was farthest from the sheriff's last stand.

But then a long yellow piece of pine came down, a rafter or something like it. It was studded with joist hangers, bent metal clips to hold connecting members of wood. They looked a hell of a lot like the footholds on a telephone pole. Danny didn't look back. She hauled herself up the rafter, bony fingers scratching and clawing and pulling her back down. She remembered the woman with her leg torn apart while she hung from the roof, and kicked out. She reached the landing, and tried to pull the improvised ladder up after her. But the zeroes were grabbing it like it meant something to them, maybe hoping to follow. So Danny kicked it away instead, and it fell among them. She watched to make sure none of them were smart enough to stand the timber back up, then scrambled away from the edge of the landing and pressed her weight against the wall.

The Silent Kid was beside her, panting. The landing had about half the roof framing spilled down onto it, with some plywood and tar paper still clinging to the structure. Snow spilled down from above like handfuls of feather down. Danny wasn't sure how long the landing would remain attached to the wall, but there wasn't much of anyplace else to go. Above them was another flight of stairs, intact except for the railing, but above that was only the blown-out steeple, two adjoining walls and the spire, the rest fallen down.

"Stay against the wall," she said, when she had her breath back. The undead were moaning and gasping down below, sucking in the scent of living flesh. They were climbing over each other, trying to scale the walls. The building shook with the fury of their attack.

The Silent Kid was checking himself over, now. Danny was glad to see that. He still planned to survive. Or cared what kind of condition he was in, at least. While he was checking himself over, Danny took the opportunity to steal a look at her leg.

The bite was just above her Achilles tendon. Reached the muscle. A piece of skin had been bitten away. She'd felt that during the struggle, the intense but blurry pain of compression between the jaws suddenly sharpening into razor-edged agony as flesh tore. The Silent Kid was also looking at the wound, his eyes wide and round. Whatever went on in his young mind, it had no outlet, no words.

"It's just a zombie bite," Danny said, and remembered she'd never been much good at reassuring children. Kelley could have attested to that, if things had gone differently. She tore a strip of duct tape off one of the rips in her jacket and pasted it over the injury. "Are you okay?"

The Kid nodded. His pale face was grave. The danger hadn't passed. This was just a brief interlude. They couldn't stay on their precarious little perch for very long, and below them were dozens of zeroes. More than dozens. The moaning was so numerous it sounded almost like ocean surf. Danny decided to have a look at their predicament and start making the new plan. There was a one-in-a-million chance they could get out of this. She'd faced worse odds.

There was a window on the landing just above their heads. The glass was broken out of it, a piece of lumber jammed clean through, and the arch at the top gave the opening a look of surprise. Danny pushed herself up the wall, and felt the throbbing injury to her leg start bleeding afresh as hydraulic pressure took over. Nothing to be done about it. She hooked an arm over the windowsill to steady herself and looked out across the dark town.

The view was ghostly in the deep falling snow. The buildings that hadn't been damaged in the fighting and fleeing seemed normal enough, but every third or fourth structure was either smoking or shot half to pieces. Not much glass in the windows. The phone and power lines were draped limply over the rooftops and snaked around the pavement. But not much of the ground was visible, because the zeroes didn't just sound like the ocean. They looked like it.

Danny didn't bother to count. However many of the undead it took to fill an entire small town from one end to the other, wall to wall, shoulder to shoulder, that was the number of them. Thousands. Some were pale as cave creatures, most filth-darkened, discolored by exposure, stained or charred. Some of the things could almost be living people, except for the blood and the chunks missing. Most of them were ragged and skeletal, often naked, but there were the incongruous heavy ones, pendulous with rotten bags of fat, and some still wore garments of bright colors that resisted the filth and corruption and wrapped their decayed hosts in cheerful patterns. The miracle of polyester. The deforming disease was everywhere in all its varieties.

Danny didn't mark any individuals or note their positions. There was nothing to note. Every damn square foot of the entire town was covered in the undead.

There was nothing to see, nothing to do until daylight came. Danny and the Silent Kid hugged their knees in the darkness and shivered, listening to the restless dead below and the ticking and creaking of the crippled structure around them. Their jackets were inadequate and wet. It was briefly warm when a nearby building caught fire and the wind shifted in their direction; Danny honestly thought they were going to die of suffocation. The smoke filled the air like stinking cotton wool and scoured their eyeballs raw. They became dizzy, coughed continuously, and the Kid puked. But at least it was warm.

Eventually the wind shifted. The reek of smoke clung to them and filled their mouths, but the air was cold and clean, scoured with snow. Once again the dominant stink was the queasy smell of decayed human flesh from below. Danny eventually thought to hold the Kid, keep him warm that way; he was fairly well-dressed but his neck and wrists were exposed. He fell asleep against her chest.

She wanted to look out the window again at the crowd of the undead. She wanted to deploy what she had left in the backpack. She wanted to climb up onto the roof and scream at the night sky. But instead she sat and waited.

22

At last there was a hint of light in the dark sky. Dawn might be a couple of hours away. Maybe less. Danny didn't know. Her teeth chattered and she could see her breath in dim gray plumes. She tested her bitten leg and found the blood was no longer flowing. It was stiff but she could use it, at least until she got gangrene. The Kid was still alive, huddled to her chest, one of his thin arms hooked around her waist. He'd had a long night.

The zeroes below seemed to have settled down. That wasn't unusual. They stopped moving to conserve their strength when there wasn't any active prey nearby. There was a gusty breeze and the rumble of fires continuing to burn out of control in the town, but no other sounds. It was time to decide what to do, before they died of exposure or the landing collapsed or some hunters showed up and figured out how to scale the ruined tower. She gently slid herself out from under the Silent Kid. He seemed to be heavily asleep. Maybe, Danny thought, he was in a smoke-induced coma and he would never wake up. Lucky him.

She turned around, kneeling, her knees screaming with stiffness, and looked through the empty window frame, keeping herself as low as possible. She didn't want to get the zeroes worked up again. Their quiet state might mean a chance of escape.

But what Danny saw struck a sheet of frozen steel right through her body, chilling her guts, her bones, her soul.

The zeroes were still down there, thousands of them. They were standing still. But they were all looking directly at *her*.

Every one of those scarred and misshapen skulls was turned precisely toward the window. Those with eyes were staring. Those without eyes had their heads tilted back to scent the air, the firelight glistening on their pulpy remains.

She saw there were a few so badly mutilated they continued to shuffle among the others, aimless, like decapitated chickens that didn't know it was over yet. Exposed brains, faceless, featureless things, stumbling among the rest. But if the zero had any motor control left, it was turned toward the only prey in town.

Danny found she was shaking violently. More than cold, a species of shock had overtaken her. She'd seen this weird behavior in the zeroes once before, long ago when she fled San Francisco and the city was about to fall. It had been a suburb—San Mateo or somewhere like that, on the peninsula to the south of the city. She'd seen thousands of zeroes, all facing in the same direction like soldiers on a battlefield awaiting an order. The difference then was they'd been snapping their jaws. All of them, snapping and chomping until the noise of it sounded like marching feet.

Danny could hear the sound in her mind, that cracking of a million yellow teeth. It was a memory so vivid . . . but it *wasn't* a memory. She watched the creatures below her. Some of their heads were rocking, snapping. They were doing it again. That awful clack of teeth.

The Silent Kid woke up.

"You know that old saying, 'from bad to worse'?" Danny whispered. The Kid nodded. "This is what they were talking about." Part of her mind was contemplating suicide in a matter-of-fact way—a grenade would take care of the two of them and there would be no more suffering.

But the train was still there at the end of town, the engine idling. The Architect hadn't left yet; he must have known he'd won. That meant the rest of the children were still in play. This thought alone was Danny's defense against the hideous noise coming from the swarm.

By now the things were all snapping their jaws. The ones so diseased that their heads were just masses of knobs struggled to make their teeth heard beneath the cancerous masses. Those whose faces had been blown off shook their heads up and down, the same instinct motivating them. What the hell was this? Some reptile memory from a billion years ago? Some little Easter egg hidden in the virus by a disease engineer? Was it God's idea of a joke? Danny had seen documentaries in which the Nazis were gathered in Nuremberg or somewhere like that, a vast plaza, and half a million steel-helmeted men stood at attention while their Führer ranted from his podium, then bellowed their *sieg heils*. This looked like that, with the champing of teeth instead of the stiff-armed salutes. Ashes from the fires mingled with the snow and drifted down on the upturned faces. The snow didn't melt, because the undead flesh was cold.

"I want you to know something," Danny said to the Kid, because it was better to talk than to listen to the jaws snapping all around them. "I'm scared shitless. A lot of people think I don't ever get scared. Probably you thought that, right?"

The Kid nodded, his big eyes wet.

"Well, I get scared like everybody else. But a lot of people can't multitask. They get scared and that's all they can think about is being scared. But what you gotta do is be scared with one hand and get shit done with the other one. Anyway, I'm kind of low on ideas right now, but what we need is a good idea. Then we can be scared and work on the plan at the same time. And if it's a good plan and it works out, you get less scared because you got something to concentrate on. That's my secret. I recommend it. But I got no ideas at the present time, so if you do, maybe now would be a good time to start talking again. We need to get those kids on that train out of here."

The Kid shook his head. Whether he couldn't talk or didn't have an idea, he didn't say.

Danny looked above them. They could see up inside the framing of the steeple, some of which had collapsed. There were two small cupola-style louvered windows up there, one of which was on the side of the main part of the church.

"Okay then," Danny said, when the clacking started to get to her again. "I'm finding it hard to think with all that noise. What say we see about getting up on the roof? It might be easier to think up there."

The zeroes continued their endless jaw-snapping. Sometimes the noise would happen to synchronize, the way clapping crowds at a concert would fall into unison; then it was one gigantic pair of jaws, biting the whole world. But it wouldn't last, and then it became the undifferentiated blanket of crunching noise again.

She was about to lift the Kid up into the framing when the Architect's voice came up through the empty window.

"Come out," he said, and the moment he spoke, the champing teeth stopped.

A quiet deep as the winter followed. Danny's ears were ringing with the silence.

She squinted out into the predawn darkness and the whirling snow. She sought the source of the voice in the crowd. Maybe it would still be possible to destroy that undead bastard completely.

"Come out," the Architect said again. But amplified. The damn thing had a megaphone. Danny searched the far reaches of the square and thought she saw him: a lone zero perched atop the remains of a pickup truck. Yes, he was holding an electric bullhorn.

"Fuck you," Danny suggested, her voice cracked and hoarse.

"You know that you cannot survive," the bullhorn said, in that flat, disinterested way of the undead. *"You will be eaten alive or you will die of thirst. Come out."*

"Clear your zombies out and I'll do that," Danny replied. She doubted the thing could hear her, her voice was so ruined. But the silence was so complete it must have carried, because the zero replied:

"They will not attack you. Bring the child. The law is one child, one life."

"Like hell I will."

"One child, one life. Or we burn the church down."

23

The walk out of the church taught Danny there was no limit to terror, no maximum fear. It could always get worse.

She went down first, pulling a rafter free in order to make her way hand-over-hand down to the ground level. The zeroes stood there, packed together like sides of rotten beef in a deep freeze. They didn't part to let Danny through. She held a grenade in her teeth. If anything happened, she would grab the Kid and pull the pin. This wasn't a fight that could be won. And while the Kid still lived, there was still a chance she could prevail.

But the zeroes honored the truce. She saw peeling black tongues rolling around in cancerous mouths, heard them snuffling the air to smell her scent. But they didn't attack. Their fear of the thinkers was too great, or their loyalty. Whatever it was, the influence held.

Danny had never been this close to the undead without violence, except for Kelley, who somehow wasn't the same. These were the stupid, nobody kind, the sharks. Even in the twilight of undeath, Kelley had been *someone*.

She pushed the grenade up the sleeve of her jacket. "It's your choice," Danny said to the Kid, when she was still alive after thirty seconds on the ground floor.

The Silent Kid came down. He was weeping, shaking like there was an earthquake only he could feel. But he came down. Danny put her arm around him, drew him in as tight as she could. They started walking.

Now the zeroes parted before them, a bubble of space following their progress through the crowd. Danny was limping; she had to transfer some of her weight onto the Kid. She felt insanity—real madness—clawing at her mind. It was too much to bear. Every face was more hideous than the last, every body more misshapen, the human frame twisted by devils into every imaginable distortion. The stench of burned and rotten flesh was over-whelming, and yet there were notes of decaying hair, of shit and urine, foul teeth, ruptured bellies. A thing with a translucent membrane for a head, filled with what looked like worms, touched the Silent Kid's hair in an almost tender gesture. Everywhere there was exposed bone, seething with insects despite the cold, and entrails hung in blackened swags. Danny abruptly vomited thin bile on skeletal feet held together only by scraps of rawhide skin. The Silent Kid threw up as well, but into his hands, as if he was trying not to discomfit anybody near him. She spat on one of the zom-bies to clear her mouth; it moaned faintly with desire.

"Listen, Kid? You heard what the zero said. One child, one life. I know what you must be thinking: I'm handing you over to save my own ass. But I'm not. I got something in this backpack he doesn't know about. I got one more move that might get your skinny ass out of trouble."

The Kid didn't respond. But he was gripping Danny's mutilated hand in his own vomit-slick fingers, and she understood he was so frightened he would cling to her even if she attacked him herself.

"So here's the deal. That zero up ahead, I was going to kill his enemy for him and then when he came around to congratulate me, I was going to kill him, too. And like always, I was too goddamned late. So he collected all the kids in that train. The last one is you. Then he'll stop up at the resort and get the rest. After that he's going to choo-choo the fuck out of here and eat you all one at a time. Right? That's what this means. I hope I'm not upset-ting you."

The Architect was working from Adolf Hitler's playbook, except he wasn't using his prisoners as free labor.

This was a buffet.

Danny and the Kid were halfway through the stinking undead to the pickup truck. She could see the thinker with the bullhorn up ahead on top of the vehicle. They'd be within earshot soon. One of the things with no face stumbled across their path; the Kid made a noise of horror and pressed himself behind Danny. She let the thing stumble by. It had nothing atop its neck except an egg-cup of skull supporting what must have been the hind brain, the medulla and cerebellum. One ear still clung to a spar of bone that jutted up above the ruined flesh. It was effectively headless.

Danny felt the madness coming again, the desire to stop and be done and die. But the part of her that planned and schemed was putting things together. She thought, if this somehow wasn't a trap, if they weren't torn to pieces in the next couple of minutes, that she might yet save the Kid. But it would be a long shot, and there were more variables than even the worst plan ought to have.

"Listen good, okay?" she whispered. "You'll be safe on the train, okay? For a while. I think that's true. Maybe a couple of days or more. Not too near here. And here's what's going to happen. If I get out of here alive, I'm going to score some wheels and follow the train. I'm going to head it off at the pass and fuck things up."

They were close. She could see the thinker watching them, his shattered face a bloodless mess of anatomical detail, the socket where his arm should have been catching the firelight. She dropped her voice even lower, speaking directly into the Silent Kid's ear.

"I promise, if I am alive, I will come for you."

Rough claws fell upon them, and there were hunters pushing through the crowd of moaners, making way, taking charge like palace guards. They were salivating freely over their leathery chins, long teeth wet.

"Do you understand?" Danny said, as the monsters pulled her away from the Kid.

"Yes," the Silent Kid replied.

And then he was dragged out of view into the swarm.

"You killed many. You destroyed the town," the Architect said. Danny limped beside him, every step a penance for her sins. None of this could be happening. She was among the zeroes and there was order, security, and discipline. She didn't know it was possible. But the moaners parted well ahead of them, almost cringing, clearing the way; the hunters were like dogs, patrolling along the edges of the mob. They hissed and snarled the moaners into compliance. Danny wondered if there was some instinct for fear being awakened in the things, which otherwise seemed to fear nothing.

"They fucked up and killed themselves," Danny said. "If you had waited another ten minutes, I would have blown up that asshole on the cross."

"You're not reliable, Sheriff. I eventually realized you would try to kill me, too."

"That's true . . . so why am I still alive?" Danny couldn't see why the Architect hadn't attacked her yet.

"That's the right question. You are still alive because you have ruined my body. I want you to know what eternity feels like. From now on to the end of your little life, you are marked. No unliving creature will harm you, not the stupidest nor the most cunning."

"Bullshit. These things will take me down the minute I'm out of sight of you."

"You'll see. You have upon you the mark of Cain. That's why they didn't kill you at the train, when everyone else was destroyed. You shall live on and on while all around you die."

"Then why did they attack me in the church?"

"I hadn't reached them yet."

Danny rejected the idea. It was too elegant. Too damn clever for this gristly creature to pull off. But still, she wasn't dead yet. It might even be true.

"Why are we talking? I don't talk to you fuckers. If that Kid dies, if you harm him—"

"He will be safe. He will reach the destination."

"And then?"

"And then you will spend the rest of your life wondering. I hope that you live forever."

They hobbled down the street in silence. Danny's head was flaring with pain now, a series of crescendos that threatened to expand into another blackout at any moment, but she forced her legs to move, limping heavily. There was still a single, slender chance for the Kid—and by extension, the rest of the children, too.

They reached the margin of town and the zero swarm was much thinner here. She might be able to run for it soon, although the hunters would come after her fast as wolves. But she couldn't run at all, if she was honest about it.

"Good-bye, Sister of the Dead," the Architect said.

"My sister was different," Danny said, and hatred bubbled up inside her like hot coal tar. "She came back and she still had something inside her. She wasn't just a shell like you."

The Architect stood at the edge of a parking lot in front of what had once been the local supermarket, the last structure inside the fence. Behind it was an army of the undead, hunters first, forming a hunched, eager rank, then the mass of the swarm behind them, pressing forward, the control of the more capable zeroes barely enough to stop them rushing at the retreating prey.

Danny stood a few yards into the parking lot, blood trickling into her boot. "Find a working vehicle and leave? That's it?"

"That is all," the zero said. "Enjoy what's left of your life. Everybody you know will either join us or die, but you"—here he ran out of breath and had to reinflate his lungs—"*you alone,* will never be eaten by our kind. You are tainted meat. All shall die or serve us, and you shall look on in despair, shunned by every kind, even your own."

"Is that all you got?"

"No," the Architect said, and for the first time, smiled. It looked like real pleasure, at least on the side of his mouth that wasn't a ruptured mass of tissue. His one eye even sparkled. At that moment Danny realized he was almost more human than she was—she couldn't feel happiness. He could.

"There's more," he continued. "When you die, you will come back. The virus is in you. And you will probably mutate, as so many of the new ones do. And you will still be shunned by the unliving. You will have eternal unlife, alone. Purgatory. Beyond hell."

Danny stared at her terrifically mutilated enemy and wondered: Would it be worse to go through eternity with a wrecked corpse or to be alone forever? That determined which of them won. And then she thought how strange it was to be trying to decide who won on points—or who won at all. If the Architect yet lived, Danny had lost forever. Her own death was of no consequence because it was already inevitable. Only the Architect had something to lose.

Danny turned around and walked away without saying a word. If she had seen what was left of the Architect's face, the smile crumpling to twisted fury that leaked black serum, she would have known that in that moment, after all, she had won.

But he had one more thing to say.

"I ate your friend Topper. Chewed real slow."

Danny turned back. A sheet of fury swept through her like the wing of some great ghost-bird. But then it was gone, wheeling through space. She did not question that the Architect had done what he said. It wasn't enough to stick a grenade down his pants now. She needed to make his brief reign in the world an absolute failure.

She hobbled across the parking lot, ankle deep in blood-speckled snow, looking into vehicle windows until she found a Chevy truck with the keys in the ignition. It took a while to start; the battery wasn't much use. But eventually it caught and choked and spluttered and ran. Danny looked back through the cloud of blue exhaust smoke, expecting to see the undead rushing at her. But they continued to stand at the edge of town, silent and waiting.

She drove away out of the accursed place, and saw a number of human corpses—the honest dead, red-blooded and still—those who had fled Happy Town during the attack, only to die within sight of the gates. Over many of them crouched gorging corpses, their throats stuffed with meat.

24

Danny drove directly away from Happy Town until she was out of sight of any watching eyes. There were scenes of horror still unfolding in the badlands to her left and right, visible in the faint light of dawn, like gray velvet; she didn't take her eyes off the road. There were wounded people crawling across the hard ground with the undead tearing the flesh from their limbs, some juggling their own steaming entrails as they tried to get away from their rotting pursuers, broken and sightless people stumbling to destruction. The undead moved with energy, but they were in no better condition, many of them stripped of skin, burned, shattered like dolls, yet still pursuing, still hungry. The uncanny discipline of the creatures within the city ended at the gates.

Out in the beyond, it was chaos of a kind Danny had not witnessed since the day mankind fell. Those who had survived the destruction of their haven but made it no farther than this were doomed. She couldn't help them. Her business was elsewhere.

She found the road that ran along parallel to the now-shattered defensive line of buckets and sentinels and turned north, the truck's wheels skidding in the snow, headlights bouncing. She was three or four kilometers from town. No sentinel would see her change course, if anyone was looking. She suspected they were otherwise engaged. She was counting on it.

Twelve minutes after she'd driven through the crumpled gates, Danny was within sight of the western reach of the train tracks. She turned again and took the maintenance road alongside the rails, heading back toward the town. She kept going until the road that led to the resort island crossed the tracks—well above the section of that route she knew to be sown with land mines. The security there was entirely for show, to keep the chooks from exploring. They didn't have the personnel or hardware to mine the entire thing. Or so she hoped.

She heard a shrill cry, and initially thought it was an air raid siren; then she realized it was the scream of the train whistle around the corner of the mountain. Her time was getting very low. She drove recklessly in the slick snow, expecting the sudden blast of a mine and the upside-down world and the pain at any instant. But her hunch was correct. In six minutes, she was deep in the forest that caped the lower part of the northern side of the mountain, and suddenly she could see the reservoir through the trees.

She twisted the wheel over and drove unceremoniously off the road into the ditch. Climbed out and dragged the precious backpack after her. She guessed the train needed fifteen minutes to get from the town to the dam across the reservoir; if it stopped there to pick up the rest of the children as the Architect had said he would, she had as much as an hour while they loaded up the boxcars. But she didn't think they planned to stop at all. The Architect was close to human. He could lie. He would know she'd try to follow the train. He had to fool her into thinking she had more time. Then they could get away.

Besides, there were so few undead on the train, they had enough kids aboard to feed them for a good long while. So she had fifteen minutes, tops.

This vigorous test of logic made the pain in her head form two red-hot horns that tapered from the back of her skull into her eye sockets. Her muscles ached, and the bite on her leg was leaking blood and hurt like a rotten tooth. The pain in her head scared her. It was the bad kind, the kind that Dr. Joe had warned her about. It couldn't be helped. She had to stay conscious, or wake up undead.

There were zeroes in the woods around her, but she saw no living survivors this way. The things saw her or smelled her, they stalked her, but they didn't attack. It seemed the Architect was right. Somehow, they all knew. She forced her unhappy limbs to pump and push her across the landscape and didn't dare think how close she was to collapse.

When she reached the edge of the trees, she fell to her knees and sobbed for lack of oxygen, blue phantoms writhing at the edges of her vision. A moaner walked past her, quite close, one of the mutated ones with the whitebeard, its head a mass of worms. It ignored her, just as the Architect had said they would. She picked up a big rock with both hands and threw it at the moaner's face. The thing's head came apart in handfuls like an overripe melon. The disease had turned its skull into mush.

Now Danny was moving again. She was hobbling like a spent jogger, trying to run, but progressing at the speed of a walk. The pain in her head was opening up like a stainless-steel claw. She felt warm wetness on her upper lip, and then her entire chin, as her nose bled freely. The blood was cold by the time it reached her neck. The pain in her skull had become burning cold, first torturing and then killing the nerves pressed against it. It became tolerable once she understood it was killing her. The problem would self-correct. Whatever else his flaws, the good Dr. Joe Higashiyama knew what he was talking about when it came to brain damage.

So Danny bled, and her skull creaked with the pain inside it, and there was nothing else to do but continue onward. She moved along behind the skirt of the woods until she came to a ridge of stone, the foot of the mountain. The dam was before her now, a long, flat line dividing the dark land from the dim sky, fringed with black trees at each end where it met the cliffs that defined the canyon. The electricity-generating plant was at the far end. That's where she needed to go. The snow on this side was deep enough that she had difficulty lifting her feet sufficiently to clear it with each step, but her shins ached with the endless grating of crusty ice against them, so she tried to lift her boots out of it rather than shove forward like an icebreaker in a frozen sea. She kept pushing along with the rock wall to her right and damn few trees sheltering her to the left from the resort.

It didn't seem like much, now that she was there. An island of three or four acres with some large, rustic-style structures, lots of windows lit up warm and yellow, the grounds gentle and manicured with clumps of ornamental trees all blanketed by snow, the island a civilized little eminence in the cold metallic water with a neat row of docks and boat slips on the far side and a narrow iron bridge on the near side. There were a couple of hundred kids in there, some ready to eat, others requiring more time to mature. When the Architect didn't stop to pick them up, the thinkers here would fall upon the children like wild animals.

Then she found herself crawling through the snow, almost swimming. She didn't remember falling to her knees. The ice packing into the wrists of her jacket sleeves revived her somewhat, and she stood up. Not long until dawn. There was a rind of pale light up behind the dam, the morning close to breaking. The blood on her face had frozen in places, and that was fine. It was easier. It stopped wetting her collar and making her cold.

The cold and the pain in her head had joined up. They had become one thing. Danny didn't think about it as she sometimes did, trying to compartmentalize the pain, break it down, blunt its edge by knowing it. This was different. She was filled with the pain. It was the thing that animated her, the way the hunger had animated her sister. The one thing that proved life, or a property like life. If the pain kept her moving, it was worth enduring. Somehow this triggered a brief memory of standing in a brown snowsuit as a girl of nine or ten, looking up at the walls of a snowplowed driveway during an especially snowy season. She remembered the good kind ache of a long day playing outdoors in the wintertime. Then the memory was gone and the vise on her skull tightened another turn.

The road that led across the dam was near. She heard voices. She would have to act quickly, once she broke cover. But as she prepared to step onto the roadway, the snow beneath her collapsed, and she was tumbling downward. The drifts had obscured a culvert that drained into the river below. She was helpless, only clinging to the backpack as she fell. Her head struck a stone and for a long moment her vision was gone, but the pain didn't increase. It couldn't. She lay on her back and looked up. Now she was below the dam, sprawled beside the river.

It was a concrete slab, battered a few degrees so the face of it was not vertical, but fell back toward the top. There were no trees at its base; Danny was out in the open. But she didn't think anyone knew she was there, or would think to look for her. Whoever was there, they would be looking for the train. She could hear it in the distance, the noise of the engine competing with the noise in her skull.

Suddenly she was pouring tea for Kelley, who was a very small girl. Danny was older, the tea set miniature in her hands. Kelley laughed at something Danny said, and Danny saw the admiration in Kelley's face, her little pearl baby teeth flashing.

Danny swiped the blood ice off her nostrils and peered around with unfocused eyes and discovered an iron catwalk that crossed the river at the base of the dam. She tugged on the straps of the backpack and felt its weight pressing against her spine. She lurched over to the catwalk, grasped the railing in both hands, and inched her way across it.

The black water below her looked fifty fathoms deep, boiling because the outlet of the electrical plant came out of culverts there. The remaining overflow spilled from a channel cut just below the top of the dam, pouring down past her. There were voices directly above, now. No cries of alarm. Then she was across the catwalk, and there was a stairway ascending the face of the dam. It seemed almost like victory, but this wasn't a marathon with cheering onlookers at the end handing out towels and Gatorade. Danny would be alone at the finish.

25

The sky glowed pink and gray, the sun almost up, rising through the twist in the canyon beyond the reservoir. Danny reached the top of the dam by the eastern slope of the valley. The road cut through the base of the cliff on that side and met the dam. She was among a stand of heavy trees clad in snow, but the top of the dam was clear and dry, salted and plowed. On the other side was the reservoir. Millions of tons of water. Plenty of water. And the electricity-generating plant was not far away on the summit of the dam. She could feel the vibration of the turbines in her skin. There were lights burning in unblocked windows in the plant. It was directly ahead of her, a carbuncle of corrugated sheds and fuel tanks and pipes rising up like castle battlements over the deck of the dam. It rumbled and hummed and the biggest structure had yellow lighted windows as warm and inviting as fresh dinner rolls.

Danny dreamed of warmth inside the generating station, a couple of small, hot rooms with clanking radiators and a stove with a shrilling kettle, mugs of instant coffee, maybe a flask of bourbon. Warm blankets and dry clothes.

But it wasn't the kettle she heard—it was a siren.

The heat and light were gone and Danny was back in the tomb of winter with the sun threatening to come up and the darkness taking on more detail, even a little color, telling her the night was over and she didn't have any more time. It would have to be now. She was done with comfort and warmth and bourbon. She swiped one of her ice-stiff gloves across her mouth and felt the blood begin to flow again. That meant her heart was still pumping. Good enough. She was on her knees once more, and there were dark strokes against the pale concrete coming in her direction. Zeroes. They had been in the middle of the span so they could see both ends of the dam at once; it did not appear anyone was inside the generator building at her end. Nobody emerged, at least.

My lucky day, she thought.

The weakest point in the dam must be the generators, she reckoned. She found herself thinking this over as if it was some great revelation. The mere act of thinking was a triumph, when the pain in her head demanded she not think, but shut down and die.

Too soon, she soothed it, and did not shut down. She reckoned it again: The solid mass of the dam was interrupted here, at the generators, because the turbines would have to be mounted inside the dam itself, where the water went through.

Danny found the slow working of ideas in her head helped drive back the agony, so she kept on reasoning. She had brought two things with her to deploy, and then she was done. The first thing was easy. She might as well do it. Danny struggled out of her backpack. The terrible weight of it was lifted and she felt a renewal inside herself. Her shoulders were no longer bent into hooks. She rocked them once, felt the relief, and then took the knife from her belt and held it in her fist and slashed the backpack open. There was no way in hell she could operate a zipper. The zeroes were halfway across the distance.

She shook the backpack, and the lead cylinder she had collected from the wrecked military train clunked free and rolled across the parapet of the dam. Danny threw herself on it. It might roll under the iron railing, through one of the curb drains, and fall into the snow below; that would be an end to everything. She scooped the thing up between her numb hands, wishing she had more fingers to capture it with. She could feel nothing at all, not even the weight. It was as if she was watching a movie of her arms. The soft lead cap on the end was finely threaded, an old-fashioned but effective way to seal such a container tight, considering the contents would eat through any kind of elastomeric gasket. Danny would not be able to unscrew it in her condition.

But that was why she had brought the hand grenades.

The contents of the pack were padded with old clothes. Danny pulled a tube sock out of the pack and stuffed the lead cylinder down inside it; it barely fit into the maximum diameter of the sock, but that was fine. She wanted it snug. She jammed one of the grenades in after it.

The zeroes approaching her were running now, or running as well as they could, with a crouching, bent-double gait that made the intelligent ones look no better than the hunters they considered so primitive. They weren't shouting at her or each other; they were more efficient than that. They didn't get excited, except when there was fresh meat. She had another twenty seconds before they reached her.

Apparently, the Architect had changed his mind about her. She was fair game, after all.

Danny discovered she couldn't work her fingers, couldn't pull the pin on the grenade. She tried to do it with her teeth, but they chattered and skated over the steel ring and would not hold it. She could make fists, though. So she took up the knife in her good hand again and stabbed the tip through the ring on the pin of the grenade, and pulled it free that way. There was more to do, but she couldn't think what it was.

The zeroes were close now, and she saw their faces. The nearest one was missing its nose and its skin was blue-black, probably from exposure to cold. It was a grim silhouette against the rapidly paling sky. Some part of Danny observed it wasn't snowing anymore.

The grenade. Throw it over the side with the precious lead cylinder. Danny dumped the sock full of metal off the side of the dam into the reservoir, as there was no question of throwing it in her condition. She heard the loud, flat *bang* of the explosion come very shortly after that—she had almost waited too long. The force of the blast felt like a slap in the face. Then a noisy shower of water sprayed up the side of the dam. The zeroes were so close they caught the spray full in the face; the reservoir was full, the waterline less than ten feet below the top of the dam.

The entire party of zeroes collapsed instantly, robbed of animation. They were steaming corpses now.

Suck it, Danny tried to say, and didn't care if her idea of a clever retort was unwitty. *Her* skin was burning now, as well. The blown-up lead cylinder contained a pellet of radioactive metal, of course. Danny had just given herself an extra-concentrated dose of poison.

The water felt hot; she didn't know if it was real heat or some property of the radiation that only felt like heat, but she welcomed it. It broke through the numbness. She could bend what fingers she had.

The siren was screaming still, and now there were figures swarming down the road at both ends of the dam. She would soon be overrun or shot dead, regardless of the radiation. Especially if there were living men among them. She didn't know if the zeroes would entrust mortals with something as vital as guarding the dam, but they might need someone to read the maintenance manuals for them.

Danny looked over the side at the water and saw a great column of steam coming up, the surface churning where the grenade had exploded. She had one more task and then she could lie back and enjoy the acid warmth of the radiation. There were auras glowing around everything, blue-green eels.

Danny crawled on hands and knees toward the electrical plant, dragging the backpack alongside her. She was within a few yards of the structure, close enough to see where the sheds dropped down into the water on the reservoir side and met two big humped shapes of dark, pitted iron, presumably the covers for the turbines below. She tried to get the pin free from a grenade, and it worked. She was so surprised she almost dropped the weapon, but managed to fumble it over the side, where it exploded at the waterline, punching a hole in the iron. Danny felt needles of ice lance her face. Water was gurgling into the hole she'd made, flowing into some hollow booming space. It might work.

She sat on her haunches and bowled another grenade; it bounced off the side of the structure and exploded in midair, doing little damage. So she shuffled forward another few feet and was able to toss the next one down between the pair of turbines. It went off with a good, metallic *clang* and there was a deep, vibrating thump from somewhere inside the dam that sounded like major damage. The dam itself was vibrating now, some great mechanical assembly grinding itself to pieces inside. She chucked two more grenades down into the gap and the noises grew. Her arm was nice and limber now. She felt like she could pitch a Little League game.

But she hadn't been paying attention to the zeroes.

They were close, dozens of them. They rushed at her, silently, faces bent into snarls; the first few reached the dark, wet slick where the first grenade had wetted the deck, and they collapsed among the others. The remaining zeroes skidded to a halt. One of them knelt to examine the wetness, and it also fell lifeless, face downward, and slipped over the side of the dam into the roiling water. The rest fell back a few paces, and one of them passed a rifle to the foremost.

They were all piss-poor shots, of course. Zeroes couldn't read, appreciate music, or shoot accurately. But Danny had no illusions about gunfire. Even bullets aimed at nothing eventually hit something. And with the pain in her head and the frostbite and the burning skin she didn't think her system could take another outrage. Not even if they just winged her.

She had two more grenades, so she rolled one of them along the parapet toward the zeroes. It exploded with a yellow flash and blew chunks out of them, twisting a section of the railing so that it hung over the side of the dam. Something hit Danny, as well. She didn't know if it was a piece of concrete, a bullet, or simply the shock of the blast. But her vision went red on one side, and then her left eye stopped working. The world went flat, like a television picture.

Danny turned her attention to the turbines again, twisting her head to see. There was a hell of a lot of grinding and banging noise down there, and above it all the rush of a very large quantity of water. She crawled to the far side of the dam and looked down: A black gout of water was spewing out of the sluiceway, bursting over the narrow banks of the river, washing away the snow as it flooded out into the valley. But it wasn't enough. She had to drain the whole bathtub, and do it fast.

The train was coming into view down the valley, bigger than Danny imagined it would be, a post of black smoke leaping up out of the exhaust stack and scouring against the cliff wall beside it. It was accelerating, just as she had thought. The Architect wasn't going to stop here.

The zeroes hadn't noticed this. They were picking their way across the blasted part of the parapet now. Danny had inadvertently removed the radioactive barrier when she detonated the grenade. They were more hideous than ever now, some missing arms or faces, all of them chewed up by the explosion, but none of them stopped. The one with the rifle was completely mobile, if pocked with craters. He would seek retribution for the wounds that did not heal, of course. Then two of the zeroes were flung to the ground—Danny saw black holes appear in their bodies. Was someone shooting at them? She began to crawl.

The fuel tanks for the backup generators were on the reservoir side of the building. Danny identified them, two thousand-gallon tanks of propane mounted on iron frames against the hull of the dam, near the high-water line so if there were a fire they would burn nothing but water and concrete. That meant they would also blow the living shit out of the dam, if they chanced to explode. Danny dragged herself toward them. Something punched her in the body, knocked her sideways. It didn't hurt, but she was having trouble breathing.

In the growing light she saw that there was blood pouring out of her chest. That explained the breathing problem. She'd been shot. Even as she marveled at this, her left ankle flew up in the air of its own accord and she saw she'd been shot again. There was a ragged hole in her boot with a pale pink mass inside that turned red as she watched.

Danny got her back up against the nearest of the elephant-sized gas tanks. *Shoot this, assholes. Go ahead.* Time was running out. It seemed to her there ought to be something important, some revelation or insight that would put it all in perspective. But there wasn't. She was half-blind and her head hurt and she was shot up and she didn't want it anymore. Might as well wind up her affairs. There were other people running in her direction now. They looked familiar. Not zeroes. She must be hallucinating. No time left to wonder.

She rummaged in the backpack and found the one remaining object she would need, the thing she had been lugging since long before she got the deadly core of heavy metal. It had been with her since she knelt in the field beside the alcohol-soaked corpse of her sister. The thing she retrieved before she set fire to Kelley's rags and watched the familiar, tragic body burst into yellow and blue flames. She could see the flames in her mind and feel the heat. Then she felt herself stepping off the cliff, falling into that terrible sorrow, falling so that her belly touched her backbone. But this time it was different. She wasn't falling, she was flying. Flying away from the cliff. The flames had become daybreak, and she could fly.

But there was something more to be done. Something back in the world.

Danny blinked and regained consciousness. The sun broke above the reservoir, the same barbaric golden eye that had looked indifferently down on the world since the dawn of mankind and the dawn of the solar system and the birth of God, for all she knew. The backpack was open between her knees. Soon she could fly all she wanted. Danny thrust her quaking hands into the bag and lifted out the precious burden. She stripped off the plastic bags that wrapped it tight and then pressed it to the bleeding crater in her chest, held it and rocked it and with the one remaining finger of her club hand she pulled the pin from her last grenade.

"I said forever," she whispered to Kelley's mummified head, and closed her eyes.

26

They heard the detonation all the way back in Happy Town. Heads turned. Thousands of zeroes twisted around toward the noise. The living who continued to flee through the badlands paused at the mighty sound, but kept on moving. There wasn't anything else; just the single explosion and then the new day was bright upon the valley, shining through a gap in the clouds, and it was time for the unliving to continue the slow progress toward immortality. They had forever, after all, the zeroes did. With fresh meat and enough padding to protect unhealing flesh, they could live, after their fashion, for eternity.

Then there was another sound, a deep roar, growing until it sounded like the ocean in a storm.

Aboard the train, the Architect, Cad Broker, and a few others in various stages of undeath were in the engineer's compartment, watching the canyon walls move past, almost to the reservoir. They had no intention of stopping, although that's what the thinkers there were expecting; this was no time to stop just because promises had been made. All of the living servants they'd brought were back with the children, keeping order inside the boxcars. They would be eaten first. The sun rose above the horizon, and they saw tiny silhouetted figures running along the top of the dam ahead. Then there was a flash of light and a greasy orange ball of fire briefly outshone the sun.

The detonation was so loud it sounded like a blow to the train itself. The Architect turned on the engineer, the one living man allowed at the front of the train.

"Stop for nothing. Stop for nothing or I will eat your eyes."

But massive chunks of stone were spilling down the sides of the canyon now, some crashing to the tracks, some pulverizing the roadway or hitting the reservoir, sending up gouts of water. The brakes of the engine shrieked and everyone was thrown forward; they could hear screams from the boxcars. Then the face of the dam seemed to liquefy, slumping into the river, and a white spray leaped through it, followed by a shimmering black mass. A wall of water, beating the rocks with a vibration like the hooves of a great herd. The river burst its banks and the tide swept past the train, no more than a dozen feet below the rails at its greatest height.

"You foolish bitch," he said to himself. "We don't drown."

The words had barely left his broken lips when the radiation exerted its influence and he fell lifeless to the floor of the engine compartment. The Architect's brief eternity was over.

The partially unliving around him cried out, for they could still feel pain, and the radioactive water was fighting with the infection for the privilege of taking their lives. They screamed and clawed at their own flesh, and then collapsed like the others. Then the flood surge was past, the river three times its natural height but well below the tracks. It roared away down the canyon, sweeping over the banks of the river and battering the cliffs.

It took twelve minutes for the flood to reach the outlet in the canyon near where Happy Town had been built. Then the surge rose over the high-class neighborhood against the hill, spilling down the streets and sluicing through backyards, turning the white snow black. Thousands of zeroes turned to face the wall of foaming destruction that sped toward them, uncomprehending. Then Happy Town was underwater, crushed by the deluge and the trees and rocks and debris caught up in the tide. The ruined church steeple was the last thing visible above the foam. Then it twisted, bent, and drowned.

27

The survivors came back. They wandered through the forest, the badlands, up the canyon in which the river was now a gurgling stream among massive wet rocks and broken trees. The reservoir had drained down to the lowest point of damage in the dam, and now the flow had little passion. People picked their ways along until someone found the train up above on the shelf of rock that bore the tracks. The children were there, walking single file, making slow progress toward Happy Town, unaware there was no longer such a place in the world.

There was a brief and violent interlude as the living humans who had been tending the children were slaughtered by the mob that found them. Their pleas for mercy were ignored; they might be innocent, but they were associated with the Architect. The train engineer was thrown into the river with broken arms. The children looked on. One group was spared—scouts from the Tribe, recognized by some other Tribespeople before they, too, could be torn apart.

"We saw somebody on the dam," Conn told the posse that had found them. "Bunch of fuckers comin' after her."

"Her?"

"Or him. Couldn't see. Anyhows, we shot them up and then the one they were after blew up the fuel tanks. Then we went after the train."

For some reason, Conn decided not to identify who he thought had done it.

Then a large party of newly emboldened citizens crossed the sludge on the exposed bottom of the reservoir to the resort island and liberated the children there. The staff who remained at the resort met the same fate as those on the train. None of the infected or undead remained animated.

Twenty-four hours after the flood, several hundred survivors gathered in the badlands in an area where the undead had fallen to the run-out of the flood. It was easy to see where such areas were; the white carpet of new snow had been turned to dark slush in long, broad fingers that extended away from town and drained into the erosion washes of the badlands.

Someone eventually realized radiation might have played a role in the destruction, and after a Geiger counter confirmed the theory, they pulled the encampment back; but away from the taint of radioactivity, the remaining zeroes began to circle.

In the end, they had to gather up any vehicle that would still start and drive away. Several thousand of the living were never seen again. Of some six hundred children collected from the living, four hundred were found, and almost half of these were reunited with some living relative.

28

"It was her," Amy said.

"It might not have been," Patrick suggested.

He was tired and miserable from a long day of listening to unhappy kids wailing at the top of their lungs. He wanted a martini. They had water, so he drank that.

Two hundred and fifteen children left over once all family and friends had taken in those they knew. They would need more volunteers to take on parenting, the toughest assignment in the ruined world. Otherwise the search for a safe place would have to continue.

But nobody believed there really was a safe place any longer.

They were staying overnight in the abandoned house where the scouts had set up camp. He, Amy, Maria, and a couple of other old-timers had left town less than four hours before the swarm descended upon Happy Town; now they just wanted to travel forever, as long as it was away from this place.

Gunshots punctuated the silence of the night; there were still scores of moaners in the area who hadn't been caught in the flood or ventured too close to the hot zone, and a pack of feral hunters was on the move through the wilderness to the north. Huge bonfires lit the night every hundred yards. Most of the unclaimed children were sleeping in vehicles or in tents, patrolled by vigilant survivors, but the Silent Kid was asleep on Amy's lap, with the little goblin-dog asleep in his, snoring.

"I can't feel her pain anymore."

"Oh, come on," Patrick said. "That's telepathy."

"Whatever. She's not there anymore. I can't feel her."

The scouts had told very few people what they'd really seen at the reservoir. They weren't sure if it would put members of the Tribe in danger or not—a lot of lives had been lost along with the lives saved.

"When Topper didn't come back, we decided to go fuck the dam up ourselves," Conn explained. "We was hiding in the rocks waiting for first light. Then we saw this chick come crawling up out of the woods. The zeroes fucked her up but she kept on coming. She fought 'em off. Then—boom."

That was the entire story, in as much detail as they would ever get. Patrick was certain it must have been Danny. But he resisted Amy's certainty. He wanted her to enjoy the comfort of *un*certainty. A little ember of hope.

That same day, several ex-Tribespeople had ventured out to the defensive line of Happy Town to see if there was some useful secret there; if they could replicate Happy Town's security, but not its society, they might yet create a real haven. But when they had found the buckets and their foul contents, mostly dumped into ditches by the acolytes to allow the zero swarm through, it was understood that they would not be using that approach.

That was how they found Topper's still-animated head.

As more and more of the survivors of Happy Town had arrived over the course of the day, fleeing south, they had been quizzed to determine if they worked for the Architect or not; those who passed muster were put into scouting teams or used as lookouts. The entire sequence of events had been so dense and chaotic it felt like years since yesterday, centuries since the fall of Happy Town.

"Danny's probably alive and well, up in the hills scalping the last of the child snatchers," Patrick said.

He took his eyes from the red light of the fireplace and looked Amy in the face. Tears were spilling down her cheeks. He wound an arm around her neck and pulled her close, but said nothing. He'd run out of words of comfort a year back.

Patrick listened to the keening grief that escaped her, a cry of anguish from somewhere so deep inside it didn't reach her vocal cords. She kept as quiet as she could, sobbing and sobbing until she got hiccups. The Silent

Kid stirred and muttered something in his sleep. Amy stayed where she was, soaking Patrick's sweater with her tears, until she could breathe again.

Amy's grief wasn't just for loved ones lost. It was also for the end of things, the loneliness of life without afterlife. Neither of them believed in anything after death anymore, except the resurrection of the hungry dead.

Amy heaved a mournful sigh, placed a gentle hand on the Silent Kid's cheek, and said, "Let's name him Danny."

EPILOGUE

So thats the store of sherif dany an her braav esploids to defeet th zeros wich ii hav root doun so al mankin wil reemembar hir 4ever. Ii los 2 fingars of mii lef hand same as sherif dany but from frosbiit not from eetin of my oon fingars as dany did wif hir oon fingars. Thats also wen ii got mii naam dany. Aftar that ii wen south wif the triib, an we had manee aventirs agaans the zeros be4 thaa dzeez wipit owt mosly. Ii got a sekand dog a big dog naamit boons wich doktar amy saas is spelt BONES but she spels th ol waa not th nu waa.

My oon chilrin heer th store of sherif dany everbode chilrin heer that store now it is famist th worl arown, but ii nu dany personal so it is difrin wif mee. Al th chilrin bleev sherif dany is stil aliiv 20 yeers arter shi was las seen gooin into th col and iis with her bakpak an wepins. Thay bleev shi stil keeps us saaf from zeros an striids the hils an valees an cant eevin dy shees so badas. But not zeero ii meen shi is imortel.

An ii ges as long as we bleev, it miit jes be tru.

—Dan Cutter, the Silent Kid

ACKNOWLEDGMENTS

Heartfelt thanks are due to many people—particularly my Gallery Books editor, Ed Schlesinger, for making this book possible; Corinne Marrinan Tripp for making *me* possible; the folks at the South Dakota Department of Tourism; Andy Nicastro, Dr. Edward Graham, Amy Davidson, Courts "Buz" Carter, and zombie fans the world over.

ABOUT THE AUTHOR

Ben Tripp has designed theme parks, urban developments, and attractions around the world for over twenty years, and is recognized as one of the top storytellers in the field. In addition, he has developed projects at all of the major motion picture studios as a screenwriter and a story consultant. He now writes novels full-time.

His award-winning first book, *Rise Again*, is a popular part of the essential zombie canon; *Below Zero* is its sequel. He also has a fantasy trilogy in the works with Tor Books, the first volume of which is entitled *The Accidental Highwayman*.

He is married to Academy Award–winner Corinne Marrinan Tripp. They live in Los Angeles with two excellent dogs.